Their Faces Were Only An Inch Apart . . .

❧

"Oh, Ben, life is so hard." The sad note in her voice touched something deep in his heart.

"Yes it is. But you're strong. You've endured a lot and still hold your head high. You'll not be whipped and cowed. You'll come out on top."

Then she was leaning against him, her cheek against his shoulder, and his arms were holding her loosely. She closed her eyes to savor the moment, and the fresh, clean scent of his leather vest crept into her senses. It was heaven, pure heaven. The palms of her hands were trapped between them. She moved them around his sides to his face. They stood for a long moment holding each other. Then he lowered his head and pressed her cheek tightly to his. It was a precious moment and a delicious weakness flooded through her.

"Ah . . . sweet, wonderful woman," he whispered, and kissed her forehead gently. His gentleness was at odds with his desire to press her tightly to him. His heart raced with the need to find her lips with his and kiss her with fierce abandon . . .

❧

"Her books are precious keepsakes."

—*Romantic Times*

"Once again Dorothy Garlock has taken pen to leather and engraved a special place for herself in 'western history.'"

—*Heartland Critiques*

ALSO BY DOROTHY GARLOCK

A Gentle Giving
Annie Lash
Dream River
Lonesome River
Restless Wind
River of Tomorrow
Wayward Wind
Wild Sweet Wilderness
Wind of Promise
Midnight Blue
Nightrose
Homeplace
Ribbon in the Sky
Glorious Dawn
Tenderness
Forever, Victoria

PUBLISHED BY
WARNER BOOKS

DOROTHY GARLOCK

Sins of Summer

A Time Warner Company

Enjoy lively book discussions online with CompuServe. To become a member of CompuServe call 1-800-848-8199 and ask for the Time Warner Trade Publishing forum. (Current members GO:TWEP.)

WARNER BOOKS EDITION

Cover design by Jackie Merri Meyer and Diane Luger
Cover illustration by Donna Diamond
Hand lettering by Carl Dellacroce

Warner Books, Inc.
1271 Avenue of the Americas
New York, NY 10020

A Time Warner Company

Printed in the United States of America

First Printing: June, 1994

10 9 8 7 6 5 4 3 2 1

For the Tulsa gang—

Joy and Mike Bruza,
Caroline and Emily

Janythe and Tim Graham
Lauren and Scott

Jennifer Carwile
Meredith and Matt

And in memory of Jack and Tony Bruza

Sins of Summer

CHAPTER

* 1 *

"We're almost there."

The man lowered his head and spoke to the girl, although he knew that she could not hear him. Five miles back he had taken her from her horse, placed her in front of him in the saddle, and opened his sheepskin coat and wrapped it and a blanket around her. They had been traveling since daybreak, stopping only a time or two to rest the horses and to eat the meat and biscuits he had stored in his saddlebags.

It was quiet and bitterly cold.

The snow seemed to go on forever. The wind worked softly, smoothing out the snow around the gray spiky trunks and naked branches that edged the road. Flakes touched the man's whiskered face and stayed there. The creases in his coat and the blanket wrapped around the girl became a web of white lines.

Around a little bend the road flattened out and buildings came in sight. The weary man sighed with relief.

A track of rutted snow and mud led to a weathered-plank, two-storied house, a barn, outbuildings, and a few shacks. Black smoke oozed out of chimneys. This was the Callahan Lumber Company headquarters, not unlike a dozen other operations in the Bitterroot Range of Idaho.

The man glanced with curiosity at the house as he passed it on the way to the barn. It was big and square with tall, narrow windows. The front door looked as if it were seldom, if ever, used. A large covered porch ran along the back of the house. Light came from the back windows.

The horse, sensing the end of the journey, walked faster, whinnied softly, and stopped at the barn door. The man shook the girl. She looked up with questioning eyes. Without speaking, he lifted her to the ground, dismounted, swung back the heavy door and motioned her to go ahead. He followed, leading the horses. It was dark in the barn. Before he closed the door, shutting out what little light the late afternoon provided, he lit a lantern.

The girl hugged the blanket around her and waited while the man quickly unsaddled the horses, wiped them down, put them in a stall and forked them some hay. Leaving the bundles he had taken from behind the saddles in the stalls with the horses, he went to the girl, adjusted the shawl that covered her head, and, with an arm around her shoulders, guided her out of the barn and across the snow-covered ground to the house.

Standing at the window, Dory was trying to decide if she had enough time to make a quick trip to the outhouse before Jeanmarie awakened, when the riders rode into the yard and stopped in front of the barn. The saddle of one horse was empty, while the other carried double. Was someone really hurt, or was it a couple of no-goods hoping to get into the house by pretending to need help? If that was the case, she would send them packing with a load of buckshot in their rears. That stupid trick had been tried before.

Dory was always apprehensive when men came to the homestead. Only the most reckless dared to come when her brothers were not at home. As she watched, a man stepped out of the saddle and reached to lift someone down. The person was small and wore a . . . skirt that came to her shoe tops. Forevermore! A woman! She went into the barn. He followed with the horses.

Dory's heart thudded with excitement. It had been months since she had talked to another woman. The last time she had been to town was before Thanksgiving, and here it was April. She waited eagerly for the barn door to open. Would they go to the bunkhouse seeking shelter for the night, or would they come to the house?

When they crossed the yard toward the house, she backed away from the window. She heard them on the steps to the porch, stomping the snow from their boots, and she opened the door when the knock sounded. A man with a dark stubble of beard on his face stood with his arm across the shoulders of a young girl. Her face was red with cold.

"Come in. It must be near zero."

Dory swung the door wide, stepped back for them to enter then quickly closed it against the biting cold. Warm air struck the man's face—air filled with the scent of freshly baked bread. Two lamps lighted the cozy, well-equipped kitchen. A black iron range dominated one end of the room, a cobblestone fireplace large enough for a six-foot log the other.

"I'm Benton Waller."

"Are you lost?" Dory lifted straight dark brows.

"Not if this is the headquarters of Callahan Lumber Company." He pulled an envelope from his pocket and handed it to her. She glanced at the writing and handed it back.

"This is the Callahan homestead. The mill is farther north—five or six miles." Her eyes went to the girl and back to him. His eyes were the color of polished pewter and she couldn't help being intrigued by their unusual color and the keen intelligence they projected. "You must be the donkey engine man from Spokane," she said with sudden realization.

"I've been hired to set up the steam donkey. I wrote that I'd be here between the tenth and the fifteenth."

"I hadn't heard you were bringing your family," she said, glancing at the girl, who hovered close to the man's side, her head barely reaching his shoulder. She was young, slight; her face stiff with cold. "Come over to the fire. There's nothing worse than a late spring blizzard."

The girl ignored the invitation until the man, with his hand against her back, urged her toward the roaring fire.

"We'll warm up a bit and go on up to the mill."

"You were promised family quarters?"

"He said there would be a cabin—"

"—The cabin Louis had in mind isn't fit for a girl. He's at the mill and won't be back until tomorrow," Dory said, not bothering to hide her frank appraisal of the girl and the tall, lean man who stood with his back to the fire. He had removed his hat the instant he had stepped inside the door, revealing thick black hair. His face was too blunt-edged to be called handsome. Despite his casual manner, she felt the tension in him and knew instinctively that he was a hardened, cautious man who had had his share of bad times.

"Mrs. Callahan, my daughter is cold and tired. I'd be obliged if you'd tell me where we can settle in."

"*Miss* Callahan. Louis, Milo, and James are my brothers—the *sons* of the Callahan who founded the company."

Ben caught the slight sarcastic note in her voice, and he studied her face. It was oval with a small straight nose, wide generous mouth, large green eyes surrounded by dark lashes. Tall and capable looking, she was not exactly pretty, but the short, untameable, sable brown curls that covered her head like a woolly cap gave her a gamine appeal.

"It was Louis Callahan who asked me to come here."

"Damn Louis! He should know a girl can't stay in one of those shacks. Lordy mercy! I could throw a cat through the wall of any of them. He didn't say a word about your bringing your family. Then again . . . why should he? I'm just a woman with barely enough brains to stay out of the fire." She stopped abruptly as if regretting her unguarded comments.

The fact that she swore didn't shock Ben as much as the bitterness in her voice when she spoke of her brother.

"He didn't know I was bringing my daughter. I just said I wanted private quarters."

The girl tilted her head so that she could see her father's face. The shawl had slipped back showing light, straw-colored hair. An anxious frown drew her brows together over cornflower-blue eyes. She put a hand on his arm and shook it. He looked down at her and spoke slowly.

"It's all right."

"Of course, it is," Dory Callahan said quickly. "She can stay in here with me. There's a bunkhouse out next to the barn. Wiley's out there. He'll show you where you can bunk for the night. Tomorrow you can talk to Louis."

"Thank you." Ben turned to the girl and pulled the blanket from around her. The coat she wore was much too big for her small frame. While he unbuttoned it, her eyes never left his face. "Stay with the lady." Again he spoke slowly. "Stay here." He pointed to a kitchen chair.

The girl put her forefinger against his chest, then pointed to another chair. "You?"

He shook his head.

She pushed his hands away and rebuttoned her coat. She shook her head vigorously and pulled the shawl back over her head.

Ben looked up and caught Dory staring at the girl. "She

can't hear.'' He spoke impatiently, yet softly as if the girl could hear him. ''She's afraid I'll leave her.''

The poor little thing.

''Then stay with her for a while. Hang your coats there by the door.'' She smiled at the girl. ''It's been a while since I've had a female visitor. What's her name?''

''Odette. She doesn't talk much,'' Ben said, shrugging off his sheepskin coat.

''She speaks?''

''When she has to. She was very sick about eight years ago, and when she came out of it, she couldn't hear. I'm trying to teach her to read my lips.''

''Can she understand me?''

''Some. She understands most of what I say, but she's used to me. She can read and write. She's no dummy.'' He said it defensively as if he'd had to establish that fact before.

Dory wanted to know more about this strange pair, but his tone told her it was time to change the subject.

''Would you like coffee and a slice of fresh bread?''

''My mouth has been watering since I stepped inside the door.''

When he smiled, lines in his whiskered cheeks formed brackets on each side of his mouth. His teeth were straight and white and free of tobacco stains, but Dory sensed that he was a hard man and not the type to be traveling around with a daughter the size of this girl.

Where was his wife?

''How far did you come today?''

''From Cataldo Mission.''

A small girl appeared in the doorway, knuckling sleep from her eyes.

''Ma . . . ma, who's that?''

''Sweetheart! You've had such a long nap.'' Dory bent to lift the child up into her arms.

"Who's that?" the child asked again.

"Someone to see Uncle Louis."

"I gotta pee-pee—"

"Shhh . . . honey. Excuse me," Dory said and left the room with the child peering at them over her mother's shoulder. Her hair was short, curly and bright red. Yet the resemblance was so strong Ben had no doubt that they were mother and child.

He looked down to see Odette staring after the woman and little girl, then quickly trying to smooth her hair back with her palms. She pulled the collar of her dress out over the heavy sweater she had worn beneath her coat.

"Are you hungry?" he asked silently, his lips forming the words slowly. She smiled and nodded. He smiled back. "Say it."

"Hungry." Her lips formed the word silently.

"Say it," he insisted and pointed to his ear.

She grinned impishly, then said, "Hungry. You?"

"You bet." He pinched her chin with his thumb and forefinger. "You little imp. You like me to nag you to talk," he said affectionately.

Dory, with the child in her arms, stood in the doorway watching the exchange between Ben Waller and his daughter. It surprised her that such a rough-looking man would be so patient and gentle with the girl. The Callahan men didn't have a patient bone in their bodies, much less a gentle one—except for James. He was young yet. Give him time and he might turn out to be as hard as Louis and Milo.

"This is *my* daughter, Jeanmarie," Dory said with pride as she lowered the little girl to the floor. The toddler headed straight for Odette and took her hand.

"What your name?"

Odette quickly looked at Ben. He silently repeated the question while the child looked from one to the other.

"Odette." The name came hesitantly.

"I'm three." Jeanmarie held up three fingers. "Soon I'll be four." She unfolded another finger. "I had a kitty cat, but . . . it run off. You got a kitty cat?"

Odette looked puzzled.

"Come here, chatterbox." Dory scooped up the child and sat her on a high stool at the table. "She'll talk your arm off," Dory said to cover the silence. "She gets pretty wound up when company comes. We seldom have visitors and never see another woman unless we go to town. I can't promise that she'll get used to your daughter and stop pestering her."

"I don't know if Odette has ever been around a child."

Dory hesitated for an instant on her way to the cupboard to get cups and plates. *He didn't know if his daughter had ever been around a child.* That was strange. What kind of man wouldn't know *that* about his own daughter? The girl might not even be his daughter. She certainly didn't resemble him in any way, although it was easy to see that she adored him. Dory gave a mental shrug. Regardless of who and what they were, their coming was a break in her dreary existence.

"Sit down. Mr. Waller, would Odette like milk in her coffee or coffee in her milk? Sometimes I color Jeanmarie's milk with coffee. It makes her feel grown up."

Ben repeated the question and Odette answered aloud.

"Coffee . . . please."

Dory Callahan flipped a loaf of bread from a pan onto a smooth board. The sleeves of a flannel shirt were rolled to her elbows. It sloped down over well-rounded breasts and was tucked neatly into the surprisingly small waistband of a heavy wool skirt that hit her legs a good six inches above her slender ankles. She wore black stockings and fur-lined moccasins. She was not a small woman, and yet she was feminine.

Ben could not help wondering about her child and why she had made a point of making it perfectly clear that she was *Miss* Callahan. Unmarried. Yet the child was her flesh and blood. A man would have to be blind not to see it.

"What your name?" Jeanmarie asked.

"Ben Waller."

"My name is Jeanmarie. I'm almost four." She held up four fingers. Ben didn't know what to say to that so he didn't say anything. "I got a doll," she said looking expectantly into Odette's face. "Uncle Louis broke her leg. Uncle James fix it. Want to see my picture book? It's got a monkey." Jeanmarie giggled behind her hand. Odette remained silent. After a long pause, Jeanmarie looked at her mother and her lips began to tremble. "She don't like m-me—"

Dory set the coffeepot back on the stove and took the chair next to her daughter. She put her palm on the child's face to turn it toward her.

"Listen to me, honey. Of course she likes you. Who wouldn't like a sweet, pretty little girl like you? The reason she isn't talking to you is that she can't hear what you're saying to her."

"I talk loud."

"It doesn't matter how loud you talk, sweetheart. Her ears have been hurt and they don't work."

"Did she fall down?"

"No, honey. She was very sick."

"Is she sick now?"

"No. But when she was, it broke something in her ears."

"They broke?" The child tilted her head to look at Odette, then quickly scooted off the stool and around the table. "I kiss . . . make 'em better." She threw her arms around Odette's neck, pulled her head down and kissed her first on one ear and then the other.

When Odette got over her surprise, she smiled with pure pleasure and murmured. "Thank you."

With her pixie face wreathed in smiles, Jeanmarie climbed back up on the stool and turned the full force of her gaze on her mother.

"Is him her uncle?"

"He's her papa." Dory sliced the hot bread, passed it to Ben and Odette and moved the butter dish to within their reach. "Help yourself to the butter and jelly."

"I ain't got a papa," Jeanmarie said. "But I got Uncle James."

Ben noticed that this announcement had no effect at all on the mother, who smoothed jelly on a slice of bread, cut it, and put it on her daughter's plate.

"Don't know when I've tasted better bread," Ben said.

"Could be you're just hungry," Dory replied. "My mother was the best bread maker in the territory. She claimed the secret to making good bread was to dissolve the yeast in potato water. In the winter she'd load a dishpan full of warm bread and take it to the cutters up in the woods. Before they started the winter cut they would make sure a path was cleared for the sleigh. Sometimes, even then, Mama had to walk a mile through deep snow. She loved the woods and—"

Her voice trailed when she realized she had been chattering like a magpie. Weeks went by when the only adult conversation she had was with old Wiley in the bunkhouse and an occasional grunt from her brothers, who took turns coming back to the homestead on Sunday.

Ben liked sitting across the table from the woman, listening to her voice. He sensed her loneliness. He was strangely comfortable with her, although he could feel the sharp edge of her curiosity about him and Odette.

Silence, broken only by the child's chatter, stretched while they finished off most of a loaf of bread. Then the thump of heavy boots came from the porch, followed immediately by the opening of the door.

The man who stood in the doorway looked down the table at Ben, then advanced a step into the room and slammed the door shut behind him. He was a big, deep-chested man wearing the clothing of a logger: pant legs stuffed into the tops of his boots, a mackinaw, and a wool cap. Snow lay on his shoulders and clung to his wiry beard. He took another step, his eyes, hard and piercing, holding on Ben.

"Who the hell are you and what'er you doin' in my house?"

CHAPTER
* 2 *

The greeting was as shocking to Ben as a splash of cold water. A chill crawled over his skin, but he met the man's angry gaze without a flicker of the emotion that tensed every nerve inside him. He pushed himself away from the table and stood.

"For God's sake, Louis! He's the man you sent for," Dory said before Ben could speak.

"Benton Waller?"

"Yes," Ben said. "I wrote that I'd be here between the tenth—"

"—And . . . the fifteenth." Louis rudely interrupted. He threw angry, suspicious words at his sister. "What's he doing in here?"

"I invited him in." Dory stood, her face red with anger and embarrassment.

"Hired hands are not invited into *my* house," Louis shouted.

"*Your* house?" Dory retorted, her voice low and quivery. "One fourth of this house is mine and I'll invite in who I please. Nothing in Papa's will gives you the right to say who comes in and who does not."

"I'm head of this family. You'll do as I say, or—"

"Or what, brother dear? James won't let you throw me out. We're two against two."

"That don't mean shit!"

"You're back a day early," Dory said lightly, then added with heavy sarcasm, "Did you hope to catch me having a high old time with old Wiley?"

"It wouldn't be the first time you've had a high old time," he sneered.

"You're pitiful, Louis. Mean-minded and pitiful."

"Thank you for the coffee and bread, ma'am." Ben felt an acute dislike for Louis Callahan, and the need to leave before his fist connected with the man's face. He reached the coat rack in two strides and unhooked Odette's coat as well as his own.

Odette followed Ben and stood close beside him. She could tell by his movements and his facial expression that he was angry. Something had gone wrong. Something Ben would tell her about later.

Louis seemed to notice Odette for the first time. "Who's this?"

"His daughter, you stupid, bull-headed dolt. You didn't tell the man he would have to share quarters with twenty or more horny timber beasts."

"Stay out of this," he snarled. "This is company business."

"I've got a one-fourth say."

"You got nothin' to say. He should've told me he was bringin' womenfolk."

"Blaming *him*! That's typical of you, Louis," Dory said scathingly.

"We'll be moving on." Ben's terse voice broke in. "If it wouldn't be asking too much, I'd be obliged if we could stay in the barn until the storm blows itself out."

Dory came around the table. "I apologize for my brother's rudeness. Let Odette stay with me and Jeanmarie until you're settled in another job."

"Don't worry about Odette, ma'am. I have the offer of another job down on the Saint Joe, less than a day's ride from here."

"Malone!" Louis shouted, making Ben wonder if the man ever spoke in a normal tone. "Is that goddamned Malone after you?"

Ben ignored the question and helped Odette into her coat.

Louis Callahan took off his mackinaw. "Waller, I was a bit hasty," he admitted grudgingly.

"Only a bit?" Dory's green eyes were large with mock concern.

"A man can't be too careful about his womenfolk in this country," he said with a meaningful look at his sister. "We'll fix up quarters for you and the girl."

"We'll be moving on." Ben steered Odette to the door. "About the barn?" He left the question hanging.

"Wait. It's best we talk this over," Louis said, pulling the cap from his head, which was bald except for a fringe of thick graying hair around the edges. "I ain't a man to go back on my word. I said you'd have private quarters and they'll be decent."

"I've never worked for a man who considered me unfit to step foot inside his home."

"You'd understand if you knew the circumstances here."

"Your family affairs are none of my business. I came here to do a job and move on."

"There's no womenfolk at Malone's," Louis said quickly.

"There are," Dory declared stridently. "You're lying and you know it."

Both men ignored her.

"We've been where there were no women before." Ben was settling his hat on his head.

"Stay. Dory would be company for your girl. And I'll pay half again more than you asked."

Dory suddenly let out a peal of contemptuous laughter.

"Hush up," Louis snapped.

"Why would you pay more than I asked for in the first place?" Ben asked.

"Because I need that engine working and a flume built," Louis said, glaring at Dory as she continued to laugh.

"I'll tell you why he's suddenly desperate to keep you." Dory's eyes sparkled with laughter. She didn't appear to be at all cowed by her huge older brother. "You said the magic words—you said you'd work for Malone over on the Saint Joe." She burst out in laughter again. "That was enough to make Louis roll over and play dead."

"We need to talk in private," Louis growled.

Ben looked down at Odette's tired, pinched face. He couldn't let his pride stand in the way of what was best for her. If the man was willing to pay half again the money he had offered, and with what he had already put away, it would be enough to set up a carpentry business for himself. Settlers were moving in by the droves, and there was bound to be a great demand for furniture, doors, window frames and flooring. He liked the mechanical work with the donkey machine, but he liked woodworking better.

Hell, he didn't have to like the man to work for him.

While Ben was mulling these thoughts over in his mind, he glanced at the child sitting at the table. Jeanmarie was perfectly still. Only her eyes, blue as the sky, betrayed anxiety. They shifted from her mother to her uncle as she waited patiently for the scene to end. Memories of himself cowering in the corner while his aunt and uncle battled verbally and physically flashed into his mind, and he felt once again the confusion this child was feeling.

"Well, Waller. Are you willing to talk it over?"

Ben looked once again into Odette's anxious face. Out of the blue the responsibility of caring for her had been thrust upon him. What had followed had been three difficult years of adjustment for both of them. Now he realized just how empty his life would be without her.

"I'll talk." Ben hung his hat back on the peg and shrugged out of his coat. "Stay with the lady," he said to Odette and was relieved when she nodded.

Without another word to his sister, or a greeting to his niece, Louis led the way from the kitchen into a hallway. Away from the fire, it was cold. Along the hall on one side was the stairway and beneath it a door that opened into a small room. Inside, Louis lit a lamp and flung open the door of a round Acme Oak heater. The firebox was full of tinder that caught when he struck a match on the ornamental rim of the stove and tossed it inside. With a grunt of satisfaction, he slammed the door shut and reached into a cabinet for a bottle of whiskey.

Ben stood inside the door of the sparsely furnished room. A rolltop desk, its contents neatly arranged, occupied one wall, a leather-covered lounge the other. The only other furniture was the glass-front cabinet that held several bottles of spirits. There were no pictures on the walls and no rug on the floor.

He accepted the half-glass of whiskey when Louis handed it to him.

"That'll warm your insides while we wait for the fire to take the chill off." Louis pulled the chair away from the desk, sat down, and motioned toward the lounge. "Sit. Not much here in the way of records," he said, indicating the desk. "We do business at the mill."

Thirty-four years of hard life had left Ben Waller little room for trust. He was especially leery of a man who flew off the handle and made quick, unfounded accusations. He waited for Louis to speak. Waiting was something Ben knew how to do. His thoughts reverted to what had led up to this abrupt change of mind on the part of his potential employer. Louis Callahan had been giving him the boot until he had mentioned working over on the Saint Joe.

Before coming here, Ben had studied the area carefully. Malone's was the only mill of any real size on the Saint Joe. Callahan's and Malone's used the same waterway to the river that flowed into the Coeur d'Alene Lake, where "boom men" would sort out logs stamped on their ends with the marks of the upstream loggers.

"I'm not a hard man, Waller," Louis said, interrupting Ben's thoughts. "It's not been easy lookin' after a woman like Dory in a place where men outnumber women ten to one." He waited for Ben to comment and when he didn't, he went on. "Dory's got wild blood. So has James. He ain't got sense enough to pour piss out of a boot. Their ma was a hot-blooded little piece if there ever was one. She was after my pa before he had time to get my ma in the ground. She got him so heated up he married up with her and from then on she was queen of the roost. She paraded around with her hair hanging down her back, a-smilin' and touchin' Pa all the time. The old fool was bedazzled. Whatever Jean wanted, Jean got."

"I thought we were going to talk about the job."

"We are. I'm tryin' to tell you why I acted the way I did." Louis set his glass on the desk, leaned back in the chair, and hooked his thumbs in the wide galluses he wore over his broad shoulders to support his britches. Ben noticed that the wool shirt Louis wore was neatly mended and wondered if the work had been done by the sister with the wild blood.

"Your family history has nothing to do with the job I'll be doing here."

"I think it does," Louis said belligerently. "Dory's already got one bastard, mister. I mean to see she don't get any more."

"You're talking pretty blunt to a stranger, Callahan." There was a hard ring in Ben's voice.

"Maybe. It ain't somethin' we're proud of."

"As I said before, your family problems have nothing to do with me."

"But now you know why I was rankled when I found you here."

"No, I don't know. Did you think I was going to plow your sister in front of my daughter and hers?" Ben stood. His tone was as cold as a frozen pond. "I don't see a way for us to come to terms, Callahan."

"Sit down, sit down. I'm a straight-talkin' man and didn't mean to rile you."

"I don't hold with a man running down a woman, especially his sister."

"Half-sister. Pa had two batches of kids. Me and Milo, then James and Dory. Hell, man! Dory ain't got no reputation to run down. Ever'body knows what she is. Ain't a decent woman in the territory that'll give her the time of day. She's got a youngun and ain't wed. You'd a heard about it sooner or later. Might as well come from me."

Ben finished his drink and put the empty glass on the desk. "Talk business or I'm leaving."

"I've put a lot of money out to get Dolbeer's engine. I heard of it back in '82. It took me three years to get a hold of one." Louis rubbed his hands on his broad thighs. "We've got plenty of big stuff cut and ready for the steam donkey to reel in. I'm building a V-shaped flume. Ever seen one?" He went on before Ben could answer. "It's a dandy. Won't take as much grease as a flat-bottom and has less chance of jamming. By God, before the end of the next year my flume will be 2,000 feet long. We'll reel the logs to the flume and let it take them to the river."

Ben's mind was on the woman in the kitchen. Her green eyes had looked straight into his. Not boldly, but with assurance and self-possession. Nothing in her manner conformed with the picture her brother had painted of her. She was all woman and Ben could understand why men would swarm around her like flies. He'd had more experience with the type of woman Callahan painted his sister to be than with any other kind, and she just didn't seem to fit the mold of a loose woman; but appearances were deceiving. He knew a banker's wife in Spokane who was as hot as a firecracker and had spread her legs for half the men in town, yet she sang in the choir every Sunday. Another more important question puzzled Ben. Why was Callahan so eager to have him believe that his sister was a strumpet?

"We're not milling near as much as we're sending down river. My brother Milo is mill boss. We float some of the plank and haul some. Our sawmill has the capacity of only about three thousand board feet of lumber a day."

Ben knew about sawmills. From the age of ten, he had been a hand in his uncle's sawmill, or in the woods with an ax, or on one end of a crosscut saw. By the time he was sixteen, he had become an expert cutter, peeler, bucker and high-rigger. At seventeen he was "bull of the woods," a camp foreman. By the next year he was recognized as the best "river pig" on the Wishkah River. He knew everything about the logging business, but the part that made Ben sick was indiscriminate rape of the forest by greedy loggers who left the hillsides exposed to the ravages of snow and rain.

Louis Callahan continued to talk.

"When we get the steam donkey set up, we'll float more logs than Malone ever thought of. By God, he'll have to sit up and take notice." Excited by his own prediction, he hastily crammed tobacco into a pipe, spilling some of it on the floor between his spread thighs.

"Before I decide to take you up on your offer of what you contracted to pay me, plus half that amount again"—Ben intended to make it perfectly clear that he expected the extra wages—"I need to know about what type of lodging you'll provide."

"Well, now, I been thinkin' on that."

Louis studied the big dark-haired man with the steel-colored remote eyes, the careful eyes of a man who knew what he wanted and walked strongly down a way he chose. If he lost Ben Waller to the Malones, it would take months to find another man to set up the steam donkey and show them how to operate it. On the other hand, he was sure that Milo wouldn't like this man; he was too independent, too sure of himself. Well, his brother was going to have to pull in his horns this time. At least until they were through with Waller.

"What I had in mind"—Louis cleared his throat—"is for your girl to stay here with Dory. She'll look after her and welcome her company."

"You're suggesting that I allow my daughter to stay with a woman of ill repute?" Ben asked with a heavy frown.

A deep red covered Louis's face. "Well, now, I didn't say that Dory was . . . that kind."

"You certainly did. You said she had wild blood and implied that she was loose."

"She ain't goin' to lead your girl off, I know that."

"Considering the kind of woman you say she is, I'm not sure I want to take the chance."

"She's got wild blood, but I was hasty when I said she was loose . . . now." Louis rubbed his sweating palms on his thighs.

"You lied?"

"Ah . . . no." Louis stammered. "She's got a bastard. That I can't deny, but—"

"—But she ah . . . uses the homestead for a brothel while her brothers are away?"

"Hell no!" Louis almost rose up out of the chair. "I never said no such."

"You implied it. How do I know my daughter will be safe here?"

"She'd be a hell of a lot safer here than in a camp with a bunch of horny timber beasts."

"There's something else you haven't considered." Ben was enjoying the man's discomfort. "Your sister may not want to take on the chore of looking after a sixteen-year-old girl."

"It don't matter none what she wants!" Louis blurted. "She'll do what she's told." He paused to take a deep breath.

"I'll put it to the women. If it's agreeable to Miss Callahan and if Odette is willing, I'll take the job. If not, we'll move on."

Louis came up out of the chair. "Good God! You'd leave a decision like that up to . . . up to the likes of . . . them?"

"Why not?" Ben grinned. "Womenfolk have good instincts about such things."

"Godamighty!" Louis sank back down in his chair.

CHAPTER
* 3 *

As soon as the door closed behind Ben Waller and her brother, Dory took a deep, painful breath. Louis would enjoy telling the man about her sinful past. She dreaded seeing the scorn in Ben's steel-gray eyes when he came back into the kitchen. Dory squeezed her own eyes shut for an instant and relaxed her features before she turned to face her daughter. She knew what to expect. Jeanmarie's little face would be puckered to cry, and somehow Dory had to head off the tears before they started. Jeanmarie never cried or made a sound during a scene with Louis or Milo, but it tore her heart to see the fear on her daughter's little face.

"We're lucky." Dory smiled brightly. "We get to keep Odette with us for a while." She helped Odette remove her coat again and hung it back on the peg.

"All night?" Jeanmarie asked in wonderment.

"All night and tomorrow."

"Oh goody! Oh goody!" The child clapped her hands.

"I think we'll celebrate and have some of that sugar candy we made the other day." Dory went to the pantry and returned with a plate covered with a cloth, which she whipped off with a flourish.

Jeanmarie laughed happily and Dory sighed with relief. She gestured for Odette to sit down, then sat down opposite her.

"Candy," she said slowly. "Sweet. Hummm . . ." She licked her lips, and to her delight Odette laughed.

"Candy. Good."

"You understood me! That's wonderful." In her excitement, Dory reached across the table and squeezed Odette's hand.

"Yes."

"I'm glad you're here," Dory said, still holding onto Odette's hand.

"Me too," Odette said, and then with a worried frown looked toward the door where her father had disappeared. "Your man?"

"No." Dory shook her head. "Brother. Br . . . oth . . . er," she repeated slowly. "Jeanmarie"—she turned to indicate her daughter—"and I don't pay any attention when he yells. Oh, goodness, you didn't hear him—"

"He's mad at Papa."

"He'll get over it. He needs your papa," she added.

"You got a mama?" Jeanmarie asked with sticky brown juice running from the corner of her mouth.

"Honey, you can't talk to Odette with your mouth full and you must look right at her and talk slowly." Dory repeated the question for her daughter, glad that she had asked it.

Odette watched Dory's lips and shook her head. "Mama's dead."

Dory nodded solemnly. "My mama too," she said slowly.

"You got a papa?" Odette liked the woman with the short ringlets all over her head. She had never seen a woman with hair so short and tried not to stare.

Dory shook her head.

"Pretty," Odette said, touching the top of Jeanmarie's head.

"Our hair is so curly that it was in a constant tangle, so we cut it. It's easier to take care of." Dory laughed down at her daughter. "It created quite a stir, didn't it, honey? We're the only bobbed-haired women in the territory."

Seeing Odette's quizzical look, Dory realized she had spoken too fast and repeated her words slowly.

"Pretty," Odette said again.

"You're very pretty too."

"Me?" Odette pointed a finger to her chest, then shook her head and picked up a blond braid that lay on her chest. "Ugh." She made a face.

Jeanmarie's laughter was cut short when the men came into the room. The child's anxious eyes went from her uncle to her mother. Dory couldn't bring herself to look at Ben, sure that she would see contempt on his face.

"Get Mr. Waller some coffee." Louis issued the order briskly.

"Your brother invited Odette to stay here with you. Before I ask Odette if that's agreeable to her, I want to know how you feel about it." Ben spoke as soon as she set the coffee in front of him.

"Hell, man. She'll do as she's told." Louis poured a cup of coffee for himself and slammed the coffeepot back down on the stove.

Dory's lips curled in a sneer and the glance she threw at her brother was one of pure hatred.

"Are you sure you want to leave your daughter in the care of a . . . strumpet, a loose woman who already has one child out of wedlock?" Dory's face hardened still more as she spat out the words. "Didn't Louis tell you that I'm a whore and that I practice my trade as soon as he leaves the house? Surely he told you. He tells every man who comes within a mile of me."

"Dory, shut up!" Louis yelled.

Jeanmarie whimpered softly and Dory moved to place her hand on her daughter's shoulder. She reminded Ben of a mother bear protecting her cub.

"Aren't you afraid that I'll lead your daughter astray?" she persisted sarcastically.

"I'm not afraid you'll have a bad influence on my daughter. Odette will not easily be led astray."

"How do you know that? I just might teach her the pleasures of the . . . flesh!"

"My God—" Louis shouted.

Dory's face was almost as red as her child's hair; her nostrils quivered and her eyes were bright with anger and humiliation.

"Odette will tell me if you do. And before we leave, I'll make sure that engine is blown to hell and back."

Louis pounded his fist on the table and roared, "You goddamn *slut*!"

Both Dory and Ben ignored him. "Jeanmarie and I will be glad to have your daughter here with us, and I'll do my best to see to it that she's not exposed to any unpleasantness." Dory spoke softly and only to Ben.

"I'll pay board for my girl. She'll not be a burden to you."

"There's no need for you to pay. It'll go with the job. Isn't that right, Louis?"

"I guess so," he mumbled.

"Odette will do her share of the work if you tell her what to do."

Ben turned and looked into Odette's anxious face. "You can't stay at the logging camp. You'll either have to stay here while I work, or we'll leave. Miss Callahan has invited you to stay with her and the little girl. We don't have much choice . . . at the moment."

Odette placed her hand on his arm and looked back at Louis standing beside the cookstove.

"I'll do what you say, Papa."

"You'll be all right here."

"You won't go away?"

"Of course not. The camp is only a few miles from here."

"Lady's nice. But . . . him—" She said the words and looked again at Louis.

"Tell her that he's at the mill most of the time."

"That's when you do your sniffin' around, huh, Dory?" Louis sneered.

Dory wanted the girl to stay so bad she could taste it. To have another woman in the house to talk to would be heavenly. The winter had been so long and so . . . lonely. But she didn't dare appear too eager or Louis would find a way to keep the girl out of the house without losing Waller.

"I wouldn't blame the girl if she didn't want to stay." Dory turned toward her brother. "But if you want this man to help you best the Malones, you'd better keep your mouth shut."

Odette studied the woman's face and the face of the little girl. The woman's clear green eyes had a lonely, pleading look, and her little girl was so still as she waited patiently for a question she didn't understand to be settled.

Odette suddenly remembered sitting on the doorstep and listening to the pleading voice of her mother arguing with a man, shivering at his harsh replies. She had known that the dispute was about her and had waited anxiously for the outcome. Finally the man had walked out, slamming the door without looking back. Then had come the sound of her mother crying. Odette had crept into the house, wet a cloth and bathed her mother's swollen face.

She tugged on Ben's arm so he would look at her. "You need the work?"

"That's about the size of it, honey."

"Then I stay."

Ben put his arm across the girl's shoulders, pulled her head to his chest, then raised her chin so she could see his face.

He spoke slowly and softly. "Maybe Miss Callahan will teach you to make bread and to sew a dress out of the goods we bought in Spokane."

Odette smiled. "You like the bread?"

"Mmmm . very much." Ben's hand smoothed the girl's hair back from her face.

Dory was mesmerized by the tender affection Ben Waller showed his daughter and by how easy it was for him to make her understand what he was saying. Tenderness between her mother and father was a treasured memory. She felt a stab of envy. It had been so long since anyone other than Jeanmarie had embraced her.

"I'll go up and light a fire in Milo's room. He can sleep in James's room or in the bunkhouse when he's home." Dory picked up Jeanmarie and set her astraddle her hip.

"Milo won't like it," Louis said in a voice so loud that Jeanmarie hid her face against her mother's chest.

"That's too bad," Dory retorted.

"The girl can sleep with you and . . . her." He jerked his head toward the child on her hip. Never had she heard him utter her child's name, and anger forced a bitter response.

"She has a name. It's *Jeanmarie*! The bunk in my room is not even a full-size bed, as you well know. Odette will sleep in Milo's room."

"I say she'll sleep in yours—"

"No, Louis. My bunk is too small."

"I'm the head of this house, goddammit!" he shouted, his bushy brows drawn together over eyes blazing with anger.

"If you don't have room for Odette why did you suggest she stay here?"

"Pay no attention to him, Mr. Waller. Odette will have Milo's bed. If I said it was raining, Louis would say the sun was shining. I'm used to his contrariness. He's always been this way. I realize it's hard for an outsider to understand the bickering that goes on here." Dory looked straight at Ben, refusing to be cowed by her brother's bullying.

"Hush your mouth! You're lucky to have a roof over your head considerin' what you are!"

Dory ignored the insult. "Stay for supper, Mr. Waller. Louis will be here to make sure we're well chaperoned."

"Mouthy, know-it-all bitch," Louis sneered as soon as the kitchen door closed behind Dory. "See what I got to put up with? Someday . . . someday—" He doubled up a fist and struck the palm of his other hand. "I'd like to—" He broke off the words and yanked his mackinaw off the hook. "Got some things to see to. Be back in a minute. If that crippled bastard's been sittin' around on his arse all week and ain't made them nails, I'll kick him out even if it is twenty below. Ain't no use havin' the best iron and best forge in the territory if it ain't used." He screwed his wool cap down on his head and slammed out the door.

Ben seethed. Was the man thinking he'd go upstairs and jump his sister as soon as he went out the door? Was that why he said he'd be back in a minute? Ben wondered if the other brothers were as disagreeable as Louis. If so, he'd pull freight regardless of the pay. Odette had not understood what had gone on between Miss Callahan and her brother. Had she heard their words, she might have been uneasy about staying here. It was hard for him to believe a man would say the things Louis Callahan had said to and about his sister even if they were true. But the woman had admitted she had a child and was not married. Maybe there was more to the story than what he'd heard so far.

Odette looked tired. Last night she had slept on a pallet on a cold floor. Ben had told the innkeeper that she was his wife, afraid he would insist that she sleep in the common room with the women who had come in on the stage. They had bedded down in a room with another couple. Ben had rolled her in her blanket and pulled her back up against his chest in an effort to keep her warm. Since they had been together he had become very sensitive to her fears.

Ben was well acquainted with fear. At nineteen he had been unjustly convicted of killing his uncle and had spent six years in prison. While there the warden had discovered that he was extremely handy with machinery, and because he had avoided trouble, he had been lent out to work with Tom Caffery. Tom, a master craftsman, was considered to be an expert in the setting up and operation of the steam donkey, which was having a profound effect on the economics of logging. The old man had taken a liking to Ben and had taught him everything he knew. When Ben had been pardoned by the territorial governor after another man had confessed to the crime, he had stayed and worked with Tom until the old man had died.

Shortly after he had buried Tom, Ben had received a letter, forwarded from the prison, from a young woman in Seattle begging him to come to her. Years earlier, when he had been only eighteen, Ben had stayed in a rooming house in Spokane and had shared a bed with her. He remembered her as a decent sort of girl, lonely as he was and more than willing to have his company. He had been fond of her, but not fond enough to tie himself to her for life, and she had not been ready to settle down either. They had had a mutual parting of the ways.

When he had reached Seattle, he had found the woman dying. To his surprise, she had introduced him to a thirteen-year-old girl and insisted that she was his daughter. The girl was deaf. Her deafness had been caused, her mother said, by a serious illness. The girl could talk but was reluctant to do so. Not certain if the girl was his or not, Ben had felt that he couldn't take the chance that she wasn't his and had taken her with him after they had buried her mother.

Other than the money he'd make, Ben had what he considered another good reason for coming to work for the Callahans now. The summer that Odette was conceived, Louis and Milo Callahan also had spent time in the rooming house in Spokane. They would not remember him, but he remembered the two of them. They had come to town to see the sights and experience every vice it offered. At the boardinghouse table they had spoken freely of the big logging operation as if they were its sole owners.

The thought nagged at Ben that one of them might have fathered the girl. During the three years he and Odette had been together, she had become an important part of his life, and he fervently hoped that she was truly his flesh and blood. He felt a strong urge, however, to know for sure, not that it would make any difference in his feelings for her. He rationalized that it would only be fair to the girl if he could prove that she came from good pioneer stock if she were not really his child.

Ben looked toward the kitchen door when it opened and watched Dory come back into the room carrying her daughter. The minute she put the child on her feet the little girl ran to

Odette and climbed into her lap. Odette's smiling eyes sought Ben's, but his attention was focused on Dory Callahan.

"Mr. Waller." Dory spoke in a low tone with her face averted to prevent Odette from reading her lips. "I'll do my best to look after your daughter while she's here with me. In spite of what Louis said, my bobbed hair, and my child, I am not a loose woman."

"It matters little to me what you are. I've no choice but to leave Odette here."

Dory's face took on a stubborn look. "It was stupid of me to think you'd believe me. Most men believe Louis."

"Your past is your business. My concern is for Odette."

"You sound as if you've known a few loose women in your day," she sneered.

"My share." Lines appeared at the corners of his gray eyes when he smiled. "Odette and I would be on our way to Malone's if not for the blizzard." He glanced at Odette. She and Jeanmarie were playing patty-cake.

"Louis and Milo have a strong dislike for me and Jeanmarie." Dory didn't understand her need to explain to this man. "One reason is that I strongly resemble my mother. She was only a little older than Louis was when my father married her. He and Milo resented her and did everything they could to make her life miserable. My father loved her dearly. She was a loving, happy woman who laughed a lot—the opposite, I'm told, of my father's first wife. As hard as my mother tried, she was never able to make peace with Louis and Milo. They even refused to attend her burial."

"Is your full brother as disagreeable as Louis?"

"No, thank heaven! James is three years older than I am. He is good at everything he does. He's the best high-climber, chopper, cutter, peeler, and river rat in the territory. And he is well liked by the men. James lives to provoke Louis and

Milo and to outdo them in anything they attempt. He's the cutting foreman of the Callahan Lumber Company only because Papa put that provision in his will."

"Then I'll be working mostly with him."

"Don't count on it. Louis will be pushing every step of the way. He's got his heart set on outdoing the Malones."

"I take it there is something personal between the Callahans and the Malones."

"You take it right. My mother was Chip Malone's foster sister. She was raised in their home. Some say that he was in love with her. And . . . Chip Malone has red hair."

Ben glanced at the red mop on the little girl's head, and then back at the mother, but she had turned away and was stoking the fire in the cookstove.

The hastily-put-together supper of fried pork, sauerkraut, boiled potatoes and dried apple pie was the best food Ben and Odette had had in weeks. While they ate, Louis talked constantly about the steam donkey. When he wanted more coffee he banged his cup on the table and continued to talk.

"By God, I bought the best cable money could buy. Steel cable. Milo wanted me to use manila rope, but I said no siree. When it's wet it stretches and is too hard to handle for hauls of more than two hundred feet. With steel cable I have the pulling range of over a thousand feet. Ain't that right, Waller?"

"If the cable doesn't kink and snap." Ben had an unexpected urge to douse the man's enthusiasm.

"I expect you to see that it don't. I'll pay you good wages to oversee the building of the flume."

"I'll set up the engine and teach your men to run it and that's all." Ben helped himself to the bread platter when Dory passed it across to him, her eyes shining with amusement and awareness that Louis wanted to argue but didn't dare.

"This coffee is as weak as a man's pecker after a week in a whorehouse. It don't have no life a-tall," Louis said, after taking a deep gulp from his freshly filled cup. He stared at his sister with a smirk on his thick lips.

Ben watched color come up to flood Dory's cheeks and felt a deep contempt for the man who so obviously enjoyed tormenting his sister. His dislike for Louis was rapidly intensifying into downright loathing, and he wondered if he would be able to stomach him long enough to set the machinery and train men to operate it.

"Such talk is for the bunkhouse, not in front of womenfolk, Callahan." Ben spoke quietly.

"Harrumpt! What'er ya gettin' in a snit for? Ya said the gal can't hear."

"Your sister can." Ben's voice held a note of irritation that went unnoticed by Louis.

"Like I done told ya, she ain't no untried woman. Ain't nothin' 'bout a man she don't know. Huh, Dory?"

Dory kept her eyes on her plate.

In the silence that followed, Louis continued to scoop food into his mouth and Ben began to wonder if his decision to stay here had been a wise one. He glanced at Odette. She was smiling at Jeanmarie, happily unaware of the conversation and the tension. His common sense told him that it was better for his daughter to stay here than to make the long, cold ride to the Malones with him not knowing what to expect when he got there.

Odette's mother had been such a woman as Dory Callahan. Perhaps he had helped to set the woman's feet on the path she had taken. He had not been her first, of that he was sure. Before she died she had told him that she had been very protective of their child and begged him to see her settled with a good man who would love and cherish her as she herself had wanted to be.

Ben came to a decision. This was a better place for Odette than in a logging camp, even if they had a cabin to themselves. He would work here through the summer. By that time, if things went right, he'd have the money to start his own business.

CHAPTER
* 4 *

Dory held herself in rigid control, afraid she would do or say something that would cause Louis to come up with a plan to house Ben Waller and Odette up at the timber camp or in one of the shacks at the sawmill. Not even when Jeanmarie upset her stool as she left the table, and Louis shouted an obscenity, did Dory retort. As usual Jeanmarie was terrified, and she scurried to hide behind her mother's skirt as Dory began filling the dishpan from the hot water reservoir on the stove.

"Goddamn brat! A man can't have peace and quiet in his own house. Come on out to the bunkhouse, Waller." Mumbling a string of oaths, Louis shoved back his chair, reached for his mackinaw and waited impatiently for Ben to get up from the table.

Odette watched Ben anxiously. She could tell by the frightened look on Jeanmarie's face that her uncle was angry. Ben put on his coat, went to her and placed his hand on her shoulder.

"You'll be all right here with the lady." He mouthed the words slowly. "I'll see you in the morning."

She nodded and watched him walk out the door behind the ugly-faced man who seemed so angry.

Dory sighed with relief when the men left the kitchen. She thought she had become used to Louis's treatment of her and Jeanmarie, but his actions tonight in front of Ben Waller had been especially vicious and humiliating. Usually Louis was satisfied with ignoring her and her daughter. Once Dory had glanced up and found Ben looking at her with eyes so narrow and so shielded with thick dark lashes that she couldn't tell if what she saw in them was pity or contempt.

Dory had just about made up her mind to leave the homestead. She didn't think she could endure another long winter here alone with just her daughter for company. Women were scarce in the timber country. She had no doubt that she could get work cooking in a lumber camp or go down the mountain to a town and find work. James would help her if she decided to go, but he wanted her to stay and hold on to what was rightfully hers. Of course, he didn't know what she had to put up with when he was away from the house.

"Louis and Milo would get too much satisfaction if you pulled out," James explained. "It's what they want. Stick it out, Sis. Give a man enough rope and he'll hang himself, as Papa used to say."

"I don't know if I can wait that long. Living here with Louis and Milo has had an unsettling effect on Jeanmarie. She gets all tense and big-eyed when they are near."

James was right, Dory thought now; but he wasn't the butt of abuse from both his half-brothers. Both men were careful not to ride James too hard. James had a quick temper, a quicker fist, and was far too popular with the men. With just one shove of a cant hook, a disgruntled man could cause a monumental jam on the narrow river. It would take days if not weeks to find and pry or blast loose the "key logs." It was a slow, dangerous process and many boom men unable to escape the sudden release of water and wood had been crushed to death or caught beneath the mass of logs and drowned.

Louis and Milo just might have met their match in Ben Waller, Dory thought, as she reached for the bar of lye soap and worked up a suds in the dishpan. He wasn't a handsome man; his nose was slightly off center in his strong-boned face. His blue-black hair and lashes were in sharp contrast to his steel-gray eyes. She had no doubt that he had seen rough, brutal action. Here was a man who would be able to hold his own with her brothers while he was here doing his job. She had dreamed of meeting such a man who would disregard her tarnished reputation and love her and her child. But it was a useless dream. Not even for her share in the business would a man like Ben Waller go partners with Louis and Milo.

Dory was acutely aware that she would have to keep a careful watch on Odette when Milo was around. It was common knowledge that he favored young girls and that he used Indian girls in such a rough way that it was a wonder he hadn't been found with a hatchet in his back. Dory had no doubt that Ben Waller would kill Milo without a second thought if he molested Odette. Although she despised her half-brother, she couldn't bring herself to wish him dead.

She turned to smile at Odette, who was clearing the table. Before the girl turned her head, Dory saw the shimmer of tears in her eyes. She quickly dried her hands and with a gentle finger turned Odette's face so that the girl could read her lips.

"He just went to the bunkhouse. He'll be here in the morning before he goes to the woods."

Odette nodded.

"Be happy here, Odette. Jeanmarie and I have been so lonely."

"Papa will come back," Odette said as if to convince herself.

"Of course, he will. He said you had new dress goods. We'll make it up and surprise him."

"I sew . . . some."

"Do you like books?"

"You have books?"

"Upstairs." Dory pointed toward the ceiling.

"Books? Ahhh . . ." Odette smiled.

"After kitchen chores"—Dory waved her hand toward the table, then the dishpan—"we'll go up."

Jeanmarie tugged on Odette's skirt. "I show you my picture book."

"Ahhh . . ." Odette said again. "You help with dishes, baby." She handed a plate to Jeanmarie to take to her mother. Odette smiled at Dory. "Baby will help."

Dory nodded happily and plunged her hands into the dishwater.

The wind blew itself out in the night. It had swept the yard clean and piled the snow against the barn and the bunkhouse.

When Dory went down to the kitchen to prepare breakfast, dawn was streaking the eastern sky and the day promised to be sunny. Wearing an old gray sweater and a yellow knit cap, she went out to the woodpile to get a few short pieces of firewood to add to the kindling already ablaze in the cookstove.

"Let me help you with that."

The voice behind Dory startled her. She turned so quickly that she almost dropped the wood she was stacking in the crook of her arm. Ben Waller, in his sheepskin coat, his brimmed hat pulled down low over his eyes, was close behind her.

"Thanks, but this will be enough to get me by until after breakfast."

"I'll fill the wood box before I go." Ben filled his own arms from a huge pile of neatly cut slabs of wood.

"I usually do it in the afternoon. It was too cold yesterday, and I had enough to last the night. Wiley cuts kindling for me," she finished lamely.

He walked beside her to the house. At the door he said, "Your brother is out in the smithy's shed. Do I dare come in before he gets here?"

She looked up to see an amused glint in his eyes.

"A sure way to get him here in a hurry is for you to pass through that door."

"Betcha a nickel he'll be here on a count of ten." Ben threw open the door and waited for her to enter.

"Make it fifteen and you've got a bet." Dory laughed up at him. She was a tall woman, but Ben topped her by a good six inches.

As soon as Ben stepped inside the door, he saw Odette. Her hair was brushed and tied at the nape of her neck, and she had a shawl around her shoulders. She waited beside the table for him to notice her. Ben went to her as soon as he dumped the wood in the woodbox.

"Mornin'."

"Papa." She mouthed the word.

Ben nudged her chin with his fist. "Aloud, you rascal."

"Mornin', Papa."

"That's better. Sleep good?"

"Warm featherbed. You?"

"Mine wasn't feathers, but I slept well." Ben shrugged out of his coat and hung it and his hat on the hook. "I take it I'm to eat breakfast in here," he said to Dory.

Loud thumps sounded on the porch seconds before the door was flung open.

"I counted to twenty-five," Dory said so low that only Ben could hear. "He's getting careless."

"What you mumblin' about?" Louis's loud voice bounced from wall to wall, making Ben wonder if the man was going deaf.

"I asked him how many eggs he wanted," Dory said irritably.

"Hurry it up. Goddamn! I can hardly wait to see that monster work. The bull-whackers brought it in a month ago. After we set her up we'll pull her up to the cutting camp. Heavy snow will be melting in the high range—"

Ben only half-listened to the man's ramblings. He wasn't saying anything that Ben didn't already know. He had studied the territory before he came here. The Saint Maries River passed through sixty miles of wild country to meet the Saint Joe, a torrent of tumbling icewater that flowed westward out of the rugged Bitterroot Range. The water below the merged rivers was calmer and boom men could sort out logs stamped on the ends with the names of the loggers upstream.

Dory dished up eggs and slabs of meat while Odette poured coffee. Louis ignored the women and talked constantly about how, with the help of the steam donkey, his logs would hit the fast water before Malone's.

Without appearing to do so, Ben watched Dory with Odette. Patient and smiling, Dory motioned to the breadboard and to the loaf of bread ready to be sliced. Odette flashed her a knowing smile and picked up the cutting knife. There was something different about Odette this morning. She was more at ease. It would make his leaving her here easier.

Ben couldn't help but feel a bit uneasy about this job. This place seemed like a tinderbox ready to explode. When the blow-up happened, he wanted Odette to be as far away as possible. His eyes fastened onto Louis Callahan's face. The man couldn't possibly be Odette's father. His features were large and coarse, while Odette's were small and fine-boned. Now he was curious to meet Milo Callahan. He wanted to find out if one of the Callahans had fathered Odette, but, he said to himself again, it would make no difference in his feeling for the girl.

In all his life Ben had never cared for anyone, nor had anyone cared for him, until Odette. It had taken him a while to get used to being responsible for a young girl. She had instantly become enamored of the idea that he was her father and had insisted on calling him "Papa."

Ben's thoughts turned to Dory Callahan and her daughter. There had been a sparkle in Dory's eyes this morning. A fascinating dimple appeared in her cheek when she smiled with her lips still pressed together. The woman had had a rough time, but it hadn't broken her spirit. He wondered why she stayed here and took her brother's abuse. Surely with her share of the company money she could live in town.

Ben looked down at his plate. He couldn't afford to feel any sympathy for Dory, but he couldn't keep his eyes away from her tall, graceful body when she moved from the stove to the table. Her waist was small, her breasts rounded and swaying gently beneath the loose shirt. Her head, with its tangle of wild, tight curls, rode proudly on her slender neck. She was a handsome, capable woman. If what her brother said about her was true, he was sure to hear about it from the other men, although it didn't matter to him what she was as long as she was kind to Odette.

It was strange, Ben thought. A man can fornicate every day of the week, but if a woman does so one time, she is branded forever as a slut.

"I said, how long will it take to get the donkey goin'?" Louis's irritated voice broke into Ben's thoughts.

"Depends." Ben drank the last of his coffee.

"On what?" Louis insisted.

"On a number of things. We can have the engine going in a week or two if you have the right tools. It'll take longer to set it in place and anchor it. Longer yet to train the men to operate it. It's a dangerous machine."

"Well, let's get goin'." Louis set his mug down on the table with unnecessary force. He stood and glared at Dory. "Don't you be lettin' in ever' jaybird that comes by. Hear?" he growled.

Although Dory felt as if her nerves were being ground to the raw ends, she ignored him and looked at Ben. "Don't worry about Odette."

"Get her to talk aloud if you can. She's real stingy with words. If there's something she doesn't understand, write it down. She reads and writes real good."

"I know. She read aloud to Jeanmarie last night."

Ben looked surprised. "She did? She's not done that before that I know of. Of course, we've not had access to many books."

Had Louis not been there, she would have told him how glad she was to have his daughter's company, but she didn't dare for fear Louis would find a way to take this little bit of pleasure from her.

Odette came to stand beside Ben, her face tilted up, her large cornflower eyes on his face. The small girl's head barely came to her father's shoulder.

"I'll be back in a few days." Ben cuffed his daughter gently on the chin with his fist. "You can count on it."

"Be careful, Papa."

"I will. Bye, honey."

"Bye, Papa."

Louis stood scowling beside the door and jerked it open

when Ben came toward him. The glance he threw his sister was malignant. Ben paused and spoke to Dory.

"Thanks for the breakfast and for looking after my girl." He spoke coolly and there appeared to be what she considered a warning glint in his eyes.

"You're quite welcome, Mr. Waller," she replied just as coolly.

As she watched the men leave, Dory pondered the coolness in Ben's voice and decided the big man would make a formidable enemy. He had a quick mind and would be a match for men such as Louis and Milo who were filled with latent viciousness. He was shrewd and tough under that quiet exterior. He was the kind of man who remained alive by knowing what to expect and from what direction to expect it.

She looked forward to seeing him again.

The next ten days were boisterous and happy at the Callahan homestead. For the two women and the child they were carefree days of fun and laughter. Dory and Jeanmarie enjoyed Odette's company so much that they were almost giddy. Dory taught her to crochet, to make bread, and to pop the corn she brought up from the cellar beneath the house. They made taffy candy one afternoon, and while pulling it, Odette laughed so hard she fell back into a chair, covering her face with her buttery hands—which evoked even more laughter. Odette taught Jeanmarie how to cut a string of paper dolls out of an old newspaper and how to lace her fingers to make a church and a steeple. In the evening after the child had gone to bed, she and Dory sewed on the new dress material.

Sid Hanes, a mill worker and one of Milo's cronies, knocked on the kitchen door one morning. He was a short man, stockily built with wide shoulders and long arms. When he came to the house with Milo, his faded blue eyes roamed over Dory like a dog salivating over a bone. She detested him.

"What do you want?" Dory demanded in a scathing tone as soon as she opened the door.

"Yore brother said stop an' see if ya was all right."

"Liar."

"I'm hungry as a bear."

"Go eat with the hogs where you belong." Dory attempted to close the door. His arm shot out and flung it open. Dory let out a muffled gasp of fury. "Step inside this door and I'll fill your belly full of buckshot!"

"I ain't no fool. I ain't comin' in without no invite. Old Wiley's got a shotgun pointed at my back. I jist want to see the dummy." His eyes moved past Dory and settled on Odette. "Bugger! Louis didn't say she was pretty as a blue-wing teal."

"Get away from this door, Sid!" Dory demanded in a strident shout.

"Air ya jealous cause she's prettier an' younger'n ya are? It makes no never mind to me. Yo're still my woman."

"You . . . varmint! Weasel! Filthy hog! Stinking pole-cat—" Dory reached for the water bucket to fling at him. When he stepped back, she slammed the door and dropped a bar across it.

"There'll come a time when I'll learn ya to keep a civil tongue in yore head." Sid's angry voice sprang boldly through the closed door.

Dory stood in troubled silence looking at Odette's quizzical face. She forced herself to laugh. "He's just . . . a rejected suitor. He's leaving." There was a note of desperation in her voice that Odette couldn't hear.

Odette smiled. The smiled faded as she went into a fit of coughing. The girl had had a persistent cough for days. Dory had made a syrup of equal parts of honey, vinegar and whiskey and every so often had given her a spoonful. It was only a temporary relief.

The next afternoon, with Jeanmarie skipping along between them, they explored the woods behind the house to get a breath of fresh air and to look for early spring flowers. The days were getting longer, the sun warmer. Two deer at a salt lick were startled by their approach and darted into the dense stand of trees.

"Come back! Come back!" Jeanmarie ran after them. "We won't hurt you."

Dory ran to catch her daughter before she went deeper into the woods. The child squealed with laughter as she was caught and pinned to her mother's side with an arm looped around her middle. As Dory turned to go back to Odette, she saw Milo coming out of the woods behind the girl.

"Boo!" he said, his mouth close to Odette's ear.

Unaware of his presence, Odette stood watching Dory and Jeanmarie as they walked toward her. The child had stopped laughing and hid her face against her mother's shoulder.

"She really *is* a dummy," Milo said, and moved around to peer into Odette's face. He laughed when the girl, realizing a man was standing close beside her, jumped back. "Scared ya, did I?"

"Stay away from her, Milo," Dory said sharply. "She can't hear, but she can read lips. She'll tell her father—"

"Sid told me she was pretty and . . . ripe. He was right as rain." He chuckled and reached to touch the blond curl that lay on Odette's cheek. She jerked her head away from his hand. "Always did like light-haired women." Milo grinned, showing a space between his big square front teeth.

Milo was not as tall as his brother Louis and had the same heavy features. He wore the clothes of a lumberjack: heavy duck pants, flannel shirt and caulked boots. He was exceedingly proud of his thick dark hair and the heavy mustache that drooped down on each side of his mouth. Dory suspected the reason he let his hair grow to cover his ears was to taunt Louis, who was bald except for the fringe of coarse springy hair that grew around the lower part of his head.

Odette's fearful eyes looked up at Dory. Dory took her hand.

"Stay away from her, Milo," Dory warned again. "She's very shy. One word from her and Ben Waller will pull out, leaving you and Louis high and dry."

Ignoring the warning, Milo stood in front of them when they attempted to pass. "Don't be in such a hurry. Does she talk?"

"Yes, she talks. I'm warning you, Milo—"

"Make her say something. I've never heard a dummy talk."

"Don't call her that . . . and get out of the way." Dory pulled on Odette's hand and they went around him.

"I'll be in for supper," he called as they headed for the house.

"Eat in the bunkhouse," Dory yelled back.

"I said, I'll be in for supper, dammit! I'll sleep in my bed too."

Dory whirled around. "It'll be pretty crowded. All three of us will be sleeping in that bed."

"It'll not be no chore a-tall to get rid of *two* of you." He laughed nastily as Dory sneered at him with disgust.

"Damn lecher!" Dory muttered to herself.

As soon as they were inside the house, Odette put her hand on Dory's arm to get her attention.

"What he say, Dory?"

"Nothing for you to worry about," she replied slowly. "He's my brother . . . and he likes to . . . tease."

"He's mean, like Louis." Odette covered her mouth with her hand and coughed.

Dory made no attempt to contradict. She sighed heavily. "I'm afraid so. But he won't bother you. I wish we could get rid of that cough."

"Throat sore now."

"Sit down and I'll fix you some hot tea."

"I wish Papa would come."

"So do I, honey."

Quietly the women went about the chore of fixing supper. Even Jeanmarie was subdued. The child sat on a stool beside the woodbox holding a doll her mother had made out of a stocking. Milo's presence at the homestead was like a dash of cold water on their spirits. The meal was only half ready when he flung open the door and came into the kitchen.

"Supper isn't ready," Dory said crossly.

"I can see that. I ain't blind." He hung his coat on the rack beside the door, hooked a chair out from the table with his foot and straddled it, resting his arms on the back. A grin spread across his broad face as his eyes wandered over Odette's slight body.

Dory saw his lecherous gaze and read his thoughts. She made no attempt to hide her opinion of him.

"You're disgusting," she snapped. "You're old enough to be her father."

"I'm shore glad I ain't. I'd say she's 'bout the age you was when you got busted. Hey, pretty girl, pour me some coffee." With her back to him, Odette continued stirring the chopped potatoes frying in the big iron skillet. "Shit! I forget she can't hear. Don't she hear anything a-tall? Hell, it don't make no difference. I think I like it. I won't get no back talk." He laughed as if he had said something terribly funny.

One brief glance at Dory's tight-lipped mouth told Odette

that she was angry at the man at the table. Had he said something about *her*? Some sixth sense told her that he was watching her and that his thoughts were less than honorable. Odette felt heat rush into her face and at the same time a cold chill traveled down her spine. She swallowed in an effort to ease the soreness in her throat.

This man was of the same breed that sometimes had come to visit her mother before she had become so sick she could no longer "entertain" them. On these occasions her mother would tell her to go to a small room off the kitchen and would lock the door. Lying on a pallet, she would wait until her mother came for her.

Odette watched Dory for her reaction to the man. She was unlike any woman Odette had ever known. Dory romped and played like a child with her and Jeanmarie, yet she was a grown woman, a mother. Odette had been delighted to know that Dory could make clay pots, and Dory had promised to show her how to form them and bake them in the outside oven Mr. Callahan had built for Dory's mother. Although Odette missed the security of being with Ben, she had truly enjoyed being here with Dory and Jeanmarie.

Odette made a wide circle around the man in the chair when she carried the bowl of potatoes to the table. On the way back to the stove she uttered a cry of alarm and moved quickly to evade the hand that snaked out to grab her skirt.

"I'm warning you, Milo," Dory said angrily, placing herself between Odette and her brother. "Keep your hands off her, or I'll brain you with a stick of stove wood."

"Ohhh . . . I'm scared." Milo held up his hands as if to protect himself.

"You came down because of her, didn't you?"

"I sure didn't come to get an eyeful of you, *sister*. Louis said she was a dummy. Sid said she was pretty as a buttercup.

I ain't ever had me no dummy and it's been a month or more since I had me a woman that ain't been broke into." He laughed loud and long at the look of disgust on Dory's face.

"You're sorry through and through. You make me want to puke."

"Sorry? What's sorry about doin' what comes natural? I have myself a hell of a time. Sid's got his eye on you. Know that?"

"You and Sid Hanes are chips off the same rotten block."

"How long's it been since you had a man? Not since that puny Malone kid got hisself killed, huh?"

"Shut up!" Dory slammed a plate of fried meat on the table. "Eat and get out."

"I ain't going nowhere . . . except up to my bed." He reached out and pinched her on the thigh.

She aimed at the side of his face with the back of her hand. He dodged the blow and laughed.

"If I told James that you pinch and slap me, he'd tear your blasted head off."

"Go right ahead and tell him if you want to see him laid out on a slab. I might take him for a deer when I'm hunting. Better yet, I might lose control of a plank and knock him into the saw blade."

"Mistake him for a deer like you did Mick Malone?"

"Mick Malone? Let's see. Wasn't he the little bastard's pa? I might of took him for a red-headed woodpecker, but not a deer."

With her back to Milo, Odette touched Dory's arm and mouthed, "Upstairs."

Dory shook her head. "Stay with me," she replied, making her mouth work slowly.

Odette nodded her understanding.

"What'er you saying to her?" Milo demanded.

"I'm telling her that you're a mule's ass and not to let you catch her alone."

"Well, now, if you'd a called me a horny billy goat, I wouldn't have cared, but mule's ass—that's going to get you another pinch," he said good-naturedly.

CHAPTER
* 5 *

The mill camp, set in a scarred clearing of tree stumps, was larger than Ben expected. Besides the mill building, there were two large three-sided sheds, the bunkhouse, the cook shack, a sturdy barn and a network of pole corrals. Beyond the camp, surrounded by dense undergrowth and young saplings, was a neat log cabin with real glass windows.

One of the buildings was a partial dugout—thirty feet long with walls scarcely four feet above the ground. A slanting ramp led down to a door on the south side of the structure. Logs reared up out of the ground to support a roof of shakes covered with evergreen boughs. From the squat stone smokestack in the center of the roof, heavy black smoke, the result of burning wood that was too green, billowed upward and hung over the camp.

Ben had spent more years of his life than he cared to remember in such a building. This was where the crew lived and slept in a field bed that extended the full length of the building. The fifteen or more men slept in the communal bed with their heads toward the wall. At the foot of the bed, between the loggers' feet and the fire, was a long flat beam called the "deacon's seat." The loggers sat on it before the blazing fire, joked and told stories to while away the long winter evenings. At bedtime each man mounted the deacon's seat to get in and out of the neighborly bed that stood two or three feet above the hard-packed dirt floor. His belongings, wrapped in a tarp or in a canvas bag, were stashed underneath.

The other fully enclosed building was the cook shack. A good cook was well paid in a lumber camp. He fed his men exceedingly well on what was the usual allowance of thirty cents a day per man. He baked, stewed, fried and roasted great quantities of meat and vegetables to assuage the appetites of men who worked hard all day in subzero weather and generated unbelievable appetites. The cook's helper, known as "bull cook," tended fire, carried water, peeled potatoes, and washed the dishes. It was also his duty to call the men to eat, which he did with gusto on cold frosty mornings.

On the morning Ben arrived at the camp, a small bookish-type man named Steven Marz was having an argument with Milo Callahan. Milo was against paying the cook's helper the wage owed him because the man needed to leave the camp without notice, having just received word that one of his children was seriously ill. Marz and Milo were not matched physically, but verbally Marz was far superior. His reasoning persuaded Milo, and the grateful bull cook left with his wages in his pocket. Marz then teamed up with the cook to prepare hot meals for the rest of the crew until another bull cook could be hired.

Steven Marz lived in the cabin. Ben liked him the moment he met him. He was a serious-faced man; slightly built, with a head of thick brown hair streaked with gray, a V-shaped mustache and wire-rimmed spectacles. It was difficult for Ben to believe the soft-spoken, highly intelligent man who kept the company accounts in a cubbyhole of an office would stay and work for such a disagreeable employer. It didn't take long for Ben to realize that the mill hands also liked and respected Steven.

Late one afternoon several days later, Ben went into the mill. The steam-driven engine had been fired up and circular saws were eating into the peeled log that sat on the carriage that carried it to the blades. The howl of the machinery, like the cry of a banshee—which was merely noise to the average woodsman—was familiar music to Ben's ears. He loved everything that had anything to do with milling lumber: the smell of the freshly cut wood, the challenge of handling the huge logs, the song of the blades and the steam-powered engine that drove them.

He watched for a moment while the dogger, a man whose muscles bunched and strained, rode the sawdust-covered carriage and levered the massive log to rest against the plank gauge. With wide shoulders, narrow hips and long powerful legs, the man controlled the log from the instant the perfectly aligned steel teeth of the blades sank into the butt until a single four-inch slab fell from the carriage. Grinning with satisfaction at the near-perfect cut, he waved at the sawyer at the controls, and another log was levered into position while the saw blades continued to sing their hungry tune.

The sawyer, Tinker Buck, a swarthy, ragged little man with a round black beard and a New England twang in his speech, handled the control levers of the huge engine. Considered to be one of the best sawyers in the Bitterroot Range, Tinker obviously enjoyed working with the man riding the carriage. A wide grin split his dark face from ear to ear, showing the gleam of a gold tooth. Through the deafening noise of the blades, he communicated with the "dogger"—the man positioning the log for the next cut—by using hand signals. The dogger watched Tinker's signals and strained every muscle of his big body to lever the log an inch or two this way or that to position it on the carriage.

Two men usually worked the carriage. Ben's eyes swept the scene for the dogger's helper and found a short, stumpy-legged man whose straw-colored hair hung beneath a leather hat. The brim was turned up in front and fastened with a feather. He stood leaning on his pike, making no move to lever the end of the log into place. The corners of his thin lips were lifted in a sneer. His eyes gleamed with hostility.

Ben returned the man's hostile gaze with no show of emotion. Beneath his calm expression his mind was working quickly. He had seen men of this caliber in every logging camp in the territory. The cruelty in the helper's face seemed to spring from some inner source of malice and hatred. Milling was dangerous work even if the team worked in unison and every man knew every move his teammate would make. In this place there were two factions working against each other. Sooner or later a catastrophe was bound to happen.

When Ben noticed that Steven had come out of his office and was trying to speak to him, he waved him toward the side door and the two walked out into the cool mountain air toward the sheds. As soon as they were far enough away from the screaming blades to hear each other, Steven spoke.

"It sets my teeth on edge to watch James work the carriage. He takes too many chances and Tinker eggs him on."

"It was James Callahan handling the logs? I thought he was foreman up at the cutting camp."

"Most of his men have been with him through six cutting seasons. They are a loyal bunch and can carry on without him. You can never tell when James will show up. He came down with the names of the extra men he hired for the summer and the supply list. When he found out Milo was gone today, he took a turn riding the carriage. There's nothing James likes better than meddling in Milo's operation here at the mill."

"It takes a powerful man to handle logs that size. He's

good, I'll say that for him. I've never seen better. I take it he and the dogger's helper don't see eye to eye."

"You take it right. Sid Hanes is Milo's man. They're thicker than thieves and both are jealous of James because he can outdo Milo or Sid in everything they attempt to do without even breaking a sweat. It sticks in their craws like a burr." When Ben failed to comment, Steven said, "How's things going?"

"I've gone about as far as I can go before I make a trip to the smithy." He paused and waited. Somehow he knew Steven had something on his mind other than the new engine.

"Old Wiley is as good a smithy as you'll find. He was a hell of a man before he got crippled up."

"Logging is a dangerous business. It's crippled many a good man."

"That it has. If you leave for the homestead now, you can make it down before dark. Milo went down this afternoon." Steven's eyes looked directly into Ben's as he spoke.

Ben stared at the other man for a long moment, then interjected in a deadly tone, "Are you telling me something, Steven?"

"Only that Milo left the mill just as we were starting a two-hour run, which is unusual unless he's got something urgent on his mind. I doubt it was Dory he was anxious to see."

"Are the tales Milo tells about his consorting with women a mere brag, or are they true?" Ben stood motionless, his gaze locked on the other man, the muscles working in his jaw.

"I don't know what all you've heard," Steven said evenly. "But if I had a girl within fifty miles of Milo, I'd keep a close watch on her."

"Thanks." Ben made a guttural sound of fury and picked

up a rag to wipe his hands. The anger on his whiskered face was ice-cold. "I'll tell you now"—he threw down the rag—"that if that bastard dishonors my girl, I'll kill him quicker than I would a rattler coiled and ready to strike."

"Dory will see that it doesn't go that far. She'll do everything in her power to protect her, but she can't stop him from pestering her."

Ben went to the barn and quickly saddled his horse. His dislike for Milo Callahan exceeded even his dislike for his brother, Louis. In the short time he had been in their employ he had learned that the majority of the men disliked and distrusted both brothers, but the younger of the two was held in especially low regard. The attitude of the lumberjacks more than their spoken words had led Ben to that conclusion. Still, a few of the men laughed with Milo when he bragged about the number of women he'd had after a day in town or about his staying power in bed, or when he took credit for a dozen or more Indian half-breeds living in the area.

The man sickened Ben. He avoided him when possible and rarely answered him even when he asked a question about the engine.

It was dusk as Ben made his way down the mountain to the homestead. His stomach muscles knotted up at the thought of Odette being scared half out of her wits by a man old enough to be her father. He'd had a gut feeling that Dory Callahan, even if she were the sort of woman Louis and Milo portrayed her to be, would look out for the girl or he wouldn't have left her there. Now, he wasn't so sure. He had heard a few offhand remarks about Dory. Once, to his friends, Milo had referred to his half-sister as "Whory Dory" and the men had laughed.

As shy as Odette was, it was hard for Ben to believe she had been raised in a whorehouse. Her mother had protected her well. Now that he had met Milo and Louis, the thought of one of them being the natural father of Odette was like salt in an open wound.

Light shone from the kitchen windows as he approached the house. He rode his horse to within a few feet of the back porch and dismounted. As he looped the reins over a bush, he heard a woman's shrill screech. His booted feet hit the porch and he flung open the door.

Milo sat astride a chair with his fist wrapped in Odette's skirt. Dory stood over him, hitting him with a large spoon. He was laughing and dodging the blows. Odette, a look of terror on her face, was holding onto the table in an attempt to keep from being drawn closer to her tormentor.

"Leave her alone! Damn, damn you!" Dory tried to wedge herself between her brother and Odette.

"Come 'ere, girl. Give me a kiss."

"Let her go!" Ben was across the room in three long strides and lifted Milo off the chair by the nape of his neck. Milo was a strong stocky man, but surprise rendered him helpless. "I ought to break every bone in your miserable body . . . you sorry piece of cow dung!" Ben flung Milo from him. The man staggered back against the open door, causing it to bang against the wall.

"Pa . . . pa!" Odette wailed.

As Ben turned to her, she ran to him, wrapped her arms around his waist and buried her face against his coat. With his hands on her shoulders, he held her away from him so that he could look into her face.

"Are you all right?" he asked slowly.

Odette nodded her head, her eyes going to Dory.

"Are you crazy?" Milo shouted, his face red with anger. "I was only funnin'. I didn't hurt her."

"If you had, you'd have had a bullet between your eyes

before she got the words out of her mouth to tell me about it,'' Ben snarled, his eyes blazing with fury.

''You're crazy,'' Milo said again. ''Get out . . . and take that dummy with you!''

''No!'' Dory's voice was shrill with panic.

''Get out! Get out! You're fired!'' Milo shouted in a cry of raw rage.

''Gladly,'' Ben replied. His eyes were steel-gray frost, his face like hard stone.

''No!'' Dory said again. ''Please . . .''

Ben's eyes flicked to her and back to Milo. ''I'll go and I'll take the pay for a complete job.''

''Like hell you will!''

Ben met Milo's hostile look and sent back his own challenge. ''That's right, like hell I *will*.'' He looked down at Odette and tilted her chin so she would look at him. ''Get your things, honey.'' Then to Dory, ''I'll take her with me up to the camp to get my gear.''

Dory's face turned pale, then red as she turned the full force of her anger on Milo.

''You low-life, fornicating weasel. I hope Louis horsewhips you for messing up his plans. You'll pay this man for a complete job or James and I will go to Judge Kenton. We have an equal vote.''

''Stay out of this!'' Milo roared. ''No man comes into *my* house, puts his hands on me and gets away with it.''

''This is *my* house and James's house. You were putting your hands on this man's daughter,'' Dory shouted back, her voice sharp, hard, and quivering with anger. ''I warned you!''

''She was switchin' her ass like she wanted it! I was givin' her what she asked for.''

''Liar! Stupid, woman-crazy liar!''

''I didn't hurt the little bitch.''

''You flap-jawed rattle-head! You scared her. You don't

have an ounce of decency.'' Dory's voice was high and shrill, her eyes full of wildness. She was on the verge of losing control.

''What do you know of decency . . . Whory Dory?''

''A hell of a lot more than a ruttin' beast like you.''

''You're lucky you and your brat's got a roof over your head . . . slut!'' Milo saw the color leave his sister's face and felt triumphant. He continued to taunt. ''You itchin' for the donkey man, Whory Dory?''

A single look at Ben Waller's set face and blazing eyes made Dory's stomach cramp with rage and sickness. The strain of years of living with brothers who hated her and her child, enduring their taunts and insults, suddenly sapped every bit of her inner strength. She had none left to face yet another crisis. Since Mick's death, a yearning had burned in Dory—a yearning to be held, loved, to have a shoulder to lean on, to belong to someone. With a feeling of chilling reality, she knew that kind of happiness would never be hers no matter how much she longed for it.

Suddenly her emotions dried to a terrible stillness. Madness skirted the edges of her mind. *She could bear no more*. Years of fear and humiliation stretched ahead—years of unbearable loneliness.

A raw cry of rage tore from her throat. With an abrupt, savage gesture she jerked a knife from the table and sprang at Milo. As quick as she was, Ben was quicker. He grabbed the wrist of the hand holding the knife, and at the same time an arm around Dory's waist swung her away from Milo, who stood in frozen astonishment. Ben took the knife from her numb fingers and tossed it onto the workbench.

''I'll . . . kill . . . him,'' Dory panted and struggled to free herself from Ben's grasp. ''He . . . they . . . ruin everything—''

''Jesus Christ! She tried to kill me!'' Milo gasped as the

possibility of personal danger sank into his mind. And before Ben could react, he openhandedly struck Dory a vicious blow across the face. His hand was drawn back to deliver another blow when Ben's fist connected with his jaw, knocking him back against the table.

"Get out," Ben snarled. "Get out before I kill you myself."

"You ain't orderin' me out of my own house," Milo said belligerently, his hand going to his face.

"Get out of my sight or, by God, you'll be crawling out of here on your belly. I know ways to break your legs before you can say your name. If you put your hands on my girl again, I'll come looking for you with a whip and a gun."

Milo staggered toward the door. "Ain't you forgot who I am? You *was* workin' for me. Be gone from here by morning and take that dummy with you or—" He left the threat hanging and slammed out the door.

Dory sank down at the table and buried her face in her folded arms. She began to tremble when she realized what would have happened if Ben had not stopped her. During the past year there had been moments when she had been afraid she would go mad. *She almost had.* Her self-control had stretched to the breaking point. There was so much hatred, pain and unhappiness in this house that had once held so much love that she feared she was losing her mind. The ache in her heart was so much a part of her that over the years she had become used to it. The coming of Ben Waller and Odette had made her realize how much of life's joy she was missing.

She shed no tears. Her pain was too great for mere tears.

Ben glanced at Odette, who stood far back in the corner with little Jeanmarie in her arms. He went to Dory and placed his hand on her shoulder.

"Are you afraid he'll come back and hurt you?"

"No." With pride and dignity Dory lifted her chin a little higher. "He only goes so far. It's strange but after all this time the words hurt more than the slap. When all else fails Milo dips into his dirty mind for a weapon to use against me. I'm sorry if you were embarrassed."

Ben shrugged. "I considered the source."

The emotional fury she had exhibited was gone. She was firmly in control once again.

"I'm not afraid of him; my room has a stout door with a bar across it." She went to Odette and took the child from her arms. Jeanmarie snuggled her face against her mother's neck. "Thank you for what you did," she said calmly, not looking at Ben. "If I had stabbed him, he would have killed me. I'm sorry I couldn't do more to protect Odette. I don't blame you for taking her away from here. The Malones will be glad to have a man of your talents. They'll give you work. Marie Malone will look after Odette."

"Papa—" Odette pulled on Ben's hand to get his attention. "Not Dory's fault."

"I'm not blaming her. Get your things, honey, and we'll be on our way."

Jeanmarie began to cry. "Don't want Odette to go," she wailed.

"Shhh . . . punkin. Shhh . . ." Dory's voice broke, only to return in a raspy whisper. "Odette has to go with her papa." Dory rubbed the child's back and placed kisses on her forehead.

Looking up at Ben, Odette was unaware of the crying child until she turned to cast pleading eyes at Dory. Sobbing, Jeanmarie held her arms out for Odette to take her. Odette took the little girl and held her tightly.

"Don't cry . . . baby. Don't cry . . . baby." Odette cast

a desperate look at Ben, then sat down on a chair with the child in her arms and rocked her back and forth.

"They took to each other right away," Dory said in way of apology. "Jeanmarie will be all right. She's gotten over disappointments before."

Ben felt a pang of indecision. Not in the three years he and Odette had been together had she expressed affection for anyone other than him. It had worried him some. He had hoped that some day she would find a good man, marry, and have a family of her own. Whatever else had happened while she was here, she, Dory and the child had become attached to one another.

Ben looked at the woman standing beside the chair. She had refused to give in to tears, but they were there, making her green eyes wet and shiny. They reminded him of a mountain pool. Her skin was pale beneath the red welt on her face. His gaze dropped to her breasts curved softly beneath the loose shirt she had tucked into the waistband of her skirt. Whatever else she was, she was a spunky woman. Dammit, he didn't want to care about her or her child. He needed time. Lord. He needed time to think.

"Do you mind if I have a cup of that coffee?"

"Of course not. I'll get it," Dory said, after she recovered from her surprise. She hadn't expected a civil word from him. They looked at each other. He watched her with eyes that revealed absolutely nothing. She met his glance unflinchingly. Suddenly they were both conscious of the welt on her face. It was slowly swelling and would soon turn into a dark bruise. Dory was aware of it because she was ashamed. Ben, because it made him angry. Pride refused to allow her to acknowledge it by touching it with her fingers although her jaw hurt when she spoke.

"Is this the first time he's hit you?"

"Oh, no." Dory's contemptuous laugh caused her to wince. "He usually pinches, but he hits occasionally." Slowly, as she felt his appraisal, a shiver shimmied down her spine. She looked away quickly before his eyes could read the misery in hers.

A short, vivid expletive broke from Ben's mouth. "What in God's name is the matter with James that he allows him to do that?"

Dory glanced at the cold-eyed man, aware that behind the calm mask was lethal fury and a will as hard as granite.

"He doesn't know, and I would be obliged if you didn't tell him." She spoke quietly with no emotion. "James would beat Milo senseless if he knew how mean he is to me and Jeanmarie. And it's likely that I would find James in the woods shot in the back. I don't want him to know," she repeated firmly as she set the mug of coffee on the table. "You'd best watch your back, too; Milo has a way of getting even with anyone who crosses him."

"I figured him for a back-shooter. I've come across his type before." His cold steely eyes bored into hers.

"Louis is mean, but in a different way. He'll not backshoot you." Dory ran her fingers over Jeanmarie's hair as she passed on her way back to the stove. "He lives and breathes Callahan Lumber. Milo follows his lead, but his only interest in the company is what he gets out of it." Unnerved by his steady stare, Dory said quickly, "You might as well eat supper before you go. It's ready."

"You needn't go to the bother. I'll grab a bite out with Wiley."

"It'll not be a bother. Don't you want to try the bread pudding Odette made this morning?"

Dory looked over at him when she spoke, and he could see dark smudges beneath her great green eyes. She looked worn out, Ben thought as his eyes roamed her face. A strange feeling began to stir in him. For Christsake! What was the matter with him? For all he knew she was what her brother said she was: a loose, wanton woman.

"I can't very well miss Odette's pudding, now can I?" In spite of his previous dark thoughts, a smile began in his eyes, darkening and warming them, and then spread to his mouth. His lips parted to show exceptionally white even teeth.

A wistful expression settled on Dory's face. He was so damn handsome, yet steady as an oak tree. Here was a man a woman could depend on. She shivered as if a flame had licked along her veins. Her mouth was so dry that her tongue stuck to the roof and her lips felt as if they were glued together. She managed to nod as she turned back to the stove.

CHAPTER
* 6 *

"What'er ya lookin' at, old man?"

Wiley had looked up when Milo had stomped into the room and slammed the door. He continued to look as Milo shook off his coat, tossed it on a chair and dabbed at the blood on his mouth with the towel he jerked from the washstand.

"Did a stick of stove wood jump up and hit ya?"

"What'a you care?"

"Wondered. That's all." Wiley brokc off a piece of bread and dipped it in his soup bowl.

"Keep yore trap shut," Milo growled. "I ain't in no mood to take no sass off a crippled old fool who don't do enough to earn his keep."

Wiley grunted and continued to eat. He had heard those words or others like them a hundred times before. How a man as good and kind as George Callahan could have raised Milo and Louis was beyond Wiley's understanding. George Callahan's first wife had been alive when Wiley had come to work for him. Milo had been a kid of eight or nine years, Louis a few years older. Even then Milo had been a mouthy, cantankerous brat, the image of his ma—a woman Wiley never heard speak a kind word from the first time he set eyes on her until the day she died. Wiley suspected that George had never had a happy day in his life until he married Jean Malone. He had fairly worshiped the woman and had gone downhill fast after she died.

Until the time of his accident, Wiley had been cutting foreman. He was injured when a falling tree split and kicked back, striking his leg with such force that it broke the bone in several places. Unable to get Wiley down the mountain to a doctor, the men in the camp had set the bones. They had done their best, but their skills were limited and their supplies scant. As a result, Wiley was permanently crippled.

When he was able to get around, George had brought him down to the homestead to help the smithy. He had taken to the job, determined to earn his keep. He was good enough now to get work most any place he wanted to go, but he hung on here because he thought he might be of some use to Dory and the baby.

Milo hooked a chair out from the table and sat down. "Get me something to eat."

Pride forced Wiley to hold his head erect and look the man in the eye.

"Soup's on the stove. Here's fresh bread." He pushed the wooden board holding the loaf of bread closer to Milo. "Thought ya was eatin' in the house."

"Keep yore damn thoughts to yoreself, ya old goat." Milo pushed his chair back and went to the stove. "What's this other stuff here in the pan?"

"Bread puddin'."

"Ya got it pretty soft, ain't ya, old man. Whory Dory bringin' puddin' an' pie so ya'll keep yore mouth shut 'bout her whorin' when me and Louis ain't here."

Wiley didn't answer. He didn't mind it so much when Milo or Louis took their spite out on him, but when they talked about Dory in an insulting way it made him want to horse-whip them. He kept his head bent over his bowl so that Milo would not see that the words bothered him. In this mood, Milo was as mean as a rutting moose and if aggravated might really hurt him. A few months back Milo had yanked a chair out from under him and he had been laid up for a week.

"I'm talking to ya. Ya deaf like that dummy in there?"

"I heard ya," Wiley muttered.

Milo brought the pudding to the table and began to eat out of the pan.

"That high-handed sonofabitch Waller will get what's coming to him for buttin' in my business. You can bet your ass on it. There's plenty a ways of gettin' even." Milo scooped up another spoonful of pudding.

"Louis is dependin' on him to set up that engine so they can snake those big'uns out of the woods."

"Hell. It don't take no brains to set up that pissin' engine. It ain't no different than the one in the mill. We ain't needin' no outsider comin' in lordin' it over us."

"I hear the donkey blows pretty easy."

"I hope the hell it does an' takes him with it." Milo's voice rose as his anger escalated. "Sonofabitch's sittin' in there eatin' at my table while I eat with a crippled up old beggar."

Resentment stiffened Wiley's back. "I'm crippled. I won't argue that. But I ain't no beggar and never have been."

"If I say yo're a beggar, yo're a gawddamn pissin' beggar," Milo shouted as he flung himself from the table, sending his chair crashing to the floor. He slammed the pudding pan into the slop bucket and jerked on his coat and cap before he stomped out the door.

Wiley sat for a moment, relieved that he was gone. Then he left the table and hobbled into the darkened part of the bunkhouse so that he could look out the window. Milo was saddling his horse. Ben Waller's horse stood by the porch. That explained Milo's bad mood and cut lip. Wiley would bet his last dime Milo had had a run-in with Waller over his daughter. The man was going to get hisself killed fooling around with young girls. It was just a matter of time.

Like a shouted warning the realization came to Wiley: Things around here were about to change—forever. Waller wasn't a man to be pushed or one who backed down. His loose-knit frame and the careless way he held his hands to his sides, the air of quiet watching, was a trifle too well-managed, too pat. Wiley had been around long enough to know that Ben Waller was a bobcat with bristles on his belly. By jinks damn! Milo might not be so lucky next time.

Wiley waited until Milo was astride his horse and heading toward the mill before he left the window and went back to the table.

He looked at the pudding pan upside down in the slop bucket and shook his head in disgust. It was a childish, irrational act to dump the pudding. It spelled out clearly what Wiley had thought all along: Milo was going crazy in the head—as crazy as his ma had been before she died.

It didn't look good for Dory and the baby unless Waller stayed around. Wiley wondered again if he should break his promise and tell James the straight about a few things. Still, if he did that and James had an *accident*, Dory would be alone. It was a hell of a mess.

There was total silence in the kitchen while Ben ate the meal Dory had placed before him. Odette had shaken her head when asked to eat and continued to hold Jeanmarie, who had cried herself to sleep. With a heavy heart Dory sat down at the table and waited for Ben to finish his supper.

She was determined to make him understand that Odette

was in no condition to make that long ride to the Malones'. The croupy cough she'd had since the day after he brought her here had held on in spite of the dosing of hot tea and honey Dory had given her. Now Odette's flushed cheeks were a sure sign of a fever. Dory couldn't blame Ben for wanting to take his daughter from this place, but oh . . . it would be so lonely here when they were gone.

For a brief moment Dory considered asking Ben to take her with him. She could stay with the McHenrys for a while. It was only fair that her daughter know her grandparents. She had no doubt that Chip and Marie would take to her baby. But would they try to take her baby away from her?

The only time Chip Malone had seen Jeanmarie was when she was a lively two-year-old. The giant of a red-haired man had stood as still as a stone in the doorway of the store and watched the little girl with bright red hair run up and down the aisles and play peek-a-boo behind stacks of merchandise. Fearing he would snatch her child and take her away, Dory had scooped Jeanmarie up in her arms. Holding her breath, she had waited to see what Chip Malone would do. He had looked at her and the child for a long while, his eyes as bright a blue as Mick's, and those of Mick's daughter's, then had abruptly turned on his heel and left. Dory remembered hearing the hollow thump of his boot heels on the plank porch of the store and thinking how lonely they sounded.

Ben got up to refill his coffee cup from the pot on the stove. He returned to the table and sat down.

"Mr. Waller, Odette isn't well. She has a croupy cough. I've been dosing her at night with hot tea and honey, but it hasn't done much good. I'm afraid of what will happen if you take her out."

Ben looked sharply at his daughter and waved his hand to get her attention.

"Honey, you sick?"

"I'm all . . . right, Papa." Odette's voiced cracked.

"She's got a fever." Dory went to her and placed the palm of her hand on Odette's forehead. "Let me take Jeanmarie." She carried the child to a big cowhide chair beside the hearth and laid her down. After covering her with a shawl, she went to the washstand, returned with a wet cloth and bathed Odette's face. "She's sick! Can't you see that?" Dory asked almost angrily.

After Odette got over a fit of coughing, Ben answered. "How long has she had that cough?"

"It started the day after you brought her here. It's gotten worse today. She needs to be in bed."

"Your brother ordered me to leave."

"Half of this house belongs to Milo and Louis. Half to me and James. I'm inviting your daughter to stay in *our* part of the house." The eyes she raised to his held cold determination. "She can sleep in my room. If Milo bothers her, so help me God, I'll shoot him."

A ghost of a smile flickered across Ben's lips. "I believe you."

Dory made an impatient motion with her hand. The warmth in Ben's slate-colored eyes made her uncomfortable. "Well?"

"I'll do what's best for Odette—to hell with my pride."

Dory went to the stove, removed a lid and set the blackened teakettle down in the hole over the flame. It immediately sent up a plume of steam. She placed two spoonfuls of honey in a heavy cup, added two spoonfuls of whiskey and filled the cup with water from the teakettle. After stirring it vigorously she carried it to the table.

"Come drink this, Odette, while I go upstairs and fix you a good warm bed."

"We stay with Dory?" Odette mouthed the words to Ben.

"We stay until you feel better."

A look of relief came over Odette's flushed face and she picked up the mug.

As Dory filled her arm with wood from the box, Ben asked, "Can I help?"

"No. I'll get the fire going in my room. See that she drinks that toddy. When I come back I'll make a poultice to put on her chest. There's a can of turpentine and one of kerosene on the porch."

Dory lost no time. She hurried up the stairs. Before Jeanmarie was born, James had brought home the Acme Champion woodstove that sat in the corner of her room. Built like a barrel turned on its side, the stove could easily heat a room three times the size of her bedroom. She shook down the ashes and placed some kindling on the glowing coals before she added the chunks of wood. When the fire was going, she closed the damper halfway. The room began to warm while she added extra soft blankets to the bunkbed.

In the soft glow of the lamplight Dory looked about the room. She would bed Jeanmarie down in the quilt box. She removed the lid and stood it against the wall. The box was almost full of quilts and blankets. She spread one of them over the others and took Jeanmarie's pillow from the bed.

Before she went out the door, she glanced back at the bed, a double bunk her father had built into the corner of the room. In all her life no one had slept in that bunk but her and Jeanmarie. The thought drew her up short. She had been caged in this house without friends or acquaintances. It was a wonder she hadn't lost her mind. The coming of Ben Waller and Odette was going to be her salvation. Affection for the deaf girl had crept into her heart, and as for Ben—she wondered if he saw her as the whore Louis said she was. Just the thought of that humiliating episode the day they arrived was enough to shrivel her soul.

Dory hurried back down the stairs. She paused as she

entered the kitchen. Ben's magnetic eyes met hers and seemed to swallow her. He was sitting in the same chair, Jeanmarie's red curly head snuggled against his shoulder, her balled fist pressed against his neck. The fingers of the large hand supporting the child's back were gently rubbing her nape.

Dory swallowed hard and concentrated on not letting him see the deep ache within her even though her eyes misted over—the result of nerves strung taut by the onslaught on her senses and the regret that her child would never know, as she had known, the loving touch of her father.

"She woke up, couldn't find you and was scared." Ben spoke barely above a whisper.

Dory struggled for the breath to answer. "Sometimes she . . . has a hard time sleeping after we've had a set-to with Milo or Louis."

"Little kids have to put up with a lot from the ones who raise them." He spoke smoothly, reasonably, with no censure in his voice.

Dory cleared her throat and tore her gaze away from the man and her child.

"She'd not have to put up with it if there was any other way," she protested, trying to collect her scattered senses.

"There's always a way."

"Louis and Milo would make my life even more of a hell than it is. I'd end up working in a whorehouse to support my child."

"Wouldn't James help you?"

"Oh, yes. But he thinks I should stay here—that I'm safer here than out somewhere on my own." Her tone was bitter. "I couldn't bear it if he *accidentally* fell into the saw blades." She looked away from his unwavering eyes. "Milo's getting wilder all the time. It's a wonder someone hasn't killed him."

Dory's face softened when she turned to Odette and placed her hand on her forehead, "Oh, honey, you're so hot."

The girl made a small broken sound and Dory glanced at Ben.

"If you don't mind holding Jeanmarie, I'll take Odette up and get her settled in bed."

"I don't mind. Odette"—he spoke when he saw the girl looking at him—"I'll see you in the morning."

"You won't go?" she mouthed the words and her eyes filled with tears.

"I'll be here." Ben felt a twinge of alarm. Odette seldom cried. During the three years he had known her, she had cried only twice: when a camp cook had wrung her pet chicken's neck, and when he once had been away longer than he expected.

"Come on, honey. We'll get you tucked into a warm featherbed and you'll feel better," Dory said, as she walked Odette to the door.

Ben's eyes followed them. Dory's arm was across Odette's shoulders. Puzzled by confusing emotions, Ben watched them pass through the doorway and out of sight. He could hear Dory's voice murmuring soft, comforting words to Odette and wondered why she spoke knowing her words were not heard.

He shifted his body slightly to form a more comfortable cradle for the child he was holding. The lamplight shone on the small face. Her lips were slightly parted, and he could feel the little puffs of warm air that was her breath. Into his puzzled thoughts came the realization that he had never before held a sleeping child, never felt a warm trusting little body against his. It was a pleasure he had not expected and an overpowering, possessive feeling came over him. He felt a tremor run through him at the thought of anyone treating this helpless little creature harshly.

Ben had been totally free of the responsibility of affection for anyone until Tom Caffery and then Odette. How had this child and her mother become so important to him? The child, not the mother, he corrected his thoughts. The child because she lived in a house of hate as he had when he was her age. But this child had a mother and an uncle, he reasoned, while he had had no one but a kindly lumberjack now and then.

Hellfire! He had enough on his plate taking care of himself and Odette without thinking about this little woolly-headed tyke—or her woolly-headed mother, for that matter.

Dory returned. "Odette is settled. I've made a place for Jeanmarie to sleep in my quilt box. She takes a nap in it now and then—for a lark," she added.

"I'll carry her up. Show the way."

"You don't have to—"

"I know, but I want to." He stood with the child in his arms and looked down at her. At the slight rasp in his voice, Dory s whole body tensed.

"Of course. You'll want to see Odette before you turn in for the night."

"That's part of it," he said slowly.

Holding the lamp to light the way and very aware of the man behind her, Dory led the way up the stairs. She pushed open the door to her room and held it back for Ben to enter. She had left a lamp burning, but with the extra light she carried, the room was brightly lit and warm.

Dory's heart was beating so fast that it seemed to fill her ears. She felt a flicker of panic at the sight of him in her room. He seemed to fill it. He was big and virile but . . . unthreatening. That was the part that surprised her. Without looking at him, she moved around him to the quilt box and hid her confusion by speaking briskly.

"Lay her down here. I'll undress her later."

Ben placed the child on the pile of quilts and watched as Dory took off Jeanmarie's shoes and covered her. When she finished and looked up, Ben's eyes were dancing and his face wore a warm smile. The charm of that smile invaded every corner of her mind.

"It just occurred to me that there would be a hell of a ruckus if Louis came in and caught me in your bedroom. After he stopped foaming at the mouth, he'd grab the shotgun and march us off to the preacher."

A flood of scarlet washed up Dory's neck to flood her face. She seemed to have difficulty swallowing, and for a moment she thought she would choke.

"You needn't worry about that," she said, relieved her voice sounded normal. "He'd rant and rave and call me every vile name he could think of, but the last thing he wants is to get me married off to a man who has an ounce of brains."

"I thought that was what all the fuss was about—you not being wedded."

"Oh, no. Louis despised me before I had Jeanmarie. Now, he's afraid I'll marry a man who'll want to have a say in the business."

He held her gaze. "Why is that?"

"James takes so many chances that they're betting he'll kill himself before long, without any help from them," she added bitterly. "Without him they'd run roughshod over me even more than they do. It would gall them for an outsider to have the right to know what went on at Callahan and Sons."

"Another man might not want to be involved with Callahan and Sons."

"Ha! You'd never get them to believe that. Have you forgotten that I'm a strumpet, a loose, immoral woman? They think the only reason a man would want *me*—to marry me, that is—is for my shares in the company."

Ben raised his brows, and piercing, sunlight-squinted eyes, that seemed endowed with the ability to look a hole right through a person, wandered over her face.

"Then they are fools," he said softly.

A curious stillness followed—a waiting, uneasy silence that deepened and pushed them apart. Only the green thick-lashed eyes and the faint color that spread across her cheeks betrayed the fact that she was shaken by their exchange.

"Why are you surprised that a man would want you for yourself?" Something like a smile crossed his face as he continued to study her thoughtfully.

"I'm not so dumb that I don't know they would want me for a few other things beside my shares in the company. Up here men outnumber women ten to one." Her voice was just a breath of a whisper, a bitter whisper. "They'd not care a whit about *me* or my feelings or my dreams or my child. Most men up here want a woman for cooking and washing and . . . bed." She scurried around him to the door. "I'll go make the poultice to go on Odette's chest."

Without thinking to pick up the lamp, she went out into the dark hall and felt her way down the stairway to the kitchen. She wished desperately she could take back her angry unguarded words. They had revealed more than she had wanted him to know. She hoped to God he was unaware of the turbulent feeling his presence inspired.

A sharp feeling of apprehension struck Dory as she prepared the poultice. Ben Waller's presence was beginning to mean everything to her. The fact that he monopolized her thoughts petrified her. He could engulf her, crush her, set a fire that would consume her, and crush what little spirit she had left. She couldn't allow that to happen for Jeanmarie's sake.

Her hands stilled and she stood with bowed head. She had to get her mind off the man and put a lid on thoughts that perhaps, just perhaps, he might be attracted to her, or she'd be in for more heartache than she could handle.

CHAPTER
* 7 *

Ben settled his horse in an empty stall and went into the bunkhouse attached to the barn. He was not looking forward to a face-off with Milo and was relieved when he saw that only Wiley was in the room. The old man was sitting on his bunk rubbing his leg. Ben shrugged out of his coat and hung it and his hat on a nail beside the door.

"Coffee there in the pot." Wiley's eyes peered up at him from beneath bushy brows.

"Thanks."

"Ya stayin' the night?" Wiley asked after Ben filled a tin cup and sat down at the table.

"Yeah. Milo leave out?"

"He hightailed it out of here madder than a cornered bobcat." Wiley's chuckle was dry as corn shucks. "Ya must'a put a burr under his tail."

"He fired me. Ordered me off the place."

"Ya goin'?"

"My girl is sick. As soon as she's better we'll leave." *My girl*. The first year he and Odette had been together he had been unable to say those words. Now they slipped out of his mouth easily . . . and he meant them. *My girl*. *My daughter*.

"Louis'll be put out."

"That's too bad."

"Milo ain't got no sense when it comes ta what's in his britches. Messin' 'round the little missy, was he?"

"That's right. He came to within a hair of getting himself killed." Ben drained his cup, sat down on a bunk and took off his boots.

"Glad it didn't happen. Least ways . . . not that way. Louis would a swore Milo caught ya fornicatin' with Dory an' stirred folks up agin ya. Might'a got ya hung."

"I didn't think of that at the time, but if I had it wouldn't have mattered. I'd a killed the sonofabitch without batting an eye if he'd forced himself on Odette."

After Wiley blew out the lamp, Ben lay down on the bunk, put his hands behind his head and stared at the dark ceiling. He had always had a boundless respect for women in spite of his unpleasant childhood with an aunt who resented every bite of food that went into his mouth. Women, as a rule, had been kind to him, even the ones considered *bad*. He figured they had been made that way by circumstances and did what they had to do to survive.

The verbal and physical abuse heaped on Dory by her half-brothers bothered him—more than bothered him. It made him want to break heads.

"Is Malone the father of Miss Callahan's little girl?" Ben voiced the question as it came to his mind.

"I reckon it was his boy, Mick." Wiley's voice came out of the darkness. "It was 'bout a year after Dory's pa died. She'd been to town for a few months of schoolin'. When she got back, James was gone an' Louis an' Milo was mean as a steer with its tail in a knot. Dory was scared of 'em an' lonesome. She started meetin' the boy. A few months later she found him with the back of his head blowed off. Folks thought he'd been took for a deer, an' some thought it was

Milo what done it, but there warn't no proof. He an' Louis got a powerful hate for the Malones."

"Was that before or after the baby was born?"

"Before. Long time before. I doubt the lad knew he'd made a babe."

In the silence that followed, Ben mulled over what Wiley had said. There was no doubt in his mind and there appeared to be none in Dory's that Milo would backshoot a man. A demon was working in Milo and sooner or later, if he stayed here, Ben was almost sure he and Milo would clash.

He suddenly thought about what he'd heard the men at the mill talking about. A few months back a young Indian girl's body had been found not five miles from the camp. She had been violated and the back of her head had been bashed in. The killer had made no attempt to hide the body, probably thinking the wolves that roamed the area would destroy it. The girl had been found not long after her death by a lumberjack who had used snowshoes to make the long trip down the mountain one Sunday to spend a few hours with his family.

Ben didn't know what had brought that to mind. There was no evidence to lay that crime at Milo's door, but as Ben remembered the look that had been on Milo's face when he had struck his sister, he believed that Milo was capable of most anything.

On the heels of that thought came another. Tonight he had been thoroughly confused by his feelings for Dory Callahan. She had awakened something in him, stirred something that left him restless. He remembered the graceful movement of her body as she went up the stairs ahead of him. She was tall and thin and swayed like a young sapling in the breeze. Her eyes were clear, honest and free of suspicion when she looked at him. He liked the proud lift of her chin, the wide green eyes and even the short curly mop that covered her head.

He ran stiffened fingers through his hair and massaged the

back of his neck. He couldn't let the attraction he felt for the woman get out of hand. He was having too hard a time taking care of himself and Odette to take on a woman and her child. Yet he couldn't help but wonder how it would be to make love to her if she were totally his. Was Dory Callahan the kind of woman her brothers said she was, or was she a woman who would love a man wholeheartedly or not at all?

His thoughts went to Odette. The sensible thing to do would be to ride out of here as soon as she was able. He'd find a place to settle, and with what tools he had, he could make a living doing cabinet work. Of course, it would mean he couldn't produce doors, window frames and flooring in quantity, but it would be a start.

He drifted to sleep with his common sense telling him to go far from this place and quick, but some unnerving, alien thing inside him told him he could not leave just yet.

The squeak of the door opening awakened Ben from a sound sleep. Before turning his head toward the sound, his hand closed over the hilt of the knife that lay by his side. A soft triangle of light came through the partly open door, then a long skirt and fur-lined moccasins. Dory, carrying a lantern, came silently across the room to his bunk.

"Mr. Waller. Ben—" Her whispered voice held urgency.

"Yes. What is it?"

"I'm worried about Odette. She's awfully sick."

Ben slung his legs off the bed and reached for his boots. "She was sleeping when I left."

"She slept for a while. But now it's hard for her to breathe."

"You been up with her all night?"

"I dozed in a chair for a while."

Ben followed Dory across the room and out the door. They

hurried across the moonlit yard to the house. The kitchen was warm and well lighted. Carrying the lantern, Dory went through the hallway and up the stairs.

As soon as Ben stepped inside the room he could hear Odette's labored breathing. He knelt down beside the bed and placed his hand on her forehead. It was not extremely hot and he felt a second of relief that turned to anxiety when her lids lifted and she gazed at him with wide blank eyes. Her mouth was open and her lips quivered as she struggled to draw air into her lungs.

"I changed the poultice and rubbed her neck with liniment," Dory said from close beside him.

"I can smell it."

"At first she would drink a little peppermint tea. She won't do that now."

"Where's the nearest doctor?"

"The only place I know for sure is Coeur d'Alene. That's a day's ride from here."

"Damn! It would take two days to get a doctor here."

"We've got to do something now. My pa died while James was going for the doctor. Maybe if we raised her up she could breathe easier."

Ben slipped his arm under Odette's shoulders and lifted her while Dory packed pillows behind her. He looked into the worried face of the woman beside him, grateful that she was with him. The silence between them was only broken by the sound of Odette's labored breathing until a loud voice came from downstairs. They heard heavy footsteps coming up the stairs.

"Dory!" Ben turned to face the man that came charging into the room like a mad bull. "What the hell's going on?"

"James, for goodness sake! Stop shouting. You'll wake Jeanmarie."

James's eyes went from Dory to Ben. "You're the donkey man?"

Ben stood slowly. "I'm getting damned tired of being called the donkey man," he said irritably. "I've got a name. It's Ben Waller."

"Sorry. Meant no offense. I'm James Callahan. It scared me when I saw the house all lit up this time of night. I thought something had happened to the little carrot-top."

"I need someone to go for a doctor. I'll pay fifty dollars a day."

Ignoring Ben, James came to peer at Odette over Dory's shoulder. "From the sound of her breathin', it's what Pa had, huh, Dory?"

"I don't know. I put a lard and turpentine poultice on her chest. I've given her whiskey toddies and she drank peppermint tea, but it hasn't helped."

James took off his coat and threw it on the floor beside the door. He leaned over Odette and put his ear to her chest.

He looked squarely at Ben. "Mister, she's got a rattle in her chest. She'll not last till a doctor gets here unless we can break up that congestion so she can breathe."

"How can we do that?" Dory asked.

"Steam. I've seen it work a couple of times. A Blackfoot Indian used it on a camp cook last winter."

"I'll be obliged for your help," Ben said. "Tell me what to do."

"Well . . . we don't have a sweat lodge. We'll have to do the next best thing. Waller, get an armload of wood and fire up the stove. Sis, bed the baby down in another room and bring up a teakettle of hot water from the reservoir."

James knelt down beside the bed and put the back of his hand to Odette's cheek. Her skin was dry and hot, her parted lips parched. He poured water on a cloth from the pitcher on the table and wet her lips. Odette's eyes fluttered open and James found himself looking into large blue eyes.

"Can you drink some water?" James asked before he remembered that he had been told that Waller's daughter couldn't hear. He squeezed some of the water from the cloth into her mouth. She licked her lips gratefully. Her eyes clung to his face. His heart galloped and he sucked in a deep breath. The girl's clear, trusting eyes seemed to be looking into his very soul. They remained open while he sponged water into her mouth. When her lids drifted down, James felt a moment of panic as if something precious were slipping away.

Ben filled the barrel stove and closed the firebox door. The sound brought James to his feet. His fingers brushed the dark-auburn curls from his forehead. For a minute or two he had lost himself. Dory came in with the teakettle. James lifted one of the two lids on the barrel stove and she set the kettle directly over the flame.

"We need something to make a tent close to the stove." James looked about the room. "She can lie on the quilt box lid. Get three chairs from the kitchen, Waller. Two to support the board, one for her feet." Ben didn't question; he hurried out of the room.

"Oh, James. I'm so glad you're here." Dory hugged her brother's arm.

He looked down and patted her hand. His brows came together in a puzzled frown.

"What did you do to your face?"

"Oh, that." She covered her swollen jaw with her palm. "I got in a hurry and bumped it on the . . . door."

James's face relaxed. "What do we have that we could spread some blankets over to hold in the steam?"

"The folding bar you bought for me to dry the baby's

napkins when I couldn't hang them outside. I cover it sometimes and let Jeanmarie play under it."

"That's just the ticket. Get it, Sis. I'll get blankets out of the other rooms."

Dory paused in the doorway of the kitchen. Ben stood with his hand grasping the back of a chair, his head bent. She went to him and placed her hand on his arm. He looked at her with eyes filled with misery.

"I've never even told her how important she is to me."

"She knows. She loves you very much."

"I'm all she has. She's . . . all I have." He took a deep breath and lifted the chair.

"James knows what he's doing."

"Thank God."

Odette was wrapped in blankets and laid on the board near the stove. The clothes rack was placed over her and covered on three sides with blankets to hold in the hot, moist air.

"Close the door, Sis. We don't want a draft." James turned the teakettle spout, and it sent out a plume of steam toward Odette's head.

Ben squatted down on his heels beside a small opening and watched as the makeshift tent filled with steam. As he listened to Odette's labored breathing, he promised himself that when she was better he would tell her how much she meant to him and how glad he was that she was his daughter. He vowed never again to wonder if one of the Callahans had sired her. It no longer mattered.

James roamed restlessly, stopping every so often to add a stick of wood to the stove.

"It's getting pretty hot in here." James peeled off a flannel shirt and unbuttoned the four top buttons of his union suit. He eyed his sister's sweaty face. Wet curls were sticking to her forehead. "You don't have to stay in here, kinky head," he said affectionately. "Go make me and Waller some coffee."

Dory went to Ben and leaned down close to his ear. "Is she breathing any easier?"

"Not yet. But her face and hair are damp from the steam so it must be going to her chest."

Dory placed her hand on Ben's shoulder and squeezed it. The action did not go unnoticed by James.

"Is there anything else we can do?" Dory asked.

"You've tried the poultice and the liniment. The only other thing I know is to burn a mixture of turpentine and whiskey in a tin can and hold her over the smoke. They say it will loosen up the stuff clogging her chest. I've not seen it tried, but one of the men said that's what his wife does when one of their young'uns gets choked up."

"Shall we do that?" Dory asked anxiously.

"Let's give this a try first."

After Dory left the room, James sank down on the floor, leaned against the wall and studied Ben Waller. There was a tough, confident look in the man's face and a vigilance in his alert eyes that looked straight into James's and refused to let him stare him down. With the trained eye of a lumberman, able to size up another human being almost in an instant, James decided Ben Waller would be a man to ride the river with. He almost smiled. Just the fact that Milo hated his guts was enough to make James like him.

"I heard you had a set-to with Milo."

"Yeah. News travels fast."

"He was roarin' mad when he got back to the mill. Said you jumped him when he wasn't lookin'."

Ben shrugged. "He can say what he wants."

James laughed. "Why'd you hit him?"

"I didn't like the look on his face."

James laughed again. "Good enough reason."

"—And he fired me."

"He's fired almost every man we've got working for us at one time or the other. Are you goin' or stayin'?"

"I'd be long gone if Odette wasn't sick."

"Can't stand the heat, huh?"

Ben's face turned hard. "Can't stand men who abuse women."

"Don't much care for 'em myself."

Ben looked steadily at the man sitting on the floor. He wanted to tell him that his brothers were meaner than a hungry wolf to his sister and Jeanmarie. But Dory had insisted that James not be told. *Hadn't the fool seen his sister's face?* He gave himself a mental shake. This was a family affair and he'd best stay out of it. Yet questions nagged at his mind. He decided to voice one of them.

"Why do the Callahans hate the Malones?"

James raked his fingers through his hair and wiped the sweat from his upper lip. He thought for a full minute before he answered.

"Our mother was raised in the Malone home along with Chip and Alpha, a girl about Ma's age. She was the apple of the old man's eye and when she died, he turned to my mother and doted on her. She was no blood kin to the Malones and he wanted her to marry his son, Chip, but she married my pa instead. That's why the Malones hate us. Louis and Milo hated our mother because she married their pa. She was considered a Malone, so they hate all Malones. Makes a hell of a lot of sense, doesn't it?"

"Most feuds start over some little thing that doesn't amount to a hill of beans."

"Most of the feuding was on the part of Milo and Louis until Mick Malone was found dead in the woods. The Malones had, for the most part, ignored us up to then."

"They think one of you killed him because he was meeting your sister?"

"It makes sense . . . if you're a Malone." Then James's eyes fixed unwavering on Ben's and there was a terrible intensity in his gaze. When he spoke again his voice was abrupt. "Don't get it in your head that my sister is a slut. It's rumored around because of Jeanmarie, but no one says it to me or makes an unwanted move toward her, or they'll get their head blowed off. Understand?"

"Perfectly."

After that one terse word, Ben looked at James in silence. How could he not know how his brothers talked to and about his sister? Hadn't he heard her called Whory Dory by the men at the camp?

At that moment a hoarse sound came from Odette and she began to cough. James jumped to his feet and threw back one of the blankets so that he could kneel beside her. He lifted her head and shoulders and leaned her back against his chest.

"It's working, Waller. Get over there and turn the spout of the teakettle so the steam comes closer to her face. Not too close, it'll burn her. There, girl, I think you're going to be able to cough up some of that stuff that's clogging your lungs."

Odette's head, damp from the steam, lolled back against James's shoulder. With long calloused fingers, he brushed the hair from her cheek. She was so slight, so helpless. The soft curves of the body against his told him she was not a child, but a very desirable woman. A strange protective feeling stirred within him.

Then her stomach began to heave.

"Get the chamber pot, she's goin' to vomit."

Holding her tightly against him, one hand on her stomach, the other on her forehead, James leaned her over the chamber pot. Liquid spewed from her mouth and with it thick slime from her throat.

"It's the peppermint tea Dory made her drink," James said, and glanced at Ben.

Odette gagged and spit. She groaned and gagged again.

"That's good, girl. Spit it out," James murmured.

Dory hurried into the room, her face anxious. "Is she choking?"

"You filled her so full of that tea she had to vomit."

Dory knelt down and wiped Odette's face while Ben stood helplessly by and watched James and Dory work with the young girl who had come to mean so much to him.

"Do you have something dry you can put on her, Sis?" James asked, as he laid Odette back down on the makeshift bed. "We can't let her get chilled."

"I'll get a nightdress. You men can go drink your coffee while I change her gown. Do you think she'll be all right?" Dory asked anxiously.

James stood and looked down at Odette's pale oval face. Her thick blond braid had come unraveled and damp strands curled about her ears. Suddenly she opened her eyes and looked directly into his. Her great blue eyes were wide open and staring . . . at him. There was a strange stillness about her. He didn't know what to say. Then her eyes drifted shut. He wanted to look into those blue eyes again. He wanted her to see him, really see him. He wanted—

"James," Dory prodded. "Will she be all right now?"

"I don't know. I sure as hell hope so. Sit by her, Sis, so she don't roll off. When we come back up, we'll put her over in the bed."

James put on his shirt and went out the door. Ben's eyes met Dory's and held. He moved to her, put his hand on her shoulder and squeezed gently.

"Thanks," he said, low-voiced and husky.

She nodded.

CHAPTER
* 8 *

Dory was bone-tired, too tired to sleep. James had urged her to get some rest. Ben was going to sit with Odette and had promised to call her if there was the slightest change.

She lay in Milo's bed beside Jeanmarie thinking that she had never, in all her life, lain on this bed. Occasionally she changed the bedding as she had done the first night Odette spent here. Other than that she seldom even came into the room. Milo didn't seem to mind the dust balls on the floor or the cobwebs on the ceiling, so why should she?

Milo was getting bolder and bolder with his abuse. Tonight was the first time he had struck her face. Usually it was a pinch or a slap some place where the bruise wouldn't show. Thank heaven James had been too occupied with Odette to really notice her face. By morning the swelling would be down and the bruise less noticeable.

When Dory heard the roosters crowing, she turned her head to look out the window. It was daylight. She eased out of the bed, tucked the covers around her daughter and felt on the floor for her moccasins. After belting her wrapper tightly about her waist, she ran her fingers through her short curls and left the room.

Ben sat in a chair beside the bunk where Odette lay, his head tilted back against the wall. His eyes were closed, his mouth relaxed and slightly parted. Dory stood for a long moment looking at him. As soon as Odette was strong enough to travel, he would take her and leave. This could be the only chance she would have to really look at him, to store away his image so that she could bring it out in the dark lonely days ahead and relive the few short hours they had shared.

His hair, dark as midnight, was thick and wavy and fell down over his ears. His cheekbones were high and his strong jaw was covered with a stubble of black whiskers. His face, she thought, was somewhat sinister looking until he smiled, which was seldom. Dory saw a great deal more than his physical good looks. She saw a kind, strong, restless man seeking to do the best he could for his daughter just as she was trying to do for hers.

Suddenly she realized his eyes were open and he was looking at her. Her heart lurched, but she managed to lift her brows in question and nod toward Odette. The girl lay on her side and from the rhythm of her breathing, seemed to be resting peacefully. Ben looked at his daughter, then back at Dory. His smile told her what she needed to know. Reluctant to leave, but not knowing what to say if she stayed, she hurried down the stairs to the kitchen. Why, she wondered, was she so happy? It was pure madness to feel so light and cheerful because a man had smiled at her.

Dory hummed as she pulled out the large wooden bowl she used to make biscuits. She whipped off the cloth and dropped a chunk of lard the size of an egg into the well formed by the flour in the bowl. Next she added salt, soda and buttermilk. With her hand she worked in the flour until she had a soft dough. From the oven she took a large iron pan she had coated with meat grease. Quickly she pinched off globs of the dough, rolled them between her palms and placed them in the pan. When that was done she set the pan on the back of the stove, washed her hands and began to form sausage into patties and drop them into the skillet. The sausage fat would season cream gravy to go on the biscuits.

She set the table for three after opening a jar of the wild strawberry jam she saved for special occasions. She was pondering whether or not to go to the cellar for apple butter when she heard footsteps on the porch. She scarcely had time to turn before the door was thrown open and Louis, his face red with anger, barged into the room.

"Waller ain't in the bunkhouse! Is he in here?" His angry voice filled the kitchen.

"There's no reason for you to shout," Dory said calmly, although she felt anything but calm.

"Answer me, damn you!"

"Keep your voice down or you'll be in for more trouble than you can handle."

"Don't you threaten me, you . . . slut."

"Me threaten you? Ha! Go ahead. Dig your own hole."

"Look at ya. Ya ain't even dressed decent. Yo're just like your ma . . . paradin' 'round . . . half naked . . . hair hangin' down."

"Are you crazy, Louis? My hair isn't over an inch long."

"Well . . . huh . . . if'n it was it'd be hangin'."

"And this wrapper is decent!"

"I ask ya a civil question and I want a answer. Is he in here? If he is . . ."

"I'm here, Callahan. What are you going to do about it?"

Dory turned to see Ben lounging in the doorway, his hair rumpled and his shirttail hung out over his britches.

Ben had been looking out the window when Louis had ridden into the yard. He had watched him dismount, make a beeline for the bunkhouse, then slam out the door and head for the house. He knew exactly what Louis's nasty mind would conjure up when he found Ben here with Dory, and he decided to see if he could irritate Louis to the point where he would show his hand. Evidently Louis didn't know that James was in the house or he'd not have called Dory a slut.

"I knew it! By gawd, I knew she'd get her hooks in ya and ya'd slack up on the job. Ya didn't get that engine half done and ya had to sneak off down here to *her*!"

"Didn't your brother tell you that he'd fired me?" Ben came into the room and faced Louis from across the table.

"Shitfire! He didn't hire ya. Nobody fires ya, but me." He turned on Dory and vented his frustration. "Ya just had to get yore itch scratched, didn't ya? Ya couldn't wait till he was done with—"

"I think you'd better shut up, Louis," Dory said, louder than she had intended. Now was not the time for James to have it out with Louis and Milo. When Ben left, it would be one against two.

"No, Dory," Ben said calmly, and placed his hand on her shoulder in an intimate gesture that he knew would further infuriate Louis. "Your brother is entitled to have his say."

"Yo're damn right I can have my say. This is my house, by gawd. Ya'll not be doin' no whorin' here. Yo're just like yore ma, a pantin' after ever'thin' with a stick 'tween his legs."

"This is *half* your house," Dory said calmly, although embarrassment was causing her heart to thump painfully. "The other half belongs to me and James." She could endure anything, she decided, as long as Ben stood beside her, his hand on her shoulder.

"Ya ain't doin' no whorin' in that half either!" Louis's anger had burst into full bloom and he failed to hear the heavy footsteps coming down the stairs, but Ben had heard them and smiled down at Dory.

"It's true I've been here with your sister for most of the night—"

Louis's anger was so great that he would have struck Dory if not for Ben. All he could do was ball his fists and sputter.

"Ya . . . gawddamn wh—" The word was cut off like a slice from a sharp knife when James came barreling into the room.

"Did you say what I thought you said?"

Louis's face turned pale as if the blood had been drained from it. He took a step back. His mouth hung open and he seemed to have difficulty drawing air into his lungs.

Ben realized the situation had suddenly turned dangerous when Dory jumped in to fill the deadly silence.

"Louis misunderstood the reason for Ben's being here, that's all. Calm down, all of you. I'll put the biscuits in the oven and make gravy. There's hot water in the reservoir. So wash up." She moved out from under Ben's hand and he let it drop to his side. "James, did you look in on Odette?"

Ben realized that Dory was desperately trying to defuse the explosion she feared would happen. James ignored his sister's question. His face was hard. It showed none of the gentleness Ben had seen last night. Narrowed eyes were on his brother's face. He looked as if he was wound as tightly as a spring that was ready to snap.

"What did you think was going on here, Louis? Did you dig down into your dirty mind and come up with only one reason for Waller being in the house with Dory?"

"Ya can't be too careful with . . . womenfolk. And ya know Dory's knowed to be . . ."

"Careful, Louis. Watch your mouth when you talk to or about Dory. You were about to call her a whore when I came in. Don't ever do that because if you do, I swear to God, I'll cripple you so that you'll walk around on stumps for the rest of your life."

Louis tried to shake off the chill that slithered down his spine. He began to sputter.

"As the eldest . . . it's my duty to . . . keep a . . . rein on her. Lone woman like her . . . is game for ever' diddler what comes along." He glanced at Ben, then away.

"My, my. When did you ever give a damn about Dory? You'd be happy as a lark if both of us dropped into a deep pit never to be heard from again."

Louis didn't rise to the bait. He turned and looked out the door and then back to see that James had pulled a chair out from the table and straddled it.

"What'd ya come down here for? Steven said ya left a list at the mill."

"I came to see Dory and Jeanmarie. Do you have any objections?"

"No. Why would I? Steven said you've got more'n two hundred logs down, trimmed and some peeled, all ready to be reeled to the flume."

"And a hundred more ready to be milled."

Louis rocked back on his heels, darting glances at Ben. Finally he said, "When'll the engine be ready to move?"

Ben took his time answering. "That's up to you. It's not my engine."

"But . . . it ain't ready yet!" Louis's voice boomed.

"No. But that's your problem, not mine."

"By gawd, you contracted—"

"I was fired. Remember?"

"Hell!" Louis snorted. "Nobody pays attention when Milo fires 'em."

Ben put his hands on the table and leaned toward Louis on stiffened arms.

"Listen and listen good. That horny, sonofabitchin' brother of yours came down here and pestered my girl. If not for your sister's keepin' his hands off her, I'd a killed him quicker than swatting a fly. A man who has no respect for a woman is lower than a snake's belly as far as I'm concerned. I'll not stay at a place where my daughter is in danger of being raped. Now you tell your brother that word travels fast in this country; and after I leave he'd better not take his spite out on Dory, or I'll blacken his name with every lumberman from here to the coast . . . that is after I come back and beat him within an inch of his life." Ben paused and then added, "Most lumberjacks feel the same as I do about womenfolk."

Ben's eyes were on Louis and he didn't see James get slowly up off the chair.

"Is that why you hit Milo?" James asked Ben.

"Among other things."

Dory began to feel a terrible dread. What would James do if he knew Milo had grabbed Odette and had hit *her* with his fist? Would Ben tell him? At that moment Ben looked at her and sent her a silent message. *Don't worry. I won't tell.* Her shoulders slumped with relief. The relief lasted only until James spoke.

"What is this about Milo bothering Odette?"

"He was probably just funnin'," Louis said quickly. "You know how Milo is."

"That's the trouble." James's voice was quiet—too quiet. "I know how Milo is with women. He's bragged about it to every man in the territory."

"That's all there is to it. Brag." Louis shrugged, trying to act indifferent, but it didn't quite come off. His shoulders and neck were stiff as a board.

"Dory." James turned to his sister. "What happened?"

With her back turned, Dory forked the sausage patties from the skillet and added a few spoonfuls of flour to the grease.

"Milo was in one of his flirting moods and as usual went too far. Odette is shy and not used to . . . to being . . . teased. Oh, shoot, my biscuits are getting too brown." Dory glanced at Ben before she bent to peer into the oven. As usual his face was unreadable.

"Waller, I'd be obliged if ya'd not take it to heart what Milo did. Get what ya need from the smithy and get the engine goin'. Yore girl'll not be bothered no more. My word on it." Louis stood on first one foot and then the other while he waited for Ben to reply.

Ben took his time answering. He weighed his options. Odette wouldn't be well enough to travel for at least a week. And, he needed the money. There was another reason for staying, too—one that, if he thought about it, would fill his mind until there would be no room for logical thinking. He hadn't even dared to bring it out and mull it over until now. *Dory Callahan and her little red-headed mite were seeping into his heart, little by little*. Maybe if he stayed long enough he would see that she was a woman just like any other and get her out of his system.

"I'll stay and set up your engine . . . if you keep Milo away from me and my girl. It should be ready to move in about a week or ten days. I don't like working for you, Callahan."

"Our money's good as anybody's and yo're gettin' plenty. I suppose ya'll go to Malone," Louis sneered.

"It's no business of yours where I go after I leave here."

Louis stomped out the door. He was smart enough not to press his luck after Ben had agreed to stay and finish the job. Beside that, he felt the need to get back to the mill and give Milo a dressing down before he ran into Waller again.

As soon as Louis left, Ben went back upstairs to see about

Odette. He returned saying she was awake and thirsty. Dory had the meal on the table and insisted the men sit down. She filled a pitcher with fresh water and left the room.

"Dory keeps things from me," James said, reaching for the biscuits. "She's just like Ma was—always trying to keep peace between Louis and Milo and the rest of us."

"Women are like that . . . I guess."

"What really happened between you and Milo?"

"You heard it once." Ben split open two biscuits and covered them with gravy. "Your sister's a damn good cook."

"Milo's got a mean streak a yard wide."

"Yeah," Ben said. "Mean and crazy to boot."

"He mouths off at Dory some, but he knows better than to touch her."

Ben lifted his head and looked James in the eye. "You don't come down here very often, do you?"

"I try to make it ever' couple of weeks. Can't always do that in the dead of winter. I've got a crew to work."

"You should get your sister and her little girl out of here. Get them set up in a town. This is no place for a lone woman."

James carefully placed his knife on the side of his plate. "You know something I don't?"

"I know Louis is mouthy, but Milo is dangerous—not only around women, but around men. He's got the devil riding on his back. His temper causes him to lose control. I'd not work with him around a saw blade or on the river. Too many things can happen accidentally."

"You think he'd hurt Dory or Jeanmarie?"

"If he was in the right mood and she crossed him."

"Dory said he teased Odette. Scared her."

"It was a little more than that, but not enough for me to kill him." Ben spoke with a certainty in his voice.

James let out a shuddering sigh. "Godamighty."

"Odette can't hear. She reads lips some but goes mostly by actions and facial expressions. She knew Milo wasn't funnin'."

"How old is she?"

"Sixteen. Almost seventeen. She's the most important thing in the world to me. She's smart. She reads and writes with a good hand. Ciphers, too. Some think that because she can't hear, she's not bright. That's not so."

James lowered his head and continued eating. He liked Ben Waller. He talked about his daughter as a father should. Ben was the first man James had met who he thought was good enough for his sister and would be able to take care of her if something should happen to him. He hoped Ben and Odette stayed a while so Dory could get to know him.

"Odette is hungry." Dory made the announcement happily. She paused in the doorway to smile at the men at the table. "Her throat is sore, so I have to fix something that will slide down easily. If we had fresh beef, I'd make beef tea. There's nothing more strengthening than beef tea. Remember Mama saying that, James?" Dory continued to chatter while she moved a skillet over to the hot part of the stove. "I think she could eat milk toast. I'll butter some bread and brown it in the skillet. Oh, shoot, I've got to run down to the cellar. Yesterday's milk is still in the pail."

James grinned at Ben and stood. "I'll get it, Sis." As he passed her, he flung an arm across her shoulders. "You've got the runnin' off at the mouth this morning, curly-top."

After James disappeared through the cellar door, Dory turned to look at Ben. Her eyes were shining.

"I was rattling on, wasn't I? I'm just so happy Odette is better. I haven't been that scared in a long time. Papa took down just like that and was gone before James could get back with the doctor."

"We're lucky your brother came home. I had heard about the Indians using sweat lodges, but I didn't have any idea it would help Odette."

"James is awfully smart. He knows a lot of things," she said proudly.

"I'm glad you've finally admitted it." James came in carrying a pail with a cloth draped over it.

Dory laughed. "Oh, you! Go finish your breakfast. As soon as I put some milk on to heat, I'll refill your coffee cups."

Dory was feeding Odette the bread and milk when James and Ben came into the room. Odette's large blue eyes went to Ben, then flicked briefly to James and back. Ben stood behind Dory and spoke slowly.

"Feeling better?"

Odette nodded. She glanced at James, then back to Ben. "You going?" Her voice came out in a whisper.

Ben shook his head. "Not till you're better."

Holding the almost empty bowl in her lap, Dory reached for James's hand and pulled him closer to the bed.

"This is my brother." She spoke slowly as her lips formed the words. "His name is James."

Odette looked at him, then turned her face away.

Dory put her fingers on the girl's cheek and gently turned her so she could see her lips.

"He is good. Not like Milo. Not like Louis." Odette's eyes clung to Dory's. "Don't be afraid of him." Dory shook her head as she spoke.

"Hellfire! I could kill those two sonsofbitches!" James snarled.

"Honey," Ben leaned over Dory's shoulder. "We're going to stay here a while. Dory will take care of you."

"Mama!" Jeanmarie came into the room rubbing sleep out of her eyes with her balled fists. "Uncle James!"

"Hello, little red bird." The child ran to him and he scooped her up in his arms.

"I didn't know you here." She planted a wet kiss on his cheek.

"You were sound asleep when I got here."

Jeanmarie turned her angelic smile on Ben. "He Odette's papa."

"Yes, I know. Odette is sick and you'll be sick too if you don't get something on your feet."

James cupped the child's small feet in his hand to warm them. He looked down at Odette. Her eyes, clear and unafraid, met his. They never flickered. He suddenly forgot the child in his arms. Even forgot where he was. The most unexpected feeling possessed him. Dear God! She was the softest, most exquisite thing he had ever seen. James did something he had cleverly avoided since he had been old enough to appreciate women. In that instant he fell in love . . . and he didn't even know it.

Odette watched Jeanmarie wrap her arms around the man's neck. His face was not that of a stranger. Now she remembered. He had bent over her, lifted her, brushed the hair from her cheeks. Her papa and Dory had been there. This was Dory's *other* brother. They had had the same mother and father. Now she could see the family resemblance even though the man's hair was dark reddish brown.

Ben watched James and recognized his interest in Odette and put it down to the fact that he probably had not been around a deaf person before—especially a pretty young deaf girl. Yet an uneasiness nagged at the recesses of his mind, an uneasiness that he shoved aside when Jeanmarie leaned from James's arms toward him.

"I kiss Odette's papa."

"There's nothing like a fickle woman," James said disgustedly as Ben lifted Jeanmarie from his arms.

"It isn't every day I get kisses from a pretty girl." Ben accepted her kiss and kissed her cheek in return.

Dory stood, shoved the bowl of milk and bread into her brother's hand and reached for her daughter.

"You scamp. We've got to get you dressed. You'll have to help me take care of Odette today."

"I kiss Odette. Make her better."

"You're sure throwing your kisses around this morning," Dory said cheerfully. "Right now you've got to get dressed and have your breakfast."

Ben reached down and took Odette's hand. "I need to talk to Wiley about making some clamps. I'll be back."

"Sis, she should eat the rest of this." James stood holding the bowl.

"Then give it to her, if she'll eat it." Dory's voice came from the hallway outside the door.

James looked helplessly at Ben. "I'll feed her the rest of this if she wants it."

Ben tried not to let the surprise show on his face as he turned to James.

"She's usually shy of strangers, especially men."

"Ask her."

"Ask her yourself. Talk slow. She's able to lip-read. She understands me and Dory."

"Ma'am—"

"Call her Odette."

"O . . . dette, do . . . you . . . want . . . any . . . more . . . of this?" James pointed to the bowl, to himself and then to her.

Odette looked at Ben with a glimmer of humor in her eyes. He smiled. She looked at James and nodded.

"You don't have to drag out each word," Ben said and edged toward the door. He looked back to see how Odette was taking his leaving. Her eyes were on James. And she opened her mouth to accept the spoonful of bread and milk.

Again, a nagging uneasiness possessed Ben. He shrugged it off. Women must fall all over a man like James. He was being kind to a deaf girl, that was all. To him she was something new.

He was just borrowing trouble.

Odette was getting steadily better. Dory was glad, but she also dreaded the day Odette would be completely well because then she and Ben would be leaving. He had promised to stay a week or ten days. Dory was sure he would not stay a day after the engine was in place.

The last two days had gone quickly. The surprise of it all was that James had spent so much time with Odette and seemed to enjoy it. The evening of the first day he had found a tablet and had drawn a picture of a man cutting down a tree and one of the same man riding the raft of logs on the river. He had written his name above the man.

Odette had taken the tablet and written, *Papa can do that.*

Is he good?

I think so.

"Have you ever had a puppy?" James asked, speaking slowly.

Reading the puzzled look on her face, he wrote the words on the tablet.

She shook her head.

He tried speaking aloud again. "I have a dog at the cutting camp. She'll have pups soon."

"Big dog?"

James was so pleased that he'd made her understand that he pressed her hand lying on the bed.

"Yes, a big dog."

"I like dogs . . . and cats . . . and horses."

While James was with Odette, Ben sat in the kitchen and watched Dory clear the supper table. Jeanmarie crawled up into his lap and nestled against him.

"Oh, honey, you shouldn't—" Dory made an attempt to lift her down.

"It's all right," Ben said. "I don't mind."

"Children are like puppies. They seem to know when they are liked." Dory carried a stack of plates to the dishpan. "Are you from a large family, Mr. Waller?"

"Mr. Waller? It was Ben the other night."

Dory grinned at him over her shoulder and repeated the question. "Ben, are you from a large family?"

"No, ma'am. I never knew my folks. There's just me and Odette."

"I've always thought it would be wonderful to be a part of a big family—where everyone got along and looked after one another. When I was little, Mama tried to make things pleasant for me and James, but Milo and Louis were always at odds with her. She could never please them. After a while she gave up and ignored them."

"Did that help?"

"No. It just made matters worse."

"Have you and James thought of selling your part of the company to Milo and Louis and starting up someplace else?"

"We thought about it, but this is our home. The homestead was a log shack when Mama came here. Papa built this house for her and she loved it."

"It's still just a *place*. Couldn't you make a home somewhere else?"

"I suppose I could."

After the dishes were done, she took Jeanmarie up to bed. When she came back down, Ben was gone.

CHAPTER
* 9 *

James guided his horse down the muddy street between the sparse buildings that made up the town of Spencer. Squatting at the base of the mountain, it was no more than a swath cut through the thick forest of pines, its buildings clustered together like a giant toadstool. Spencer and towns like it had sprung up all over the northwest to provide settlers, trappers, loggers and mill operators with a place to spend their spare time—and lose their money.

Here many a lumberjack had spent his entire winter's pay in one day of wenching and boozing. Boozing led to brawling—the most ferocious kind of brawling. It was not unusual for a man to crawl away minus an ear or the tip of his nose, or with a hunk chewed from his hide. As long as he was on his feet, he was fair game. Cheers were for the victor regardless of which fighter was right. But when a man was down, the fight was over. Only the most vicious of men would try to cripple a fellow lumberjack.

In the middle of the day Spencer looked like a lazy little town. Dogs and chickens roamed the muddy street between the two rows of buildings—eight on one side of the street, seven on the other, with the Idaho Palace saloon at the end facing a street so narrow a man could spit from one side of it to the other.

The hooves of the big black that James was riding made a sucking sound as they pulled at the mud, and he wondered why he had come here. He hated mud.

He had left the homestead early this morning to check out a stand of new growth on the eastern slope. He liked the solitude of being a timber-cruiser. It was like prospecting for gold, except that his gold was a stand of timber that would produce thousands of board feet of lumber. He had looked, made a few notes on the card in his pocket, then turned his horse on down the mountain.

Until a few days ago he had been content at the camp, working his crew, testing his skills by facing some reckless dare, competing in contests where he had gained a reputation of best all-around lumberjack. He made an occasional visit to town to drink and brawl and relieve himself with the good-time girls.

For the first time in years he had caught a glimpse of something more. His thoughts for the last few days had been taken up with a small, blond slip of a girl. The protective longing he had for her was a new feeling. He needed time alone to think, to try to understand if it was that he felt pity for her because she was deaf, or that he hadn't been in the company of a pretty young woman for a long, long time.

James passed the harness shop and the smithy, where the blacksmith, a huge Negro, was hammering forcefully on a red-hot piece of iron. The smell of fish came from Bessie's restaurant when he passed it. She was standing in the doorway and waved. James wondered how a woman so thin she looked as if the wind would blow her away could run an eatery.

He stopped behind a wagon in front of the mercantile, tipped his hat to the woman on the seat and grinned at the two children sitting on feed sacks in the back. Their eyes were round with the excitement of being in town. The boy smiled and waved. The little girl clapped her hand over her mouth and ducked behind her brother.

Amos McHenry had been the first to come to Spencer. He had built his store on land given to him by Silas Spencer, a trapper and woodsman long laid to rest, and had honored the old man by naming the town after him. McHenry was a Scotsman who looked as if he could swing a bull by the tail and not work up a sweat. His massive, stooped shoulders were crossed with wide suspenders over a faded flannel shirt. His walrus mustache was thick, but his sandy hair, parted in the middle and slicked down, was sparse. Even though he spoke in a soft voice, he was ready to face down any man who gave him trouble.

"Howdy, James. 'Tis a pleasant day we be havin'."

"It is that, McHenry."

"How be Miss Dory an' that sweet lass of hers?"

"Doing all right. You got any more young'uns since I was here last?"

McHenry laughed heartily. "Got one on the way. 'Twas a long winter, laddie."

"You're going to overpopulate the territory, McHenry. Will this be nine or ten?"

"Ye be losin' count, mon. 'Twill be one more'n a dozen. 'Tis a laddie I be lookin' for. Eight lovely lassies is 'nuff for any mon."

James removed his hat when Mag McHenry came in from the living quarters that adjoined the store. She was big like her husband, a tall, broad-shouldered, wide-hipped woman with coal-black hair which she wore in a single braid. Her dress hung straight from those broad shoulders to the tops of her shoes. Dark eyes, bright as shoe buttons, honed in on James.

"Is that the Callahan I be hearin'?"

"You have an ear for voices, Mrs. McHenry."

"How be Dory and the bairn?"

"They're fine."

"Glad to be hearin' she has the donkey mon's lassie to keep her company. It's hearin' I am that the poor little mite's deafer than a doornail." She clicked her tongue sadly.

It irritated James for Odette to be referred to as "poor little mite." But he reasoned silently that Mrs. McHenry was just repeating what she had heard.

"Aye, it's terrible what's goin' on. 'Tain't safe fer mon, woman nor beast now days. I be thinkin' 'bout Dory all by her ownself wid jist ol' Wiley thar ta stand 'tween her an' that devil what's murderin' those poor souls."

"What do you mean?" James looked from McHenry to his wife.

"Ain't ye heared 'bout the women bein' murdered?"

"I heard about an Indian girl found in the woods a month or two ago."

"Been two since then that we know of, mon. One in Pitzer, one down on the Saint Joe River. All since Christmas. Strangled with bare hands they were an' heads bashed in. 'Tis tryin' times we be havin', laddie."

Mrs. McHenry clicked her tongue again. "Could be more under the snow. They be harlots all but human bein's jist the same. For a fact 'tis a devil what's doin' it."

James reached into a jar, took out a handful of stick candies and placed them on the counter. McHenry rolled the candies in a paper and tied them with a string, talking all the while.

"I wrote ta the territorial governor, I did. Asked fer a marshal ta come. Ain't heared a word."

"Give me some of that chewing tobacco Wiley likes and a couple cans of peaches."

James paid for his purchases.

"Be keepin' yer eyes on Dory and the bairn till this devil what be doin' this terrible thing be caught." Mrs. McHenry spoke as James settled his hat back on his head.

"I'll do that, and I'll tell Dory you asked about her."

The wagon with the woman and two kids was still in front of the store. James stopped, unwrapped the candy and handed each of the children a stick. The woman turned and smiled her thanks.

"Thank the man," she urged.

Each of the children murmured something. James tipped his hat to the woman, stashed his purchases in his saddlebag, and mounted his horse.

He rode on down the street to the Idaho Palace, dismounted, and stepped down onto a walkway of split logs that was slowly sinking into the mud. He wrapped the horse's reins around a post and crossed the porch to the door.

There were a half-dozen people in the saloon: the bartender, two men at the bar and a woman sitting with two men at a table in the corner. All except the woman and the bartender were strangers to James.

"Howdy, Callahan. What'll ya have?"

"Beer." James tilted his hat to the back of his head and propped his foot on the footrail. "How's things, Mel?"

"Slow. Ever'thin's mudded in. Damn! I hate mud. Ever' spring it's muddier and deeper," he grumbled.

Mel was a fat man with freckles and a fringe of sandy hair around a bald spot. For years he had driven a mule train. He was rough and he ruled the goings-on in his saloon with an iron hand. He set the glass on the counter and wiped away the foam that spilled over the top.

The men at the end of the bar had turned sideways and were looking at James. One was a short, barrel-chested man with arms that reached almost to his knees. His friend was younger, slighter, and taller, with sideburns that reached the straggly beard on his jawbone.

"Air ya the Callahan?" The man's voice was unusually loud in the quiet room.

"One of 'em." James turned his head slightly and glanced at the men. The one that had spoken had a mean look on his face; the other had watery eyes that shifted uneasily.

"Well . . . which one?" The man's voice rose belligerently. His friend put a hand on his arm in an attempt to calm him down.

"Why do you want to know?" James answered testily, watching the man in the mirror over the bar.

" 'Cause if yo're the one I think ya are, I'm goin' to beat yore brains out."

"You mean you're going to try."

"Don't ya be pissin' 'round with me, boy."

James turned, faced the man, and looked at him with careful eyes. "Who put a burr under your tail, mister?" he asked quietly, but coldly.

"Ya did. Name's Lyle Kirkham, brother to a gal down in Scottsworth. She said it was a Callahan what . . . forced her. A Callahan strong as a bull with plenty a brag. Beat 'er up good."

James turned back to face the mirror. "I haven't been to Scottsworth in a couple of years."

Boot heels sounded on the wooden porch and two men came into the saloon. One was a big red-headed man with heavy shoulders, slim hips and long legs. James saw him in the mirror and wariness tightened his nerves. This was a hell of a time for Malone to show up.

"Don't ya turn yore back on me, ya pisser!" Kirkham's voice rang harshly. "I ain't done with ya yet . . . I ain't even got started. Fer all I know ya can be the one a killin' them—"

"That's enough, Lyle." Mel's sharp words rang with authority. "I ain't havin' no trouble in here." He reached under the counter for a shotgun and placed it on the bar. "Any trouble in here'll be of my doin'. Howdy, Chip, what'll ya have?"

"Whiskey and two glasses." Chip Malone leaned on the bar, watched the two men in the mirror and realized he had walked in on something about to happen. James rested his elbows on the bar, his hands clasped loosely around his beer mug.

Kirkham moved past Chip to stand behind James.

"Yo're goin' ta pay fer what ya done." He dropped a heavy hand on James's shoulder.

James exploded in full fight. "You son of a bitch!"

As he spoke, he spun and swung. The blow was a powerful, wide-armed punch straight from his shoulder to Kirkham's mouth. It set the big man back on his heels and left his lips a bloody pulp.

"Don't ever put your hands on me unless you're wanting a fight," James growled through gritted teeth.

Kirkham regained his balance and charged. James sidestepped, grabbed him by his hair and shoved his face down hard on the bar. Blood spurted from his nose.

"What the hell's eating you, mister? I don't know you. I don't know your sister. I haven't been to Scottsworth in years. Now get the hell away from me."

When Kirkham's face came off the bar, he found himself looking into both barrels of Mel's shotgun.

"Get!" Mel's face was red and his jaws quivered. "Get and don't come back."

Lyle staggered back to his friend, who shoved a red bandanna into his hand.

"Dammit, Lyle. I told ya he warn't the one. That'n was older, shorter, an' had a gap 'tween his teeth. Come on, let's get outta here."

James accepted the wet cloth Mel handed him and wiped the blood from his knuckles. He used it to mop the blood from the bar, then handed it back.

"What was that about?" Chip asked.

"He took me for someone else." James drained his glass and moved it across to Mel for a refill.

"I can imagine who." Chip set his hat on the bar and ran his fingers through red hair streaked with gray.

James straightened and looked into bright blue eyes beneath red-brown brows. Both men had square chins and stubborn jaws. James's height was equal to the other man's, though he was of a lighter build.

"Stay out of my business."

"I intend to. But first, a word of advice. Stay clear of Milo's hangouts. He'll get you killed."

"And my, how you'd grieve," James retorted sarcastically.

"Boss, I'm goin' on down to the blacksmith." The man with Chip spoke.

"Go ahead. I'll be down."

Mel moved to the end of the bar and Chip took a step closer to James.

"I got . . . sort of a favor to ask."

James looked up in surprise. "You want me to put my head on a stump so you can cut it off. No deal. I think I'll keep it a while."

"I've nothing against you, James. I never thought for a minute that you had anything to do with Mick's death."

"But you've got plenty against the rest of the family, including Dory. Blood's thicker than water, Malone."

"Let that rest for now. There are times when hate can eat a man alive. It's what's happening to Louis and Milo."

"What do you want? I've got things to do."

"It isn't for me. And get this straight—I'm askin', not

beggin'. You understand?'' James didn't say anything and Chip went on. ''Marie is ailing. She hasn't left the house since before Christmas.''

''What's that got to do with me?''

''She wants to see the little girl.'' The last few words tumbled out in a rush. Chip picked up his whiskey glass and drained it.

A smile spread over James's face and a pain of regret struck deep in Chip Malone's heart. Dear God. His face was so much like Jean's. Right down to the way his lips lifted higher on one side.

''So you want to see Jeanmarie. Dory named her after our mother and Mick's. But you knew that, didn't you?''

''Yes, I knew that. Marie was pleased. It meant that Mick would not be forgotten.''

''Bring Mrs. Malone out to the house.'' James's chuckle was humorless. ''Now wouldn't that be a hullabalooser! The Malones calling on the Callahans.'' He drank from his glass and wiped his mouth with the back of his hand.

Chip was silent. He turned his empty whiskey glass around and around between his fingers. Mel came along the bar, refilled his glass, and went back to the end of the bar before Chip spoke.

''I can't do that. Marie hasn't left her bed for a month now.'' There was real regret in Chip's voice. He hadn't loved the woman as a man should love his wife, but she was a good woman. She had borne him a son, and since the boy's death her health had gone steadily downhill.

''I'm sorry to hear it,'' James said sincerely. ''She's been decent to Dory, and Jeanmarie treasures the gifts Mrs. Malone sent her.''

''Ask Dory if she'll come. Come with her if you're afraid she won't be treated right.''

"You can bet your life I'd do that . . . if she comes." He looked squarely into Chip's eyes. "I want you to know something else. I'll fight you to hell and back if you make one move to get Jeanmarie away from her."

"All I want is to give Marie the pleasure of being with her granddaughter."

"So you acknowledge that she's Mick's."

"Hell, yes! One look at her was proof enough. And I've never heard that Dory denied it."

"No. Dory doesn't deny it. And Milo and Louis don't let her forget it."

"Too bad it turned her into—" Chip broke off his words and drained his glass.

"Into what?" James's voice was scarcely above a whisper. His fists knotted. The face he turned to Chip was taut with anger.

Chip knew he had made a mistake. The man was ready to explode again.

"I'm sorry, James. I over-spoke. I don't usually pay attention to rumors. But this one hit close to home. She's the mother of my grandchild."

"Let me tell you something, Malone. Milo has spit out a few slurs about my sister. He hates her . . . and me, because of our mother. But there's not a man alive that can brag that Dory has ever done a thing to deserve those slurs. She was a sad, lonesome kid when she did what she did with Mick. No one would have known it if she hadn't got caught. And there's something else. She doesn't regret it. That little girl means the world to her. The only thing she regrets is that Mick didn't live to see her." James took a deep breath to calm himself. "If I hear of you putting a dirty name to my sister, you or your wife will never see Jeanmarie again if I have to ship them off to . . . China."

"It wasn't me that put the name to her. If you want it stopped, talk to Milo and Louis."

"I'll do that."

The woman who had been sitting at the table had come to stand on the other side of James.

"Howdy, goodlookin'. You goin' to be in town long?"

James turned and flashed her a grin. "Not long, sugarfoot. Ya been pinin' away for me?"

The woman laughed and squeezed his arm. She was short and blond and had an abundance of curves in all the right places. She also had bad teeth and a few wrinkles she tried to hide with rouge.

"Of course. Can't you see I'm down to skin and bones?"

James loosened his arm from her grasp and tossed a coin on the bar. "Fix Clara up with a couple of drinks, Mel. I've got to be going."

"Bye, honey. Don't stay away so long."

"Be good now." James laughed into her eyes.

"I'm always good," she replied in a coarse husky whisper.

He pulled his hat down snuggly on his head. "See ya, Mel."

Chip followed James out onto the porch.

"Got the donkey engine set up yet?"

"Just about." James stepped into the saddle. "Louis is sure he's going to beat you to the fast water."

A light came into Chip's eyes. "He'd better not bet on it even if he did get the best man in the country to set up his engine."

"You know Waller?"

"I've heard of him. Tried to get him myself, but for some reason he went your way."

"Yeah. We were lucky." James pulled on the reins to turn his horse.

"James," Chip called. "Dory will be treated with utmost respect."

"Yeah," James said again. "I'll tell her."

Chip Malone watched James ride away. Dear God, how many years had it been? Yet each and every time he saw him, his longing for Jean was stronger than before. If things had turned out just a little bit in his favor, James would be living in his house, working in his cutting camp, having his grandchildren.

Chip headed for the smithy. It had been hard to ask the favor, but he had promised Marie. Now it was out of his hands.

CHAPTER
* 10 *

James had left right after breakfast. He seemed to have a lot on his mind. Dory was too busy to wonder what was bothering him. Time flew by and before she knew it, it was mid-morning and time to punch down the bread dough and put it in the pans to rise.

Ben had spent a few minutes with Odette and the rest of the morning with Wiley. When Dory went out to call both men in for a noon meal, they were busy at the forge hammering out clamps, hooks and braces for the donkey engine.

Wiley and Ben talked during the meal. Ben admired Wiley's smithy skills, and the old man basked in his admiration.

"You do a good job, Wiley. I've not had better hooks made anywhere."

Dory set a pan of rice pudding, along with a pitcher of cream, on the table. She dished some out for Jeanmarie.

"They can just sit there and brag on each other," she said to the child while pouring thick cream in the bowl. "We'll eat the pudding."

Ben winked at Jeanmarie and she giggled happily.

"Wal, now. I ain't missin' this puddin'." Wiley reached for the bowls Dory had brought to the table. "Reckon we can talk about smithin' any time a-tall. Though it's pure pleasure to have my praises sung."

"Leave me some of that pudding," Ben said, winking at Dory. "And I just might sing you some more."

"That'd be mighty pretty to my ears." Wiley grinned his snaggle-toothed grin at Dory. She felt happy chuckles form deep in her chest and roll up into laughter.

Next to Jeanmarie and James, Dory loved Wiley best. She'd known him all her life. She had always thought that if she ever moved away from here she would take Wiley with her—that is if he wanted to go.

When she saw Steven pass the window, she got quickly to her feet and went to the door. Something was wrong or Steven wouldn't be here this time of day. He tied his horse to a hook on the side of the barn and headed for the bunkhouse. Dory stepped out the door and called.

"Come on in, Steven. Wiley and Ben are in here."

Steven turned and came toward the porch.

"Howdy, Miss Dory." He removed his hat as he spoke. "Hello, Wiley. Hello, Waller."

"Howdy," Ben nodded.

"Have you had dinner?" Dory asked. "We were just finishing up."

"Yes, ma'am. I had dinner early. I thought Louis might be here."

"He was here yesterday morning. I haven't seen him since. Is there trouble at the mill?"

"Nothing Louis can't take care of. Milo is on a tear. He fired three men this morning, but I told them not to go, just stay out of sight for a while."

"It's not unusual for Milo to be on a tear, is it? Come have some rice pudding."

"It's tempting, but I think I'd better get on back and try to keep things going until Louis gets back to calm him down." Steven pulled a big gold watch from his vest pocket, flipped open the lid and looked at the time. "Louis takes these little trips occasionally to spy on the Malones."

Dory grinned. "I don't doubt it, Steven. Let's hope he doesn't get caught."

"There'd be trouble aplenty. I'm not sure Malone is guilty of all they accuse him of."

"You'd never make Louis believe that."

"I wouldn't even give it a try. Sorry to have interrupted your dinner. Good day, Miss Dory." Steven stepped out the door with his fedora hat in his hand. On the porch he paused and set it squarely on his head.

Dory watched him ride away before she came back to the table. She had a worried frown on her face.

"I hope James stays away from the mill if Milo is having one of his crazy spells."

"Crazy spells?" Ben asked.

"Crazy, my foot. It's pure old meanness, is what it is," Wiley said. "Milo ain't got much sense to start with, but when he's all liquored up and gets it in for a body, he ain't got no more sense than a pie-eyed mule. He'd as soon beat a feller to death as look at him."

"Steven seemed nervous." Ben helped himself to the cream in the pitcher. "Do you think Milo's giving him trouble?"

"Could be. Ever' once in a while Milo gets it in his head that Steven's cheatin' 'im and Louis."

"Can't they look at the books and tell if he's keeping straight accounts?"

"Nope. Milo and Louis don't read or write much. That's why they keep Steven. He was a young feller when he came here. Bright as a new penny too. George, Dory's pa, took to him right away and hired him. He's been here since. George was fond of him. Mighty fond. So was Jean."

"Papa stated in his will that Steven could work here as long as he wanted to. If he was fired for any reason, the company had to pay him for two years' work."

"I think that if I was Steven, I'd find an excuse to bash in Milo's head so I'd get fired."

"That wouldn't do it," Dory laughed. "He tried it once and Louis wouldn't agree to fire him. They know he keeps straight books. The banker comes out every couple of years and checks them. Not once has he found anything that wasn't right."

"He looks more like a banker than a tally keeper," Ben said, and stood.

Wiley reluctantly moved his chair back from the table. "He ain't changed a bit since he come here. Neat and gentle-man-like. Never thought he'd last out the week." Wiley reached for his battered hat and slammed it down on his head. "Hit was a mighty fine meal, Dory."

"Thanks for the dinner. I don't know when I've had better," Ben said. "I'll run up and see Odette for a minute before I go back to work."

"Me, too. Me go see Odette." Jeanmarie held out her arms to Ben. Her big eyes had a pleading look he couldn't resist.

"All right, little curly-head." Ben lifted her up to sit on his arm. She grinned at her mother over his shoulder.

"You're spoiling her, Ben."

"Little girls are supposed to be spoiled. Isn't that right, curly-head?"

"Uh-huh," the child replied.

Dory stood clutching the back of the chair. Having Ben and Odette here had been wonderful, not only for her, but for Jeanmarie. Her child was basking in their attention.

"Good man, Dory. I wish he'd stay on here." Wiley was watching her intently. "The young'un took to him."

"They'll stay until the engine is set up. Then they'll go. Ben would never work permanently for Louis and Milo."

"You an' the young'un could go with him."

"For goodness sake, Wiley. He hasn't asked me. Hasn't even hinted of it."

"He ain't got no wife. Can't ya—"

"—No, I can't. He either stays because he wants to or not at all."

Steven could hear the big saw blade singing before he reached the mill. Milo must have quieted down, or Tinker wouldn't have started the saws going. Damn Milo. He had come back to camp with cut lips and full of fight. The story he told about his fight with Ben Waller convinced no one but his closest cronies. After a day of drinking, he had ordered the men to load the firebox so that he could start up the donkey engine. Fearing that the boiler would blow up, they had refused.

Milo had become raving mad and kicked over the stove in the bunkhouse. Luckily there had been enough men around to put out the fire that had started when the hot coals had come in contact with a stack of blankets and a straw-filled mattress. Then, while the majority of the mill hands were at breakfast, he had climbed up on the platform and pulled the lever that set the two large circular saws whirling in midair. Above the blades was a system of belts and pulleys, any one of which could break or grow hot and burn through. Free of a log, the saws had begun to sing a high unwavering note that had brought Tinker on the run.

Strong as an ox, Tinker had wrested the controls from Milo, shut down the machinery, and pulled him off the carriage.

Steven had been tempted to send someone to the homestead, but he knew Waller was down there and he was afraid Waller and Louis might have had a set-to over Dory. It was best that the workers know as little about that situation as possible, so he had gone himself.

Steven rode to the barn and handed his horse over to a muleskinner who sat on the rail fence waiting for his animals to drink.

"Louis back?"

"Not yet, but Milo drank enough to pass out. Cook kept pouring it to him. That damn Milo's goin' to get hisself or somebody else killed. I got a notion to hie my tail on over to Malone and see if he needs another muleskinner."

"What happened after I left?"

"He started a fight with Tinker, and Tinker put a headlock on him. When he yelled at Tinker that he was fired, Tinker laughed. Milo went crazy, jumped on the boiler and started hitting it with that twenty-pound maul. It took four men to hold him. He's plumb crazy."

Steven walked to his cabin, unlocked the door, went inside and carefully wiped his feet on the floor mat before he placed his hat on the hatrack beside the door. This had been his home for sixteen years. His first two years at Callahan Mill had been spent in the bunkhouse with the men. They had been the most miserable years of his life. Then, with two years' wages in his pocket, he'd had the cabin built during the off season and had gone to Coeur d'Alene for the furnishings. His cabin was off-limits to everyone in the camp, including Louis and Milo.

Steven went to the glass-fronted cabinet and poured himself a brandy. Carrying the short-stemmed goblet to the window, he stood and looked out over the mill site.

How long was he going to have to stay here? Was it going to take the rest of his life to repay his debt to George Callahan?

He had said when the time was right, do what you think best. Steven glanced at the false-fronted bottom of the cabinet where the heavy iron safe was hidden. He sighed. He owed George Callahan his life. The best he could do was to give him a few more weeks or months of it. Things were coming to a head. He could feel it.

Dory was preparing the evening meal when James rode into the yard, dismounted, and led his horse to the barn. She hoped he had worked out in his mind whatever the problem was that had been bothering him when he had ridden away that morning. It worried her that he might have become aware of just how cruelly Louis and Milo treated her. James was so dear to her. If anything should happen to him, it would break her heart. She and Jeanmarie would be alone. The only thing she could do then would be to throw herself on the mercy of the Malones. She shivered at the thought.

James came directly from the barn to the house.

"How is Odette?" he asked, as he flung his saddlebags over the back of a chair.

"Feeling much better. Jeanmarie is with her." When James frowned, she added, "Odette doesn't mind. She's very patient with her. The last time I looked in, Jeanmarie was drawing the first four letters of the alphabet on the tablet. Doesn't that beat all?"

James looked at his sister's smiling face. *She was pretty.* Her eyes glowed, her cheeks were flushed. She appeared to be happier than he had seen her in a long time. Did it have anything to do with Ben Waller? It had occurred to James only recently how lonely it must be for her here. It was obvious that she and Jeanmarie had formed an attachment to Odette. Had it extended to Odette's father?

"There's something I want to talk to you about before Ben

and Wiley come in and while the little mop-head is upstairs. Lordy, that kid is so smart, I'm sure she knows a lot more than we think she knows about things."

"What do you mean?" A shiver of dread had traveled down Dory's spine.

"She's a talkative little imp, yet I've never heard her say a word to Louis or Milo. She took to Ben like a duck to water."

"Well . . . you've heard the old saying that children and dogs know when people like them. Jeanmarie senses that our brothers don't bear any love for us. Is that what you wanted to talk about?"

James washed his hands in the basin and slushed water onto his face with his cupped hands.

"No," he said while drying his face. "It's something else." After hanging the towel on the bar above the wash-bench, he ran a comb through his hair and straddled a chair. "I saw Chip Malone today."

Dory's hands stilled. "You went there?"

"I saw him in Spencer—at the saloon. Chip has always been fairly decent to me. A couple of times he's called his men off when they would have picked a fight with me and some of my men."

"Louis hates him with a most unreasonable hatred. It gets worse as the years go by. I realize that I'm partly responsible for that even though Louis doesn't hate them out of any love for me."

"Regardless of who hates who and why, I'm getting sick of hearing about it. Louis pushes so we'll have more logs in the river than Malone, so we'll cut more board feet at the mill. I was for getting the donkey engine. We'll be able to snake the timber out easier and faster, but I'm not going to push my men to work sixteen-hour days in order to beat Malone to the river."

"Is that what you and Chip talked about?"

"We talked about you and Jeanmarie."

"Oh." Dory couldn't conceal the shudder of fear that went through her.

"Mrs. Malone is poorly. He wants you to bring Jeanmarie to see her."

Dory drew in a deep breath. "He what?"

"Mrs. Malone wants to see her granddaughter."

"So he admits that she's Mick's child? That's the first I've heard of that." Dory whirled around to face her brother. "I don't trust him."

"I don't think he has anything in mind other than giving his sick wife the pleasure of being with Jeanmarie. He was sincere. I'd stake my life on it."

"He was sincere all right," Dory sputtered. "Sincere about getting me there and keeping my baby. If he did that it would take an army to get her back."

"Think about it, but don't think too long. Mrs. Malone hasn't left her bed for a month."

"I'm sorry to hear that, if it's true. Mrs. Malone has been . . . kind. But, James, how do we know he's telling the truth?"

"There's ways of finding out. I talked to McHenry at the mercantile. He said that she's not been in lately and the Malones have bought supplies for a sickroom."

"I hadn't thought of Mr. McHenry. Nevertheless, I don't dare go to the Malones. It would be like sticking my neck in a noose."

"Would you go if me and Waller went with you?"

"You and Ben? He wouldn't go."

"You want to bet on it? Well, think about it. It's up to you."

Dory changed the subject when she heard voices on the porch. She always grew edgy when the Malones were discussed.

"Steven was here today looking for Louis. Milo is on one of his tears."

"How many did he fire this time?"

"Three, but Steven told them to stay and to keep out of sight until Milo sobered up."

"It was stupid of Louis to leave the mill if Milo was drinking."

Wiley and Ben came in. Ben's head was wet and he had on clean clothes. He had bathed—something Dory had longed to do for the past several nights, but there was no chance with James and Ben in the house.

"How did it go today?" James asked after they had hung their coats on the pegs.

"Good. I'll head back to the mill in the morning and get that monster ready to pull up to wherever you decide you want it." Ben clapped Wiley on the shoulder. "This old man knows his stuff."

Wiley beamed and shifted his chaw of tobacco from one cheek to the other.

"Wiley Potter, you spit out that chaw before you come to the table," Dory said firmly, her smile taking the edge off her sharp words.

"Lucifer! I forgot 'bout it." Wiley headed for the door and stepped outside. "Sure hate to waste a fresh chaw," he said when he returned. "Ben took so long with his bathin' I got tired a waitin'. It ain't healthy to be washin' so much. It ain't stunted his growth none . . . yet, but it might'a addled his head."

"Just when I was fixing to take this old codger with me and make him a partner in my own milling business, he has to go ruin things by talking against me. I'm going to need a good man to make hinges and hasps for doors and—"

Ben's steel-gray eyes, alight with humor, flashed to Dory and darkened with concern. Her feet seemed to be glued to the floor. Her hand paused in midair, and her face was drained of color. Her eyes were flooded with tears.

"You can't take Wiley," she said with a sob. "You just can't—I'd be here all alone."

Then, to the amazement of the men watching, she burst into tears and ran out of the room.

Ben was stunned.

Wiley's mouth dropped open.

James hurried after his sister. Ben could hear the low murmur of his voice coming from the darkened hallway leading to the stairs. He felt as if the wind had been knocked out of him. He would remember the haunted, desperate look in her eyes for as long as he lived. He had to put things right.

At the end of the hallway Dory was turned to the wall, her face buried in her bent arm. James stood behind her with his hand on her shoulder.

"I'm . . . sorry. I'll be . . . all right. Just give me a . . . minute."

"You'll not be left here alone, Sis. Wiley will stay as long as you want him. He dotes on you and Jeanmarie."

"Ben will go and . . . take Odette."

"Ah, Sis. We have no control over that. I didn't realize you'd been so lonesome."

"May I talk to her?" Ben asked.

James's hand dropped from his sister's shoulder. He looked into Ben's face with a puzzled frown on his, then turned and walked back into the kitchen.

Ben moved to stand close behind Dory. He lifted his hand to touch her, but let it fall back to his side.

"Dory, I didn't mean to upset you. I was just talking to hear my head rattle. I'm not much for chit-chat and at times I talk without thinking. Not for the world would I lure Wiley away from you. He wouldn't go anyway. He thinks the world of you." He put his hand on her shoulder. "Please don't cry, Dory. Please."

"I'm . . . not . . . cryin'."

He turned her around and wiped a finger across her cheek. "Then what is this wet stuff on your cheeks?" he asked lightly.

She sniffed. "I don't know what got into me. I'm . . . so ashamed."

He gripped her shoulders with both hands. "You carry a load here on these shoulders. You've nothing to be ashamed of."

"Sometimes I wonder if this is all there is to life . . . just existing from day to day."

Standing there, close to him, a naked hunger to be held possessed Dory. Her face was lifted to his. He was looking down at her. She could feel his warm breath on her wet cheeks. Their faces were only inches apart.

"Oh, Ben, life is so hard." The sad note in her voice touched something deep in his heart.

"Yes, it is. But you're strong. You've endured a lot and still hold your head high. You'll not be whipped and cowed. You'll come out on top."

Then she was leaning against him, her cheek against his shoulder, and his arms were holding her loosely. She closed her eyes to savor the moment, and the fresh, clean scent of his leather vest crept into her senses. It was heaven, pure heaven. The palms of her hands were trapped between them. She moved them around his sides to his back. They stood for a long moment holding each other. Then he lowered his head and pressed her cheek tightly to his. It was a precious moment and a delicious weakness flooded through her.

"Ah . . . sweet, wonderful woman," he whispered, and

kissed her forehead gently. His gentleness was at odds with his desire to press her tightly to him. His heart raced with the need to find her lips with his and kiss her with fierce abandon. As he held her he felt as if he had found a part of himself that had been missing without his even being aware of it.

Dory didn't know how much time had passed until she became aware that she was holding him tightly and moving her hands over his back. His whispered words had sent her senses reeling. She knew then that he was everything her soul had longed for. For just an instant she felt his lips touching her hair. Then he was holding her away from his strength, the warmth of his body. She kept her eyes on the hollow at the base of his brown throat.

"Feel better now?" he asked. "Are you still sore at me?"

"I wasn't sore at you. I just felt as if I was losing everything. So much has happened lately."

"You work hard and haven't had much sleep."

"I did last night. Odette is much better."

"The thanks go to you and James. I would have lost her if not for you."

"I don't want thanks, Ben. James doesn't either." She wiped her eyes with her sleeve. "I think he likes Odette. He's awfully concerned about her."

Ben was still while thoughts ran crazily through his mind. Finally he said, "I appreciate his concern."

"Would you object if it was more than just . . . concern?" Dory asked quietly.

"It wouldn't come to that," Ben said, not quite believing what he was saying. "James is a man and Odette is just a kid."

"She said she'd be seventeen this summer. Some women have a couple of children by the time they are seventeen." Dory didn't think it necessary to mention that her own child had been born when she was that age.

"That may be, but James—"

"—James is twenty-four. He's been doing a man's work since he was fourteen. There's not a better man anywhere than James even if he is reckless . . . at times. He's good and kind and works hard."

"Hold it." He shook her shoulders gently. "You don't have to sell me on your brother. I like him. I'm grateful for what he did for Odette. Don't you think we're getting the cart before the horse?"

Ben tried to make his voice light even though a premonition of rough water ahead engulfed him. He couldn't let a man-woman attachment develop between Odette and James without his knowing for sure who her father was. How the hell could he explain that to Odette? There was another side of the coin, too. He had been with her for more than three years, and if it turned out she wasn't his daughter, a lot of people would read something wicked in that, and it could spoil Odette's chance of marrying a man of her choice.

CHAPTER
* 11 *

Dory filled a plate with food for Odette and Ben took it up to her. By the time he returned, supper was on the table, and he took his place beside Wiley. Jeanmarie, excited about having so much company and blissfully unaware of the tension at the table, chatted on and on until Dory gently reminded her to eat her supper. The little girl was enjoying herself. The grown-ups were not yelling at one another.

Dory listened to her daughter's chatter with only half an ear. She was consumed with thoughts of what had happened between her and Ben in the darkened hallway. For a brief, wild moment she had known his closeness, his warmth, smelled his scent, had felt safe, even cherished. Then it was over.

Even while her body was touching his, she had felt him drawing away from her. And when they had talked about an attraction between Odette and James, he had drawn even farther away and had put up a shield between them. He obviously didn't think her brother good enough for his daughter. Dory's disappointment in him had been acute. She had felt as if the breath had been sucked out of her.

If James isn't good enough for his daughter, a woman with

an illegitimate child would certainly never be good enough for him.

Dory raised her head. Her eyes were caught and held by Ben's. Sober eyes beneath straight dark brows searched her face. She felt something stir in the marrow of her bones and in the corner of her heart she had kept locked away. She recognized it for what it was: a hunger for love, a yearning for someone to share her thoughts, her dreams, her burdens. She lowered her eyes to her plate, afraid that her emotions would be too clearly revealed.

In her thoughts she talked to him. *Because of my reputation you think I'm tarnished, and I suppose I am to a certain extent. But I'm not one bit sorry for having been with Mick. He needed me and I needed him. It just happened and afterward we both knew it had been wrong. Please don't hold that against me. Out of my sin that summer came the most precious thing in my life. How could I be sorry for that?*

Dear Ben. Give yourself the chance to know me. I would love you with all my heart and soul—love your daughter as if she were my own—stand beside you through good times and bad—work beside you all the days of our lives—

"Mama. Mama—"

"Sit still. I'll get it, Sis."

Dory looked up at James. "Get what?"

"Milk. Jeanmarie wants buttermilk."

"I didn't hear her. I must have been daydreaming."

"It's a easy plan, Ben," Wiley was saying, and Dory wondered how long she had been in her dream world. "I could make ice tongs, if I had a way to smooth them down."

"I've no doubt of that. Your nails and wedges are as good as any I've seen anywhere."

"Careful, Ben. Brag on this old buzzard too much and he'll get to thinking he's worth cash money." James set a small glass of buttermilk beside Jeanmarie's plate and took his place at the table.

"Thank Uncle James, honey," Dory prodded gently.

"Thank you." Jeanmarie giggled happily. "I want to see Odette." She tried to wriggle off her stool.

"Finish what you have on your plate first."

Ben listened to Dory talk to her child. Her voice was musical as if she were trying to soothe an excited animal. She *is* a good mother, he thought, remembering his aunt reaching across the table and rapping his knuckles with a spoon if he as much as dropped a crumb on the table or left a bite on his plate. Dory had not even spoken harshly to the child when, during the noon meal, Jeanmarie had waved her spoon around and flung food over the table. Dory had taken the spoon from her hand and reminded her that it should be left on her plate when she wasn't using it.

Jeanmarie put the last bite of food from her plate into her mouth and looked expectantly at her mother. Dory lifted her off the stool.

"We'll go see how Odette is doing."

James waited until he was sure his sister and Jeanmarie were on the way up the stairs before he spoke.

"I heard some news in Spencer today. McHenry told me that two more women have been killed—strangled and their heads bashed in. One in Pitzer, one down on the Saint Joe. That makes three that they know of since Christmas."

"Hell and damnation!" Wiley exclaimed. "Off and on fer the last few years there's been stories 'bout murdered women. It's been laid to drunk Indians. One feller was hung 'cause he was last with a whore what was found in her bed with her throat cut. Feller swore with his dyin' breath he didn't do it."

"The latest were whores too." James leaned back in his chair. "All the women were killed within twenty-five or thirty miles of each other and according to the way they were killed, by the same man. McHenry has written to the territorial governor asking him to send in a marshal.''

Ben's quick mind honed in on one thing and fear washed over him like a wave of ice-cold water.

''Could it be a coincidence that the slain women were whores, or could it be that the killer chose them because of it?'' Ben looked James full in the face when he spoke.

''I hadn't thought about it.''

Ben leaned his arms on the table. ''I think we'd better think about it.''

''If you've got something on your mind, spill it.''

''The day I came here Louis told me that Dory's child was born out of wedlock. He said her reputation was anything but lily white, and said a few more things about what he suspected went on here when she was here alone.'' As Ben talked, his expression became angry, almost brutal. ''At the camp I heard Milo referring to her as Whory Dory. The men, most of them, have no reason not to believe Milo and think Dory is . . . well, that kind of woman.''

James jumped up from his chair. His dark face had turned livid with tight-lipped fury. He paced back and forth and Ben wondered if he had been wise to lay it on the line all at once. Not *all*—he wouldn't break his promise to Dory—but enough for James to realize the danger his sister was in.

''Those two are rotten to the core. There isn't anything too mean for them to do. Wiley said their ma was the same. Today I saw Chip Malone, and even *he* hinted that Dory was a loose woman.''

''Some people like to spread a story like that. Coming from a relative they believe it must be true.''

James paused. ''What you're saying is that if the killer is looking for whores, he might come after Dory.''

''It's a possibility.''

"Hellfire!" James sat down hard on the chair.

"Men talk. It's reasonable to think that what's been said about Dory has spread throughout the territory."

"You don't believe it?" James stood and looked down at Ben as if he could kill him.

"Hell no! Do you think I would have left my daughter here if I did? If she was in that trade, she would have left here and gone to where there were more . . . customers."

"What can I do? What the hell can I do? I can't take her and Jeanmarie up to the cutting camp." James sat back down and leaned his forearms on his thighs, his hands dangling between. "I never realized they hated her so much because nothing like that was ever said around me. They're seldom here when I am," he said as if talking to himself. "We're not like other families that gather at Thanksgiving and Christmas."

"I ain't much good on my feet as ya know, but I can handle that ol' shotgun a mine." Wiley's sharp old eyes went from one man to the other. "Done it a few times, too, when some polecat come a smellin' 'round. Did it the other day when that no-good Sid Hanes come a callin'. If he'd a made a move to push in the door, I'd a nailed him to the wall with a double round from ol' Bertha." The old man's whiskered face had taken on a wolflike expression.

James turned to Wiley. "I've not . . . Dory's not said anything about men coming here to the house thinking that she . . . that she—"

"Dory ain't wantin' to trouble ya none, boy."

"I'm sure as heck glad I didn't know about the shotgun the night I arrived in that snowstorm," Ben said, and his lips quirked at the corners.

"I had my eye on ya. Ya'd a not made it to the porch if ya ain't a had the little missy with ya, and that's a fact if there ever was one."

"Dory's kept all this from me," James said as if he were bewildered. "Why didn't she tell me?"

"She didn't want you to end up in the woods with a bullet in your back," Ben said bluntly.

James was staring at the floor, deep in his own thoughts.

Wiley cut off a chaw of tobacco with his pocketknife, stuck it inside his jaw and watched Ben carry his coffee cup to the stove, refill it and return to his chair.

"Hellfire!" James jerked his head up. "We'll sell out to Louis and Milo. I'll take Dory and Jeanmarie and go to California."

"You'll what? James, what are you talking about?" Dory stood in the doorway with Odette's tray in her hands. She carried it to the counter and went straight to her brother. Her hand gripped his shoulder. "James, did you say what I thought you said? You'd sell out to Milo and Louis?"

He tugged on her hand and she sat down in the chair beside him.

"Sis, wouldn't you like to leave here? Go to California or Washington? If we sold out to Milo and Louis we could go anywhere we want to go."

"What brought this on? They don't have the money to buy us out. There's just enough cash money to run the company until fall. Steven explained that. The surplus went to buy the donkey engine and the cable to go with it."

"We could sell on contract and have them pay us so much each year."

"James, they wouldn't pay us a dime after we left here and you know it."

"Steven would see to it," James argued.

"They would pay Steven his two years' wages and get rid of him before they'd pay us. Why are you so all-of-a-sudden set on selling?"

"I want to get you and Jeanmarie away from here," he blurted angrily. "I'm responsible for you."

"There's something you're not telling me and I want to know what it is." Dory looked only at James. With fingers on his cheek she turned his face so that she could see his eyes. "What's happened, James? Why are you wanting to get me and Jeanmarie away from here?"

James leaned toward his sister and took her hands in his. "Sis, there's been four women murdered near here since Christmas. Three that we know of. There could be more. It's reasonable to believe that if there is a madman on the loose, he'll not stop until he's caught. I want you away from here until then."

"That's terrible . . . those poor women."

"McHenry wrote the territorial governor asking him to send a federal marshal. We both know that don't mean diddly-squat. Finding the man here in the timber country will be like finding a needle in a haystack. When word gets out, everyone will be looking for him, and he may leave the country. But we can't count on it."

"I understand your concern and love you for it. But Wiley is here, and Ben and Odette . . . for a while. Don't worry, Brother. We'll be all right."

James got up from the chair and went to the water bucket. He drank from the dipper and let it fall back in the pail.

"Have you thought more about going to see Mrs. Malone?" he asked when he turned.

Dory glanced at Ben, then at Wiley before she answered. "No. I haven't had time to think about it. You want me to go, don't you?"

"I'm thinking it would be the decent thing to do," he said tiredly.

"I'll think about it, James."

Dory held her breath for fear he would ask Ben to go with them to the Malones. She would die of embarrassment if he refused. To her relief he let the subject drop.

James opened his saddlebag and took out a couple of packages. He tossed one to Wiley.

"McHenry happened to have your favorite on hand." He untied the other package. "Have a candy stick, Sis." He placed one on the table in front of her as he passed on his way to the doorway leading to the hall. A second or two later they heard his footsteps going up the stairs.

Afraid to look at Ben, afraid of his reaction to James going up to see Odette, Dory began clearing the table of the supper dishes. Her back felt as though it had a steel pipe run through it. Her head thudded and her stomach was churning.

James stood in the doorway of the bedroom watching Odette and Jeanmarie. He was surprised to see that Odette was up, dressed, sitting in a chair and reading to Jeanmarie, who was cuddled in her lap. Her voice was soft, sometimes a mere whisper, and the words came hesitantly at times.

Honey-colored hair hung down over her shoulders and curled slightly. Her body was slim, her breasts generous. A slight rosiness tinged her cheeks.

James became aware that she was looking at him, her eyebrows arched in surprise. He couldn't make up his mind if her eyes were sky-blue or the color of a mountain lake.

He made a motion for her to continue, then stepped into the room and sat down on the end of the bunkbed. She looked back down at the book, and after a slight hesitation, she began to read again. At first her voice quivered and she stumbled over the words. After a few lines her voice steadied, and, unaware that Jeanmarie had fallen asleep, she continued to read the story about a fairy princess.

She is remarkable, James thought. A soft, sweet, courageous woman. *She was reading and couldn't even hear her own voice*. He feared she would look up, catch him watching her and stop reading. But she didn't. When she finished the story, she closed the book and placed it on the floor beside the chair. She looked down at Jeanmarie's red curly head resting against her shoulder and placed a gentle kiss on her forehead before she shifted her gaze to the man sitting on the bunk.

Fragments of light shone in the incredible blue of her eyes. The corners of her lips lifted in a half-smile as she gestured to the sleeping child. James felt as if he were suspended in time and space and almost feared that if he closed his eyes, she would disappear. The silence was deep as they looked at each other without any awkwardness.

He wanted to tell her that it gave him much pleasure to hear her voice, but he didn't know how.

"I'll be back."

She nodded that she understood him and he left the room. He returned quickly with a copy of his favorite book, *The Deerslayer* by James Fenimore Cooper.

Kneeling beside her, he opened the book to the first page and placed it in her lap.

"Will you read to me?" his lips moved silently.

"You don't read?"

He shook his head. "Not very well. Too slow." Which was true. He'd had more important things to do at that time of his life than to sit in a school and learn to read and write. He knew enough to get by, but that was all.

"Practice. You go fast."

"Read it to me . . . sometime," he urged and smiled. He could almost feel her warm gaze on his mouth.

"Sometime." She handed the book back to him.

"You keep it," he said and placed it on the floor beside the other book. He stood. "Let me take the little mop-head. You must be tired."

"Jeanmarie's not a mop-head," Odette said, and ran her fingers through the child's red curls.

James was so delighted to be talking to her that he wanted to keep her talking.

"Then what is she?"

"Ah . . . let me see." Odette tilted her head from side to side, her lips pursed. "Jeanmarie is a little strawberry top."

"That's good. How about little red bird?"

"That's good too." Odette laughed. It was a soft little sound.

James lifted the child from her arms and placed her on the bunk.

"Take off shoes, James."

When Odette's voice came from behind him, it washed over him like a warm spring rain. It gave him such pleasure that he closed his eyes for an instant before he turned his head and nodded to her.

After covering the child, he again knelt beside Odette and placed the packet in her lap. Her eyes brightened with pleasure as she watched him unwrap the candy.

"For you and Jeanmarie." James's lips formed the words without sound. He stuck the end of one of the candy sticks in her mouth. She responded by sticking one in his mouth.

He smiled deep into her eyes. The smile she gave him in return was one of startling girlish sweetness, warm with the glow of complete trust.

His heart soared like a bird in flight.

The silence in the kitchen was as deep as a well. It went on and on, broken only by the small noises made by clinking dishes as Dory washed them and put them in the pan to be scalded with the water in the teakettle.

"Thank 'ee for supper, Dory." Wiley put his hat on and went to the door.

"Welcome, Wiley. See you in the morning."

Dory was acutely aware that she and Ben were alone. When he got to his feet, she held her breath for fear that he would follow Wiley to the bunkhouse. He went to the stove, picked up the teakettle and poured the boiling water over the dishes in the rinse pan.

"You don't need to do that," Dory said when he reached for the drying towel. His nearness caused her heart to thump painfully.

"You think I can't wipe dishes? I have washed and wiped a barn full of dishes in my day. When I was just a tad I was cook's helper in a timber camp. We cooked for twenty men, three times a day."

"How old were you?"

"I was eight or nine."

"That's awfully young. Didn't you go to school?"

"Not much." Ben slipped a fork beneath the edge of a plate to lift it out of the hot water. "Jehoshaphat! That water's hot!"

"Usually by the time I finish washing and am ready to dry, the water has cooled."

They worked in silence, and gradually Dory's heart returned to its natural rhythm.

"I don't understand why James is so worried about me and Jeanmarie being here alone. Heavens! Papa's been gone almost six years and I've been here alone most of the time. Besides, I'd never let anyone in the house I didn't know."

"If a man wanted in, he'd get in even with Wiley out there riding shotgun. Then again, the man doing this could be someone you know or have seen around."

"No one I know would do such a terrible thing," she said with conviction, and slid a cup down into the hot water.

"Don't be too sure. Crazy people don't always look crazy. I betcha a nickel he won't have a wild look or run around in the woods dressed in an animal skin."

"How do you know so much about it, Mr. Smarty?" She threw him a teasing grin.

"Well, Miss Smarty. I saw a man once who had killed five women. He was a quiet, skinny farmer who went to church every Sunday with his mother. All the women he killed had blond hair. He cut them up and buried them behind his barn. He might never have been caught, but his dog dug one of them up and carried an arm up to the church yard to chew on while he waited for his master."

"Glory be!" Shudders shook Dory's shoulders. "That gives me goose-bumps. What did they do to him?"

"Hung him."

"I don't want to hear any more about that. I won't sleep a wink tonight."

"I didn't tell you that to scare you. Just be careful. You and Odette stay together, even when you go to the necessary. Wiley will keep an eye out in the daytime. I'll come back here at night as long as Odette and I are here."

I wish you didn't have to go. Oh, I'll be so lonesome when you're gone.

They finished the dishes in silence, both occupied with their own thoughts. When the last dish was dried and stacked on the counter, Ben hung up the towel. Dory emptied the rinse water into the dishpan. Ben carried it to the end of the porch and threw the water out into the yard. While Dory wiped the pan and hung it on the end of the washbench, she worked up the courage to say what she wanted to say.

"There's more coffee. It should be about the way you like it. It's been on the stove since morning."

"Is it strong enough yet to float a railroad spike?"

"Pretty close to it."

"I was hoping you wouldn't kick me out after you got me to do all that work."

"*All* that work?" she said teasingly. Relief that he was going to stay made her almost giddy. "I was going to reward you with half my candy stick."

"In that case, I'll get the coffee."

"Laws! You don't have to wait on me."

"Sit." He put his hand on the top of her head and pushed her down onto the chair.

Dory prayed for a miracle that would keep him and Odette here at least for a few more weeks. She watched him, wanting to remember every detail of the time they spent together, to hold it in her heart to bring out and enjoy again and again after he was gone.

CHAPTER
* 12 *

"You've given me the biggest," Ben protested when Dory placed a piece of the candy beside his coffee cup.

"You're bigger than I am, and . . . you're company." Her voice was light. A teasing smile played upon her mouth until a dimple appeared in her right cheek. She sucked on the candy stick, still smiling.

"Being big paid off this time."

His light eyes held hers; he touched the edge of the cup to his smiling mouth and took a swallow.

"Two more days and it'll float a horseshoe." His eyes were twinkling with introspective humor. It was an expression that would never leave her mind.

They sat and looked at each other. There was no tension, no hurry to talk. They were content to sit together. Ben sensed that there was something she wanted to say and waited with that infinite patience he had. Dory couldn't gather her thoughts and was unable to form a plan on how to approach the subject.

Looking into Dory's eyes, Ben could almost ignore the nagging worry about Odette and James. James had gone upstairs to give Jeanmarie the candy. After all, Ben reasoned, this was his home and he could go where he pleased. It worried him that Odette might be flattered by the attention of a man like James and misjudge his intentions. From that standpoint it was good that they would be leaving soon. Even if they stayed in the area, it wasn't likely they would see much of the Callahans. Somehow, though, that thought didn't appeal to him as much as it would have a week ago.

Dory fidgeted. She looked at him and away. Minutes passed and she didn't speak. He decided to help her.

"Something is bothering you, Dory. You can't decide if you want to tell me or not." His gaze was intense, and her heart began to beat quickly, like a trapped bird's.

"I want to tell you. I've got to decide something before James leaves." Then, after a pause. "You heard James say he wanted me to go to the Malones'."

"Yes, I heard that . . . and wondered about it."

"He saw Chip Malone today in Spencer. James and Mr. Malone have talked from time to time."

"And you?"

"I haven't been around him that much. When I was small, I was always with my mother, and he avoided us if he could. Mama would go out of her way to speak to him. Oh—but it's a long story."

"I have the time if you have." The smile had left his eyes. She seemed utterly vulnerable to him, undefended.

Dory drew a quivering breath and told him about her mother having been raised in the Malone home and how she had defied the man who had been like a father to her and married George Callahan rather than Chip Malone. She explained that her mother and father had loved each other very much and that her mother had died after a difficult pregnancy that had resulted in a stillborn child. Her father had died a few years later.

"I had been going to boarding school down in Coeur d'Alene for six months out of the year and finished the spring before Papa died. It was lonesome being here alone. James was away most of the time and the only people I saw for weeks at a time were Wiley and Louis and Milo. My brothers were not as bad then as they are now, but they made no bones about hating me.

"Mick Malone was about my age. I met him at school. Sometimes we laughed about our families feuding like the families in a Shakespeare play. He would call me Juliet and I'd call him Romeo. One day after Papa died I saw Mick at the store in Spencer. He told me he had made something for me. We arranged to meet about a mile from here where a little flat-bottomed creek comes down from the mountain.

"Mick was afraid of Indians, but I wasn't. We've lived here a long time and have never been bothered at all. Papa always said that if we leave them alone, they'll leave us alone. Poor Mick. He was afraid of everything, his father most of all, because he believed that he was a disappointment to him. Mick was small and thin and had the reddest hair you ever saw. He wanted to make beautiful jewelry out of the rocks he found. He called them agates. Chip ridiculed him and let the men make fun of him. I will never forgive him for that.

"The present was a silver bracelet Mick had made from one of his mother's silver spoons. He had hammered it flat and etched it with a floral design. It's beautiful. Mick had the makings of a wonderful artist.

"That summer we met six times. He told me about his father and how Chip would hold James up as an example because by the time James was twelve he was doing everything from riding the rafts to high-climbing. Mick liked art and reading, while James hated school and did as little as possible. One day Mick came to our meeting place with a bruised face and cut lips. A bully had jumped him and Chip had just stood there and let the boy beat him. I think that hurt Mick most of all. He was so heartsick he cried. We held each other and comforted each other . . . and it . . . just happened. We both knew it was wrong, but it . . . just happened," she said again.

"Understand that I'm not apologizing for what I did. Because of that, something wonderful happened to me. I got Jeanmarie. How could I be sorry?

"The next time I saw Mick he was lying face down beneath the tree where we met." Dory looked at Ben with huge tears in her eyes. "He was trying to get up the courage to leave. Mick was a sweet boy. He didn't deserve to die like that."

Ben reached across the table and covered her hand with his. Dory turned her hand palm up, interlacing their fingers.

"Months later I discovered that I was pregnant. Child that I was, I didn't know until I talked with Mrs. McHenry. The news spread across the country like a forest fire. People knew that I had been meeting Mick because I was the one who found him.

"Marie saw my baby when she was six months old. I thought she would swoon. Mrs. McHenry had sent word for me to come to the store. Later I learned that she had arranged the meeting. Since that time Marie has seen her granddaughter once or twice a year. Chip saw her one time. I was so scared he would snatch her up and take her away from me that I almost died right there on the spot."

The flesh of the hand in his was warm and soft. Ben looked down at it and then at her face. Her green eyes were clouded with worry.

"Now James wants you to take her to the Malones'," Ben said. "Why?"

"Marie is very sick and wants to see her granddaughter. But I'm afraid I'll get there and they won't let Jeanmarie leave. You have a daughter, Ben. Wouldn't the thought of losing her tear you up?''

''Of course. Does James plan to go with you?''

''He'll go. He would not consider our going if he thought the Malones would try to keep Jeanmarie. But he's only one man. Chip has dozens of men working for him. Rough men that will do most anything for money, and Chip has plenty of that.''

''James must trust Malone to keep his word.''

''I don't know if his word is good. Chip's, I mean. My mother used to say that he was wild and reckless, but that deep down he was a good man. She just loved my papa more than she did him.''

''Would you feel better about it if I went along with James?'' Then he added with a teasing twinkle in his eyes, ''We could take Wiley and his shotgun.'' Ben had wondered briefly about the wisdom of getting more involved with the Callahans, then had tossed caution to the wind when he had seen the look of misery on Dory's face.

''Oh, Ben. Would you?'' Her eyes shone like stars through her tears. ''I'd feel so much better if you were there.''

''It will take a week for me to finish up my job with the engine. By then Odette should be well enough to travel.''

''Where will you go when you leave here?''

''I haven't decided.''

''I wish that you . . . and Odette could stay.''

''It wouldn't work, Dory.'' Ben felt her grip his hand tightly. ''If I stay around your half-brothers, I would kill one of them or they would kill me. I had an inkling of it the night I came here. The weather was bad and Odette was tired or I would have gone on to Malone's.''

''But you left her here with me in spite of what Louis said.''

''I wasn't completely sure about you then. But I knew

Odette. She wouldn't be easily led into something she knew was wrong."

"Are you—"

"—Sure now?" he finished for her when she couldn't say the words. "I'd stake my life on it."

"Oh, Ben, thank you." A tear escaped from the corner of her eye and rolled down her cheek. "Doggone it! I hate it when I bawl."

Ben nudged her chin so she would look at him.

"I suppose you've had plenty in your life to bawl about." He put his hand on the top of her head, allowing her hair to curl around his fingers. "But this isn't one of them."

"Women cry at the craziest times. I wouldn't cry in front of Milo or Louis if my life depended on it. And here I am bubbling like a fountain in front of you."

"Well, dry it up before James comes down. He'll think I caused it and knock my block off."

"Oh, you—"

Dory went to the washstand and wiped her face with a wet cloth. She felt light, as if pounds had been lifted from her shoulders. *Ben didn't think she was a loose woman. He said he would stake his life on it.* She was going to enjoy each minute she had with him and try not to think about his leaving. When she turned, she was smiling.

"I feel so much better about everything. Thank you, Ben."

"You're the thankingest woman I ever met," he said, chuckling. "I'd better go up and see Odette, then head for the bunkhouse."

"And I've got to put Jeanmarie to bed."

They went out into the hallway and up the stairs. Ben felt a strong urge to take her hand but suppressed it. At the same time, Dory wished he would take her hand and was disappointed when he didn't.

They stood in the doorway. If James knew they were there, he paid them no attention. He was sitting on the floor beside Odette's chair. She had the tablet in her lap and was watching James's mouth as he spoke.

"I know that," James said, looking into her face and pointing to something on the page. "But I don't know that." His finger slid down the page. "I don't know the sixes."

"It not hard. Two sixes are twelve. Three sixes are eighteen. I'll write them down." A head of blond hair and a head of dark auburn bent over the tablet in Odette's lap. "Four sixes are twenty-four. Or think two twelves and you get the same." Odette talked aloud as she wrote.

James smiled when he saw Ben and Dory. "She's teaching me to cipher. I never did learn to multiply past the fives. She knows up to the twelves and can figure fractions and board feet. Did you know that?"

Ben was speechless for a moment. Odette, relaxed and smiling, was completely at ease with James and was carrying on a conversation as if she heard every word he said.

"I knew it."

"She's going to write the tables out for me."

"I'm sure you could find them in a book, if you really want to learn them."

The tone of Ben's voice as well as his words told both Dory and James that he was not pleased at finding his daughter and James in this cozy situation. James stood. He lifted Odette's chin with his finger so she would look up at him.

"I'm going. Thanks for the lesson."

"I'll write the tables for you, James."

"All right. I'll get them the next time I'm here." James left the room and Ben moved into it.

"Feeling better?" he asked, after he had squatted down on his heels beside Odette's chair.

"Much better, Papa."

"That's good. I'll see you in the morning before I go back to the mill. Good night, honey. Good night, Dory."

Ben left the room and went down the stairs and through the kitchen to the porch. James was standing there.

"You didn't like me being there with Odette. Did you think I was going to rape your daughter while you and my sister were in the kitchen?" His tone was belligerent.

"No, I didn't like it," Ben said in an equally belligerent tone. "I don't want you playing flirting games with her. She won't understand it and might take you seriously."

"I wasn't playing a flirting game. I like her. She's pretty, and . . . sweet."

"And not for you, bucko. Leave her be."

"Goddamn you! I was good enough when she was sick—"

"And I appreciate it. There are things here that you don't know, James. Things I can't tell you about." Ben's tone had softened. "It's nothing against you."

"Like hell it isn't. You think I've got bad blood because of Milo and Louis."

"I've never believed in bad blood. If I had, I would have given up trying to make something of myself long ago."

"I would never do anything to hurt her."

"I believe you would never *intentionally* do anything to hurt her. But because she reads the words on your lips and does not hear the tone of your voice, she could take something you say teasingly in a different way. I won't risk having her heart broken." *Or risk her marrying a man who could be blood kin.*

James stood on the end of the porch looking up at the night sky. He had met the woman he wanted to spend the rest of his life with. She was peace, goodness. He had wanted to lay his head in her lap and feel her fingers in his hair. In the short time he had known her, she had taken over his heart—and he had not even seen her standing on her feet. Now a man he had come to like, to admire, was telling him to keep his distance. Life was hell sometimes.

He turned to Ben. "I'll not hurt her."

"Thank you. James," he said, as James stepped off the porch. "Dory told me about the Malones. I'll go with you if you want me to go."

"I'd be obliged. It'd make Dory feel better."

James walked off into the darkness, leaving Ben standing on the end of the porch hating what he had done, what he'd had to do.

In the room at the mill where the Callahan brothers lived when not at the homestead, Milo sat on the side of his bunk, swearing and nursing his head in his hands. He complained to Sid Hanes, who was sitting on the other bunk, that he had what was the grandpappy of all headaches. He had just come in from outside, where he had retched violently.

"Oh . . . shitfire! My head is killin' me. Where'd ya get that rot-gut ya gived me?"

"It's from the same batch ya always get. Ya jist downed the whole jugful is all."

"I've drunk a jugful before," Milo grumbled.

"Ya've been mad as a peed-on rattler since ya got back from the house. Ya guzzled her down too fast. Makes a feller sick ever time."

"That goddamn bitch tried to kill me, ya know that, Sid? She come at me with a knife."

"Ya told me." Sid lifted the lid on a squat wood stove and spit a chaw of tobacco into the flames. " 'Bout a dozen times," he muttered under his breath.

"She ain't gettin' away with it. I'll tell ya right now. I'll get her an' Waller too. That sonofabitch hit me when I wasn't lookin'."

"He did, huh?" Sid wasn't fooled by Milo's account of the fight but was smart enough not to say so.

"Betcha him an' old Whory Dory is havin' a high old time 'bout now. He ain't come back, has he?"

"No. What ya reckon he's doin' down there?"

"What'a ya think, ya dumb shit? What would ya be doin' if ya was there?"

Sid ground his teeth in frustration. Since the first time he had laid eyes on Dory Callahan, he had wanted her. She was the reason he had become one of Milo's cronies. It certainly wasn't because he admired the man. He was a means to get what Sid wanted. Dory's shares in the company were an added bonus, but he'd take her without them. Yeah, he thought. He'd take her and take her and take her. Just thinking about her made him hard as a stone.

Sid realized Milo was talking again and expected him to listen and side in with him.

"I ain't forgettin' that damn Tinker either. Bastard pulled me off a that machine. It ain't his'n. He ain't workin' here no more. I fired his ass."

"Ya've the right. Yo're the owner. Hell, I'm as good a sawyer as Tinker. 'Nother thing, Waller ain't no mechanic to my way a thinkin'. If he was, he'd a had that engine goin' by now. He's too busy sniffin' 'round Dory is what he's doin'."

"Well, if yo're wantin' Whory Dory so bad, why don't ya get her on her back and plow 'er good? Then we'd take us a half-ass preacher down there. Gol' damn! Wouldn't that be rich? Old Whory Dory'd be wed to ya afore she knowed what end was up. It'd serve the snotty bitch right for what she done."

Sid's grin was wide, but it suddenly vanished.

"James'd be fit ta be tied iff'n she warn't willin'. That sucker ain't got no quit a-tall when he digs in his heels."

"Don't worry none 'bout James. I'll take care of him. You take care of Whory Dory."

"It's what I been tryin' to do. What with that old man with a double barrel breathin' down my neck, and Louis poppin' down there all the time, I can't get to her. You'd think Louis was keepin' her fer himself way he hovers 'round."

"Hush up that kinda talk." Milo shielded his eyes with his hand as he lifted his head to glare at Sid. "That's trash talk. I said she'd wed ya and she will. We'll go down there one of these nights and give ya a chance at her. I aim to have me another go at that dummy."

"Her pa's tougher than a boot an' got a short rein on his temper. He'll kill ya."

"Not if I kill him first," Milo said matter-of-factly. "I ain't forgettin' what he done."

Sid was elated at the turn of events. He would be a member of the Callahan family. By God, the men would sit up and take notice—or else. Tinker would be out on his ass, that was sure. Next to go would be that uppity Steven, with his clean shirts and slicked-down hair. Hell, Steven was just a hired hand like the rest of them. With Steven gone he'd use that fancy cabin when he was here at the mill, which wouldn't be often. He'd be boss. He'd live down in the big house—

"Louis go down the mountain, or to the house?" *My* house, Sid almost said.

"How the hell do I know?"

"Did ya hear 'bout the whores that was killed—one down on the Saint Joe, the other'n near Pitzer?"

Milo stared at the floor. "What of it?"

"Maybe we could pin it on Waller."

"Shit! He ain't got the guts ta cut a woman's throat."

"How'd you know they was cut?"

"I heared it."

Sid started to say something, then clamped his mouth shut. He had heard the news barely an hour ago while Milo had been lying flat on his back, dead to the world.

Suddenly the door was flung open so hard it bounced back against the wall. The noise cut through Milo's aching head like a knife. With hands cupping his head, he sprang to his feet and glared at Louis standing in the doorway.

"Goddammit! Can't ya see my head's 'bout to fall off?"

Louis's small bright eyes swung to Sid. "Get out."

Sid picked up his hat, scurried around behind Louis and left. Louis slammed the door shut.

"Damn you, Louis. I said—"

"—Shut up an' listen to me." Louis shrugged out of his coat, then threw it and his hat on a chair. "What the hell were ya tryin' to fire up that donkey for? Ya've been liquored up fer two days and two nights. Soon's I turn my back yo're raisin' hell 'round here."

"Suppose Steven was fillin' yore ear," Milo sneered.

"Steven ain't wantin' that engine, or the carriage or the donkey to be buggered up. It's money outta his pocket too."

"He ain't got no say. He ain't owner here."

"He knows that if we don't make it this year, we're liable to be took over by the bank."

"Shit. He says that ever' year."

"We got the means now to get the river clogged before Malone gets there. I ain't havin' ya a-fightin' with the crew an' gettin' 'em all riled up. Hear?"

"That's all ya think 'bout—beatin' that goddamn Malone."

"Malone'd burn us to the ground if he got a chance."

"Where ya been? Over spyin' on 'em?"

"What if I have?"

"All night an' all day? Must a been a lot goin' on."

Louis grunted, sat down on the bunk and unlaced his shoes. His eyes caught the edge of something under the bunk. He pulled out a shirt, stiff with dried blood.

"What's this?"

"Gimme that." Milo yanked the shirt out of Louis's hand, lifted the lid on the stove and dropped it inside.

"Why'd ya do that for?"

"It ain't no good no more."

"That was blood on that shirt."

"Yeah. I beat the shit outta a smart-ass peeler and he bled all over me."

"Yeah?" Louis looked down at his brother's bent head. His faint smile was as cold as his eyes.

CHAPTER
* 13 *

The honeysuckle and bridal wreath, once black and brittle from winter's freeze, were green again. The tops of the Ponderosa pines surrounding the homestead swayed in a light, warm wind. A robin was building a nest in a sheltered place beneath the eave of the outhouse, and sparrows, busy searching for nesting material, flitted from ground to branch with beaks stuffed with dry grass, bits of string and horsehair.

It was Sunday. James and Ben had come down the night before and both agreed that this was as good a time as any to make the trip to the Malones'.

Odette and Jeanmarie sat in the back of the wagon, Dory on the seat beside Wiley. Even though Dory was apprehensive about visiting Marie Malone, she was excited to be leaving the homestead for the first time in months.

The wagon, with Ben and James following, rolled down the timbered hillside and on toward the green sward. The heat from the sun was cupped in the sheltered valley, and the fragrant blooms of spring were everywhere. Flocks of robins rose as the wagon approached. Birds were a source of delight for Dory. She watched the flocks gather to migrate in the fall and looked forward to their return every spring.

"You've never said what you think about us making this trip, Wiley." Dory smiled at the old man, who sat with one foot on the guard rail, his battered old hat square on his head.

"Don't see that it could hurt none." He leaned over the side of the wagon and let loose a stream of tobacco juice into the fresh green grass.

"You don't think Chip will . . . try anything?"

"Chip ain't no fool, Dory. The only claim he's got that the young'un's Mick's is the red hair." He looked at her, his leathery old face creased with a frown. "Spite of all ya hear, I ain't ever knowed of Chip bein' underhanded. He's ornery an' schemes ta best Callahan Lumber, but ya ain't ort ta hold that agin him, considerin' what Louis does."

"He flat scares me. I don't think I could ever like him because of the way he treated Mick."

"Likin' an' toleratin' ain't the same. Jist tolerate an' ya'll get by without causin' a ruckus."

When Jeanmarie became restless, James took her to ride in front of him on the horse. Her clear, childish laughter rang out. Her chatter was continuous. She was having the time of her life and Dory was glad that her daughter was enjoying herself. She could count on one hand the number of times the child had gone visiting.

The time went quickly. It was well past mid-morning when they approached the Malone ranch. The buildings were set in a valley surrounded by flat grassland where cattle grazed. The house and outbuildings gleamed white in the bright sunlight. Mick had told her about his home, but Dory had not imagined that it was so grand, so well tended. The main part of the house was square and two-storied. A wing out one side had a slanting roof that covered a small porch. The wagon track branched, one lane going around the house to the barn, the other going to the front of the house.

As they approached the fork in the track, it occurred to Dory that this was where her mother had spent her girlhood. She had left this place to marry her father and live in what she had later described as a two-room log cabin. She had never returned, not even for a visit. She had left too much bitterness behind.

The door opened and Chip Malone stepped out. His red hair, dulled with gray, was thick and curly. He wore a dark flannel shirt. Wide, white suspenders held up his duck britches. This was his domain. He owned everything in sight and the large logging operation in the mountains beyond.

An icy hand clutched Dory's heart, and a knot of apprehension twisted her stomach when she realized he was looking directly at her. She didn't know why she knew that. The distance between them was too great for her to see anything but a clean-shaven face. It made her want to grab her daughter and hold her close to her side. She looked over her shoulder for reassurance that James and Ben were still there. They had moved up close to the back of the wagon. Dory's eyes caught Ben's. He nodded, acknowledging her anxiety.

Wiley stopped the team in front of the door. Dismounting, Ben and James tied their horses to the end of the wagon. Dory's heart was beating like that of a trapped rabbit, but her face showed none of what she was feeling about coming to this place she had heard so much about but had never seen. It did nothing for her nervousness when Chip came around to the side of the wagon to help her down. He extended his hand. She hesitantly put hers in it.

"Thank you for coming, Dory. It'll mean a lot to Marie."

Dory said nothing. As soon as her feet were on firm ground, she pulled her hand from his. Ben lifted Odette down and James took Jeanmarie. From her position on James's arm, Jeanmarie looked at the man and smiled.

"My name's Jeanmarie. What's your name?"

For the space of a few heartbeats, Chip was unable to respond. Then he said, "My name is Chip."

"She'll talk your arm off," James said. "Howdy Chip. This is Ben Waller."

Chip extended his hand and Ben shook it.

"—And his daughter, Odette."

"Welcome to our home, ma'am."

Odette didn't know what he said, but she smiled and nodded.

"How'er you doin', Wiley? You old coot, I think you're going to live forever."

"I aim to, Chip. Jist to spite ya."

"Take the wagon and horses on around to the back. One of the men will take care of them. Come on back to the house and we'll have dinner."

"Thank 'ee kindly. I'll do that."

Dory was surprised at the welcome. She had expected hostility. It's what she would have felt if the situation had been reversed.

"Come on in," Chip said, leading the way to the door. "Marie knows you're here. I got a look at you through the glass when you came down onto the flatland." He held open the door.

Dory walked in, followed by Odette, then James carrying Jeanmarie. Chip and Ben came last. They were in a wide hallway that divided the house. An open stairway was at the end. Chip closed the door and waited while Dory took off her bonnet and then Jeanmarie's. James set the child on the floor and took off her coat. Unaware that she was the focus of the strange man's attention, Jeanmarie reached out to touch an embossed red rose on the wallpaper. She tilted her head and smiled at him.

"Pretty."

Bewildered by the look of pain and regret on Chip Malone's face, Dory quickly looked at Ben. His calm face and steady gray eyes looking back at her were reassuring. Then Chip was moving down the hallway.

"James, if you and Waller will wait for me here"—he opened the door to a room that looked like a small parlor—"I'll take the ladies up to see Marie. I know she's anxious."

Holding firmly to Jeanmarie's hand and beckoning to Odette, Dory followed Chip Malone up the stairs. He led them down the upper hallway to an open door.

"Marie, look who came to see you."

Another person was in the room, but Dory had eyes only for the woman on the bed who lay propped up with pillows. The soft brown hair Dory remembered was almost completely gray, and the fine-featured face so like Mick's was creased with wrinkles. Marie Malone looked twenty years older than when Dory had last seen her six months earlier. She hoped and prayed that the shock she felt was not reflected on her face.

"Hello, Mrs. Malone." Pulling Jeanmarie along with her, Dory went to the end of the bed, aware that Chip lingered in the doorway.

"Hello. I'm so glad you could come." She paused for a moment to catch her breath. "Chip, is Consuela preparing dinner for our guests?"

"She started as soon as I saw them coming."

Dory was relieved when she heard his footsteps going back down the hallway.

"Come closer so I can see you," Marie said in her breathless voice. "My, my, Jeanmarie, you're getting to be a big girl."

"I'm almost four." The child went around to the side of the bed and held up four fingers.

''Almost four? And you can count, too.''

''Mrs. Malone, this is Odette Waller.'' Dory took Odette's hand and pulled her up beside her. ''She's been staying with us. Her father is working here for a while.''

''Chip told me about the . . . the donkey engine.'' She paused to get her breath again. Then to Odette, ''I'm glad you came.''

''Odette hasn't been able to hear for quite some time. She reads lips after she gets used to a person. She's been reading to Jeanmarie out of the books you gave her even though she can't hear her own voice.'' Dory turned so Odette could read her lips. ''Mrs. Malone gave Jeanmarie the books.''

''Baby loves the books,'' Odette said and smiled.

''Odette is very stingy with words . . . sometimes,'' Dory said. She turned to Odette and smiled. ''I told her you are sometimes stingy with your words.''

''You're teasing me now.''

Marie saw that the girl's magnificent blue eyes were looking at Dory with affection. She was a pretty girl, somehow fragile looking, while Dory was a beautiful woman. If only Mick had lived, she would have been so good for him.

''I'm glad you have . . . company. I've wondered how . . . you've stood it up there alone.''

The other person in the room had placed a chair beside the bed. She was a small, plump woman with shiny black hair that hung in a braid down her back. She wore a loose-fitting dress and moccasins.

''Another chair, Rita, please. For Odette.''

After they were seated, Jeanmarie attempted to climb on the bed. Dory lifted her onto her lap.

''You better sit here, punkin.''

''Let her on the bed. Please. I've so little time with her. I want to . . . feast my eyes on her.'' After a pause, she said, ''Rita, will you get the box?''

Dory lifted Jeanmarie to sit beside Marie on the bed. The child looked at her mother with bewilderment.

"This lady is your grandmother. Remember the story Odette read to you about grandmothers? She wants you to sit beside her. You'll be still, won't you, honey?"

"That red hair, so like Mick's and curly like yours, Dory." Marie gasped for air. "Eyes are blue like Mick's and . . . Chip's." Rita returned with a box and placed it on the floor on the other side of the bed. "Isn't . . . she pretty, Rita?"

"*Sí*, Maria. It is so." Bright, expressive eyes moved from the woman on the bed to the child. "Chin like yours, I think."

"My granddaughter," Marie said, her eyes filling with tears. "A part of Mick. Thank you, Dory, for . . . bringing her."

"There, there, Maria. This is happy time." Rita bent over the bed and pressed a handkerchief into Marie's hand, then took a paper-wrapped package from the box and placed it on the bed beside her.

The tears miraculously vanished and Marie smiled. "I can't waste time feeling sorry for myself. Jeanmarie, I won't see you on your birthday, so I'll give you your present now." She placed the package on the little girl's lap.

Jeanmarie looked in bewilderment first at her mother, then at Odette, then down at the package, but made no attempt to open it.

"She's never had a wrapped present," Dory explained. "She's not sure what to do with it."

"Open it for her, Dory."

Dory folded back the paper, being careful not to tear it. "Oh, look, Jeanmarie. Your grandmother has given you a beautiful doll."

Jeanmarie looked at it for a moment, then a big smile

covered her pixie face. "For me?" she asked as if she couldn't believe it.

The doll was like no doll Dory had ever seen. Its head was china with painted black hair, large blue eyes and red lips. The body was soft kid and the lower arms and hands were of china, as were the feet. The doll wore a blue dress trimmed in white tatted lace.

Jeanmarie was staring into the doll's eyes as if fascinated.

"Look under her dress," Marie urged. "Rita made . . . her dress and . . . her underdrawers."

Peeking beneath the dress, Jeanmarie began to giggle. "Looky, Mama. Looky, Odette, drawers like mine." She scrambled off the bed, placed the doll in Odette's lap, lifted the doll's dress and then her own. "See, Odette?"

Odette laughed. "They are like yours."

Jeanmarie attempted to lift Odette's skirt. "You got underdrawers?"

Odette held her skirt down. "Of course. I'll show you when we get home."

Dory turned to Marie. "Jeanmarie is very aware that Odette can't hear. Sometimes I'm amazed at how much she understands."

"Mick was sensitive to other people's disabilities too."

Dory pulled her daughter close and whispered to her.

Jeanmarie looked at Marie. "Thank you for the doll."

"You're very welcome, child."

After a pause, Dory whispered again.

"Thank you for the . . . underdrawers," Jeanmarie said to Rita. Then, holding the doll tightly against her chest, she headed for the door.

"Honey, stay here." Dory got to her feet.

"Want to show Odette's papa and Uncle James."

"Maybe . . . later."

"Rita will take her down and bring her back." Marie saw the anxious look on Dory's face. "Don't . . . worry. Sit down, Dory. I know what you're . . . thinking. She'll not disappear, I swear it."

"It's just that I get scared sometimes when she's out of my sight." Dory sat down. She could hear Jeanmarie's chatter as she and the woman went down the hallway.

"You've been afraid we'd try to . . . take her. To tell the truth we thought . . . about it." Marie paused to catch her breath. "Stories about you caused Chip to . . . think you were not . . . a good woman. 'Course your bobbed hair . . . doesn't help." Marie breathed rapidly, then smiled.

"If my hair hung to my hips, it would be the same. People believe what they want to believe," Dory said drily.

"Yes. Chip believes his son was . . . murdered. Nothing will change his . . . mind."

Dory remained quiet. She believed with all her heart that Milo had killed the father of her child, but she couldn't tell this to Mick's mother. Nor could she tell her that Chip's disapproval had made his son so unhappy that he had been planning to disappear from their lives. Marie Malone had enough grief to bear.

"Chip is an . . . honorable man for all his rough ways. He has promised me . . . that he will . . . never"—she had to pause—"never try to separate you from your . . . daughter. He will keep his promise." By the time Marie had finished, she was so out of breath that her thin bosom heaved as she gasped for air.

"You're tired." Dory covered the thin hand that lay on the bed. Marie turned it and grasped Dory's fingers. "Rest and let me talk for a while."

"One more thing. The . . . box. Presents for Christmas . . . for birthdays. And some things . . . Mick loved. A pin he made for me." Tears were rolling down Marie's cheeks and she breathed rapidly. "I'd be happy if she wore it . . . on her . . . wedding day."

Tears flooded Dory's eyes and fell on their clasped hands. "I'll not let her forget her father . . . or you."

"Thank you." Marie sighed and closed her eyes.

Odette placed a handkerchief in Dory's hand. Dory first blotted the tears on Marie's face, then wiped her own wet cheeks.

Marie opened her eyes. "I must not sleep," she said in her weak, breathless voice. "I don't want to miss . . . a minute . . . of your visit."

Dory stood and faced Odette. "Tell Jeanmarie's grandmother what you've been teaching her while I get a drink of water."

"Fresh water . . . in the pitcher."

Odette seemed to know Dory needed time to get her emotions in order. She moved to the chair closest to the bed and began to talk.

"Baby learns fast. She can count to ten." Odette held up all ten fingers. "She knows the letters in her name and writes some of them. She can't put them in order yet. Jeanmarie loves the music box and the books you gave her. Oh, my how she loves books. She likes Mother Goose rhymes best."

Listening to Odette talking to Marie about Jeanmarie, Dory wished that Ben could hear his daughter. When they first had arrived, he had constantly urged her to talk aloud. It occurred to Dory that she and Jeanmarie had been almost as good for Odette as Odette had been for them.

Dory thought about how afraid she had been to come here and how glad she was now that she had come. She was no longer afraid the Malones would try to take Jeanmarie. Marie was dying. After she was gone Chip would lose interest in his grandchild. Dory only hoped that while they were here James would be civil and they could leave without further hostility.

The room where Ben and James waited for Chip's return was clearly his domain. It was a masculine room with deep leather chairs, a heavy walnut desk strewn with papers, and a bookcase, sideboard and liquor cabinet. The walls were covered with paintings of log-rafting, bull-whackers, skid-greasers, buckers and fallers. There were several mountainous landscape scenes, and one painting showed this very valley in the dead of winter with the house and buildings in the background. The painting on the wall over the desk was of a man standing with his foot on a freshly felled log, an axe on his shoulder. The face was unrecognizable, but the red hair identified the man as Chip Malone.

Ben moved closer to study the paintings. He realized they were very well done even though he was not an experienced observer of the arts. In the lower right corner of all the paintings, so small one had to look closely to see them, were the initials M.M.

''You like the pictures?'' Chip spoke from the doorway.

''Very much. I don't know a lot about art, but I know what I like.'' Ben moved back from the wall. ''Do you know the artist?''

''My son. We found them hidden away after . . . his death.'' Chip went to the liquor cabinet. ''Drink?''

''Not for me, thanks,'' Ben said.

''Not for me,'' James said curtly.

Chip lifted his shoulders in a shrug, poured a small amount of whiskey in a glass and tossed it down before he turned. ''Sit down. We have a short wait before mealtime.''

''You don't have to feed us.'' James sank down onto the chair nearest to him.

"That's right. I don't *have* to do anything, but when people come to my home, on my invitation, we offer them a meal. Get the block off your shoulder, James. The only motive I had in getting you here was for Marie to see the little girl."

"I'm thinking the invitation was a long time coming."

"Yes. I admit that. Time has a way of lessening grief. Marie has only a short time left. A few weeks at the most. I'm doing everything I can to make those weeks as happy for her as I can. Lord knows, the woman has had a lot to put up with."

"I'm sorry about your wife. As far as I know she's been decent to Dory and Jeanmarie when they've met."

"Yes, I know about the meetings arranged by Mrs. McHenry. Frankly, I was furious at first, considering—"

"—Considering that my sister is a whore?" James jumped to his feet.

"Sit down, James. I was going to say considering the circumstances under which Mick died."

"Hell. I had nothing to do with that."

"I know. You were in Coeur d'Alene that week."

"You checked on me."

"Of course. Wouldn't you have checked on me if the situation had been reversed?" Chip turned to Ben, abruptly changing the subject. "Where are you from, Waller?"

"Over near Spokane—and north along the Pend Oreille Lake."

"I've heard that the Pend Oreille River is a mean one for log driving." Chip's eyes went to James, then back to Ben.

"Not as mean as the Wishkah. There loggers have built a splash dam to hold their harvest. The problem is when they open the gates there's such a rush of water that many of the logs get hung up along the riverbank. And you know what that could mean. A massive jam."

"I've not been over around the Wishkah." Again Chip's

eyes darted to James. This time they stayed. "You been over there, James?"

"No."

Chip shrugged again, and turned back to Ben. They discussed weather, Indians, politics, the war between the states and every other topic Chip could think of without bringing the Malone or Callahan lumber companies or the donkey engine into the conversation.

Ben realized that Chip was trying to keep the conversation impersonal and was relieved when Jeanmarie and a woman of Indian or Mexican descent appeared in the doorway.

"Señor, I'll be back for the niña after I speak to Consuela in the kitchen."

Jeanmarie peeked from around the woman's skirt and saw James. She darted across the room to him.

"Looky what the lady give me, Uncle James. I can take her home." She placed the doll on his lap. "She's got hands and feet and ever'thing," she said excitedly. "See her underdrawers. They're like mine. See." She swiftly lifted her dress past her knees to reveal the legs of white drawers. "They're like Odette's too. She's goin' to show me when we get home."

Trying to keep the grin off his face, James pulled the doll's dress down and cradled the china head in his palm as he inspected her face.

"What'a ya know. She's even got a nose."

"Uncle James! You're . . . silly." Jeanmarie giggled and grabbed the doll. "I got to show Odette's papa." She went to lean against Ben's knee. "Want to see her underdrawers?" The child's laughing eyes looked up at him expectantly.

"Why sure. Hmmm . . . they match her dress."

"Does Odette's match her dress?"

"Well, ah . . . Odette's a big girl. Guess I'll have to ask her."

Ben glanced at Chip. His eyes were riveted to the child. James was trying not to laugh.

"The lady that made the dress and the drawers said the dolly's head will break." Jeanmarie held the doll close to her, reached up, and pulled Ben's head down so she could whisper. "I'm not goin' to let Uncle Louis see her."

Ben didn't know what to say. He was sure the other two men had heard the child's words. In the quiet that followed, he gave her a gentle push toward Chip.

"I bet Mr. Malone would like to see your doll."

Ever friendly, Jeanmarie tilted her head to look at Chip.

"You got red hair," she blurted, then giggled. "Mama said my papa had red hair. Want to see my dolly's drawers?"

Something like a smile flitted across Chip's face. "It's been a while since I've seen a young lady's drawers." He flipped up the doll's dress. "They are very pretty."

"You got a little girl?"

"No. The lady that works here has a little boy."

"I don't like boys. When they grow up they're mean. But not Uncle James and Wiley and Odette's papa."

"I guess some grow up mean, but not all."

"Are you mean like Uncle Louis and Uncle Milo?"

Jeanmarie leaned against his knees and looked up at him with eyes so like Mick's that Chip looked back at the child as if seeing her for the first time. He ruffled the red curls on her head, then took her small hand and held it between his. He had to swallow hard several times before he could speak.

"I sure as hel . . . heck hope not."

He was grateful when Rita appeared in the doorway.

"Señor, the meal is ready. I will take a tray to Maria, and send the others down."

The good-byes were said in the middle of the afternoon. Ben and James insisted that they get back to the homestead before dark. Dory was misty-eyed when she left Marie's room with the precious box of mementos Marie had put in her care. James took it and Odette to the wagon while she put on her bonnet and Jeanmarie's. Without looking directly into Chip Malone's face, she thanked him for the dinner.

"Thanks for coming and bringing Jeanmarie. I want you to know that we don't hold any bitterness toward you and the child." After he finished speaking he squatted down and spoke to Jeanmarie. "Take care of that young lady," he said, touching the doll she held clasped in her arms. "And thank you for showing me her underdrawers," he whispered.

Jeanmarie giggled and hid behind Dory's skirt.

Holding tightly to her child's hand, Dory went out to the wagon, which Wiley had brought to the front of the house. Odette was already seated in the back. James lifted Jeanmarie up to sit beside her and then helped Dory up over the wheel and onto the seat.

The dreaded visit was over. She had been afraid when she arrived, and she was leaving with a heavy heart.

Why was it that it was the good people who had to die?

CHAPTER
* 14 *

Dory stood on the porch. Oh, how she loved spring. She liked the gentle touch of the warm wind on her face, the smell of the pines, the promise of seeds and bulbs parting the earth, reaching for the sun. Odette, completely recovered from her illness, was taking the clean dry clothes from the line. Jean-marie followed along behind her cuddling a kitten that had mysteriously appeared in the barn after James's last visit.

Dory was happy—almost.

Since James had told her about the murders, he or Ben had come to the homestead each evening just after dark and left again at dawn. It was a long journey for both of them. Dory had tried in vain to convince them that it was a trip they didn't have to make.

"It isn't that we don't trust Wiley to do his best to protect you," James said. "If someone got to him first, you would be on your own."

"Someone could get to both of you," Dory argued.

"It's not likely before one of us got to him."

Tonight would be Ben's turn. Would the pattern be the same? Would he visit for a few minutes with Odette and then go to the bunkhouse? It was as if Ben and James had decided between them to spend as little time as possible with them. On the nights James came to the house, he played for a few minutes with Jeanmarie, then cautioned Dory about barring the doors, and then departed, leaving a disappointed Odette looking after him with troubled eyes.

Dory was sure that Ben was responsible for her brother's attitude toward Odette. What had he said to him the night he had hurriedly left the room and followed James downstairs? James had looked happier that evening than he had in a long time. He had ignored Odette the day they went to the Malones', and since then he avoided her as if she had the plague. Poor Odette. She didn't understand why.

Tonight Ben would be later than usual. The donkey engine was to be moved. Teams of oxen would pull it five miles over a treacherous trail to where the big logs were trimmed and peeled and made ready for the chute that would take them downhill to the river.

"I will be late, but I will be here," Ben had said, then had added drily, "Louis is so excited he is almost pleasant to be around."

"That would be a sight to see," Dory had said laughingly, hoping to get a smile from Ben. But it wasn't to be. The distance between them was widening. It was as if he had never held her in that darkened hallway, sheltered her in his arms, or buried his lips in her hair.

Standing there on the porch, she suddenly realized that the sun had been gone for a while now and all that remained was a red glow in the western sky. The air was cooling rapidly. The twilight time of evening was short in the mountains.

Odette had brought in the clothes and gone back out to play with Jeanmarie and the kitten.

Dory called to Jeanmarie. "It's time to come in. Tell Odette."

She watched the child tug on Odette's hand and motion to her. Odette looked up and waved. Dory beckoned and waited until they started toward the house before she went inside to light the lamp and tend to the beans she had left simmering on the stove.

Odette and Jeanmarie ran to the house. They were laughing and breathless when they entered the kitchen. Jeanmarie had the black and white kitten in her arms.

"I've put some beans in a bowl for us," she said, looking directly at Odette as she spoke. Then to her daughter, "Put the kitten in the box behind the stove, Jeanmarie, and wash up. I'll take the beans out to Wiley. He'll keep them warm until Ben gets here." Dory wrapped a rag around the bail of the pot and lifted it from the stove.

"You want the bread?" Odette asked.

"Oh, yes. Jeanmarie, come along and carry it."

"I'll set the table," Odette replied. She wrapped a pan of bread in a cloth and placed it in the child's outstretched arms.

Wiley was at the washbench when Dory opened the door and called, "Here's supper." She set the pot on the stove.

"Got bread," Jeanmarie announced proudly.

"Bet ya baked it all by yoreself." Wiley wiped his face, then walked over and put his gnarled hand on the child's head.

"Huh-uh. Odette did. Mama showed her."

"Wiley, do you have plenty of butter and jelly?"

"Got plenty."

"I churned today. I can bring you some fresh buttermilk."

"Got some of that, too. Ben'll be later tonight. Eat yore supper an' get yoreself up to that room and drop the bar."

"Oh, Wiley—"

"Don't ya be oh, Wileyin' me. It's what Ben said fer ya to do."

"But . . . I've lived here all my life and I've never had to lock myself in at night. Somehow it goes against the grain."

"Times is changed, missy. There's goin's-on 'round here that ain't been before."

Dory looked down and saw her daughter looking up at her with large, curious eyes and decided to end the conversation.

"I put the last of that ham you smoked in the beans. We'll have to find us a hog or two to fatten up for winter. Come on, puddin' pie. Let's go see if Odette has the table ready."

It was almost dark when they left the bunkhouse. Walking along the path to the house, Dory heard a horse snorting a greeting to the horses in the pen beside the barn. She turned, expecting to see Ben coming out from behind the screen of pines. Instead she saw two riders. Milo was on his big buckskin. The other rider was unmistakably Sid Hanes.

Scooping Jeanmarie up to straddle her hip, Dory hurried toward the house, hoping the men hadn't seen her.

Sid let out a whoop.

"Yore a-goin' the wrong way, Dory. Ain't ya goin' to come to meet me?"

Dory's heart was racing by the time she got to the porch. Odette met her with a worried expression on her face. Dory handed Jeanmarie to her.

"Go upstairs and bar the door."

"No," Odette shook her head. "Stay with you."

"I'll be all right. Go. Bar the door and don't open for anyone but me. I don't think they'll bother you unless they are drinking. Understand?"

"Understand."

Dory wondered whether or not to tell her about the loaded rifle that lay on top of the wardrobe but decided against it. She and Odette had not talked about guns and she didn't know if Odette knew how to fire one. Tomorrow, she told herself, tomorrow I'll show her how to load and fire.

Things had come to a pretty pass when a person had to think about taking a gun to her own kin.

By the time Milo and Sid had turned their horses into the corral and headed for the house, Dory was well on the way to getting her nerves under control. It wouldn't be any different, she told herself, from any of the other times Milo had come down to the homestead in the middle of the week, except that he would be more mouthy. He always showed off when one of his cronies was with him.

She watched the men approach the house and felt a moment of relief when both of them appeared to be steady on their feet. Milo was bad enough when sober, but drinking he was as unpredictable and as dangerous as a wild dog. Sid was fairly dancing along beside him, his short legs pumping to keep up with Milo's longer stride. And he was listening to Milo with a silly grin on his face as if every word were hilariously funny.

The first words Milo said were, "Where's the dummy?" He stood inside the door looking around. Sid crowded in behind him.

Dory's velvet green eyes glittered with a cold light. She looked first at one man and then at the other with raised brows, all the contempt she felt for them revealed in her expression.

"She is *not* a dummy and she isn't here."

"That's a pile of horseshit. You got her up in that room with the bar across the door. Hell, it don't make no never mind 'bout that. We got all night to get in there, ain't we, Sid? A few blows with a sledge'll do it. Fix us some supper, Whory Dory."

His words sent a chill of fear over Dory. Milo was different tonight. He was always mean, but tonight he was mean without the usual pretense of humor that went with his meanness.

"Beans and bread are on the table."

"That ain't enough ta feed a horsefly," Milo complained.

"I didn't know you were coming."

"Fry us up a batch of eggs."

"I don't have any. The hens have quit laying."

"Goddamn, Sid. She ain't goin' ta be decent a-tall. Yore goin' ta have ta learn her ta have grub ready when her man comes home."

"I plan on it. I sure as hell plan ta whup her in line." Sid's eyes were bright as stars and his thick lips spread, showing tobacco-stained teeth. He was more cocky than usual.

Dory felt the hair rising on the back of her neck. "What are you talking about?"

"You'll find out. Get a jug a sorghum and a crock a butter. If'n we got to make out with this we need somethin' to fill in. We got work ahead. Ain't we, Sid?"

Sid snickered.

The uneasiness that had crept over Dory was now full-fledged fear. Milo and Sid were up to something that included her and Odette—something unpleasant.

Ben, please hurry.

Dory brought the butter crock to the table and went back for the sorghum. Out of the corner of her eye she saw the kitten come out from behind the stove, stretch, and amble toward the table. She hoped that Milo wouldn't see it.

"If it ain't a cat!" Milo reached down and grabbed the kitten by the scruff of its neck. "There ain't nothin' I hate more'n a goddamn cat."

"Give it here. I'll put it back in the box." When Dory reached for it, Milo threw the kitten to Sid. "Give it to me," Dory demanded.

"Give me a kiss first."

"I'd sooner kiss a warthog! Why don't you hightail it back to the dung heap you crawled out of?" Her voice was coldly wicked and cut into Sid's pride like a finely honed knife.

"I'm goin' to have to learn ya some manners after we're wed," he said, and tossed the kitten back to Milo.

"Wed? Ha! You filthy mule's ass. I'd sooner wed a pole-cat," she spat the words contemptuously and hurried around the table, but by the time she got there, Milo had the kitten on the floor with his heavy boot on its head. The kitten was mewing and thrashing in an attempt to free itself.

"That's cruel. Let it go." Dory stooped to pull the cat out from under Milo's boot.

"Leave it be, or I'll squash its brains out," Milo said in a low, mean voice.

Dory looked up. The eyes that looked into hers told her that he hated her with every fiber of his being and that he would do exactly as he said.

"Why are you doing this?"

" 'Cause I want to. Do as I tell ya or I'll grind its head into the floor."

"What is it you want me to do?" Dory tried to stay calm and close her ears to the kitten's pitiful cries.

"Me and Louis has give ya to Sid to wed. I want ta see ya kissin' him."

Dory was stunned, but only for a moment. "Have you lost your mind? You think I'd marry a filthy piece of horsedung like him? Not if my life depended on it!" Her voice rose until it was a strangled screech.

"Ya . . . ya . . . bitch," Sid snarled. "Ya just better watch out what yo're callin' me."

"It just might not be yore life dependin' on it," Milo said calmly. "It just might be that brat of yores."

Oh, sweet Jesus, he's crazy!

The hatred that blazed in his eyes struck her like a lash.

Horror and outrage washed over her. She wanted to smash his hateful face.

Sid moved in behind her, put his hands on her arms and tried to pull her back against him. She elbowed him in the gut as hard as she could. He merely laughed.

"It's up to you . . . whore." Milo's voice was low and strangely calm. "Ya been lettin' ever'thing with a stick 'tween his legs feel ya up. Now, it's Sid's turn."

Terror knifed through Dory. Then her fright turned to anger. She would have spit in his face but for the hand that shot out and gripped her jaws. Milo's fingers bit into her cheeks.

"Stand still. Old Sid's horny as a two-peckered goat."

Sid's wet mouth began to nuzzle her neck. "Yo're goin' to behave, ain't ya sweet thin'? Yo're goin' to like old Sid's lovin' oncet ya get used to it. I got somethin' in my britches just itchin' to get in yores. It might be jist the biggest one ya ever had."

Dory remained still as a stone, her eyes locked with Milo's. Her intense hatred of him was like a festering boil, but the emotion rioting through her was wholly concealed behind the noncommittal expression on her face. She could hear the small mewing cries of the kitten beneath his boot heel and forced herself to stand still, even though Sid was rubbing his hardened crotch against her hips.

When Sid's hands moved around to cup and fondle her breasts, Milo's expression changed to a smirk. When Milo dropped his hand from her face, he scratched his crotch and laughed.

Thinking about the kitten under Milo's boot heel, Dory endured the humiliation of Sid's fingers pulling at her nipples and the hand that moved lower to her mound to press her back against his crotch.

"I like titties," Sid murmured. "I like 'em best if they've been nussed."

Encouraged by her lack of resistance, Dory's tormentor became bolder and moved his mouth around to hers.

The smell of his foul breath caused her stomach to churn and sickening bile to come up into her throat. Suddenly she had taken all she could take. In a haze of red rage, rationality exploded. Rebelling against this indignity to her body and mind, she groped for a knife on the table. Her fingers closed around the handle of a three-tined fork. She gripped it, and with all the force she had, she drove the sharp tines into the hand pawing her breast.

"Yee . . . ow!" Sid screamed.

Dory broke free and ran for the door. She was fast, but Milo's long reach caught her as her feet hit the porch and he dragged her kicking and screaming back into the kitchen.

"Ya dammed bitch!" He slapped her with such force it spun her around. She crashed into a chair before she hit the floor. He yanked her to her feet and struck her again and again.

"Bitch! Slut! Whore!" Sid yelled, holding his injured hand. Blood poured through his fingers. "Ya'll pay fer this flat on yore back. I'll screw yore damned eyes out!"

The rage that boiled up in Dory gave her strength. Half-mad with pain and fury at what was being done to her, she jerked away from Milo and grabbed the fork.

"Don't hit me again . . . or I'll kill you!" She hissed and spit like a cornered cat, but her strength was no match for his.

"With that?" he sneered, and struck her so fast and so hard that she had no time to use her weapon. She reeled back against Sid. He yelled and shoved her against the table. She stumbled, hitting her cheek on the edge of the table as she fell heavily to the floor.

It didn't occur to Dory to stay down. She was more angry than she had ever been in her life. Her rage was a holocaust sweeping up from deep inside her, ridding her of all fear, robbing her of dignity. She managed to get to her feet, only to be knocked down by a blow from Milo's fist. She lay stunned. When her senses returned she found herself crawling to a chair so that she could get to her feet again.

In a daze of confusion and pain, she heard Wiley's voice, loud and strong.

"Hit her again an' old Berthy'll cut ya slap-dab in two."

"Ya gawddammed ol' fool," Milo roared. "Get the hell outta here."

"After you," Wiley said calmly.

"I'll cut yore heart out."

"Maybe. But not now. Get out."

"Ya ain't orderin' me outta my own house."

"I ain't. Old Berthy is. Get out and take that ruttin' warthog with ya. My finger's gettin' itchin' to empty both barrels."

As Milo moved around the table, Dory inched back to keep him from getting behind her and using her as a shield. Her head felt as if it were in a cellar with a thousand bells ringing at the same time. She could hardly focus her eyes.

"Ya goin' ta let 'im run us off?" Sid blurted. "Shit. We could take 'im."

"Ya yellow pup. Ya couldn't knock a pimple off a jaybird's ass. Come on, make yore best try 'cause one's all ya'll get."

Milo's face was beet-red except for the white around his mouth. Stiff with rage, he kicked a chair out of his way, snatched a towel off the washbench and threw it at Sid.

"Yo're a dead man," he snarled at Wiley, then to Dory as he went out the door, "Ya stupid whore! Ya'll wed Sid or that kid'll get what the cat got."

Sid sent a silent threat to Dory that he would be back,

wrapped the towel around his injured hand, and trailed out after Milo.

Wiley followed them to the porch and watched as they crossed the yard to the corral. He could hear the murmur of their voices as they caught their horses and saddled them. Wiley was as sure as anything that his fate was sealed.

Milo would kill him.

Hell, he was an old man anyway. If he'd ever done anything worthwhile in his life he had done it tonight. Milo had turned ugly mean, like a rogue steer, and Wiley doubted that even Louis would be able to control him now.

As he waited on the porch for the sound of the horses leaving the homestead, Wiley heard a rifle shot and at the same time heard the plop as the bullet sank into the porch post beside his head. He dropped to the floor and shouted to Dory to blow out the lamp. Seconds later there was darkness, except for the small slice of moon that hung over the treetops.

After rolling over so he could get the shotgun in position, Wiley waited. The only sound was the stamping of the horses in the corral. It's a hell of a place to die, he thought. He'd always thought he would die in bed, not flat on his belly on a board porch. Straining his ears for a sound, he heard Dory's whisper.

"Wiley! You all right?"

"Yeah. Stay in the house."

"I've got the rifle—"

"Shhh . . ."

There was a long silence, then Milo's voice came from the side of the yard where the sumac grew.

"Did I get ya, old man?"

"Come and find out, ya shithead." Wiley felt good. If he could get Milo, there'd be one less worry for Dory. After a minute of silence, he yelled, "Hey, yellow-belly. Ya feared of a crippled-up old man? Yo're mighty brave at fightin' women."

Milo answered with a shot that passed over Wiley's head.

"Shit! A blind man could do better'n that. Hell, ya couldn't hit a bull in the arse with a shovel," Wiley taunted, hoping Milo would fire again. The flash would give away his position and old Bertha would do the rest.

In the quiet that followed, the sound of a running horse was heard, followed by a nicker from a horse in the corral. Then silence.

"Someone's comin'," Dory whispered from just inside the door. *Oh, God! Don't let Ben walk into this.*

It seemed to Dory the silence went on forever. She leaned against the wall with the rifle in her hand. Could eternity be this long, she wondered. There wasn't a sound from Wiley on the porch. Dory's mind raced to Odette and Jeanmarie. Odette would not have heard the commotion or the gunshots, but Jeanmarie would have. She prayed that Odette would not be persuaded to come downstairs. She prayed that it was Louis out there in the dark and not Ben.

When the sound of the shots came, Dory's heart plunged to the pit of her stomach. Logic told her that Milo would not be shooting at Louis. *Please, God, Please. Oh, Ben, I've not even had a chance to tell you I love you.*

That awful silence again. It went on and on until it was broken by the sound of a horse leaving the yard. *One horse.*

A minute passed, then she heard Ben's voice.

"Wiley. Dory. It's Ben."

Dory's legs melted from beneath her. Limp, she sank to the floor and rested her forehead against the rough wall beside the door.

"Up here on the porch," Wiley called. "Watch yoreself. There's two of 'em."

"Only two?" Ben said, and shoved his Smith and Wesson into the scabbard that rode on his thigh. "There's only one now and he took off like a scalded cat."

"Which one'd ya get?"

"Sid. He shot at me. I didn't give him another chance. You hurt?" Ben squatted down beside the old man.

"I ain't hit, but I shore as hell twisted my leg when I dropped to the porch."

"I'll give you a hand."

"No. Leave me be for a while an' see 'bout Dory. She's just inside the door."

Inside the kitchen, Ben struck a match so he could find the lamp. He lit it and turned to see Dory huddled down beside the wall.

"Dory? You all right?" Ben knelt beside her and tried to turn her toward him. She resisted and put her hand up to shield her face. "Odette and Jeanmarie?" he asked.

"They're all right."

Ben took hold of her wrist and pulled her hand away from her face.

"Godamighty!" he exclaimed. "Did Milo do this?"

Tears of pain and humiliation rolled down Dory's cheeks. One eye was almost swollen shut. The cut on her cheekbone, where she had hit the table, was open and oozing blood. Her mouth was cut, her cheeks and jaw bruised and swelling. Blood from her nose had run down her chin and onto her shirt.

A soft whimper of pain came from her lips. She leaned her forehead against his shoulder. Ben held her gently, not knowing where all she was hurt.

"Is Dory all right?" Wiley called anxiously from the porch.

"She's beat up pretty bad," Ben answered in a tight angry voice.

"Fool that I be, I ne'er thought he'd do such a thin'. I come runnin' soon as I heared her yell."

"He's been hittin' on her for some time. Didn't she tell you?"

"Nary a word," Wiley said. "Lucifer! James'll kill 'im."

"He won't have to. I will." Ben's words were cold and harsh and strangely void of anger.

CHAPTER

* 15 *

Ben gently stroked the head of short tight curls pressed to his shoulder. She had fought Milo to keep him away from Odette. She had endured her half-brothers' slurs and physical abuse in order to protect James. She was a proud, brave woman and he wanted to rage with savage destruction at the men who had done this thing to her.

"I'm . . . sorry . . ." Dory whispered in anguish.

"Sorry? You've done nothing to be sorry for. You're the spunkiest woman I've ever known."

"But . . . I've got blood on your shirt." She rolled her head back and forth.

"It'll wash." Ben had almost forgotten that Sid's bullet had torn through the fleshy part of his arm above his elbow. It was his blood she was seeing on his shirt.

"Ben . . . Ben . . ." She said his name in a breathless whisper and looked up at him with unfocused eyes.

"I'm here, honey. And I'm staying. Don't worry. They won't be back."

Dory's eyes cleared. She grabbed a handful of his shirt. "He'll kill Jeanmarie if I don't . . . if I don't marry Sid! I've never seen Milo so mean! He'll do it. He was going to kill the kitten if I didn't . . . didn't . . . let Sid—"

"Dory, listen to me." He shook her shoulders gently. "Sid is dead. I killed him."

"You . . . killed him?"

"Yes, I killed him. He was trying to kill me," he said, looking intently into her face.

"Milo said . . . he said . . . that he'd—" She choked up and couldn't say more.

"He'll not hurt Jeanmarie."

"But . . . I'm so afraid!"

"I know you are. Can you stand up? I'll get you to a chair and help Wiley up off the porch."

"Is he hurt?"

"He hurt his leg when he dropped down."

There was a momentary catch in her breath when she moved, followed by a faint moan. It was a steady hurtful sound. Every bone and muscle in her body hurt. Her teeth hurt, her eyelids, and her tailbone. The room tilted when she stood, and she held tightly to Ben. He eased her down onto a chair and took her a wet cloth.

"Hold this against your face while I help Wiley."

The cold, wet cloth felt good. It came to her befuddled mind that she needed to clean herself up before Odette and Jeanmarie saw her. There was so much blood on her shirt. Where had it come from?

Wiley hopped into the kitchen leaning heavily on Ben.

"I'll sit here by the door, Ben. Get me ol' Berthy. If the bastard comes back he'll get a dose of lead. You all right, Dory? Gawddamn that bastard," he exclaimed when he saw her face. "I ort ta a kilt him . . . wish I had."

Ben retrieved the shotgun, picked up the rifle, checked to see if it was loaded, then stood it beside the door.

"Ben, did ya get hit? Blood's runnin' down yore hand."

"It's nothing. Sid's bullet grazed my arm. If I get a nick I bleed like a stuck hog."

"You've been . . . shot?" Dory jumped up out of the chair so fast that she was dizzy. She stood swaying and grabbed the table to steady herself. Looking down, she saw the lifeless body of the kitten, its head a bloody pulp. "Ohhh . . . ahhh—" She gagged, slapped a hand over her mouth and stumbled toward the door.

Ben caught her with an arm about her waist and helped her to the edge of the porch. The contents in her stomach spilled out of her mouth in gushes. She moaned and gagged and vomited until there was nothing to come up. When the sickness was over, she hung limply on Ben's arm until the dizziness passed.

"Poor little kitten." She began to cry. Tears rolled from her eyes and fell on her blood-stained shirt. Ben turned her in his arms.

"Don't cry, honey. Don't cry. Please don't." His words thickened and ran together.

"I'm trying," she whispered, her lips trembling so that she could scarcely say the words. "It was so awful. Milo had his . . . foot on the kitten's head and it was crying. He made me stand and let that sorry excuse for a man . . . paw me." She shuddered and began to cry again. "It was degrading. I didn't know what else to do. Oh, Ben, I feel so dirty—."

"Sweet, brave woman, you did what you had to do."

"When I couldn't stand it any longer, I . . . stabbed Sid with a fork and ran to the door to get outside. Milo caught me and hit me. I fell against the table and grabbed another fork, that's when he really beat me. Milo hasn't been like that before. He's always been mean, but it's only the last year that he's pinched and slapped me. Tonight I could feel how much he hated me. I think he wanted to kill me."

"Were he and Sid drinking?"

"No. I'm sure they weren't. Milo asked about Odette as soon as he came in the door. He wants her."

"I'll kill him first," Ben said quietly.

"Or he'll kill you. He's a back-shooter, Ben. I know he killed Mick. He laughs every time it's mentioned."

"You and James are going to have to make some decisions. You can't stay here. That's certain."

"I forgot about James," she gasped. "He'd go crazy if . . . he saw me."

"Don't worry about that now. James can take care of himself."

Her hand touched his wet sleeve. "You're hurt—"

"—It's not bad at all." His hands gripped her shoulders and held her away from him.

"Are you sure?" Her voice trembled.

"I've had worse from a mosquito bite. Will you be all right here on the porch while I take care of the kitten?"

Dory stood with her arm hooked around a porch post. After a few minutes, Ben came out of the house carrying a bundle and walked off into the darkness. When he returned, he took Dory's arm and they went back into the house. She glanced at the place where the kitten had died. On the floor was a wet spot where Ben had scrubbed at the stain.

Dear Ben. She would thank God every day for the rest of her life for sending him here.

Moving slowly like a tired old woman, Dory went to Wiley. Tears mingled with blood on her cheeks. She pressed his hand.

"If you hadn't come, they would have beat me down and then gone upstairs for Odette. Milo said he was going to . . . ah . . . have a go at her. I don't know what they would have done to Jeanmarie. I'm so glad I didn't lock myself in up there. If I hadn't been down here they would have gone up there right away. I delayed them long enough for you to get here. Oh, Wiley, I'm afraid for you. Milo said he'd kill you."

"There, there, gal. It ain't goin' to be easy gettin' ol' Wiley." Embarrassed, yet touched by her attention, Wiley attempted to be cross. "Get on with ya and get yoreself cleaned up. You'd scare the daylights outta the young'un if she saw ya in such a mess."

"I'm hoping she's asleep by now. Mercy! If Jeanmarie's asleep, Odette won't hear us and open the door."

"Odette might know more about what's going on down here than we think," Ben said. "I'll go up."

He picked up one of the lamps and left the room. At the top of the stairs, he held it up so that the light was on his face. Just as he suspected, the door to Dory's room was open a crack. It opened wider when Odette saw Ben.

"Papa?"

Ben held the light to the side so she could see him clearly and beckoned. Odette stepped out into the hall, her eyes fastened on his bloody shirt.

"Papa! You're hurt!"

"It's just a scratch. You can tend to it later."

"Milo and a man came. Dory sent me and Baby up here."

"Milo hurt her. She needs you."

"Bad?" Odette asked and waited anxiously, her eyes on Ben's lips, for his reply.

"She won't die," Ben hastened to say, and he saw his daughter's shoulders slump in relief.

Odette hurried down the stairs to the kitchen. She paused in the doorway and gasped when she saw Dory's face.

"Dory . . . Dory—" she exclaimed.

Dory tried to make her swollen lips form words Odette could understand. "I'm all right." She had to repeat the words several times.

"Ah . . . Dory." Odette took Dory's hand and held it to her cheek. The look in her large sorrowful eyes was almost Dory's undoing. "Milo do this?"

Dory nodded, trying not to cry again. She pointed at the bloodstain on Ben's shirt.

"He hurt Papa too? Ohhh . . ." Odette stamped her foot with more anger than Ben had ever seen her express. "He's mean like a snake—James will beat him for this!"

Dory's eyes flew to Ben. He was staring at his daughter's angry face with a puzzled look on his own. She reached for Odette's hand to get her attention, and pointed to Ben's sleeve again.

"Ben, my lips are swollen and she can't understand me. Take off your shirt so we can see to your arm." Dory made a move to get up. With a hand on her shoulder, Ben pressed her back down on the chair.

"Tell me where the things are. Odette can take care of this. She's patched me up a couple times before."

Dory and Wiley watched as Odette expertly rolled the sleeves of Ben's shirt and union suit up past his elbow to the bulging muscles of his upper arm. After washing the wound, they could see that the bullet had cut a path across the flesh and required stitches. Swiftly and skillfully, Odette cleansed the lacerated flesh with Lambert's Listerine from Dory's medicine box, and after pouring boiling water over the needle and thread, she unhesitantly closed the wound with four neat stitches. She wet a compress with the listerine, pressed it to the wound and bound his arm with strips of clean cloth.

Dory was impressed by Odette's calm, efficient manner, and so it seemed was Wiley.

"Wal, now, if'n I get me a gunshot, I know where I'm a'goin."

"She's wonderful," Dory spoke slowly, thc words coming

distorted from her puffed lips. "You should be proud of her, Ben."

"I am." Ben watched his daughter empty the bloody water from the pan, wash it, and refill it from the teakettle.

"Your turn, Dory." Odette set the pan on the table and gently cleaned Dory's face with a warm, wet cloth. After washing away the blood, she soaked a cloth with the Listerine and dabbed at the cuts. Dory winced as Odette pressed the cloth to a cut on her cheekbone.

Odette wanted to cry. Her friend's face was almost unrecognizable. One of Dory's eyes was swollen shut. Her lips were cut and almost twice their normal size. Bruises, already dark but getting darker, covered her cheeks and chin.

Ben sat quietly watching. Dory had stayed here and taken Milo's abuse in order to protect Odette and Jeanmarie. He realized that Dory had awakened something in him—something no other woman had even stirred. Her compassion, her understanding, her courage had reached some longing deep within him, something he was not even aware of. He had never cared for another human being until he had met the old man who had taught him about the engine; then Odette. He had gone his lonely way thinking that love, home and a family were for other men. Now he wondered if it were possible . . .

Ben knew one thing for certain. He was not going to take Odette and ride out of Dory's life. Maybe once in a lifetime a man met a woman of her caliber. He had to stay near her, protect her, until he found out if fate had purposely arranged for their paths to cross.

His reverie turned to the attraction between James and Odette. It could be a fleeting thing. Perhaps he was making more of it than he should. He was becoming more convinced than ever that Odette could not have been fathered by one of the Callahans—but he wasn't sure and probably never would be. He might be forced to take James into his confidence. He would hate for Odette to learn that he was not sure if he had fathered her or not. She might be so hurt that she would slide back into the scared, silent girl she had been when he had first met her.

When Odette had done all she could do for Dory's injuries, Dory pointed toward the tablet and pencil at the end of the table. Odette took them to her and she began to write.

I'm so glad you are here. I don't know what I would have done without you to take care of Jeanmarie and now me. Milo killed the little kitten. Help me think of a way to make Jeanmarie understand.

Dory finished writing and handed the tablet to Odette.

"Poor kitty. He's so mean!"

Did Jeanmarie know what was going on?

"No. Baby sleep."

Dory had just reached for the tablet to write another message when Wiley's voice stopped her.

"Horses comin'." Wiley leaned forward, turning his ear to the door. "Sounds like more'n two."

Ben moved quickly and blew out first one lamp and then the other, leaving the room in total darkness. With his hand against Odette's back he urged her toward Dory.

"Dory, hold onto Odette."

"Might be that Milo's stirred a bunch up agin ya 'cause of Sid," Wiley said in a low voice.

"That's what I'm thinking. I'm going out. Dory, if you hear shots, you and Odette get on the floor."

"No, Ben. Don't go. Please . . ."

"He's gone, missy," Wiley said softly. "He knows what he's doin'."

"They'll . . . kill him."

"Ain't likely."

Dory groped for Odette's hand and held it tightly. Fear squeezed the air from her chest. Even in her near panic she realized that Ben had been right to get out of the house. They would have a better chance if they were not bunched together. She also realized that she would be more hindrance than help in her present condition. She doubted if she could even get to the rifle by the door.

The riders rode into the yard and stopped, evidently confused by the darkened house.

"Stop right thar," Wiley shouted. "Who air ya?"

"Wiley? Ya gawdamned old fool." There was no mistaking Louis's loud, strident voice. "It's me, Steven and Tinker. What the hell's goin' on here?"

"Come on in. Ya got ya a mess to clean up here, Louis." Wiley struck a match. "Can ya light the lamp, Dory?"

Dory reached for the matchbox and put it in Odette's hand. When the room was alight from the soft glow of the lamp, Wiley spoke again.

"Tell her to light the other'n. I want Louis ta get a good look at what Milo's been up to."

"Louis won't care what Milo's done to me. I don't want Steven and Tinker to see me."

"Tell her to light the other'n," Wiley said stubbornly.

Dory pointed to the other lamp, and by the time the men stepped up on the porch, the room was brightly lit.

"Where's Waller?" Louis stood back out of the path of light that came through the doorway.

"He's out thar some'ers. Come on in. Hell, the shootin's over 'less *you* start it up again."

"Milo said he killed Sid."

"Guess he did. I didn't see it, but he said he did."

"What the hell'd he do that fer?" Louis came in, followed by Steven and Tinker.

" 'Cause Sid shot 'im. It's what I'd a done."

There was sudden quiet. Three pairs of eyes stared at Dory. She longed with all her heart to cover her face with her two hands. Pride forced her to hold her head up and stare back at them—with the one eye that she could still see out of.

Steven removed his hat. Tinker rocked back on his short stubby legs and whistled through his teeth. Louis stared and said nothing. Steven came to Dory, knelt down in front of her, and took her hand in his.

"Dory, honey—"

"Don't touch me, Steven. I hurt in places I didn't know I had. I may have a cracked rib," she said, holding herself carefully erect, taking in short gulps of air through her mouth.

"We should get you to a doctor."

"No. Odette will take care of me."

"Harrumpt!" The sound came from Louis. "It'll learn ya not to come at a man a tryin' ta gouge his eyes out."

"Is that what Milo told you?" Dory asked.

"Him and Sid stopped here for supper. By Gawd, it's his home as much as yores. Ya ort to a fixed it."

"What else did he say . . . dear brother?" Dory's voice was heavy with sarcasm.

"Ya stabbed Sid with a fork an' come at him."

"He's lying and you know it!"

"Yo're the liar!" Louis shouted. "Just like yore ma. Lyin' to get in here, lyin' to get Pa to push me 'n' Milo out."

"It's always back to that, isn't it?" Anger made Dory forget her sore jaws. "You mean, stupid, thick-headed dolt! You're so damned dumb you can't see that it's Milo who lies. He did this to me because I wouldn't stand still and let Sid paw me and slobber on me."

"Liar!" Louis bellowed.

"He was going to let Sid rape me. He said . . . he said my baby's life depended on me marrying Sid. He's crazy, and if you weren't as crazy as he is, you'd see it. He'd have killed me if not for Wiley. He and Sid would've killed all of us if Ben hadn't come when he did."

Louis took a step toward her, his face red, his jaws shaking, his fist knotted.

"Don't talk to me like that you . . . you . . ."

"Whore. Go on, say it. It's what you call me to my face and behind my back. You and Milo were dragging my name through the mud even before I had Jeanmarie."

"What else would ya call a woman with a kid and ain't wed?" Louis roared.

"I've taken all I'm going to take from you and Milo. I'm going to Judge Kenton and have him divide the property. Half to you and your crazy brother and half to me and James."

"By Gawd, ya'll not!"

"By God, I will! I didn't know it was possible until a few days ago."

"It's that gawddamn Waller. He's put ya up to it!"

"I read about it in one of Papa's books." Dory hoped her lie was convincing. Her jaws hurt so bad she could hardly get out the next words. "Judge Kenton can do it, can't he Steven?"

Steven was turning his hat around and around in his hands. "We can ask him."

Louis's fury was real. It pushed him beyond the bounds of reason. His nostrils flared and his jaws quivered as color drained from his face. He threw out an arm and pushed Steven out of his way so he could get to Dory.

Tinker sprang forward and grabbed the arm Louis had drawn back to hit her, but it was Ben's voice that stopped him.

"Callahan!" The word exploded in the room. "Touch her and I'll blow you to hell."

All eyes turned to the doorway. Ben stood there, his hand

inches from the gun on his thigh. Louis saw the smoldering look of anger in the steel-gray eyes. He noted Waller's loose-limbed stance. *The man was ready to kill him.*

There was deadly quiet in the room. Tension was thick. Everything in Louis rebelled against backing down.

"I warn't goin' ta touch her." Self-preservation had won over his pride.

"That isn't all." Ben's light eyes looked like two frozen ponds; his voice was unnaturally quiet and its very gentleness kept all eyes focused on his face. "Don't ever call her a whore or a slut again. And if I hear of you saying any of the things you said about her the night I came here, I'll come looking for you. Is that understood?"

"So that's the way it is," Louis sneered. "Yo're thinkin' to get yore hands on her shares."

"That bothers you, doesn't it? You were going to marry her off to Sid because you could control him *and* her shares."

"It's the only way she could get a man to wed her."

"You're as low-down as any man I've met. Watch what you say about her," Ben warned. "I'll not kill you, but if I tear into you, you'll wish I had."

Louis could barely control his anger. "Ya killed Sid. The law will hear about it."

"They certainly will. I'll tell them."

"You'll hang."

"Not for killing a man who shot me first."

"Ya can't prove Sid shot first."

"He shot me in the arm. I shot him between the eyes. How could he *not* have shot first?"

Now is the time, Ben thought, for Louis to bring up the fact that he'd been in prison—that is if he knew about it. Wanting the engine set up, he would have overlooked that detail until now. Ben waited. Louis said nothing.

"That should be the end of it, Louis," Steven said. "Where's the body, Waller?"

"Out by the barn."

"We'll take him back up to the mill. There's a graveyard of sorts up there." Steven took the lantern from the hook beside the door and lit it. "Coming, Louis?"

Louis shot a belligerent look in Dory's direction, then an even more hostile look at Ben.

"You're fired."

Ben laughed, but made no retort.

"I'll send down your pay and your tools in the morning." The tone of Steven's voice doused any opposition from Louis.

"I'm staying until James gets here and he and Dory decide what they want to do. Tell that to Milo. If he wants trouble, I'll oblige him. A word of advice, Callahan. Most of the men who work for you are good, *decent* men. I'd hope, if I were you, that they didn't find out what Milo did to his sister. You know how loggers feel about womenfolk. It doesn't take much to foul up an operation—an iron wedge left in a log will cause a blade to fly into a hundred pieces, a single jab with a pike can cause a pileup. Overload that donkey engine and it will blow to smithereens."

"Are ya threatenin' me?"

"No. I'll not cause any of those things to happen. I'll be right here."

Ben followed the men to the porch and stood there until they had slung Sid's body over the back of his horse, mounted, and left the homestead.

CHAPTER
* 16 *

As the horse carrying Sid's body passed, the men who had gathered in front of the bunkhouse removed their hats in respect for the dead. Tinker, Steven and Louis dismounted at the corral. Louis stomped off toward his room, leaving Steven and Tinker with the job of preparing the body for burial. They went through Sid's pockets and removed several small coins, a pocketknife, a silver toothpick, and a picture of a very plump naked woman. After taking off Sid's gunbelt, they rolled the body in a blanket and placed it on a wagon bed to await the service in the morning.

The area in front of the bunkhouse was well lighted with torches. The men stood around in bunches and talked. Many of them had disliked Sid Hanes, but now that he was dead, he was, so it seemed, everyone's friend. Angry voices spoke of riding down to the homestead and confronting Ben Waller. Some said hanging was too good for a man who would shoot down a man without cause; others said it could just as well have been one of them that lay on the wagon bed waiting for a holc in the ground.

Milo had done a good job stirring up the men against Ben.

"Sid were mouthy . . . but he didn't mean no harm."

"Sid never was no gun hand."

"Couldn't hit a mule in the ass at ten feet."

"Waller ain't ort to a gunned him down like he done."

"Ain't no law up here. Poor Sid ain't got no folks to speak up fer him."

"Jist never thought of Waller as a killer. We ain't ort to let him get away with it."

"Ya can't tell 'bout quiet fellers like him . . . could be wanted by the law for all we know."

"I think we ort to go down and have us a little talk with 'im."

Tinker listened to the talk and became more and more disgusted with the fools who couldn't think for themselves. You can lead them like sheep, he thought. Like damn dumb sheep. Finally he spoke up.

"I'm thinkin' if ya want to do something for *poor* Sid, ya can get ya a shovel and start diggin' a hole."

Heads turned. Tinker was as well thought of as any man in camp. All were eager to hear what he had to say.

"Ya ain't thinkin' Waller ort to get away with this, air ya, Tinker?"

"Get away with what? Ya dumbheads! Ain't ya got brains enough ta see that Milo's usin' ya ta get back at Waller? Waller come in on him tonight and broke up the little get-together he and Sid was plannin' with Miss Dory and Waller's girl."

"Milo didn't say nothin' 'bout womenfolk bein' there."

"What the hell do ya think they went down there for? A church meetin'?"

"Wal, even if they did have courtin' on their minds, Waller didn't have to kill Sid."

"What would ya a done if somebody shot you? Stand there and let him shoot ya again?"

"That ain't the way Milo told it an' he was there."

"He lied to cover up the meanness he done down there. Two shots were fired. One from Sid's gun, one from Waller's. Sid hit Waller in the arm, Waller hit him between the eyes. Figure it out fer yoreselves."

"Milo didn't say nothin' 'bout Sid firin'. Said there was one shot."

"Milo's lyin'. I found the shell by Sid's body. How ya think it got there? It shore didn't jump ten feet outta Waller's gun. Found Waller's shell too. Right where he was standin'."

"Wal . . . I'm wonderin' why Milo lied. Sounds fair ta me."

"Shit! I didn't want ta believe Waller was a killer."

"Should'a knowed Milo'd try an' make him an' Sid look good."

"Milo's been talkin' 'bout Waller's girl. Said he liked it cause she couldn't hear. Said she was deaf as a stump."

"That shows ya where his brains is," Tinker said with disgust. "If ya want to know what kinda man yo're workin' fer—ride down and take a look at what Milo done to Miss Dory. It'll make ya want to puke." Tinker turned on his heel and walked away.

Standing on the fringe of the crowd, Steven listened to Tinker talk to the men and noted that none of Milo's cronies were among them. After the sawyer left, they lingered and talked among themselves for a while, then began to put out the torches and head for the bunkhouse.

Steven went down the path to his own quarters. Inside the cabin he lit the lamp, dropped the bar that secured the door and closed and locked the inside shutters.

Now that the time had come to make a move, he felt strangely calm. Nevertheless, the need for a drink of good brandy sent him to the liquor cabinet. With glass in hand he stood in the middle of the room and looked around. He had been comfortable here. Almost happy. Now that he was leaving it, he would have to plan carefully, because once he left, he wouldn't be back. It would be too dangerous. If he showed his face on this side of the mountain after doing what he was honor-bound to do, his life wouldn't be worth a plug nickel.

He finished his drink, rinsed and wiped the glass, and then knelt down and removed the false front of the cabinet that concealed the safe.

Only a foot and a half square, the heavy iron safe was small but adequate. It held a thousand dollars of cash money, all of it earned while working for Callahan and Sons, and two packets of letters. Steven took one of the packets to the table, adjusted the lamp, opened a letter, and began to read.

Dear friend Steven,

Of all the men I know, you are the one I trust to do what is best for my loved ones. Wiley is my dear and loyal friend, but what must be done would be too great a burden to put on a man of limited education. I realize you may not want to stay here after I am gone—in fact you have told me so. Please stay for a while and if you think things are going as we hope they will I want you to destroy the document. If not, and I fear it will not, you must take these papers to Judge Kenton.

Steven continued to read the letter he had read a dozen or more times before. When he finished, he folded it carefully, and then read the next letter in the stack. It was from Jean Callahan. George had given him the letter along with his own. The letter started with: *Dear friend Steven.*

Steven could almost recite the words from memory. Still

he read it through, folded it, and put it with George's letter. There were four more letters and a legal document in the stack. The letters were old and bore such postmarks as Bay Horse, Cracked Rock, and Two Shoes. Steven didn't read them. One time had been enough. He wrapped the packet of letters and the document in a piece of thin leather and tied the bundle securely with a shoestring.

The other packet of letters was personal. Steven looked at them and asked himself why he had kept them all these years. He knew the answer. They were a connection with his past. Oh, yes, he'd had a past before he'd come to the Bitterroot Mountains. He'd had a family who loved him, a mother who worried, a father and a brother who despised him—at the end. They were gone now. He had read in the San Francisco newspaper about his father's ship going down. His mother and brother had been on board as well. He had grieved—for his mother.

Looking back he wished he had stayed, faced the disgrace and worked to clear his name. Realistically, he knew that he had done the only thing he could have done: run. It was folly to think he could have cleared his name while in prison. The cards were all stacked against him. Even his own father and brother had thought him guilty when thousands of dollars were missing from his father's shipbuilding company.

His wild lifestyle of drinking and gambling and the fact that he kept the company books had made him the logical suspect. The family had been shunned by lifelong friends, and irate stockholders had hired men to kill him. He'd had several narrow escapes before he had wandered cold, sick, and hungry to the Callahan homestead and Jean and George Callahan had taken him in.

When he had recovered, they had offered him the job of keeping the books for the small but growing lumber company.

Before accepting, he had told them his story and prepared to move on, not wanting to bring trouble down on his new friends. They had persuaded him to stay. He had changed his name and settled into a life far more primitive than the one he had left behind.

Several times over the years, bounty hunters had come looking for him. The picture they showed no longer resembled the man who kept books at the mill. No one had ever heard of a man named Maxwell Lilly.

Reminiscing was painful even after almost twenty years. Steven kindled a small fire in the pot-bellied stove that sat in the corner of the room. When the flames were high, he tossed in one scrap of paper at a time: a letter from a girl he had been engaged to marry, newspaper clippings, and wanted posters. He couldn't part with the note his mother had left on his bed the day he had been accused. She told him that she loved him and believed him innocent. He tucked it and a ledger sheet from the books he had kept so long ago into an envelope and put them back in the safe. He had kept the ledger sheet thinking that maybe someday it might be useful in clearing his name. It no longer mattered. He was Steven Marz now. He stirred the ashes with the poker until they fell through the grate. Nothing remained.

Maxwell Lilly no longer existed.

Louis was in a rage. Milo lay on his bunk, his hands behind his head, and stared up at the ceiling.

"Ya done it now. Ya really done it. Ain't I told ya to stay clear a Waller's girl? Ain't I told ya? Ya had to go down there, just had to go, and ya got Sid killed."

"How'd I know Waller'd gun him down?"

"Don't ya be tellin' me more lies. Gawdammit! Ya said one shot was fired. There was two. Sid shot first."

"I heard one shot."

"Then yo're deaf as a doornail! Tinker found a shell by Sid's body and smelled the barrel of his gun. Sid shot Waller in the arm. Waller's aim was better."

"Ya believin' me or hired help?" Milo sat up on the bunk, an ugly scowl on his face.

"I saw it. Steven saw it. I don't give a shit about Sid. What's this about him weddin' Dory? Who thought a that?"

"I did. We'd better get her wed to someone who'll do what we say, or she'll up and wed someone like that Waller. That'd be real trouble."

"Real trouble'll come when James sees what you done to her. He's a tail-twister when he's stirred up an' this'll rile him aplenty."

"We ort ta a took care of that sonofabitch long time ago. I been tempted more'n once. Always too many around. But I'll get the pecker yet."

"Ya'd better get ta him afore he gets ta you. He'll tear down yore smokehouse."

"Harrumpt! I got friends here what owe me. We could take him an' his bunch with both legs tied together." Milo snorted and lay back down on the bunk.

"I ain't wantin' the men takin' sides. And that ain't all, damn ya to hell. Sit up and listen to me."

"What'er ya harpin' on now? Don't want to hear no more 'bout Whory Dory. She got what was comin' ta her. Stabbed Sid with a fork. Would've stabbed me if she'd got ta me. If'n that old man hadn't butted in, I'd a let Sid have a go at 'er, teach 'er some respect fer her betters. His pecker's big as a stump. *Was* big as a stump. Don't guess it 'mounts ta much now."

Louis looked at his brother for a long moment, then sat down on his bunk and held his head in his hands. Things were piling up on him too fast, and this brainless brother of his was no help at all.

"She wants Steven to go to Judge Kenton an' try an' get the company split up in half. Half would go ta her an' James an' half ta us. Ya know what that'll mean? It'll mean we'll have ta buy 'em out ta hold onta what's ours. We ain't got a pissin' cent that ain't tied up."

Milo was silent for a moment. Then he grinned.

"Might not be a bad idee. They could buy us out. We could go ta Seattle or San Francisco. See the sights."

Louis jumped to his feet. "Have ya lost yore mind? I ain't sellin'."

"Calm down. I'm just a talkin'. Kenton won't do that nohow. Ain't no way he could divide it up even. If'n he did, it'd take a year or two to get it done. All ya got ta do is keep yore eyes on Steven so's he can't get to Kenton to ask him."

"You ain't worried a tall, air ya? I worked my ass off an' I ain't givin' up nothin'. The chance has come to get even with Malone—"

"—It's all ya think of—gettin' even with Malone."

Louis sat down and tried to speak reasonably.

"Air ya forgettin' that fer three years in a row, he's clogged the river an' got the best price fer his logs? And we got the leavin's? Have ya forgot that it was a Malone whore what come in here an' took our maw's place an' gived the old man a couple of bastards that get half of what's ours? Have ya forgot it was a Malone what ruint Dory an' dragged our name through the mud? I ain't forgot—"

"I ain't forgot old Jean. That's certain. She was a hot little heifer. I can still hear them bedsprings a squeakin' an' the old man a gruntin'."

"Shut up!" Louis shouted. "I ain't wantin' to hear 'bout no whore."

"Why is it ya never want ta hear 'bout Jean an' the old man? I used to think ya was kinda sweet on her an' jealous of him a gettin' what ya was wantin'. Guess it was ya hated her, huh? Whory Dory reminds me of her. Both of 'em built to give a man a good ride."

"Is that all ya think of? Pluggin' a woman?"

"Ain't nothin' better to think 'bout." Milo laughed. "Sometimes I think 'bout ridin' 'em like a wild bronc or bouncin' on 'em like a featherbed, or pokin' it down their gullet. Now old Sid, he liked to nuss titties—"

Milo's voice droned on. Louis pulled off his boots, blew out the lamp, and lay down on his bunk. He had a lot to think about, plans to make. Milo had his cravings. He had his. One thing was certain. He wasn't going to let Milo's cravings interfere with his.

It was decided that Ben and Wiley would spend the night in the house. Ben had put his horse in the barn and fetched Wiley's crutch and the pot of beans Dory had cooked for their supper. They sat at the kitchen table. Odette and Dory had gone upstairs while Ben was outside.

"Ain't no need me bein' in here, Ben. Milo ain't comin' back here tonight. 'Bout now Louis is a gnawin' on his arse like a dog on a bone. Not that Louis cares what he done to Dory, but he's scared a what Dory said 'bout the dividin' part."

"I think she just pulled that out of her hat to rile Louis. If the judge did anything at all, it would be to force one party to buy the other out. If that couldn't be done, he'd sell the whole works and divide the money."

"James'll go plumb outta his head when he sees what Milo done to Dory." Wiley had finished his plate of beans and was on his second cup of coffee. He didn't have much of an appetite. His leg hurt like hell.

"I've been thinking about that. If it wasn't for that killer running loose, we could take the women down to McHenry's. I don't think Dory would go to the Malones'. She'd be too ashamed for them to see her all beat up."

"When James sees her, ya can bet he'll be on Milo like a chicken on a junebug. One of 'em might end up dead. If it's James, that gal ain't got nobody."

"She'd have somebody." Ben's fork paused on the trip from his plate to his mouth.

"I be a old man, son. 'Sides, Milo'll back-shoot me first chance he gets."

"Not if I can help it."

"Wal . . . yeah . . . an' I thank ya. But I ain't wantin' James ta go off half-cocked an' get hisself killed."

"I'm not wanting that either. He's going to wonder why I'm not back in the morning and think something's happened. I'm hoping he comes here before he goes to the mill."

"Will his crew be knowin' how ta run the engine?"

"One of the men up there has worked with steam. He knows to watch the gauge and not to fill the firebox too full. I could have stayed on a day or two longer, but as of now, my job is done. They're on their own as far as I'm concerned." He spread butter and honey on a thick slice of bread and ate it before he spoke again. "How do you think Steven figures in this?"

"Never been able to figure him out. Stays to hisself. Don't take sides. Been a big help keepin' the company goin'. George thought a heap of him, is all I know."

"Papa—" Odette spoke from the doorway and came into the room to stand beside Ben. "Dory is frettin'. She's afraid for Baby. She's scared for James and Wiley—for all of us."

"Have you had supper, honey?" Ben tugged gently on her hand and she sat down.

"Baby and I had one of James's candies."

Ben spooned beans onto a plate and set it in front of her. "Eat. I'll go talk to Dory."

After helping Dory to wash, Odette had wrapped a cloth tightly around her bruised ribs. She had slipped a nightdress over Dory's head and helped her into the bed. Odette's fingers were wonderfully gentle as she dabbed at the cuts on Dory's face with a pad soaked with witch hazel. When that was done she had sat with her. Grateful not to be alone, Dory had reached for her hand and held it tightly.

Because of her swollen lips Dory was unable to speak so that Odette could understand her and had written on the tablet, *I'm afraid for my baby and James . . . for you and Ben and Wiley.*

"Don't worry, Dory. Papa won't let anyone hurt Baby. James will come and help him. Papa likes you and Baby."

"I hope so. Oh, I hope so," Dory said, knowing Odette didn't understand her. She wrote on the tablet. *I'll be all right. Go eat supper. Put the lamp on the table in the hall.*

The dimly lit room was lonely after Odette left. Dory's worst fantasy had become a living nightmare. What had caused Milo to act so irrationally? He had always been mean, but not as he was tonight. She wasn't surprised at how Louis had reacted. He never admitted that Milo was in the wrong even if he saw it with his own eyes. Her immediate fear was for James. He would be crazy mad when he saw what Milo had done to her. She prayed that Ben would be able to talk sense into him.

Suddenly all that had happened to her was too much to hold inside her. Her aching face twisted as she sought to hold back the sobs—the only sound in the quiet semi-darkened room. She managed to choke them down, but she couldn't have stopped the faint grieving moans that bubbled up out of her misery if her life had depended on it. In all her life she had never felt such crushing anguish.

"Dory . . . shhh . . . don't cry. Hush, pretty girl, don't cry—" The words were murmured; the voice was deep and moving.

Dory wanted nothing but to cling to the man who knelt beside the bed. His hand stroked her shoulder and arm. She groped for him. Gentle hands held her. It was wonderful to be close to someone who cared. Not just someone . . . Ben.

"Oh, Ben—"

"Don't worry. Things will work out. They always do." He spoke softly into her ear. His arms were holding her gently. She was cradled against his chest, sheltered by strong wide shoulders.

"Not . . . for me. Ben, what'll I do? He said he'd do to Jeanmarie what he did . . . he did—"

"Shhh . . . don't think about it. Milo is full of talk. He won't hurt Jeanmarie. He'll never hurt you again. I don't think he'll be so brave facing a man."

"You don't understand. He doesn't fight fair! He doesn't know the meaning of the word. He's got . . . friends."

"And you've got me and James and Wiley," he said quietly.

"He'll see that James has an accident. He'll catch Wiley away from here and shoot him in the back like he did Mick. He'll kill . . . you." Forgetting her sore jaw, she raised her voice and clutched his upper arm.

"You don't have much faith in me, do you?" he said teasingly.

"I do! I do! But you'll go and take Odette. She was so good to me. I . . . I—" She could say no more for the sobs that clogged her throat.

"Hey, now. Don't cry. Odette and I are not leaving just yet."

"She's so level-headed—"

"—And you're about the bravest woman I've ever known. You fought like a wildcat down there."

"Your arm! Am I hurting your arm?"

"Naw. I could still hug a pretty girl if I had stitches in both arms." He had a smile in his voice.

"Ben, I'm ugly."

He laughed. "What brought that on?"

"I don't want you to think I'm ugly."

"You're not. You're as pretty as a speckled pup—that is when you don't look like you've tangled with a buzz saw." His chuckle vibrated through his chest.

"Oh, Ben—" Her arm slipped around his waist and she nestled closer. "I'm sorry to be such a baby. I haven't cried this much since Mick was killed." She took a shuddering breath and let it out slowly.

"Did you love him so much?" She could feel his warm breath on her face.

"Yes. I loved him like I love Jeanmarie. He was so lonely, so misunderstood. If you could have known him, you'd understand. He was fragile and hated himself for not being what his father wanted him to be."

"I think Chip understands him now. The walls of the room we waited in were covered with Mick's paintings. Chip seems very proud of them."

"He told me he painted, but I never saw his pictures. He liked making jewelry and gave me a pin he made. He made one for his mother, too. She gave it to me to save for Jeanmarie."

"The next time you go to the Malones' you should see the paintings. They're very good."

"I'll not go again. Marie is dying—"

"I have the feeling that Chip wants to put all that behind him and accept Jeanmarie as his granddaughter."

"No. I'll never forgive him for the way he treated Mick. If he had been more understanding of him, Mick wouldn't have had to sneak off to meet someone he could talk to who would not ridicule him. He'd not have been killed, shot down in the woods as if he were no more than an animal."

"And you would have married him?"

"Yes," she said slowly. "With Jeanmarie on the way, there's nothing else I could have done. Although the love I had for Mick was not like the love my mother had for Papa." The sob came back into her throat.

"Poor little girl. You've had a load to carry." His voice was the merest of whispers. "Go to sleep. Things will look better in the morning."

She felt his lips on her forehead. She wasn't dreaming because she could feel his breath, warm on her wet face, and she could smell a faint woodsy scent on his vest. Not wanting to leave the warm security of his arms, but knowing she must, she pushed herself away from him and lay back down on the pillow.

"Thank you, Ben."

"You don't have to be thanking me, Dory." His voice was strained and light, his face a blur. He stood. "Wiley and I will be downstairs. You've nothing to worry about. Sleep, so you'll get your strength back."

Dory listened to his footsteps going down the hallway and wished he hadn't had to go.

CHAPTER
* 17 *

Dory was out of bed before Jeanmarie awakened; and while washing and dressing, she looked at herself in the mirror.

She was too shocked to cry.

Both of her eyes were blackened. They looked like two burnt holes in a blanket. One eye was open, the other swollen shut. The skin on her face was either black, blue, or red where the skin was broken. Her upper lip was almost twice its normal size. Both lips had been cut against her teeth, and it was difficult to drink without water dribbling down her chin.

When she removed her nightgown and the binding Odette had wrapped around her rib cage, she discovered dark bruises on most every part of her body. She thanked God that Wiley had come before Milo had broken an arm or a leg.

Not wanting to face Ben, Dory lingered in the room, dreading going down to the kitchen where Odette was preparing breakfast. But when she could stall no longer, she walked determinedly down the stairs and stood in the doorway, her knees shaking. Thank heavens, Odette was alone. She saw Dory as she carried dishes to the table.

"Dory? You all right?" Odette's soft blue eyes were filled

with compassion. "Oh, Dory . . . Dory—" She hurried to her and took her hand. "Sit down. I'll do everything."

"I should move around or I'll get stiff." Odette's eyes questioned and Dory repeated.

"Poor mouth. I get the tablet." She ran from the room. When she returned she said, "Baby waking up."

Dory wrote swiftly, telling Odette to tell Jeanmarie before she brought her downstairs that her mama had hurt her face, and that the kitten had gone to find its mother.

Odette nodded and went back up the stairs.

Dory wandered to the door and out onto the porch. It was a beautiful spring morning. There wasn't a cloud in the sky. The sun was warm and the birds were singing. A pair of mourning doves searched for seeds in the patch of grass beside the water trough.

Such a peaceful scene. It seemed impossible that so much ugliness had happened here just a few hours earlier. A man had died, and her own kin had enjoyed humiliating her, had used his fists on her, hating her, wanting to kill her.

Wiley was sitting on a box beside the bunkhouse door, his shotgun across his knees. Did he and Ben expect Milo to return with his sidekicks to finish what he and Sid had started last night? Or were they still thinking that whoever was murdering women would come in broad daylight? Dory stepped down off the porch and called to him.

"Wiley, have you had breakfast?"

"Yup. Couple hours ago."

"Where's Ben?"

"He's 'round some'ers. Said fer ya to stay in the house till he gets back."

Gets back. Fear erupted inside Dory. Her brain began to buzz. *He wouldn't go to the mill alone. If he went at all, he'd wait for James to go with him.*

"Where did he go?" Dory stepped off the porch and started across the yard.

"Stay in the house, Dory. Ben said so."

She stopped. "Did Ben go to the mill?"

Wiley didn't answer. The longer he was silent the more frightened she became until she felt as if her heart would gallop out of her chest.

"He went to the mill," she answered for him and held her breath while she waited for him to deny it. Wiley said nothing. "Oh, Wiley. Why did you let him go? If they don't kill him they'll beat him to a pulp . . . maybe cripple him for life!"

"It warn't fer me to say, Dory. I'm thinkin' he ain't no slouch when it comes ta lookin' after hisself."

"He's got stiches in his arm where Sid shot him. He won't have a chance against Milo." Through her mind raced the brutal realization of what Milo could do to him.

"He ain't a man ta go off half-cocked. He knows what he can do an' what he cain't."

"Does Odette know he went there?"

"I ain't a knowin' that, but I'm a thinkin' not."

Dory felt a numbness in her chest. She looked toward the trail that led to the mill for a long while before she started back to the house. She stepped up on the porch and turned to look back at the old man sitting on the box.

"When did he go?"

"Before daylight."

"Why, Wiley?"

"Ya'll have to be askin' him that."

Ben and Wiley had talked long after the women had gone to sleep. Wiley told Ben what he knew of the family, much of which Ben had heard before. Ben urged the old man to lie down in one of the other rooms and get some sleep. Wiley refused.

"Wouldn't sleep nohow," he said. "Guess in my old age I ain't wantin' to waste time sleepin'. I'll sit here an' count my blessin's that Milo didn't blow my head off."

Ben spread a bedroll on the floor. He had trained himself to catch a few hours' sleep whenever he could, but tonight thoughts of what Milo had done to Dory kept him restless. When he could shut them off, he lay thinking about her. Dory's arm had been around his neck, her soft breasts against his chest. How good it had felt to hold her. Was what he felt for her the love a man felt for his mate? The only thing he knew about that emotion was what he had read in the classics introduced to him by his old friend, Tom Caffery. He had known then that someday he wanted to be loved as Cathy had loved Heathcliff, but he had held out little hope for it.

He wondered if Dory would be shocked to know he thought of her naked in his arms, her belly pressed to his. Did she even suspect that her sweet, caring presence was beginning to fill that vacant place in his heart?

Ben could feel the swelling in his groin as he thought about her. He was a man of strong sexual hungers, but he didn't regard this physical change in his body as a sign of love. He liked her, liked to be with her.

Waller, he asked himself just before he gave himself up to sleep, what happened to your plan to set your sights on a woman only when you had something to offer her? And how do you know she'd even have you after she learns that your daughter's mother was a whore and that you have to guard the girl against involvement with James because he may be her uncle?

It was still dark when he awakened. The birds were chirping, a sign that dawn was near. He got up and rolled his bedroll. He heard the plop of a chaw of tobacco hitting the can and knew that Wiley was awake.

"Ready for some coffee?" Ben asked.

"I'd give a dollar fer a cup."

"It won't cost quite that much."

Ben got the fire going and put the coffeepot on. While waiting, he cleaned and checked his gun and strapped on his gunbelt.

"Ya goin' huntin'?" Wiley asked.

Ben didn't answer until after he had set the pot of beans on the stove to heat and sliced bread from the loaf on the table.

"I'm going up to the mill. I figure it'll be better for me to settle with Milo. If I take care of it there'll be no need for James to go storming off up there. The men would be sure to take sides, and that's the worst thing that can happen to a logging crew. Some of them could end up under a raft heading down river, or traveling down a sluice with a couple tons of logs on their tail."

"Milo's got a bunch of ornery sidekicks up there that's jist full of cussedness."

Ben shrugged. "I figure there's some of the other kind too."

After they ate, Wiley made a painful trip to the outhouse, then settled on the box beside the bunkhouse door. Ben led his saddled horse out of the barn.

"Tell Dory to stay inside and keep Odette and Jeanmarie with her," he said, as he stepped into the saddle.

The sky was beginning to lighten in the east. He reached the trail to the mill and took a few precautionary minutes before venturing onto it. The thick growth of pines on each side could easily conceal a predator. That was a risk he would have to take. A cathedral-like stillness hung over this timbered trail. Every few minutes he stopped to listen for riders coming toward him. His ears were alert for any sound or lack of sound as he moved the horse on up the hillside.

A gray dawn hovered over the mill site when he reached it. His eyes searched the area carefully, but he could see no movement except at the cookshack, where the men had gathered for breakfast. His timing had been just right. He tied his horse to a sapling, walked to the cookhouse, and opened the door.

A dozen or more men, Milo and Louis among them, were seated at the two oilcloth-covered tables wolfing down slabs of meat, cornmeal mush, and biscuits, and taking great draughts of coffee to wash down each mouthful. Only the cook noticed Ben standing in the doorway.

"Have a seat, Waller. Fresh batch of biscuits coming up."

"Thanks, but I've had breakfast. I've got business with Milo. I'll wait until he's finished."

Idle talk ceased abruptly and all eyes turned to stare at Ben.

"Business with me?" Milo's big jaws continued to chomp on the food he had in his mouth. "I ain't doin' no *business* with a killer. Ya come to the buryin'?"

"You know why I'm here. Finish your breakfast and come on outside."

Milo laughed, but his eyes were mean. "Now wouldn't that jist put the frost on yore balls? The donkey man's callin' *me* out and *he* done the killin' a poor Sid."

"That isn't what this is about and you know it."

"I think ya kilt old Sid 'cause yore whore was shinin' up to 'im. Ya scared ya'll lose yore pecker hole, *donkey man*?" Milo laughed extra loud. The look he gave to his friends produced a chorus of guffaws.

Controlling himself with great effort, Ben spoke calmly. "You've not only got a filthy, rotten mind, you're a mewling coward. Only a low-down, sneaking sonofabitch shithead fights a woman."

Ben's words had the effect he intended. His contempt

washed over Milo in a chilling torrent, and Milo jumped to his feet, his eyes wild, his teeth bared. He felt the steel-gray eyes stabbing into him, but he was too angry to realize the danger he was facing.

"Yo're fired!" he shouted. "Get the hell off my land."

"I don't work for you. I quit the minute I saw what you did to Miss Dory. You low-life bastard, you beat her almost senseless." Ben took a few deep breaths. It wouldn't do to let his anger rule his head.

"That's family business and none of yores," Louis shouted.

"And that makes it all right?" Ben shouted back, his aroused voice overriding Louis's. "For Christ's sake, Louis, use the few scrambled brains you lay claim to. It's any man's business to protect a woman from a goddamned snake." Ben's blazing eyes never left Milo's flushed face. "I want to see if this flap-jawed loudmouth who uses his fists on a woman has the guts to face a man."

"She had it comin'. She's just a slut, a whore an' not even a good'n."

The muscles along Ben's jaws rounded into hard knots. He took a long, deep breath to steady himself.

"You'd goddammed better believe that the next time you call her a whore you'd better hang onto your balls. Because if you hit her with that word again, it'll be the last time they'll be of any use to you." He spoke in a low, controlled voice.

Milo stared numbly at the cold-eyed man, shocked by the lethal hatred in his face. He opened and closed his mouth as if he were strangling. He glanced at the men around from him. There were very few smiles or encouraging grins on their faces. Despite his bravado, Milo wondered for the first time if he had bitten off more than he could chew.

"By gawd, I'll call 'er what I want. Come on, boys. Let's learn this flop-eared jackass some manners."

Several men got up to follow Milo, then stopped in their tracks. The man in the doorway had dropped into a crouch, a revolver in his hand.

"You"—Ben waved the gun at the men behind Milo—"stay out of it. It'll be just me and him." His voice and his eyes were coolly threatening.

"Ya talk big with a gun in yore hand," Milo sneered. "Hell, I ain't no slick-handed gunfighter."

"And I'm not going to be jumped by a pack of wolves. Call off your dogs. If you don't have the guts to take me on, say so, and I'll shoot your pecker off here and now and be done with it."

Tinker and several of the men got to their feet.

"They'll not jump you," Tinker said. Then to the men standing with Milo, "Stay out of it. Hear? If they fight it'll be fair—no gouging of the eyes, no biting. Fists and feet, that's it. I'll shoot the first man that noses in on either side."

"Sounds fair to me." Ben slammed his gun down into the holster.

"There ain't goin' to be no fight," Louis roared, his face fiery red and contorted. "I ain't payin' wages fer ya to stand 'round watchin' a hard-peckered rooster a fightin' fer a hen. Get to work."

Ben was suddenly out of patience with the senseless exchange. He ignored Louis. His eyes, glittering like sunshine on steel, were pinned to Milo.

"Just you and me, *horseshit*, unless you're scared."

All eyes were on Milo. He glanced at the faces of the men who stood with Tinker and knew that what Waller had said had set them against him. He still had his friends. He couldn't lose face in front of them. Every man in the cookhouse was waiting to see if he would accept the challenge. He outweighed Waller by thirty pounds and had the longest reach of any man in the camp. With the dirty tricks he knew, he should be able to whip him. Then the sonofabitch would pay for sticking his nose in where it didn't belong.

"I'm goin' ta bust ya up; I'm goin' ta stomp yore ass in the ground." Milo laughed harshly and headed for Ben.

"It'll take more than bragging to do it."

Ben backed out of the doorway and into the space in front of the cookhouse. It was now daylight. Milo came out, followed by Louis and the rest of the men. They quickly formed a loose circle.

Ben took off his vest and turned up his shirt sleeves, being careful not to reveal the bandage on his arm. While he worked at the buckle on his gunbelt, a fierce love of battle welled up inside of him. During his six years in prison, he had fought to stay alive; fought older, bigger and stronger men. He had learned to fight with his brain as well as his fists. He never underestimated an opponent and always avoided getting in close until he found out if he was up against a puncher or a grappler.

"Ya'll never work in the Bitterroot again," Louis snarled. His eyes blazed with a queer, leaping light and his teeth bared a little. "I'll see to it. We didn't pay ya wages to go sniffin' round a bitch in heat."

"Only a sorry piece of stinking horseshit would talk that way about his own sister," Ben said, his voice heavy with contempt. He took the few steps necessary to hand Tinker his vest and gunbelt, then turned to see Milo charging him with a bellow of rage.

Ben just had time to sidestep and swing a jarring right to the mouth that flattened Milo's lips against his big square teeth. The blow would have stopped a bigger man, but it merely slowed Milo. Roaring with anger, he swung a huge fist that caught Ben in the jaw. As Ben rolled with the punch, his foot lashed out, the heel of his boot connecting with Milo's shin.

Ben threw up an arm to weather the windmilling attack of arms and fist. A fist landed on his wounded arm and another on his chin. Pain shot through his arm like fire. He backed away. Milo lowered his head for another charge and Ben let him come on. Before Milo could land a blow, Ben's fist came at him with such force that his head snapped up and his body arched backward. Milo staggered, then planted his feet wide apart and became as rooted as an oak tree. Before Ben could back away, Milo's big fist thudded against his cheekbone, opening a gash.

Milo was bleeding from the nose and mouth. Ben moved around him, then came in low, hitting him so hard in the stomach with his head that Milo lost his balance and fell heavily to the ground, dragging Ben down with him. Gnashing teeth tried to grab at some part of Ben's face or neck. Milo's arms were locked around Ben's body. They rolled. Milo brought his head forward in short raps, striking Ben in the face. Blood spurted. Ben brought his knee up between Milo's legs, but without leverage the blow rendered only enough pain to cause Milo's arms to drop from around him. Agile as a cat, Ben sprang to his feet.

A rock-hard fist caught the slower-moving Milo in the mouth as he got to his feet. He staggered back, then plunged in to throw punches. Milo was a rough-and-tumble fighter. Ben had spring steel and rawhide in his rangy frame. He moved in and hit, but danced away from Milo's grappling arms.

Suddenly Milo grabbed Ben by his arm, his wounded arm, and slammed him against the wall of the cookhouse. Ben's head hit hard, then the ground flew up and hit him. Milo moved in to stomp his face with his heavy boots. Ben rolled and staggered to his feet. He blinked, shook his head to clear it.

The determination to survive that he'd known while in prison surged through him in full force. He'd not let this hunk of low-life beat him down. He ducked under Milo's swinging arm and lashed out with his fist. Milo caught the rock-hard fist in the mouth and reeled back. A tooth was sheared off. He backed off in surprise, and spit it out of his bloody mouth.

"Is this the best you can do, you stupid ox? Now I know why you only fight women." Ben taunted and waited. Blood flowed from the deep cut above his eye, from his gashed cheekbone, and from his nose, where Milo had battered him with his head.

Realizing that a front tooth was gone, Milo roared with rage and charged. Ben crouched and put all his strength behind the fist he sent into Milo's stomach. Milo's head came down as he grunted. A knee rose up to meet his chin; a fist hit him behind the ear. He went down on one knee. A boot heel caught him on the jaw, knocking his head to one side. He swayed, but didn't go down.

It was only during this brief breather that Ben heard the cheers from the men. He didn't know if they were for him or for Milo.

Milo was not finished. He quickly scooped up a handful of loose dirt and flipped it with a quick motion toward Ben's eyes. Ben shuttered his eyes just at the right time and took the dirt in his face. Almost babbling now with pain and insane rage, Milo rose and barreled toward his enemy. Ben stepped aside and with as much strength as he could summon, aimed a blow at the place he realized was Milo's weakest spot: the pit of his stomach. He heard the whoosh as the air was knocked out of him. Milo doubled up, grabbed his gut and fell heavily to his knees.

Ben was on him lightning fast. He grasped a handful of

Milo's hair and held the battered head erect. Then, holding him there, he slapped him until his face streamed with blood. The first slap was a backhanded blow across his mouth that split his lips and Ben's knuckles even more. The second blow, a hardened cupped palm, smacked him across the ear, stunning him.

"Now, you son of a bitch, you know how Dory felt when you were hitting her."

Showing no pity, Ben delivered blow after blow. They rocked Milo's head on his shoulders until it bobbed as loosely as a cork on a string. When his eyes glazed over, and wet began to seep through his duck britches, Ben stopped. He put his foot against Milo's chest and shoved hard. Milo toppled face down in the dirt. For a second or two Ben stood looking at him. Milo had wet his britches and from the smell of him, his bowels had let loose too. With his foot on his head, Ben pressed his face into the dirt.

"You filthy pile of horseshit, you sorry excuse for a man, this is where you belong, in your own filth, in the dirt, like a damned belly-crawling snake."

Ben staggered as he walked away. There was a period of taut silence while he scanned the faces of the men gathered to watch the fight. There were sly grins and furtive glances in Louis's direction. Ben understood that. Louis had the power to send them packing, and most of them needed the money they earned to support their families.

"Get the hell off this land!" Louis charged up to him, but was smart enough to back away when Ben raised his fist. "Ya ain't movin' in an' takin' over down there even if ya are sleepin' with that whore!"

Ben took a giant stride forward and hit him. As tired as he was, the force behind the blow sent Louis reeling back in surprise, his heels digging into the ground for purchase. When he righted himself, he put his hand to his mouth and brought away blood.

"That's a sample. You'll get a hell of a lot worse if I hear of you calling her that name again. And . . . I won't stop until I . . . gouge your eyes out."

The dead certainty in Ben's voice hit Louis like a blow between the eyes. The threat left him standing with his mouth open. He watched as Ben took his gunbelt from Tinker and strapped it around his hips. With his vest in his hand he went to the horse tank and doused his head in the water, lifted it, and doused it again.

Ben took his time leaving, and when he did, the crowd of silent men was still watching him. He mounted his horse, turned him toward the trail, and rode back toward the house.

From where Steven Marz viewed the fight, it seemed to him that the majority of the men were rather pleased—more than pleased, even elated—that Milo was getting the beating of his life. The sight also afforded Steven a great deal of satisfaction. What the man had done to Dory was unforgivable and had been the driving force in the decision he himself had made.

By the time the fight ended, Steven realized the camp was like a powder keg ready to explode. Unless Waller could talk some sense into James, he'd kill Milo over what he'd done to Dory.

It isn't going to work, George. Wishful thinking will not make it so.

He needed to plan a way to leave without having to explain why he was going. Louis would see to Milo, then make tracks for the high country to watch the men use the steam engine to reel logs to the flume.

He decided to make his move during the noonday meal

while the men were in the cookhouse. He was leaving sooner than he had expected, but there was nothing to be gained by waiting. He was glad that he had planned ahead. Fifteen or twenty minutes was all the time he needed to get his things together.

Steven walked leisurely back to his cabin.

CHAPTER
* 18 *

The hours after Dory learned that Ben had gone to the mill were the longest, most miserable of her life.

At first she was angry that he had not mentioned that he was going. Then she feared that he would not return. She, more than anyone, knew the odds against Ben's getting away from the mill without being hurt—possibly injured for life. Milo was not one to fight his battles alone when he could get help from his lackeys.

She had a sick, uneasy feeling in the pit of her stomach. Logging camp fights were vicious. She had seen men come away from them without teeth, an eye gouged out, ears bitten off, or an arm or leg left useless. Dory took a small measure of comfort from Wiley's words. *He ain't no slouch at takin' care a hisself.* The words stayed with her and she clung to them for reassurance.

Dory decided that Odette should know that Ben had gone to the mill. If something should happen to him, it wouldn't be such a shock to her. Odette read what Dory had written and stood looking at it for a moment before she lifted sorrowful eyes from the page.

"Papa will be careful. Don't worry," she said, although

her eyes had filled with tears. "He will be careful," she said again slowly, as if to reassure herself.

Dory moved a chair to the door so that she could see into the yard. Odette brought her cold, wet cloths to hold against her face in an effort to reduce the swelling. On the floor beside her, Jeanmarie played quietly with her doll. Odette mixed up a batch of bread and set it aside to rise. With Dory's written instructions she made a cobbler from a can of berries and put it in the oven. When that was done, she pulled a chair close to Dory, sat down, and reached for her hand.

Dory held Odette's hand tightly, needing physical contact with someone who loved Ben. The fragile girl with the enormous blue eyes had become very dear to her; she was like a sister, a cherished friend, and far wiser than anyone would suspect.

The morning wore on. The shadows of the trees receded as the sun rose higher in the sky. Neither Odette nor Dory wanted to talk as they watched and waited.

Dory was not sure when she first realized that Ben's horse was in the corral and that Wiley was no longer sitting on the box beside the bunkhouse door. She got to her feet, her heart racing and making her short of breath.

"Dory— What is it?" Odette stood, her eyes questioning.

Dory grabbed the tablet. "Ben's horse?" she said, as she wrote the words.

Odette's eyes followed Dory's pointed finger. "Ranger. Papa's horse."

He had circled the homestead and had come in on the other side of the barn. He didn't want us to see him!

Dory stood only a minute trying to fight the feeling of despair that threatened to swamp her. A soft sound from Odette galvanized her into action. She gave Odette a gentle push toward the door, grabbed Jeanmarie's hand and pulled her out onto the porch. They hurried across the yard to the bunkhouse.

All of Dory's senses willed that Ben be all right.

The instant she opened the door she saw him. He was bare to the waist and lying on the bunk with a wet towel over his face. Before the three of them could get inside, he had swung his feet over the side and was sitting on the edge of the bunk. He had been in a fight, a vicious fight. His face was bruised, swollen and cut. The stitches Odette had put in his arm had broken loose and the wound oozed blood. Ben's knuckles and the backs of his hands were torn and bleeding.

"Papa—" Odette went to him and knelt down.

"I'm all right, honey." He looked into her face to reassure her. "How did you know I was here?" he asked, looking up at Dory.

"Your horse . . . in the corral. You don't look all right."

"I've been in worse shape."

"You fought Milo?"

"Yes."

"And won?"

"He didn't get up."

"Good! I hope you knocked his teeth out."

"I did. A front one." He grinned in spite of his swollen lips.

"Now that we've seen you, you might as well come up to the house and let Odette patch you up."

"Good idee, Dory," Wiley said. "He's a needin' more stitches in that arm."

Dory tilted her head better to see Ben's battered, rugged, almost primitive-looking face, scarcely aware that Jeanmarie was holding tightly to her skirt, her big questioning eyes on Ben's face.

"You don't look so good." She tried not to grin; it hurt too much.

"At least I've got all my teeth." He wiggled his jaw and winced.

"You're going to have a black eye, maybe two of them."

"Yeah. You and I make quite a pair." His grin was lopsided and his eyes glittered devilishly.

A pair. Oh, Ben, Ben--

Dory took a deep breath that quivered her lips; her eyes softened and caressed his battered face. She had an urge to run her fingers over his rough cheeks and into his hair and press his head to her breast. Her eyes were lost in his intent gaze.

Ben watched the expressions flit across her face. She was proud and beautiful but, oh, so vulnerable. The thought that she had felt Milo's fist was gut-wrenching. He had an almost irresistible urge to bury his aching face in her skirt so that he could feel her all through him. He'd had the strange feeling when he'd left the mill that he was coming home, home to love and understanding and everything the word stood for. The world fell away for a moment as he and Dory looked at each other. But the moment had to end.

"Your poor hands," Odette said, with so much emotion he thought she would cry. She held one of his swollen hands in both of hers. "Broken?"

"No." Ben shook his head and wiggled his fingers.

"I'll kiss 'em and make 'em well." Jeanmarie moved between Ben's spread knees and bent to place her lips on his hand, then looked up at him with great blue eyes shining with love. Seconds piled on top of each other to make a minute before he was able to speak.

"Thank you, little . . . sweetheart." His throat was so clogged he could scarcely whisper. He put his arm around her and drew her close. Jeanmarie nestled against him, her cheek against his bare chest.

Ben could feel his heart beating against his sore ribs. He

remembered the many times he had dragged himself to his bunk after a battle and had lain there without as much as a word or touch from another human being. Here, with Odette, Dory, Jeanmarie and the old man, he felt as if he were with . . . his family.

"Where is that bloody shirt?" Dory said briskly, trying to keep the tremor from her voice. "We'll have to soak it in cold water before we wash it."

Ben sat quietly on a kitchen chair. Odette hovered over him and gently washed the cuts on his face and hands. After she bathed them, she dabbed them with a cloth soaked with witch hazel lotion. As soon as Odette moved away to empty the pan of bloody water, Jeanmarie went to Ben and leaned against his thigh. She reached up to touch his cheek.

"Odette make it better?"

"She sure did, curly-top."

"She's making berry pie."

"For dinner?"

"Uh-huh. Want to see my dolly's drawers?" She giggled behind her hand.

"Is she still wearing the same ones?"

"Uh-huh. Odette's gonna make more."

Dory wanted to cry when she realized how starved her child was for male attention and how sweet and patient Ben was with her.

Odette returned and made ready to restitch Ben's arm. Ben took Jeanmarie's hand and moved her to the other side of him.

"Stay by me, honey. Hold my hand. Odette's going to sew me up again."

Jeanmarie took Ben's hand. "Don't hurt him, Odette," she said in a commanding tone.

"I'll try not to, Baby." Odette tried to keep from laughing. "I think she likes you, Papa."

Working as if this were something she did every day, Odette made neat stitches to pull the wound together. After soaking a pad in Listerine, she wrapped a bandage around Ben's arm to hold the pad against the wound.

"This isn't the end of it, you know," Dory said, while Odette was repacking the medical box. "Louis may bring a crew of men down here to run you off."

"Don't worry about that. I'll go only if you and James tell me to go and not until then."

Dory's eyes traveled over his face and down to his bare chest, then back to lock with his. She saw tension there, but something else that she thought she had seen before. Could it possibly be that he yearned for some of the same things she yearned for? Love. Someone to call your own. Someone to share the joys and the sorrows of life.

"Why?" she asked softly. "Why are you taking this risk?"

Her words hung in the air between them. She watched the puzzled look come into his eyes. It was as if her unexpected words had thrown him off balance.

"It just seems to be the right thing to do," he answered simply.

"I don't want you staying here out of pity for me." She closed her eyes and shook her head from side to side. When she opened them he had moved closer to her and was looking down into her face.

"You want me to go?"

"Heavens, no! I'm afraid for you. For Odette."

"And I'm afraid for you. For Jeanmarie." The very softness of his voice caused her eyes to fill with tears.

"James will be so angry when he sees me. I don't know what he'll do."

"I'll talk to him. The two of you must decide if holding onto your shares in the company is worth all this."

They heard the sound of Wiley's crutch on the porch, then his voice.

"Rider comin' up from the south. I think I'll set me down here on the porch."

Ben went to the door. "Know him?"

"I can't be tellin' yet. Sits high in the saddle. I'm guessin' he's a stranger or he'd not be wearin' that big-brimmed hat."

Ben stepped out onto the porch and flexed his fingers, not sure how they would work if he had to use his gun. Behind him he could hear Dory telling Jeanmarie to be quiet.

The horse approaching was a long-legged dun moving in an easy, space-eating stride. The man riding him sat easy in the saddle as if he had spent half his life astride a horse. His hat was pulled low over his forehead, and he was wearing a canvas-colored duster. The rifle in the saddle scabbard had a shiny wooden stock and was within easy reach.

"He's a lawman," Ben said in a low voice.

"How ya be knowin' that?"

Ben didn't answer. The rider pulled the horse to a stop, tilted his hat back and wiped his brow with the sleeve of his coat.

"Howdy. It's a mite cooler up here, but not much. Mind if I water my horse?"

"Help yourself." Ben stepped off the porch.

The man touched a heel to the dun and moved him toward the watering trough, keeping his eyes on Ben as he dismounted and held the reins while his horse drank. He was a man with a rugged, weathered face who appeared taller when in the saddle. When the horse had had enough water, the man led him toward the porch.

"Tie him thar at the post an' come wet yore own whistle," Wiley called.

"Don't mind if I do. Name's Norm Kraus. You one of the Callahans?" He directed the question to Ben.

"Ben Waller." The man's eyes flicked to Ben's cut and swollen hands and nodded. "This is Wiley Potter," Ben said. "He can tell you what you want to know about the Callahans."

"Howdy." Kraus extended his hand to Wiley.

Wiley shook his hand. "Ya lookin' fer one of the Callahans?"

"Not especially."

Ben stepped into the kitchen and returned with the water bucket and the dipper. He held the bucket while the man drank. His eyes were sharp and assessing, and Ben had the distinct feeling that Kraus knew who he was. When Kraus finished, he dropped the dipper back into the pail.

"Much obliged."

When Ben returned with the water bucket, Dory motioned to him from the far corner of the room.

"Who is he?" she asked when he came to her.

"Says his name is Kraus. I think he's a lawman."

"Ben! No." Dory clutched his arm. "Will he arrest you?"

"He hasn't had time to hear about Sid. He's probably here looking for whoever is doing the killings."

"Will you tell him what happened . . . last night?"

"Yes. I'd rather he hear it from me. Shall I invite him to eat?"

"I don't want anyone to see me like this."

Ben took her hand in his. "You've nothing to be ashamed of. Milo is the one who should feel shame, not you."

"You're right." Dory lifted her head a little.

"It might not be such a bad idea for him to see what kind of a man Milo is. Before he leaves, he'll ask what happened to you. It's his job to find out things."

"You think we should ask him to eat?"

"It's mealtime. It's the custom. We don't want him to think we're hiding something."

"All right. Ben," she said when he dropped her hand and started to turn away. "I'm so glad you're here."

"So am I." He brushed the curls over her ear with his fingertips. "Don't worry. When James gets here, we'll figure out something." As his hand slid around and cupped her cheek, just for a moment Dory felt cherished.

"Dory?" Odette said as soon as Ben left them. "What did Papa say?"

Dory took the tablet and began to write. *He thinks the man is a lawman. He wants him to eat with us.*

"Papa likes you," Odette said, looking into Dory's face. "You like him?"

Yes, I do. Very much. Dory wrote on the tablet. *Do you mind?*

"No. I want us to stay with you and Baby and . . . James."

I wish it were possible. Oh, I wish it. Dory put her arm around Odette and hugged her, then wrote, *Let's get the meal ready.*

On the porch Wiley was talking to the stranger about the Callahan Lumber Company.

"George Callahan come to the Bitterroot more'n forty years ago. He'd lumberjacked some in Michigan an' I guess loggin' was in his blood. Good man, George. Give a man the shirt off'n his back if he needed it."

Kraus had removed his duster. He was a big-boned man, weighing about two hundred pounds, most of it in his chest and shoulders. His thick, sandy hair was neatly trimmed, as was his handlebar mustache. A big silver star was pinned to his vest. Ben congratulated himself on reading the man right.

"Loggin's a hell of a lot easier now than in George's time." Wiley paused to spit. "Waller, here, brought in the donkey engine and set it up. That bugger'll snake a log big around as a wagon wheel into a flume. Sure do wish old George had lived to see it."

"I've seen John Dolbeer's snorting donkey operate. It's a awesome sight to see a log six feet through and forty feet long come bounding through the woods, breaking off some trees as if they were twigs. The machine has been a boon to the logging industry." Kraus's sharp eyes honed on Ben. "Is that what brought you to the Bitterroot, Waller?"

"Partly. Miss Callahan asked me to invite you to the noon meal," Ben said, hoping to steer the conversation away from himself. "It will be ready soon."

"That's very kind of her." The marshal's eyes were sharp but cautious. Ben had the impression that they saw everything, read everything, and that the man was well aware of the discord among the Callahans. Could he know, too, that Ben was an ex-convict?

"Air ya here seein' about the murders of the whores?" Wiley asked.

"Among other things. The way I see it, the women killed were whores, but their murderer should be caught as well as one who murders a parson."

"Ain't had nothin' like it go on since I been here an' that's been a spell." Wiley leaned over the side of his chair to spit in the can.

"How long is that?"

"More'n thirty year."

"There's been a lot of new folks moving in, but you must know about all the old-timers."

"I do. The good 'uns as well as the bad 'uns." Wiley spit again.

"Hummm. How about you, Waller? You staying in the Bitterroot?"

"Maybe a few weeks."

"Where you from?"

"North of Spokane."

The door opened and Dory stepped out onto the porch. Her head up, her shoulders back, and she looked directly at the marshal.

"The noon meal is ready. Come in and wash up." She stepped forward and held out her hand to Marshal Kraus. "Marshal, I'm Dory Callahan. Welcome."

When Norm Kraus stood and looked at Dory, he blinked rapidly. Ben wanted to smile. Dory's composure, in spite of her battered face, shook the man.

"Thank you, ma'am," he said, as he took her hand.

Dory led the way into the kitchen. Odette was pulling pans of hot bread from the oven. Meat, swimming in brown gravy, was cooking in the heavy iron skillet. The room was filled with the delicious aroma of the freshly baked bread.

The cloth-covered table was set and fresh towels were at the washstand.

"Marshal, this is Odette Waller, Mr. Waller's daughter." Dory made the introduction.

"Howdy, miss."

"Happy to meet you, sir." Odette smiled.

"And this is my daughter, Jeanmarie. Honey, say hello to the marshal."

"Howdy, young miss."

"Hello. What's that?" Jeanmarie pointed to the star on his vest.

The marshal was taken aback for a minute. He looked at the tight short curls on the child's head and then at the mother. The child's curls were as red as a sunset, the mother's soft brown like the pelt of a young otter.

"It's my badge," he finally said.

Dory indicated the washbench. "After you wash, please

be seated. Come, I'll set you on your stool. I'll explain to you about the badge later."

Norm Kraus had a hearty German appetite. He ate large helpings of sauerkraut, boiled potatoes, venison and fresh bread. Odette waited on the table. She and Dory communicated by eye contact and hand signal even as Dory spoke the words aloud. Ben doubted the marshal was aware that Odette couldn't hear. He caught him looking first at his face then at Dory's, and knew that sooner or later he would ask the question.

The table conversation centered on the heavy winter snow and the flooding in the lowlands due to the runoff. Dory and Wiley were eager for news. Kraus was a good talker. He told them about the fire that had almost destroyed Idaho City, formerly called Bannock, and about the clashes between the Mormons and several other Christian denominations. He explained that a group of men were working on making Idaho one of the United States and the capital would be down in the Boise Basin.

"Wal, now. Wouldn't that jist be somethin'? Ideeho, a state with a gov'ner an' all." Wiley seemed pleased with the idea.

"It isn't going to happen right away," Kraus cautioned.

Ben was content to listen. He was having trouble eating because his jaws were sore, and he couldn't chew the venison. He noticed that Dory was having trouble too. She ate only potatoes and the soft part of the bread.

Odette set the cobbler on the table. The pie was golden brown with juice bubbling in the slits she had cut in the crust. She set a pitcher of cream beside it and looked up to see the admiration in Ben's eyes. She blushed prettily and winked.

"This is your favorite, Papa," she said, touching his shoulder. Then to Dory, "Sit still, I'll get the coffeepot."

Ben was proud of her. What had become of the shy, almost

speechless girl he had brought here? That she had blossomed was due to being with Dory. She even looked older, more woman than girl.

The meal ended. The men pushed back their chairs, went to the porch, and then walked out toward the barn.

CHAPTER

* 19 *

The marshal stopped to light a thin Mexican cigar.

"Which one of you wants to tell me what's been going on here?"

"Harrumpt!" The sound came from Wiley.

"What makes you think something has been going on?" Ben grinned a lopsided grin.

"I'm not blind. Someone tried to beat the hell out of that woman in there, and not long ago either."

"Last night. Any other woman that I know of would have stayed in bed. I don't think there's a bone in her body that doesn't ache."

"If it was you who did it, she gave you as good as she got," the marshal said drily.

"It sure as hell wasn't me. I have plenty of faults, but beating women isn't one of them. It was her half-brother, Milo Callahan."

"Why?"

"The bastard had a low-down skunk with him who wanted to . . . ah . . . use her," Ben told him angrily. "When she refused and stabbed the skunk with a fork, Milo beat her. He might have killed her if Wiley hadn't stepped in."

"*Verdammen!* Her own brother was going to let a man rape her?"

"Exactly."

"Where do you fit in all this?"

"Because a woman killer is on the loose, James Callahan and I have been taking turns spending the night at the homestead. Wiley watches during the day. Last night was my night to come down."

Ben told the marshal the events of the night before and that he had gone to the mill site this morning and had given Milo the beating he deserved.

"Can you prove what you say about the killing?"

"Talk to Steven Marz and a man named Tinker. They heard two shots fired. Sid shot me in the arm; I shot him in the head."

"I'll do that. I plan on riding on up to the mill."

"There's one more thing," Ben said, and glanced at Wiley. "I served six years in Washington Territorial prison. Another man confessed to the killing or I'd still be there. I don't go around talking about it because some folks think once a convicted murderer always a murderer."

"I know about that. I recognized the name Ben Waller. I was a young deputy at the time of your conviction and a marshal when you were freed. For what it's worth, more than a few lawmen thought you'd been railroaded."

"It would have been nice to have known that at the time," Ben said drily.

"Is Milo Callahan at the mill?"

"The last time I saw him he didn't appear to be in any shape to travel."

"What about the brother, Louis Callahan?"

"Mean and ugly. The only thing on his mind is how to clog the river and irritate Chip Malone."

"Who else is up there? How about the man who keeps the books? Is he there?"

"As far as I know."

"How long has he been working for Callahan?"

"I don't know. I've only been here a few weeks."

Later Ben was to remember that Wiley hadn't answered any of the marshal's questions.

"One more question. My aim is not to raise any hackles, and I'm half ashamed to ask the question after meeting the lady—but it's my job to find out as much as I can about people. I've been told that Miss Callahan is a prostitute."

"You want to know if she's a whore." The words came from hard-clamped jaws. Ben felt himself stiffening, his chest getting tight. The emotion rioting through him was not wholly concealed behind his usually noncommittal expression.

"Damnation!" Wiley snorted. "Them bastards has spread that stink 'round since Dory was knee-high to a pup. She had a young'un an' warn't married 'cause one of them cusses kilt her man. She ain't no more a whore than I am."

"A crazy man looking for whores to kill wouldn't know that. It's believed, and I was told several times, that Dory Callahan is a whore. You've got to admit that you don't see many bobbed-haired women in this part of the country that aren't in the business one way or another."

Ben stood on wide-planted legs, his gaze locked with that of the marshal. When he spoke, his angry words were ground out from between clenched teeth.

"What the hell has bobbed hair got to do with it? I'm telling you that she isn't that kind. She's a good, decent woman caught in a hell of a mess. Her two half-brothers hated her mother and for some ungodly reason hate her. They're determined to ruin her. They're the ones who've spread the stories about her."

"Nice family."

Ben snorted. "You don't know the half."

"The main reason I rode up here was to check out Miss Callahan." Marshal Kraus swung into the saddle and sat looking down at Wiley and Ben. "Now I want to see what kind of man tries to force his sister into degrading herself."

"I don't think he's too much to look at right now."

The marshal cracked a smile. "As far as I can find out, there's only a half-dozen women in the pleasurin' business left within a twenty-five-mile area. Until this killer is caught, I'd keep my eye on Miss Callahan."

"I intend to do just that."

Ben and Wiley watched the marshal ride away.

"Harrumpt!" Wiley snorted. "I ain't got much use fer lawmen."

"He seems to be a good, steady man doing his job."

"Wal, he ain't goin' ta catch no body ridin' round with that star on his chest askin' fool questions."

"I'd say he knows what he's doing. Wiley, I'd like you to keep what I said about being in prison under your hat. I'll tell Dory when the time is right."

"I ain't 'bout ta go blabbin' what ain't none a my business."

Two hours later James rode in on a lathered horse. Ben and Wiley were working on the tin chute that carried water from the well to the horse tank. Because Ben's hands were in such bad shape, Wiley was doing the work and Ben was telling him how.

"Hellfire! Here comes trouble, Ben. Hope ya can talk sense inta that boy."

James jumped off his horse and left the reins dragging.

"Where's Dory? By God, if that bastard's hurt her I'll kill

him." James stepped around his horse, stopped, and stared at Ben. "What the hell happened to you?"

"It's a long story. Come on into the bunkhouse and I'll tell you about it."

"I've got to see Dory."

"She's all right. There are things I want to tell you before you see her."

"Go on, son. I'll take care a yore horse." Wiley limped over and took the reins.

James didn't move. He stood as if his feet were planted in the ground.

"Odette? Did he hurt Odette?"

"No. She and Jeanmarie were upstairs. Dory got them out of the way."

"I'll beat the living hell out of that sonofabitch. I'll stomp his guts out!"

"I've already done it. Well, I didn't stomp his guts out, but you can bet your bottom dollar he knows he's been in a fight."

"I should have been here. I've done a piss-poor job taking care of her."

"Stop whipping yourself. What's done is done. Dory is worried you'll go off half-cocked and get yourself killed. How did you find out so fast? I didn't expect you until tonight."

"Tinker sent a man up to tell me as soon as they got back to the mill last night. I was up in the high timber and didn't get back to camp until about noon." James reluctantly followed Ben to the bunkhouse.

For the second time that afternoon, Ben related what had occurred the night before.

"You'd better know this, too. Louis blames Dory because she stabbed Sid. He drew back his fist to hit her. If he had, I'd a killed him. I came within an inch of it. Tinker stepped in and Louis backed off. He ordered me off the place—again.'' Ben's grin had no humor in it.

''He'll set the law on you for killing Sid.''

''That's been taken care of. The marshal rode in just before noon today. I explained, and he'll talk to Tinker.''

''I didn't know there was a marshal within a hundred miles. Is he the one McHenry sent for?''

''I expect so.''

''I'd like to have seen you beat the shit out of Milo. Why did you do it? It was my job.''

''Think a minute and you'll figure it out. Part of the men would have sided with you, part with Milo. They have to go out as a team and work together. If I've learned one thing about working a crew, it's that they don't work well together if they're at loggerheads with one another. It's too easy for accidents to happen.''

''Did many of the men side with Milo?''

''A few. Tinker kept them in line. I had counted on him doing that.''

''This blows the lid off. I'll never work a crew again for Callahan and Company.''

''A couple of your men have worked with a donkey engine before. I don't think they'll have any trouble if Milo and Louis leave them alone. It'll handle just so much pressure. Over that, it'll blow.''

''I don't care if the thing blows clear to hell.''

''I do. I don't want to see a man killed.''

''Shit! I should have taken Dory and got out of here years ago.''

''Dory told Louis that she was going to ask the judge to divide the company property in half, part for you and her and part for Louis and Milo. Louis got so angry he frothed at the mouth.''

"That would kill him. He lives to best Chip Malone. I've never figured out why it's so important to him. I wish it were possible to divide the company, but it isn't. One part can't make it without the other. The only thing we could do with our half would be sell to Malone. I don't give a damn about the company right now. I'm worried about Dory. I never thought either one of them would go so far as to . . . hit her."

Ben stood looking down at James's bent head. He was a good man. It was hard to believe that he and Dory were kin to Milo and Louis.

"I'm breaking my promise to Dory when I tell you this. What happened here last night has been coming on for a while. The night Odette took sick, Milo had been here. Dory fought him to keep him away from Odette. He slapped her. Hard. I was surprised you didn't notice her face. He has been hitting her for a year or two. She didn't want you to know. She was afraid you'd end up with a bullet in the back."

The eyes James raised to Ben's were remarkably like Jeanmarie's. They were filled with smoldering anger.

"He wanted Odette? The bastard! Why didn't you tell me? Why didn't Dory tell me what had been going on?"

"You were all she had . . . then. She was scared to death that she would lose you."

"Are you in love with my sister?"

"I don't know what being *in* love means. I like her a hell of a lot. Do you have any objections?"

"No." James stood, went to the window, and looked out. He was far more calm than Ben had expected him to be. "Chip Malone sent word that Marie had died. The funeral is tomorrow. I think he's hoping Dory will go and take Jeanmarie."

"She won't," Ben said. "You'll know why when you see her."

"Are you going to stay around for a while?"

"I should take my daughter and get the hell away from here, but I'm staying. I have money coming and my tools are still at the mill."

"Is that the only reason?"

"No. When I'm dealt a hand, I play it out. If you decide to take Dory and pull out of here, you'll never get a cent of your inheritance. If you stay, I'll stand with you. If you go, I'll help you as much as I can. I owe your sister a lot for what she's done for Odette."

"I'm obliged to you," James said quietly.

Ben stood by the window and watched James walk across the yard to the house.

"The boy's settlin' down," Wiley said from behind him. "I seen the time when he'd a gone tearin' up there and done somethin' foolhardy. He ain't never had no fear a nothin', even when he was a tyke. He's changed. He's scared a leavin' Dory all by her ownself."

"Maybe he's learned to use his head for thinking instead of ramming."

The cook's helper took warm water to Milo's room and cleaned the blood from Milo's battered face and hands while suffering the man's insults. When he finished, Milo demanded a looking glass and the boy took him one. When he saw himself with a missing front tooth, he threw the glass across the room, and obscenities of every description rolled from his swollen mouth.

Louis paced the room and swore. "Ya dumb head. If ya hadn't a took Sid down there, this wouldn't a happened."

"Ya was the one that hired Waller. Ya was so crazy to get that damn donkey." Milo's words were slurred. He kept running his tongue into the hole where his big front tooth had been.

"And ya was crazy to get in his girl's bloomers. Now, damn you, Steven'll go to old Kenton—"

"—Steven ain't goin' nowhere. I'll put the word out. He steps a foot outta this camp, I'll know it, and I'll break his scrawny neck."

"I can't be lollygaggin' 'round here all day. I got to get up to the cuttin' range."

"Go on. I ain't keepin' ya." Milo was sitting on the side of his bunk in a clean union suit. He had shed his soiled clothes as soon as he had come into the room. The humiliation of wetting and messing his drawers sat harder on him than the beating he'd taken from Waller. His ears still rang and his stomach was in a constant state of upheaval.

If he never did another thing in his life, he would get even with Ben Waller. *It didn't take Milo long to figure out how he was going to do it.*

Long before Norm Kraus reached the mill, he could hear the singing of the massive steel saw blades as they cut into the logs on the carriage. As he rode up to the mill, he saw smoke, thick and black against the blue sky, belching from the smokestack atop the building.

The machinery suddenly ground to a screeching halt and the quiet was absolute. The marshal removed his duster and flung it across his saddle. Then he tied his horse to a sapling at the edge of the clearing and walked to the sprawling sheds that were the mill.

A crew of men with pikes were working a log down the chute toward the carriage that would carry it to the blades. A short man with a heavy black beard, using a wrench, was turning a pipe on the steam engine that drove the spinning steel disks.

All eyes turned to the marshal. The big shiny star on his chest never failed to catch a man's attention. The men with the pikes stopped working. The black-bearded man straightened and wiped his hands on a greasy rag. He called a greeting.

"Howdy."

"Howdy." The marshal walked toward him. "You Milo Callahan?"

"No. Tinker Buck, head sawyer. You lookin' for Milo?"

"Him or the other Callahan."

"Louis went up to the high country this mornin'. I ain't seen Milo about. Must be back in his room."

"Where's that?"

"Ya can go through that shed to get to it"—he flung an arm to his right—"or there's an outside door on the north."

"Much obliged."

Norm Kraus retraced his steps to the outside, rounded the sheds and knocked on the only door that faced the north. He heard no answer and rapped again. After a decent time had elapsed, he opened the door.

His eyes swept the room. The first thing he noticed, after discovering that the room was vacant, was the stench. The room smelled like someone had used the chamberpot and left the lid off. One side of the room was fairly neat, clothes were hung on a peg above the bunk, the bedcovers were on the bed. The other side of the room looked like a boar's nest. Empty liquor bottles, spit cans and foul-smelling clothes littered the bed and the floor around it. On the wall facing the foot of the bed was a picture of a naked woman lying on a couch in a lewd position.

Kraus backed out of the room, closed the door and went back to the main building. As soon as he stepped through the door, the sawyer came to him.

"Wasn't Milo in any shape to talk?"

"There was no one there."

"The hell ya say." Tinker scratched his beard with a greasy

finger. "I'd swear he was there. I'd swear he'd not move from that bunk of his for a day or two after the beatin' he took this mornin'."

"You'd a lost if you'd a bet on it. He probably went off somewhere to lick his wounds. Where'll I find Marz?"

"Steve's usually in that little cubbyhole yonder where he keeps his ledger books. I noticed them gone this morning. I suspect he's working on them down at his place. He does that sometimes."

"Where's that?"

Tinker went to the door and pointed to the far side of the clearing. "That's Steve's place."

Kraus nodded his thanks, stepped out the door and walked toward the neat log cabin that was set back against a thick grove of Ponderosa pine. He rapped on the door, and rapped again when there was no answer. He waited a minute more, then looked into one of the two glass windows.

The room was well furnished, with heavy tables, a desk, a bookcase, and lamps with fancy painted shades. He went to the other window, shaded his eyes with his hand and looked in. This was the bedroom. The furnishings were equally fine. The poster bed was high off the floor; the wardrobe was rich walnut. A handsome dark-emerald-green carpet was on the floor.

"*Verdammen!*" Kraus muttered to himself. "You can tell a lot about a man by seeing the way he lives. This one's lived high on the hog for most of his life."

The marshal went back and tried the door. It was locked. He paused for a few minutes, carefully removed the pleased smile from his face, and went back to the mill. Tinker Buck was waiting for him outside the door.

"Wasn't Steven there?"

"No. His place is locked up tighter than a drum."

Tinker cocked his head to one side. "That's funny. Steven

seldom leaves the mill; and if he does, he lets me or cook know it. I'll go ask cook."

"I'll go along." On the way to the cookshack, he asked, "How long has Marz been here?"

"He was here when I hired on ten, twelve years ago."

"He's got a nice place down there."

"Yeah, he's a quiet one. Keeps to hisself, but that don't mean he ain't friendly."

"Big man, is he?"

"Naw. Doubt he could lick a pussycat."

Neither the cook nor his helper had seen Milo or Steven since shortly after sunrise. After the fight Milo had been helped to his room and Steven had gone back to his cabin. At the barn the wrangler said one of Milo's friends, a man named Rink, had come for Milo's horse, saddled it and led it around the corrals to the back of the mill.

When asked about Steven, the wrangler, a gray-haired man of undetermined age, refused to talk.

"I ain't seen him." The old man's eyes went to Tinker and away.

"You sure, Billy?"

Billy stuck his hand into his pocket and felt the silver dollar Steven had given him. Even without the dollar he would have turned a blind eye to Steve's leaving just because the man asked him to. Hell, there wasn't a man in this camp that had been more decent to him than Steven Marz.

"Is his horse here?" Kraus asked.

"Hell, I don't know. Go look."

"*Verdammen!* How'd I know which horse was his?"

"Dang-bustit, Billy, tell the marshal what he wants ta know," Tinker said impatiently. "That sonofabitchin' Milo has left camp. You know that he hates Steve's guts an' there ain't no tellin' what's on the bastard's mind."

"Ya think Milo'd lay fer him? Hell an' damnation, Tinker, Steve'd not have a chance, even with Milo all busted up like he is."

"Every man in this here camp knows Milo's been actin' crazy. He started up the donkey and pert nigh blowed it up. He messed with the engine in the mill an' buggered it. There ain't no tellin' what he'll do next."

"Well—" Billy stalled for a minute or two. Then his fear for Steven overcame his promise not to tell that Steven had left the mill site. "He came 'round through the woods an' in the back. He asked me to saddle his horse and not say nothin' to nobody 'bout his leavin' camp. He tied a satchel on his saddle and left."

"When was this?"

"Maybe half an hour ago. Everybody was in the cook-house, but me. I was aiming ta go after I went to the privy."

"Which way did he go?"

"Trail that goes west a ways, then branches up toward the cuttin' camp or down the mountain toward Spencer."

"That the only way to Spencer?"

"There's a way along the upper shelf, but Steven wouldn't go thataway. He'd have to cut back to cross the river."

"He'll be back in a day or two," Tinker said. "He never stays away long durin' the season."

"Was he on good terms with the Callahans?"

"It's accordin' to what ya mean by good terms. He puts up with 'em. Steve's a good man. There's not a man here, less'n it's Milo an' Louis, that don't like him even if he is a prissy, city-type feller," Tinker said. "He stays out of any trouble beween the Callahans. Got good business sense, an' Louis listens—sometimes. If not for him the mill would'a shut down a year after the old man died."

"Why don't the Callahans like him?"

"They don't like anybody that I know of. Not even each other."

"You can't tell about these quiet types. He might be running off with the money."

"Hell," Tinker snorted. "There ain't no money here. The mill just squeaks by."

"How are the men paid?"

"By the season. Season's just started."

"Guess that leaves you to tell me about the killing last night."

"I can do that an' tell ya 'bout the fight this mornin' too."

"I don't need to know about that. Ain't no law against fighting; just killing. Was it fair, or was it not?"

"It was fair."

"Good enough for me." Kraus turned to the wrangler. "One more thing. Did the man come for Milo Callahan's horse before Steven Marz left or afterwards?"

"After. Right after."

Deep in thought, the marshal went back to where he had tethered his horse and mounted deftly. He walked the horse a distance down the trail, then kicked him into a gallop.

CHAPTER
* 20 *

Steven had been called on to read a scripture over Sid Hanes before he was put in the ground. Out of respect for the dead, even a man as disliked as Sid, the crew with the exception of Milo and Louis had gathered at the gravesite.

Louis had left the camp shortly after Milo had been taken to his room. When Steven had seen him ride out, he had gone to his office and carried a couple of ledgers back to his cabin lest anyone wonder about his absence from the mill.

Now, Steven was reasonably sure he hadn't been seen leaving the camp by anyone other than Billy. After eighteen years it was hard to believe that he was finally leaving this place. He had become fond of Dory and James, and he was proud of the fact that he had not allowed that fondness to shade his judgment.

He wondered what had prompted him to sew the important documents into the lining of his coat. Was it a gut feeling that something could happen to him on the way to Coeur d'Alene? The company ledger sheets, his personal papers and a few treasures he couldn't part with, along with a change of clothing, were in the satchel tied to his saddle.

As Steven rode down the narrow trail he thought that

George and Jean Callahan would have been sick to their very souls if they had known what Milo had done to Dory; and if they had known the extent of Louis's hatred for anything related to Malone, even to despising Dory's child. More than likely one of the brothers had killed Mick Malone. Steven had known that he was standing at the center of a gathering storm since that day. Looking back, he knew he shouldn't have tarried. But how was he to know it would progress this far this fast?

The trail wound downward. These hills and the valley, Steven knew, comprised a vast listening gallery that most men never noticed. It was a place where a man might be closely watched by a dozen pairs of eyes. A tingling feeling came over him. Unease caused him to turn and scan his backtrail. He was unable to see very far because of the turns and twists of the trail in that heavily wooded area. At times he passed beneath locked branches that made a canopy overhead. There was a restlessness here in this shadowy place—an unnatural quiet that pervaded the very air.

Steven moved the horse a little faster and tried to shake off the jumpy feeling. The trail wound down for a mile or more beneath a shelf that hung over a basin thick with wildflowers. A scattering of spruce and foxtail had crept up to line the slope and trail.

It all happened so fast. A fox darted out from the brush and spooked his horse. As the shying animal sidestepped, Steven was struck a wicked blow on his back, then one on his arm. Only a second passed before he realized someone was shooting at him from the ledge above. He threw himself flat along the horse's neck just as another shot went through his thigh and along the shoulder of his mount. The animal squealed with fright, wheeled, almost throwing Steven off, and raced down the trail.

Searing pain tore through Steven. He grabbed wildly for the saddlehorn, clutching it with a desperate grip. As he heard the fourth shot, his hat was torn from his head. He slumped in the saddle, knowing he had to hold on or be thrown to the ground. The scent of blood set the roan wild. Steven twisted both hands in the horse's mane and held on through the roaring in his head and the threatening darkness.

There was silence except for the sound of the roan's hooves on the pine needles and the mount's labored breathing. He glimpsed the river and something moving on it. His befuddled mind heard a shout that faded, or was it an echo in his head? It seemed an eternity before the horse slowed, then stopped, its foam-covered sides heaving. Steven raised his head. He could see the river off to his left. Fighting to stay conscious, he relaxed his death grip on the horse's mane, kicked his feet from the stirrups, and slid to the ground. He crawled into the underbrush and collapsed.

It was still daylight when Steven fought his way back to consciousness. He lay in a nest of dried grass and pine needles. He was flat on his back. The sky overhead was blue and dotted with fluffy white clouds. Memory returned. Someone had tried to kill him. Four shots had been fired. Were they out there looking for him now? Afraid to move, he turned his head cautiously. He was lying half under a bush. His horse was cropping grass nearby.

Had someone watched him leave the mill and taken the rocky, treacherous shortcut down the mountain to overtake him, someone who had wanted to kill him? It could only be Milo. He was the more vicious of the two brothers. He might be worried that Steven was going to Judge Kenton to inquire about dividing the property. Other than Milo, he didn't know of anyone who disliked him enough to kill him.

Steven drifted in and out of consciousness. When he became alert, excruciating pain knifed through him. The best he could figure was that the bullet that had hit him in the back had gone in under his left shoulder blade. One had torn away the fleshy part of his upper right arm, one had skidded along his thigh bone. Luck had been with him. An inch or two either way and any one of the bullets would have killed him.

When he awoke again, it was twilight and a few stars were out. As the air cooled, he began to shiver. He rolled over carefully and pushed himself to a sitting position. The pain in his back and thigh was agonizing. With great effort he managed to focus his eyes. Blood soaked his clothes. His thoughts were hazy, but his mind told him that he had to leave this place or he would die here.

Because his throat was so dry, he had to try several times before he could whistle for his horse. Sound finally came. He whistled and waited. He whistled again. He could have cried with relief when he heard a soft nicker and the sound of the horse coming to him.

"Good girl. Good girl. You're the best damn horse in the world," he muttered when the horse loomed over him.

He held onto the stirrup and pulled himself to his knees. Then slowly and painfully he got to his feet. Pain like white fire shot through him; the world tilted and swayed. He hung his left arm around the horse's neck and leaned on him while his heart pounded and his mind accepted what he had to do. It seemed almost forever before he felt he had enough strength to try to get into the saddle.

Having to stand on his injured leg while he put his foot in the stirrup was so painful that he cried out. Clenching his teeth and using both hands on the saddlehorn, he pulled himself up, swung his leg over and eased himself onto the saddle. Exhausted, sick to his stomach from the effort and the pain, he sat there with his chin on his chest. His head felt as if it weighed a ton.

Where was he? Since instinct told him to follow the river, he urged the horse out onto an animal path that ran alongside. Small grunting sounds came from him as he rocked with the motion of the horse. What seemed like hours later, he waded the horse across a shallow creek that flowed into the river, and he knew he was not far from Spencer. He was shaking with pain, no longer conscious of the cool night air because fever burned through him. He hung limply in the saddle.

I'm dying and no one knows or cares.

When next he opened his eyes, the stars overhead were dancing and swaying. A serpent of fire surrounded his back, his chest and his arm. Blood had run down his leg and into his shoe.

His horse was walking slowly into Spencer.

Steven's head cleared momentarily. The town was dark except for the saloon at the end of the street. He turned the horse to walk behind the stores. Fighting to stay conscious, he pulled the horse to a stop behind the mercantile and sat there. He tried to move, and when he did, a haunting cry of agony tore from his throat.

The door opened and McHenry, carrying a lantern, stepped outside.

"Who be ye?"

Steven looked at him with tears rolling down his cheeks. "Help me," he whispered.

"Steve! Ah . . . mon. Whatever has happened to ye?" McHenry stuck his head in the door and called, "Mag, here." He set the lantern on the ground and was beside Steven in two strides. "Aye, ye're bleedin'. Air ye hurt bad?"

"I may be dying."

"Nay, nay. Can ye get off, mon?"

"I don't know."

" 'Tis no never mind. I be strong as a ox. Lean to me, mon."

"Wait," Steven whispered. "Papers in my coat lining. Hide them."

"What ye be sayin'? Ya. Sure I be doin' that."

"Someone wants me dead. Take them to Judge Kenton in Coeur d'Alene if I don't make it."

"Ye can be countin' on it."

Mag McHenry appeared beside them. "Who be it, McHenry?"

"It's Steven Marz. He be hurt bad."

Mag let out a keening cry. "Oh, poor mon. Bring him in, McHenry. Bring the poor mon in."

Steven tilted himself toward McHenry's waiting arms and slipped into merciful darkness.

McHenry was sitting beside him when he awakened. He was lying on a bed and he felt no pain. His eyelids seemed to weigh ten pounds each; it was such an effort to hold them open.

"I can't feel," he whispered.

"It be the potion Mag give ya to ease the pain while she tended ye."

"Am I hurt bad?"

"Aye, bad enough. Ye be most drained a blood an' need ta be drinkin' water, Mag say." He held a glass of water and poked the end of a dried reed in his mouth. "Suck it up."

Steven drank and closed his eyes wearily, then opened them.

"The papers?"

"Hid away like ye said. Yer horse be in the barn an' nobody know ye be here."

"Important. Get them to Judge Kenton."

"I be doin' it. Who shot ye, mon?"

''Someone on the upper trail.''

''The marshal I sent for is here. He rode out, but be comin' back. I'll be askin' him to see 'bout who shot ye.''

''No! God, no! Don't tell him. Please, McHenry. Don't tell the marshal. Don't tell anyone I'm here.'' Steven tried to rear up in bed. McHenry, with a deep worried frown on his face, gently held him down.

''If that's what ye want, mon.''

Steven closed his eyes and drifted into unconsciousness.

Ben didn't go to the house until the evening chores were done. He wanted to give James and Dory time alone together. When he did go in, he carried a pail of fresh milk and the eggs Wiley had gathered from the hen house. Odette was in the kitchen preparing supper, and Jeanmarie sat at the table drawing pictures on the tablet.

''Hello, Papa,'' Odette said.

''Hello, Papa,'' Jeanmarie echoed and scribbled on the paper, her tongue sticking out the corner of her mouth.

A soft expression of warmth and gentleness came over Ben's face. He could only marvel that he was not shocked by the child's greeting.

''What are you doing?'' Ben asked, looking over Jeanmarie's curly red head to the paper.

''Making a pussycat. See the whiskers?''

''Sure do. I see the ears too.''

Jeanmarie drew a long line that curled at the end. ''That's the tail.''

James came into the kitchen. ''I persuaded Dory to lie down for a while. She feels pretty bad about Marie Malone. I've been going through the desk in the study. Louis has taken everything out that amounts to anything.''

''What did you hope to find?''

''I don't know. I guess I'm just looking for anything that

will help us decide what to do." James sat at the table and stared at his clasped hands.

Ben sank down in a chair beside him and spoke in a low tone, not knowing how much the child would understand.

"It seems to me you have two choices. Go or stay. If you go, you'll have to leave your shares in the company behind unless you can get that judge to divide the property. If you stay, you've not only got to fight Milo and Louis, but to guard Dory against this crazy killer until he's caught."

"Dory doesn't want to go. She's more determined than ever to hold on to what Papa left us. She feels she would be turning her back on all that he worked for if she left it to Milo and Louis. Without Steven, they would have run it into the ground in no time at all."

"What do *you* want to do?"

"It isn't what I want to do, it's what I've *got* to do. I don't give a hoot and a holler about the company. I'm not working for the Callahan Lumber Company ever again. I've got to look after Dory until she's settled with a good man who will take care of her." James looked into Ben's eyes. "Why don't you marry her, for God's sake?"

"That wouldn't solve the problem. Even if she would have me, she still wouldn't want to leave here. It would be you and me against the other two; and before a month went by, one of them or both of us would be dead. Besides that, I don't think two people should marry unless they want to be together and build a family."

"Don't you want to be with her? You'll not find a better woman anywhere," he said, and his eyes dared Ben to contradict him.

"It's more complicated than that."

"Maybe you're believing what's been said about her." James's eyes turned frosty.

"Climb down off your high horse. You know that isn't so. I don't want her to agree to take me under these circumstances. Oh, hell. I want a woman to want *me*, love me. Can't you understand that?"

"I thought you said you didn't know anything about love."

"Damnation! My personal life isn't the problem."

"What the hell do you think we should do?"

"I'll tell you what works for me. In case of doubt—don't. I wouldn't do anything just yet. I think the two of us can find enough to do around here to keep us busy for a while. They say possession is nine-tenths of the law. If she wants her home, she'll have to stay in it."

"Louis doesn't care about this place."

"It'll irk him if he's kept out of it."

"He'll be as mad as a peed-on snake."

Both men looked up as Dory came into the room.

"I went to sleep. I haven't slept during the daytime for years." Some of the swelling had left her battered face and the bruises around her eyes and cheekbones had darkened. One side of her mouth was still so swollen that it looked as if she was poking her cheek out with her tongue.

"Sit down, Dory. Supper is ready." Odette carried a stack of plates to the table. "Papa, call Wiley."

Ben noticed how pretty Odette looked. Her face was rosy, her eyes bright. Her hair was tied back with a ribbon. He saw James looking at her often. The unease that skittered around in Ben's mind intensified when he saw the way Odette looked at James. He had never seen her gaze at anyone so openly. An expression of warmth and happiness shone on her face. *She's smitten with him.* Good Lord! He couldn't let much more time go by before he got the man aside and set him straight about a few things.

Jeanmarie chattered throughout the meal. Wiley, wise old

man that he was and realizing the others had plenty on their minds, filled in the voids.

James and Dory were quiet.

Ben looked up once and saw Dory's eyes glistening with tears. She quickly batted them away. *She's grieving for her lover's mother*. Ben was unaware of the frown the thought provoked. He didn't like to think of that long-ago boy being her lover.

As soon as the meal was over, Wiley picked up his shotgun and ambled off toward the bunkhouse.

"He doesn't go anywhere without that gun," Dory said. "He thinks Milo will try to kill him."

"I have a feeling that old wolf can take care of himself." Ben moved back from the table. Jeanmarie slid off her stool and climbed onto his lap.

"Oh, honey, don't. Ben's been hurt." Dory reached to lift her down.

Ben shifted the child higher onto his lap, moving her so that she didn't lean on his injured arm.

"You're not hurting me, are you, curly-top?"

Jeanmarie grinned up at her mother, snuggled closer to Ben and put her head on his chest. Her small hand moved up to rest against his neck.

"He likes me, Mama."

Dory's eyes flashed quickly to Ben's. They looked as if they were seeking something. Sadness sagged the corners of her mouth as she turned away.

Ben held the child and watched the women remove the empty bowls and plates from the table, wash the dishes and put the kitchen in order. He feasted his eyes on Dory's slim, neat figure. He knew she was hurting, but she kept her back straight and her head up. A wave of possessiveness came over him. Suddenly what he wanted was clear in his mind. He wanted Dory to be his. He wanted this child in his lap to be his. He wanted to belong to the two of them.

James was restless. He smoked several cigarettes, thumbed through a *Police Gazette*, and finally went outside.

Deep in thought, Ben was unaware that Jeanmarie was asleep until Dory came to him.

"I'll take her upstairs."

"I'll do it. You shouldn't lift her until your ribs have healed." He shifted the child to lie against his shoulder and followed Dory out of the kitchen and up the stairs.

To Dory's surprise, Ben stayed in the room while she undressed Jeanmarie, slipped the nightdress over her head, and tucked her in bed. From time to time she glanced at him. He leaned against the wall and watched her.

Dory began to wonder what kind of a lover he would be. Would he be gentle or would he pounce on her and demand his rights? If she were married to him, those hands, so generously sprinkled with fine black hair, would touch her in her most intimate places. He was looking at her, his head tilted to one side, his eyes as deep as the sea. Not a muscle twitched in his face, nor did a smile appear on his lips. Because he was looking at her so intently, the blood rushed to her face and she felt a bit giddy.

"We brought the mattress in from James's room so Odette could be in here with me and Jeanmarie." She had told him that before, but she said it again to break the silence.

When Ben didn't speak, Dory cleared her throat. It felt as dry as dust. She purposely kept her eyes on the wall beside his head. Just when she thought he would never move, he straightened and held out his hand. Dory looked at it stupidly at first, then put her hand in his.

He pulled her to him, put his arms around her and held her in a gentle, protective embrace. Leaning on him, she closed her eyes, feeling the beat of his life's blood, his breath on her upturned face. This was a moment she would keep in her heart forever.

Ben reached out and turned the lamp wick until there was only the barest light in the room.

"Will we bother the baby if we talk in here?"

"Nothing bothers her once she's sleeping."

He led her over to the mattress on the floor, sank down and pulled her down beside him. He sat with his back to the wall, his long legs stretched out in front of him, and, with his arm around her, drew her close. Dory laid her head on his shoulder with a sense of wonder that this was happening.

Was he only offering strength and comfort?

Had she come into his arms willingly or because he had fought for her?

CHAPTER
* 21 *

"I don't know where to begin," Ben said softly. "I'm not good with words."

Dory found his hand and gently rubbed her fingers over his bruised and broken knuckles.

"You did all right last night. Louis believed you."

"I meant every word I said to him. What I want to say to you is much more important."

"Then say it," she whispered fearfully.

"I want a family." The words came out shakily. He paused, and when he spoke again his voice was firm and full of purpose. "Tonight the baby called me papa. I want to be her papa. I want the two of you and Odette to be my family."

"Oh, Ben! I want that too." Dory felt as if she had been lifted out of a black pit.

"You must know some things about me before you agree to spend your life with me."

"Your past has nothing to do with now. If you're willing to take me and my child— Oh, Ben, I've hoped and prayed for a man like you."

"Wait, Dory. I want you to know about me before you

make a decision that will affect your life and mine for as long as we live."

"I've already made it. Nothing you will say will change my mind."

"I was thrust upon my aunt and uncle because there wasn't anyone else to take care of me," he began doggedly, ignoring what she had said.

"Oh . . . Ben." She hated the idea that he had been a lonely little boy.

"They had no children of their own, didn't even like them. I was ten years old before I realized that there were families that laughed together, cared for one another."

He told her about being sent to prison for murdering his uncle.

"How awful for a young boy."

"Honey, I might have been a boy in years, but by the time I went to that prison, I was a man and knew how to take care of myself. If I hadn't had to scratch and claw all my life, they would have broken me. You've no idea what goes on in those places."

"Thank God you got out!" Dory leaned back so that she could see his face. "I want to cry when I think of you there."

"After the first couple of years it wasn't so bad. In fact, the years with Tom Caffery, who was like a father to me, were the best of my life up to then. He's the one who taught me about the engines. When I met him, I could hardly read and write. He taught me to appreciate fine paintings and good books. He made me see that I was worth something, that other people would see me as I see myself. Now I know that I loved that old man. At the time I didn't know it. The last few years of his life he was in constant pain. I like to think that I partially repaid him for all he had done for me."

"You don't have to tell me any of this."

"I want to. We've got to level with each other."

Dory's heart soared. Utterly happy, she curled against him. He told about meeting the girl at the boardinghouse and about the letter he received thirteen years later.

"Odette was the surprise awaiting me. The woman swore that she was my daughter. At first I didn't believe it, but given Odette's age and birthdate it could be true. I decided I couldn't take the chance that she *wasn't* mine. She's been with me three years."

"She's a daughter you can be proud of."

"There is no way for me to know for sure if Odette is of my flesh and blood, but she is my daughter. She'll always be my daughter." It nagged at his mind that he should tell her of the possibility that Odette could be Milo's or Louis's daughter, but he couldn't bring himself to talk about it.

"Oh, Ben. You are a good man. A truly good man."

"Well, there it is. I'm no prize, but I'll take care of you and your daughter the best I can and I will never, never hurt you." His stroked her cheek tenderly with his fingertips.

The vow was made so sincerely that Dory wanted to cry. In this moment of closeness, with his arms around her, she wanted to tell him that a miracle had happened. All her life she had longed to belong to someone whole-heartedly and to have him hold her as if she were something precious.

"Are you asking me to marry you?" she whispered. She tipped her head and touched his neck with her lips.

"I'm asking you to think about it. Give yourself a little time to think about what I've told you."

"I don't have to think about it. I've waited for you all my life."

"I want no part of the Callahan Lumber Company. You

can give your shares to James. We'll take Odette and Jeanmarie and start up over near Spokane or go south to Boise. I've got money put back to start a small business."

"You don't want to stay here?"

Dory's happiness began to fade. Did he want to take her where people wouldn't know she'd had a child out of wedlock?

"If I stayed, I'd end up killing one or both of your half-brothers. It could land me back in prison."

"What about James?"

"He'll no longer be responsible for you. He can do as he pleases."

Dory felt tears building behind her closed lids. How could she go from here and leave James? Yet, she loved this man with all her heart and soul.

"Ben, you haven't said you . . . cared for me. I won't marry just to have someone take care of me."

He tilted her chin with a gentle finger.

"I like you more than any woman I've ever met. I've never even thought about spending my life with one woman until now. I want to live with you, take care of you, grow old with you. I want to sleep with you in my arms every night for the rest of my life. I want to see your belly swell with my child—a son or daughter with a mop of curly hair. I want you for my wife."

He hadn't said the love words she wanted to hear. She tried not to be disappointed.

"Thank you for telling me," she whispered.

"I want to kiss you, but I don't dare. I'm afraid I'll hurt you."

"Your lips are as sore as mine. I'd hurt you too."

He wrapped her in his arms with gentle strength and nuzzled his face in her hair.

"I need to know if you care for me," he whispered with a nervous catch in his voice.

"I love you," she said simply. "I'd not even consider marrying you if I didn't love you. I knew when you came here that you were a man I could love. That's why I was so afraid you wouldn't stay."

Ben was awed. No one had ever said those words to him before. He sat there, holding her gently, rubbing her back, and he knew that this was where he belonged: here with her.

"Mama and Papa loved each other," she said dreamily. "They seemed to know each other's thoughts. When she died, the light went out of his life."

Ben cupped the back of her head with his hand and let his fingers slide up into the thick curls. He had not known how sweet it would be to hold her. Through the layers of clothing, his and hers, he felt her soft breasts, her hip tight against his, and a current of passion flowed through him, hardening his groin.

Would Dory be shocked if her hand dropped to his lap? Or would she enjoy that part of their life together? Dear God, he hoped so. The only woman he had ever been with who had wanted *him* was Odette's mother long ago. The others had wanted the coins he placed on the table.

Dory was experiencing a heady feeling of pleasure in being held in Ben's arms. She refused to think about anything but the present. He loved her even if he couldn't say the words. She would wrap him in her love so that he would never be lonely again.

"You're a sweet woman, Dory." His voice came softly again. She could feel his face in her hair.

"You don't mind my bobbed hair?"

"I like it. There'd not be much danger over a campfire or of being hung up in a briar patch." She felt the silent chuckles against the cheek pressed to his chest and heard the steady thrum of his heart.

"Jeanmarie loves you and Odette. Thank you for being so patient with her."

"You don't have to thank me for that. I like the little tyke. I'm thinking you were like that when you were her age."

"I had a mama and a papa."

"She'll have a papa."

Dory felt a peace like the calm following a vicious storm. She wanted to see his face and tilted her head. The silver-gray eyes looking down into hers were warm and caring. He moved his face until his lips could reach her mouth. The touch was feather light. Dory felt as if she were drunk with happiness.

"Ben, I don't care what you've been." Her voice was choked with emotion. "What you are now is what I love. And you wouldn't be, if you hadn't lived your life as you have so far. Do you understand what I mean?"

"Right now I'm having trouble understanding anything. It's hard to think clearly holding you like this." His hand stroked her arm, and where her hand rested against his side, she felt him tremble. "I picked a hell of a time to hold you. We're both sore from the banging we took. I keep wanting to touch like this"—his fingers stroked her breasts—"or kiss your lips—"

"—You can."

"I don't dare. I wouldn't want to stop." He pulled her up onto his lap, cuddled her against him. She lifted an arm to encircle his neck. "I'll be content with this . . . for now."

Odette lingered in the kitchen when Ben didn't immediately come back after carrying Jeanmarie upstairs. She sat down at the table and opened the book James had given her to read, but she couldn't keep her mind on the written word. Her eyes kept going to the door. She wished with all her heart that he would come back in while she was here alone.

With her head bent over the book, she stared at the page and relived every minute she had spent with him, what he had said, the touch of his hand, the warm look in his eyes. She had thought he liked her, but since she had recovered from her illness, he had been distant. At times he ignored her.

Glory! A man like James wouldn't want a girl who couldn't hear. He would want a pretty girl, a girl he could talk to in the dark, one who didn't have to see his lips to know what he was saying. Misery washed over her. She had been foolish to dream that someday he would come to her, take her in his arms and tell her he loved her.

She looked up and he was there . . . looking at her. Her face turned fiery red. *Had she said aloud the words she had been thinking?* She jumped to her feet to flee. He was across the room in two bounds and took her hand before she could reach the door. Gently, he turned her face up to his so that she could see his lips when he spoke.

"Odette! Are you afraid of me?" He spoke slowly, but anxiously.

"No." She shook her head.

"Did Ben tell you to stay away from me?"

"No."

"Stay with me awhile. Please. Talk to me. Tell me about yourself."

Odette studied his lips carefully. He had such a beautiful mouth, and the way his lips formed the words made him easier than most to understand.

"I lived with my mama till she died," she said after they had sat down. "Papa came and here I am."

"Where did you live?"

"Seattle."

"I've been there."

"See ships?"

"I went to Victoria on one."

Odette smiled. "Me too."

James picked up the book. "You like it?"

"Very much. Baby don't." She shook her head and laughed.

James couldn't take his eyes off her. She was so pretty and fresh and sweet, and when she laughed, her eyes were like stars. He reached out and took her hand again. They gazed at each other; he at her incredible blue eyes and soft mouth made for kisses, she at his handsome face and dark auburn hair.

"Odette, has anyone ever kissed you?" The words came out before he could bite them back. He held his breath for fear they would frighten her away. Relief made him weak when she tilted her head, looked into his eyes, and seemed to be thinking of how to answer his question.

"Mama did."

"I mean a man. Have you been kissed the way a man kisses a woman he likes?"

"No, James. No man liked me that way."

"I like you that way."

"You want to kiss me?"

"Only if you want me to."

Her lips parted and her breath came quickly. She closed her eyes and moved her face close to his.

James stood and pulled her to her feet. Her eyes flew open. His heart was galloping like a runaway horse.

"I might not get to do this but once, sweetheart. I want to do it right."

"Sweetheart?" she said, as if that was the only word she understood.

"Yes, sweetheart. I want you for my sweetheart."

A brilliant smile came over her face. "I want you for my sweetheart too."

James put his arms around her and pulled her to him. In all his life he had never felt anything as incredibly wonderful as this sweet, soft girl against him. It was more than a sexual feeling. He knew what that felt like. He had experienced that at different times. This was loving and giving and sharing, and he knew in his heart he would die to protect her. All these thoughts went through his head as he lowered it to her waiting lips.

His hungry mouth found hers waiting, and held it gently. It was so warm, so soft, and she gave of herself so freely, that logic fled his mind. He held her and kissed her with fierce possessiveness. When he broke away, she gasped for breath and clung to him as if to melt into his hard body. She breathed in the scent of him and savored the taste of him. There was a strange sense of rightness being here in his arms, as if it were where she was meant to be.

"Sweetheart, sweetheart—" he murmured thickly. His mouth parted over her lips, his breath cool as mint, his cheeks pleasantly rough on her face.

This is what it means to be kissed by a man you love, Odette thought. The taste of him, the feel of him is wonderful. His tongue circled her lips, coaxing them to open, then darted inside. Her skin tingled. Every tiny hair on her body seemed to stand at attention. She wanted it to go on and on. When James moved, she was disappointed. His hands moved to her upper arms and his mouth was no longer on hers. He turned so that the lamplight shone on his face.

"I love you. I want to marry you."

Odette was in such a daze she couldn't think, but something deep within her stirred. She shook her head.

"You don't want me, James. I can't hear."

"I don't care about that."

"Maybe not now. But later."

"Honey, I love you. I want you to be my mate for life. We'll make our own family—have babies."

"I won't hear our baby cry." Tears filled her eyes, making them sparkle like diamonds.

"You can see him cry."

"I talk funny."

"No. There's nothing wrong with the way you talk."

"A girl said so. Said I talked bad."

"She was jealous 'cause you're so pretty."

"They call me . . . dummy." Tears rolled down her cheeks and he sipped at them with his lips.

"You're smart and sweet and wonderful. Sweetheart, I love you the way you are."

"I love you, James. You make me happy."

"Darling girl. This is new to you, I know. We'll go slow. Let's keep this to ourselves for a while. Don't tell Ben. Don't tell Dory."

"Why, James?"

"Because I want to talk to Ben first."

"I'll tell no one. You sure you want me?"

"I was never more sure of anything in my life."

He tilted his head, then spoke to her without sound.

"Ben and Dory are coming down. I'll leave you, sweetheart, but I'll take this with me." He placed a quick kiss on her forehead and went out the door.

CHAPTER
* 22 *

One thing was certain. Dory, with her bruised and swollen face, could not attend the burial service for Marie Malone.

She and James had talked it over and decided the decent thing to do would be for him to go instead. He would simply tell Chip Malone that Dory wanted to come but was unable to. She sent a pink rosette made from a satin ribbon Jeanmarie had worn on her bonnet the first time Marie had seen her. James was to lay it on the grave, a token from Marie's granddaughter.

During the early morning hours the sister and brother had labored over a letter to Judge Kenton. They thought it better not to involve Steven in their plan to ask the judge about dividing the property. Milo and Louis were very capable of making his life miserable should they find out that he had advised them.

After the burial James would ride into Spencer and ask McHenry's son Howie to deliver the letter. They told of the events of the past few days and of the prior abuse Dory had endured. They stated that it was no longer possible for them to continue being in partnership with their half-brothers.

Howie McHenry was an eighteen-year-old replica of his

father and just as trustworthy. The journey to Coeur d'Alene and back would take most of three days—longer than James wanted to be away from the homestead.

A large crowd had gathered at the churchyard by the time James arrived. He tied his horse to the rail and went to stand in the back of the crowd. Chip, with his hat in his hand, stood at the foot of the grave while the preacher spoke of the good things Marie Malone had accomplished during her lifetime. He said a prayer, then led the group in singing the hymns, "Rock Of Ages" and "Shall We Gather at the River." When the voices died down, Chip threw a handful of dirt on top of the box. Then a crew of men with shovels quickly filled in the grave.

Almost the entire town of Spencer had come to pay their respects. Marie Malone had been well liked. She had wheedled Chip into building the schoolhouse and paying the teacher out of his own pocket. She had been responsible for the paint on the church and the bell in the tower and had helped to raise the money for the hymn books. The mourners filed past Chip, offering their condolences, then drifted to the wagons and buggies that lined the lane alongside the church.

James waited until Chip stood alone beside the grave before he approached him.

"I'm sorry about your wife, Chip." On impulse James held out his hand. Chip grasped it quickly and gripped it hard.

"Thanks for coming, James. Marie suffered greatly the last week or so. I'm thinking it was a blessed relief to her to get it over."

"Dory wanted to come, but couldn't. She sent this from Jeanmarie." James took the rosette from his pocket and placed it on the mound of dirt alongside a bouquet of wild crocus and one of buttercups.

"That was kind of her." The two men stood silently for a moment, both looking at the mound that covered the grave. When Chip raised his head, there was a look of bleakness in his eyes.

"Can you come out to the house, James?"

"No. I've got a few things to see to in Spencer and then I have to get on back."

"This is a busy time. Who's working your crew?"

"You wanting to hire him away from us?"

"No." Chip smiled. "I've got all the foremen I need unless you're looking for a job."

"I'm not looking."

"If you ever decide you want to get with a good outfit, let me know." Chip pulled two cigars out of the inside pocket of his coat and offered one to James. When James shook his head, Chip put one back, bit off the end of the other, and struck a match to it. "A few days ago a marshal was here asking questions."

"What kind of questions?"

"He asked about people in the area. Mainly he wanted to know how many whores were in the area. As far as he knows, four have been killed since the first of the year. A couple of Indian women have been found dead, but there is no way of knowing if they were whores."

"I suppose you told him he could find one at the Callahans," James's eyes turned ice cold. His voice was heavy with sarcasm.

"I told him nothing of the kind," Chip replied stiffly.

The words that formed on James's lips died between hard-clamped jaws. This was not the time or place to get into an argument.

"He's been to our place," James said, then added, "I didn't see him."

"I've been wondering about how safe Dory is out there by herself. As far as reputations go, undeserved as it is, she's considered one. Now don't get your hackles up. You know it as well as I do."

"Don't lose a minute's sleep over Dory. She's not out there alone. Old Wiley guards her like she was a gold nugget. Ben is there. We'll take care of her."

"She's always welcome to come stay at my place for a while. Rita, our housekeeper, is always there. The families of some of my men live nearby. There would be children for Jeanmarie to play with."

"How do I know she'd be safe there? Maybe you're the one going around killing the whores."

"Or you." Chip grinned, and James's answering smile lent a fleeting warmth to his features.

"If it's me, Clara at the Idaho Palace is safe. I'd see that nothing happened to her." Even to James the words sounded false and he wished he hadn't said them. Hell, he'd been with Clara one time and when it was over he couldn't get away from her fast enough.

Chip smiled again and put his hand on James's shoulder. They started walking toward the hitching rail.

"That marshal is nosy. He had a half-dozen wanted posters he wanted me to look at. Guess he's trying to rack up some bounty money while he's here."

"See anyone you know?"

"Not even close."

"He's a piss-poor marshal if all he's doing is going around the country counting the whores and showing wanted posters."

"The murderer, whoever he is, is crazy, but crazy like a fox. He'll be hard to catch. I'm glad Waller is with you and Dory. I was hoping he'd take a shine to her." Chip's slow smile altered the stern cast of his face. "Milo and Louis would find that a bitter pill to swallow. I bet going up against Waller would be like bucking a whirlwind."

"Yeah. I guess he's got no quit a-tall when he's riled." He was tempted to tell Chip about the beating Ben had given Milo, but he knew it would bring up the question of *why*. He went to the rail, untied his horse and prepared to mount. "Be seein' you, Chip."

"Thanks again for coming, James. Tell Dory to take good care of my granddaughter."

For a moment James sat gravely looking at the man he had heard about all his life, but had never really known. Then finally he nodded and put his heels to his mount.

Chip watched James ride away and suddenly felt more lonely than he ever had in his life. When James was out of sight, he went slowly to his buggy. One phase of his life was over. The next phase looked bleak indeed.

James had plenty to think about as he rode toward Spencer. He didn't like Chip Malone very much and searched his mind for a reason. Chip was a fierce competitor. He would crowd the river if he could to get his logs to the big sawmills first and get the best price. Hell, he couldn't blame him for that. Chip had been a hell-raiser in his day; he had drunk, fought, gambled and been an all-around disappointment to his father. Chip was a rough, arrogant man who had expected his son, Mick, to be the same.

James's mother had said that down under all that rowdiness Chip Malone was a good man. Once he had married Marie he had seemed to settle down and had put all his energy into the business. That was why he had been so successful. It was said that he was a rich man. He paid his men well and they were fiercely loyal to him.

James kicked his horse into a lope and shoved Chip Malone

to the back of his mind. It was more pleasant to think about Odette. She occupied his thoughts a lot lately. For the life of him James couldn't understand why Ben was so against his courting her. Did he think he just wanted to get her in bed? He had to admit that it had crossed his mind. He was a male and his desires were as strong as any man's. The memory of her soft body against his caused a turgid swelling in his groin. She was so sweet, so fresh, so fragile. He'd be so gentle with her, so careful.

Hell, how could he say any of this to her father?

When he reached Spencer, the merchants who had attended the burial were reopening their doors for business. The warm sun had dried the streets that weeks earlier had been a quagmire. The sign of spring was evident on the porch of Bessie's restaurant. The sweet potato vine that had been growing from a pot in the front window during the past few months was on the porch, and woe to anyone who dared pluck a leaf from the vine. More than the usual number of people were on the street. Most had attended the funeral and had stopped to make a few purchases before heading home.

A hoop being rolled by a cotton-headed boy came toward James from out of a side street. It frightened his horse; the animal squealed and shied. The giggling youth grabbed the hoop and ducked out of sight behind a building.

James dismounted in front of the mercantile. He spoke to the men he knew, tipped his hat to a lady, and went inside the store. Several customers were lined up at the counter. While James waited to have a private word with McHenry, he looked at the goods piled on the tables and arranged on the shelves that lined the walls.

McHenry's, like most mercantiles in the Northwest, carried everything from garden spades and barbed wire to ribbons and silk underdrawers. One table held dress goods, another shoes and hats. On the ribbon and lace table James saw a small red-satin heart-shaped thing edged in white lace. It was stuffed to resemble a small pillow. On it the words *I love you* were embroidered in white. When James picked it up, the scent of roses wafted up to set his heart thumping. The scent was the same as the one he had smelled last night when he had held Odette in his arms.

"Howdy, James." McHenry had come up beside him.

"What's this?" James held out the small pillow.

"'Tis called a sachet. Womenfolk tuck them in their . . . uh . . . bosoms so they be smellin' sweet. Ye wantin' to buy it?"

"Yes," James growled, red faced. "And don't say a damn word. Hear?"

McHenry held his hands up. "I ain't sayin' nothin' 'bout it atall. But ye better set it down 'cause here comes Watt Bell an' he'd have aplenty to say. I be goin' ta see Mag fer a minute. Be right back and wrap it . . . fancy-like."

McHenry had seen James at the church and had been sure he would be in town before he headed back home. As soon as he got back to the store, he had gone in to speak to Steven. The man had been sleeping and Mag had refused to allow McHenry to awaken him. The burden of caring for Steven without anyone's knowing he was here lay heavy on McHenry. What would he do and how could he explain to the marshal if the man died?

Iris, McHenry's daughter, sat by the bedside. He had insisted on naming his daughters after flowers because, he said, they were the flowers of his heart. Iris looked up when her father entered.

"Is he still sleepin'?" he whispered.

"I'm not asleep," the weak voice answered from the bed.

"How be ye, mon?"

"As well as can be expected, I guess." Steven's eyes were feverish and his cheeks were sunken.

"James is in the store. Let me be bringin' him in."

Steven's eyes went to the girl, who had moved away from the bed, then back to McHenry.

McHenry nodded in answer to the silent question. "On the way. Early this mornin'."

Steven sighed and closed his eyes for a moment.

"Let James come in, but say nothing."

"Ya got my word, mon."

"I appreciate what you're doing. It might cause you a heap of trouble if I died on you. We'd better tell James."

"My Mag be as good at doctorin' as any I be seein'. She says ye got a chance. Ye hold on and stay awake. I be fetchin' James."

McHenry stood outside the door and allowed his shoulders to slump with relief. It was a burden he and his family were carrying, but one that he had taken on willingly. Steven Marz was a good man. He had helped McHenry straighten out his books more than once and would never take a penny for his trouble.

"McHenry, I need a word with you in private." James was leaning against the table that held the heavy duck britches when McHenry came into the story.

"What be on ye'er mind?"

"I'd like to hire Howie to take a letter to Coeur d'Alene."

" 'Tisn't possible, mon. Howie left this mornin' to take my list a needs ta be filled afore the freight wagons be headin' this way."

James chewed the inside of his cheek for a second. "Well, that's that."

"It's sorry I be, James. Howie left at daylight wantin' ta be in town afore nightfall."

"It's all right, McHenry. It's nothing that can't wait until I can make the trip myself."

"Now 'tis my turn ta talk ta ye, but let me see if me girls is takin' care of me trade."

James waited impatiently. He wanted to get down to the saloon and have a beer. If word of what had happened to Dory and the fight at the mill had gotten out, he would be sure to hear about it at the saloon. And he was anxious to be heading home to the golden-haired girl who now consumed his thoughts.

McHenry came back with a small wrapped package and handed it to James.

"How much?" James tucked the package inside his shirt.

"Five cents ta ye."

"How much to anyone else?"

"Three cents," McHenry said and grinned.

"Fine way to treat your friends," James grumbled and slapped the coin in his outstretched hand.

McHenry looked to see if anyone was watching them, then motioned James to the farthest corner of the store.

"Steven rode in last night. He be in bad shape. All shot up he is."

Stunned by the news, James took a second or two to absorb it.

"Godamighty! Who did it?"

"He wouldn't be knowin'. Was ambushed on the trail down by the river."

"Might be he was mistaken for someone else."

"Three shots hit. That be no mistake."

"Will he be all right?"

"One bullet into his arm, one his leg. My Mag dug the other outta his back. She thinks he'll be makin' it if fever don't take him."

"Where is he?"

"In the room yonder. My lassie be sittin' with him. There be more I need ta tell ye. Steve don't be wantin' anybody knowin' he's here. He fears the one who did it will come ta finish what he started and do harm ta the family while he's about it."

"The marshal you sent for is here. He should be told."

"No, laddie. Steve wants no marshal ta be knowin'. Made me swear, he did."

"Why, for God's sake?"

"I wouldn't be knowin' that. I respect the mon's wish. Nobody but my family be knowin' he's here."

"It's strange. Why was he coming to town? This is the busy time at the mill."

"Ye'll have ta be askin' him that."

With McHenry leading the way, they walked down a short passageway that divided the store from the family quarters. He opened a door and beckoned to his daughter to come out before James went in.

This didn't seem quite real to James. He had known Steven for most of his life but had not realized how small the man was. His slight body made only a small hump beneath the patchwork quilt that covered him. The whiskers on his cheeks were speckled with gray, and James realized the man was old enough to be his father. He eased himself down in the chair where Iris had been sitting.

"Steven?" He waited until the man opened his eyes. "What the hell happened to you?"

"James." Steven lifted a hand from the bed and let it fall back. His eyes were bright, but clear. "Hell of a note, isn't it?"

"Do you have any idea who did this?"

"I can only guess. Someone who thought I was going to inquire about dividing the property."

"That would have to be Milo or Louis. It's hard to believe they'd go that far."

"Greed causes men to do many things."

"Louis lives and breathes for the company, but I never figured him for a back-shooter. Milo, on the other hand, is crazy as a loon at times. I know Dory believes he killed Mick, but there's no proof."

"After Waller got through with Milo, he wasn't in very good shape. Course, he's got his bully-boys who would do anything he asked them to do for a dollar."

"It looks like Mag did a good job doctoring you. Hell, I'm sorry about this. Is there anything I can do?"

"Yes. Keep quiet about it for a while. Whoever shot me probably thinks I crawled off into the bushes and died. My horse spooked and took off. I don't know how I managed to stay in the saddle. I vaguely remember passing a raft on the river and hearing a shout. It's probably what kept the gunman from running me down and finishing the job."

"I'll say nothing if that's what you want. But don't you think the marshal should know about it?"

"Especially not him!"

During his waking moments Steven had thought of the marshal and the wanted posters he would be carrying. The dread of going to prison was worse than the death he was facing.

"Can you give me a reason why the marshal shouldn't be told? It's his job to know these things."

"Not now. Someday. I'm not wanted for murder or anything like that, if that's what you're thinking."

"I'm not thinking that at all. If you don't want him told, it's good enough for me. Christamighty. I hate going back home and leaving you here. But the way things are, I can't leave Dory to face Milo and Louis alone. Louis will be fit to be tied when he can't find you. He depends on you to keep things on an even keel at the mill."

"I've done all I can do—all George asked me to do." Steven closed his eyes wearily.

"Steven?" James said anxiously.

Steven opened his eyes. "I'm not ready to kick the bucket yet, James." There was a little humor in his eyes.

"I hope not." Relief was evident in James's voice. "Hell, I remember when you came to the homestead. Pa thought you were the smartest man he'd ever known."

"Smart doesn't always cut the mustard. It takes luck too. I'm lucky enough to have such good friends as you and the McHenrys." His voice sounded weary and James could see that he could scarcely keep his eyes open.

"I'm going now, but I'll be back soon."

When Steven didn't answer, James knew he was asleep and went quietly from the room. As he passed through the store, he spoke for a moment with McHenry, telling him that he would be back in a day or two.

There were only a few wagons and buggies left on the street when he reached it. He stood in front of the store for a moment before walking down the boardwalk toward the saloon. Had Louis's greed and desire to best Malone pushed him beyond reason, or had Milo's crazy mind invented a plan to get rid of Steven? James doubted the ambusher was Louis. Louis knew how valuable Steven was to the Callahan Lumber Company.

To James, coming in out of the bright sunshine, the Idaho Palace was quiet and cool and dim. He stood inside the doorway and allowed his eyes to scan the room. A group of card players occupied one table, two men drank beer at another. At the end of the bar, a man with a large star on his chest stood talking to the bartender. Tipping his hat to the back of his head, James went to the bar.

"Howdy, James." Mel drew a mug of beer from the keg and placed it on the bar. "Come in for the buryin'?"

"Yeah. Figured the Callahans ought to be represented."

"Biggest buryin' since I been here."

"Everyone liked Mrs. Malone."

"Have ya met the marshal?"

"Can't say as I have."

"Marshal, this here's James Callahan, the best all-round lumberjack in these parts."

The marshal was large in the shoulders and chest, but short in the legs. When he moved down the bar, he had to tilt his head to look at James.

"Kraus," the marshal said, and held out his hand. After shaking hands with James, he moved back a few steps and leaned an elbow on the bar.

James acknowledged the introduction with a handshake and a nod and picked up his beer.

"I stopped in at your place the other day. Your sister served me a good meal."

"Dory's a fine cook."

"Went up to the mill. Talked to a man named Tinker about the man Waller killed."

"From what I hear, he had it comin'."

"Wanted to talk to the other witness, but he wasn't there. Do you know where I can find him?"

"Who'er you talking about?"

"Steven Marz, the man who keeps the books at the mill."

"Steve gets tired of the racket at the mill and goes off for a day or two. He never stays away long. Is there any doubt that Waller was justified in shooting Hanes?"

"No. But for the report, I should have statements from two witnesses."

"Well, stick around a while and Steven will show up."

"I intend to."

James set his empty mug on the bar. "Got to be goin'. Nice meetin' you, marshal. See you later, Mel."

James didn't breathe deeply until he was out of town and on his way home. He felt a restless stirring and knew that something unpleasant was about to happen. He was uneasy about the marshal. He sensed the man was here for a reason more important to him than catching the man responsible for the murders.

CHAPTER

* 23 *

There was much to mark this morning as different from other mornings. It was light, but the sun was not yet up when Ben came into the kitchen with an armload of stove wood.

"James is on his way?"

"He wanted to get an early start." Dory looked at Ben, reveling in the wondrous new feeling of belonging to him and knowing that he was hers.

Ben dropped the wood in the wood box, came to her and put his arm around her.

"How do you feel this morning?"

"Much better. And you?" Dory felt light-headed and foolish and happy.

"I'm fine. Let me see your face." His eyes were warm and shining and looked long and deliberately at her bruised face. "The swelling is almost gone." He dropped a quick kiss on her lips and then another that lingered. His sparkling eyes teased her. "That was worth waiting for."

"You're in fine fettle this morning," she said in a breathless whisper.

"I slept like a log last night. It's a good thing James was

sleeping in here. I'd not have heard an army storming the house."

"It was all that exercise you got up at the mill."

"That wasn't it and you know it." Amused smile lines fanned out from the corners of his eyes, and the creases deepened on each side of his mouth. "When I left you last night, I felt like I could lick my weight in wildcats if you were there waiting for me."

She looked into his silver-gray eyes and bracketed his cheeks with her palms.

"I love you. I'll always be waiting for you. There's no problem we can't work out if we're together."

"Dory, Dory, why didn't I come here sooner?"

"When are you going to tell Odette?"

"Now. We'll tell her together. How about James?"

"He knows that something wonderful has happened to me. I couldn't keep the smile off my face."

When they told Odette, she was delighted. She hugged Ben, then Dory. Jeanmarie, her nightdress dragging the floor, came in rubbing sleep from her eyes. Odette scooped her up in her arms and danced around the room.

"Will Baby be my sister?"

"Your stepsister." Dory spoke slowly. When Odette beetled her brows, a sign that she didn't understand, Dory wrote it on the tablet.

"I don't like *step*. Sister!"

Ben and Dory laughed. She reached for his hand. It was a natural, unconscious gesture—and it felt so wonderful to be free to touch him. Although she hadn't tried to explain their new situation to Jeanmarie, the child seemed to know. She went from Odette's arms to Ben's and wound her small arms around his neck.

"Odette's papa. Jeanmarie's papa."

An emotion flooded Ben's heart like none he had felt before. He hugged the child tightly to him and kissed her soft cheek. His eyes met Dory's, and he silently vowed that he would love and protect them for as long as he lived. *Love.* He was looking into Dory's green glistening eyes when the word popped into his mind. *He loved her! He loved them!* Love was a new word for him. But, by God, he loved her!

Ben wanted to set the child down, go to Dory and tell her, but the little arms were wound tightly around his neck. As if knowing he wanted her close, Dory moved over beside him. He put his arm around her and pulled her tightly to him. Over her head he spoke silently to Odette, who watched with large questioning eyes. *Come here, sweetheart.*

With his arms around the two women and the child, Ben felt as if he had the entire universe in his arms. Right here was everything he had ever hoped to have. This woman would be the hub around which his life would revolve. He lowered his face into her short tight curls, breathed deeply the clean, sweet smell, and promised to do everything in his power to keep her safe and happy. He wanted her never to regret her decision to give herself to him.

Finally Odette moved away and Jeanmarie wiggled to be let down. Ben held Dory to him for a little longer, reluctant to lose the joy of holding her.

Odette dressed Jeanmarie while Dory cooked breakfast. Her hand shook as she poured water into the cornmeal. She couldn't prevent her eyes from seeking Ben. When she caught him watching her with tender amusement, he smiled. The thrill of that smile reached all the way to her toes, and her heart leaped with joy.

It was the same throughout the morning as they went about the chores of everyday living. Ben filled the wood box and chopped a supply of kindling. He set the iron wash pot up in the yard, filled it with water and built a fire under it. Dory gathered the clothes to be washed while Odette churned and amused Jeanmarie.

When Ben was near Dory, their eyes caught and clung as if they shared a glorious secret. It seemed to her that nothing could happen to dampen her spirits. But something did.

Louis arrived at mid-morning. Dory was at the washtubs on the porch. She saw him the instant he came out of the woods and toward the house. Odette, in the yard poking at the clothes in the boiling water with a long stick, was unaware of him until he rode past her on a sweaty horse. Her frightened eyes searched for her father. With relief she saw him come out of the barn and toward the house.

Dismounting and leaving his horse loose to wander to the watering trough, Louis came to the porch. He had an ugly scowl on his face.

"Where in the goddamn hell is that damn James?" he demanded. "Is he here?"

"Hello, Louis. Nice morning." Dory continued to rub the neck of Wiley's shirt against the scrub board.

"Goddammit! I asked you a question. I want an answer. Where's James?"

"He's not here."

"He ain't at the camp. Ain't been there fer a couple a days."

"He isn't here," Dory said calmly.

"Damn you! You know where he's at. He don't take a piss without tellin' you. He left them men on their own ta get them logs to the river an' most of 'em don't know shit 'bout that engine."

"You'll have to discuss that with James." Dory twisted the water out of the shirt and dropped it in the rinse water.

"Is that goddamn Waller still here? Or did you take in that dummy of his?"

"What I do in my own house is my business."

"Yore house! Yore house! Why you . . . you—"

"If you say it, I'll do my best to knock every tooth out of your head."

Hearing Ben's voice behind him, Louis spun around. "I told ya to get off Callahan land. I ain't tellin' ya again."

"I told him to stay."

Louis turned back to Dory and shouted, "I ain't talkin' to ya, so keep your mouth shut."

"But I'm talking to you," Ben said. "I'm staying until James and Dory tell me to leave. Even if they did that, I'd still stay until I got the money coming to me."

"Ya didn't finish the job."

"I did what I said I'd do."

"Ya caused more trouble than it was worth. I wish I'd never heard of the goddamn machine."

"I'm glad you did." Ben's eyes flashed a secret message to Dory.

"Where'd James go to?" Louis demanded in his loud voice. "I can't be runnin' both places. I got to get to the mill."

"Why can't you run both places? You've been interfering at the cutting camp for years." Dory's tone of voice showed her contempt.

"Keep outta this! Ya done already gone an' got a man killed!"

"A worthless no-good little weasel who was going to rape me!" Dory's aroused voice overrode that of her half-brother, who was spitting and sputtering with rage. "And look what happened to me because I resisted."

"Rape? Ha! Ya wanted it! It's what ya get fer swishin' yore tail an' gettin' a man stirred up."

"You stupid lout! I don't know what holds your ears apart. It sure isn't brains."

Louis looked at Dory with a face distorted with pure hatred. His eyes were wild.

"Ya got what ya had comin'. If we'd done our duty an' whipped ya in line long ago ya might not a turned out like ya done."

"If either of you lift a hand to me again, I'll blow your head off." Dory's expression said that she meant every word.

Louis was so angry that spittle came from the corner of his mouth. He stood first on one foot and then on the other.

"Yore just like *her*! Ya ain't nothin' but a . . . slut!"

Ben hit him.

He had kept out of things up to now. He landed two blows before Louis fell: a tight fist to his stomach and an uppercut to his chin. Louis reeled back a step or two, then hit the ground like a fallen timber and sat there with a look of disbelief on his face. The only sound above his labored gasps for breath was Jeanmarie's tinkling childish laughter, which stopped when she darted behind her mother's skirts.

With more patience than he realized he possessed, and in spite of the storm of anger that flowed through him, Ben waited for Louis to get up. He had hit him mainly because of what he had called Dory, but also because he didn't like him or his attitude. He was glad Louis had given him the excuse.

"Be careful how you talk to my *wife* or about her from now on," Ben said, his voice icy cold, his eyes iron hard.

Almost choking on his fury and keeping his eyes on Ben, Louis rolled to his knees, then stood and backed away. He rocked on unsteady legs, holding his belly. His mouth worked and his chin quivered.

"I thought as much. Ya want it all, just like *her*," Louis hissed, his small bright eyes fixed on Dory with an icy glare that reminded her of a poisonous viper. With a jerky stride he went to his horse and mounted, then yanked on the reins cruelly. The animal squealed in protest, then dug in its hooves and took off toward the mill.

"There's a few things I wish I'd said to that mule-brained, stupid, block-headed jackass. He's rotten buzzard bait and a pissant to boot!" Dory sputtered.

Ben stepped up onto the porch, a teasing sparkle in his eyes. "Honey, I think you've said everything that needed to be said."

"By jinks damn! He makes me so mad! He's always comparing me to my mother. He hated her, so he hates me. I'm glad you hit him. I wanted to hit him myself."

"You're like a feisty little rooster when you get riled up. I'm going to have to watch my step."

"Men like Louis and Milo think women are nothing but dumb heifers to breed and take their pleasure on."

"Cool off, sweetheart."

"Oh, Ben." Dory dried her hands on her apron. "Are you sure you want a bobbed-haired wife who shoots off her mouth like a drunken river pig?"

"I'm planning on getting me a big old hickory switch and putting it over the door. I'll use it when my wife calls me a mule-brained stupid jackass."

"Oh, you!" Dory's arms went around his waist. Her insides warmed with pleasure when his arms tightened around her and a delicious joy invaded her innermost being as it did each time she was close to him.

"I like your spunk," he said close to her ear. "I'm proud of the way you stood up to him." He pressed his lips to the curve of her neck. The warm moist lips traced a line to her jaw. Love and tenderness welled within her. Aware, but not caring, that Odette and Jeanmarie were watching, they stood quietly as if to absorb the feel of each other. When Ben pulled back he lifted her chin with a forefinger.

"I'm helping Wiley put a rim around a wagon wheel, but I'll keep an eye out."

"I know. We should know in a few days what's best to do. James thought it would take about three days for Howie McHenry to get to Judge Kenton and back."

Before it was time for the noon meal, the clothes were drying on the rope line that had been strung from the porch post to the windmill and back to the corner of the house. The tubs, except for the one containing the soapy water to be used to scrub the kitchen floor, were emptied and hung on the nails on the porch.

Odette had been unusually quiet and Dory wondered if she were uncomfortable with the display of affection between her and Ben. As one side of her mouth was still swollen and it was hard for Odette to understand her, Dory got out the pencil and tablet.

Do you mind that I love your papa and he loves me?

"No, Dory. Papa is happy. I've not seen Papa so happy. He smiles."

You are dear to your papa. He loves you like I love Jean-marie. The love between a man and a woman is different.

Odette read quickly. "I know that," she replied. "I am a woman. I love James. James loves me. I don't think Papa will like for me to love James." Dory gave Odette a hug then began to write:

James will talk to him. Ben might think James too old for you. He is almost twenty-five.

"I will soon be seventeen. Eight years is not so much." A worried look crossed Odette's face. "I wish that papa would be happy for me."

After the noon meal, Ben and Wiley went back to work in the barn and the women scrubbed the kitchen and hallway. The house needed to be thoroughly cleaned, the windows opened and the curtains washed. In other years Dory had enjoyed spring cleaning, but not this year. She couldn't get into the mood for it.

The possibility that she and Ben might be going away from here weighed heavily upon her. But where her husband went, she would go. James was in love with Odette. Dory had known it almost from the time he had tended to her when she was sick. If Ben didn't approve of James for his daughter, would she be able to go away with them, leaving her brother broken-hearted?

James returned in the late afternoon, sooner than Dory had expected him. He unsaddled his horse, turned him into the corral and went into the barn. Minutes later he came out followed by Wiley and Ben. The men came toward the house.

James's eyes found Odette the minute he stepped into the kitchen. He winked a greeting. Flustered, Odette began to wash the dust from the fireplace mantel.

"Give me some coffee and something to tide me over till supper, Sis. I haven't had a bite since I left here."

"For heaven's sake! Why didn't you stop at Bessie's? You know she dotes on you. She always gives you big helpings."

"I didn't have time. She's got her potato vine out and spread across the front of the restaurant."

"That's the sign that spring is here. It wouldn't dare get cold after Bessie puts out her potato vine," Dory explained to Ben. Then to James, she said, "Why were you in such a hurry you couldn't take time to eat?"

"I wanted to get back." He looked at Odette, who was lingering by the fireplace. "Come sit," he said when she looked at him. Odette took a chair beside Ben and across from James so she could see his face.

Dory set a plate of bread and apple butter on the table in front of her brother, then sat down. She wished that she were near Ben and could hold his hand. She was afraid that what had brought James back in such a hurry was something unpleasant.

"I went to the burying," James began. "Chip was quite decent. He said to tell you to take good care of his granddaughter." Dory raised her brows in a noncommittal gesture and James shrugged. "Howie left for Coeur d'Alene this morning before I got there. McHenry sent him to buy goods for the store. While I was at McHenry's he pulled me back into a corner and told me that Steven was there. Someone laid for him and shot him three times. He's in bad shape."

Dory drew in a trembling breath. "Oh, my goodness! Who would do such a thing to Steven?"

"I talked to him. He thinks it was someone who thought he was going to Judge Kenton to get the property divided."

"It's my fault," Dory exclaimed. "I should never have taunted Louis with that possibility."

James continued. "I doubt it was robbery. Steven never carries cash money to speak of. Whoever shot him wanted to kill him. They shot four times." He repeated word for word his conversations with McHenry and Steven. "No one knows he's there except the McHenry family and now us. Steven doesn't want it reported to the marshal. Of all people, he doesn't want the marshal to know where to find him. He said he would explain later."

Wiley shuffled his feet and moved restlessly in his chair. Ben saw the old man's hands shake when he took out his pocketknife to cut a chew of tobacco.

"What do you think of it, Wiley?" Ben prodded.

Wiley took his time putting the chaw in his cheek and returning his knife to his pocket.

"I'm thinkin' that if'n Steven don't want the marshal ta know 'tis his business, he bein' the one what was shot."

"It's a big responsibility for the McHenrys," James said. "Steven is afraid that if someone comes and tries to finish the job, some of the family could be hurt or killed."

"Milo or Louis wouldn't risk that, but they could have hired someone," Dory said.

"Louis knows that if it wasn't for Steven the company would have gone under. What surprises me," James said, "is that they haven't tried to get rid of me."

"You're the best cutting foreman in the Bitterroot," Dory said. "You get more work out of ten men than Louis or Milo can get out of twenty. Another thing, they didn't think that you or I could persuade Judge Kenton to divide the property, but Steven could, because the judge likes and respects him."

"Makes sense to me." Ben was watching the way James's eyes kept going to Odette. Her silent adoration of him was obvious. *I'll have to tell him. Only he can put a stop to this before it goes any farther*.

"What shall we do?" Dory reached down and lifted Jean-marie onto her lap.

"I'll go back down to Spencer the day after tomorrow. By then Steven should be better . . . or worse. Howie will be back by then and I'll have him take the letter to the judge."

"Louis was here today looking for you," Dory said.

"Yeah?"

"He had been to the cutting camp and was in a rage because you weren't there."

"If I'd been here, I'd a told him where he could put the whole damn company. I'm tired of it." James got up and refilled his cup. "I'm tired of playing games with him and Milo. I'm tired of keeping away from here when I think they're here, and I'm tired of wondering if I'll be shot in the back and you'll be left alone," he said to his sister. "All my life, and yours too, Dory, we've had to walk on eggs to keep peace, even when the folks were alive. They made life miserable for Ma and Pa, and now they are doing the same to us." James ran his fingers through his hair. "I want a home and a family to work for, and I don't want people thinking that all the Callahans are trash. Is that too damn much to ask?"

James went to the door, looked out and came back to the table.

"The entire town turned out for Marie Malone's funeral," he said, looking at his sister. "How many would come to yours, Dory? Or mine? It isn't our doing. We just happen to be Callahans. It makes a person stop and think."

"I'm not one bit ashamed of being a Callahan," Dory said quietly, her eyes mirroring her distress. "Papa was a good and decent man. He did the best he could for Milo and Louis and for us. We can't help the way they are. I realize that I contributed to the way people think about the Callahans—I had a child out of wedlock. I'm sorry if I've disgraced you. But James, you can make what you want out of your life in spite of your relatives."

"Oh, Sis. It isn't you and Jeanmarie. If you had married Mick, even if you were big as a barrel, folks would have welcomed you with open arms because you'd have been a Malone. After Mick was killed, it would still have been all right if Milo and Louis hadn't been so busy spreading stories about you."

"What's done is done, James. We can't go back and change things."

As Ben listened, he knew that he had made no mistake choosing this woman to share his life. His mind filled with pride, his eyes with admiration when he looked at her. He saw behind her pride and courage, to the misery inside her.

James paced back and forth and Dory's worried eyes followed him. Suddenly he stopped, looked at Ben, then moved around the table, took Odette's hand, pulled her to her feet and drew her into the hallway.

When the door closed behind them, Dory looked at Ben. Her heart sank. His brows were drawn down in a scowl. She was vaguely aware that Wiley had got to his feet and was moving toward the door.

She wanted to cry.

CHAPTER
* 24 *

The kitchen was as silent as a tomb after Wiley left. Dory looked down at her daughter sleeping in her lap and brushed the curls from her forehead. She wasn't even aware that she was miserable. She just knew that what she'd thought she had a moment ago had vanished and once again she was alone. There was a difference now. Now she knew how wonderful life *could* be.

She didn't look at Ben. She didn't want to see the disapproving scowl on his face. Into her mind floated a dozen unanswered questions that merged into one. Why did he not want James to court his daughter? It could only be that he didn't think James good enough; that he thought brutality was ingrained in all the Callahans. If that was true, why did he want *her*? She and James were full brother and sister; the other two had only their father's blood.

"Ben?"

He didn't look at her. He was looking at the stove as if it were something he hadn't seen before. He was thinking that he had not realized that James was so serious about Odette even though she was smitten by him. Odette had had no experience with boys her age, much less with a man like

James. It was natural for her to be flattered by his attention. Damn him! She would never understand now when James broke things off between them. He couldn't tell Odette that there was a chance he wasn't her father, that one of James's half-brothers may have sired her.

Ben turned to Dory and saw the hurt on her face. It was like a blow in the gut. She had gone through so much, and now this.

"Why, Ben? Is it that you think James has bad blood? I have the same blood."

"It isn't that. I don't believe in bad blood. Never did, never will."

"He isn't like Milo and Louis. He's got the softest heart in the world. He'd never hurt her."

Ben was silent. He didn't want to discuss it with Dory until after he had talked to James. This could be the death of his dreams as well as Dory's and Odette's. But he couldn't let it go on. It was too risky.

Dory took his silence as a rebuff and said no more. They sat in silence and waited for the door into the hall to open. When it did, Ben got to his feet. James had an arm around Odette and a beautiful smile lit the face that looked up at him.

"I want to talk to you outside, James." Ben spoke before they had taken two steps into the room.

Smiles faded from the couple's faces.

"Now?"

"Yes, now," Ben replied and headed for the door.

"Papa?" Odette had not caught all the words, but she knew from the look on Ben's face that he did not like what was happening.

With a finger on her cheek, James turned Odette's face toward him.

"It will be all right," he said silently, his lips moving with the words. "Don't worry."

Ben waited for James beside the woodpile. The younger man walked purposefully toward him, his face set in angry lines of resentment.

"Here I am! Whatever you've got in your craw, spit it out."

"I have nothing against you. Under different circumstances I'd be happy for Odette. I blame myself for letting this go this far, because it can't go any farther."

"I asked Odette to marry me. I'll love her and protect her. We will go away from here so that she'll not have to put up with my half-brothers."

Ben knew there was no easy way to say what he had to say, so he said it as bluntly as possible.

"I *may* not be Odette's father. Her father *could* be Milo or Louis."

For a moment James looked as if he had been poleaxed; then his face turned fiery red.

"What the hell are you talking about?"

"The summer I was eighteen, I slept with a woman in Seattle. Milo and Louis were there at the same boardinghouse. Thirteen years later the woman named me as Odette's father, but there is no way for me to know for sure if she's my flesh and blood."

"You knew Milo and Louis back then?"

"I didn't know them. I sat at the table with them and listened to them brag. They were so full of themselves they paid no attention to a skinny bashful kid."

"Does Odette know?"

"Of course not! She's been with me almost four years now. I don't know what it would do to her if she even thought that I doubted she was mine. I've been the rock she's clung to. She was a silent timid little thing when I first saw her. She wouldn't look anyone in the eye and didn't speak a word for months. She's changed since we came here. She talks and isn't so ashamed that she can't hear. I give credit to Dory and Jeanmarie for that."

"Oh, God." James turned his back to the house and looked off into the woods surrounding it. A single choked sob tore from his throat. "Oh, God," he said again.

"I'm sorry, James. I should have told you the night I asked you to stay away from her, but I didn't want to bring out the reason if I didn't have to."

"We've got to find out for sure," James said tensely. "I'll ask them if they slept with a woman that summer."

"No," Ben said firmly. "You can't do that. Think of what it would do to Odette, and we still wouldn't be sure."

"But . . . I love her!" James blurted.

"So do I. That's why I can't let her marry you and have your children."

Ben was silent after that. One part of his mind told him that he should take his daughter and leave this place. The other part asked him how he could leave without Dory if she refused to go. As loyal as Dory was to her brother, Ben was sure she'd not leave him here to battle his half-brothers alone.

The hell of it was that he couldn't leave either because of what had happened to Steven. The same could happen to James and Dory would be alone. If she felt differently about Chip Malone, she could go there and let Chip and James figure out what to do.

"It's a hell of a mess, James. I'd give anything if I didn't have these doubts. At first I was going to take Odette and leave, then all this trouble came down and I realized that I love your sister. I won't go and leave Dory to face those two and she won't go with me and leave you here to face them."

James turned. The look on his face reflected the misery in his soul.

"Don't go until Dory will go with you. She deserves more than living here and taking their abuse. I'll be around, but I'll stay out of sight until this trouble plays out. Tell Odette that I went to the mill. After a while, when I don't come back, she'll forget me."

"She won't forget you, but time will ease the hurt."

James walked quickly to the barn. Ben stood beside the woodpile dreading having to face Dory and Odette. Knowing he had to do so sooner or later, he put his feet into motion and headed for the house.

Both Dory's and Odette's eyes were on him the instant he came through the doorway. He felt their anxiety and would have given anything to be able to tell them that things were all right.

"James said he was going to the mill."

"Papa?"

Ben went close to Odette and repeated what he had said.

"Why did James go to the mill now?" she asked.

Ben shook his head. The hurt in her eyes cut him to the core.

"Papa? You don't like James?"

"I like James," he spoke slowly.

"No. You are mad at me and James." Odette shook her head and huge tears flooded her eyes.

"No, honey. I'm not mad at you." He pulled her to him and hugged her. He looked at Dory over her head. Dory's face was set and the eyes that looked back at him were ice-cold and accusing. He stepped away from Odette and reached for the water bucket. "I'll get some fresh water."

Outside, he threw out a half-bucket of water and hung the bail of the bucket on the pump spout. He worked the pump handle until the water came gushing out and continued to work the handle until the bucket filled and overflowed.

When Dory called Ben and Wiley to come in to supper, her voice was even, but underneath Ben detected anger. It was evident, too, in the way she stood, shoulders back, head high. She had practiced this for so long that it came naturally to her not to allow her hurt and anger to show.

While at the table, Wiley talked and tried to act as if the tension didn't exist. Dory spoke when she was spoken to, Odette not at all—her eyes going constantly to the doorway. The meal was finished in silence. Ben got up to leave when Wiley did.

"Good supper, Dory." Ben waited for her to say something, and when she didn't, he followed Wiley out the door.

"Lucifer!" Wiley exclaimed as soon as they reached the bunkhouse. "It was colder'n a well-digger's ass in there."

James was stretched out on a bunk, his clasped hands beneath his head.

"Do you want me to tell Dory you're here?" Ben asked. "She'll save some supper for you to eat later."

"Suit yourself."

Ben passed through the bunkhouse and into the barn. He leaned on a stall rail. His horse came up to nudge his arm. Absently he rubbed him between the eyes and stared unseeingly at the animal. His action, or lack of it, might have destroyed any chance for happiness not only for himself, but for Dory, Odette and James. He would explain his actions to Dory when the time was right. If she was the level-headed person he thought she was, she would understand.

How long he stood there, he did not know. When he became aware that it was pitch dark in the barn as well as outside, he went back into the bunkhouse. James hadn't moved. He lay on the bunk staring at the ceiling. Wiley sat on the edge of his bed in his union suit, one leg rolled up. He was rubbing a foul-smelling salve on his injured leg.

"Phew!" Ben wrinkled his nose. "It smells like something's dead in here."

Wiley laughed. "I smelled it fer so long, it don't even stink no more."

Ben went to the door, opened it and looked toward the house. The light was burning in the kitchen. He saw Dory go past the window. Later, after the women went upstairs to bed, he would go bed down in the kitchen. The danger to Dory was still there. He must not let other matters overshadow that.

Wiley blew out the light. He had not asked the cause of James's depression nor tried to prolong a conversation. For that Ben was grateful. He liked the old wolf, really liked him. In his younger days he must have been a man to reckon with.

Ben sat in the dark, his chair tilted back against the wall, absorbed in his thoughts. Putting the problem of James and Odette to the back of his mind, he tried to figure out why Steven would be going to Spencer in the middle of the week when this was the busiest time of the season for a mill. Prices were highest in early spring. The teamsters were ready to haul out the sawed lumber as soon as their loads were ready.

Another thought crossed Ben's mind: who was in charge at the mill? Milo was supposed to be; but without Louis there to back him up, the men didn't seem to pay much attention to him. And with Steven gone, who was keeping the tally and writing out the bills of lading?

"Ben! Ben!" Dory's frantic scream reached him and sent the front legs of the chair crashing to the floor. He shot out of the door and into the yard. James was right behind him. "Ben! I can't find Odette." Dory was running toward him.

He caught her in his arms. "What did you say?"

"I can't find Odette."

"Calm down, Sis. What's this about Odette?"

"James! I'm so glad you're here." Dory let out a strangled sob. "I went up to put Jeanmarie to bed. Odette was finishing up in the kitchen. When I came down she wasn't there. I went to the end of the porch to see if she was emptying the dishwater because I knew she wouldn't hear me if I called. I found the dishpan on the ground."

"Get a lantern, James, and get Wiley out here to stay with Dory." Ben gripped Dory's upper arms. "Would she have gone to the outhouse?"

"No. She's scared to go out there alone even in the daytime."

"Are you sure she's not in the house? She'd not hear you if you called."

"I know that," Dory replied with irritation in her voice. "She went out to empty the dishwater. She would not have left the dishpan on the ground and gone back in the house."

"Does she do this every night?"

"Yes. She pours the rinse water into the dishwater and throws it out off the end of the porch." Dory explained as if talking to a child. "Don't just stand here, Ben. Do something. If Milo came and took her, he'll rape her or let some of his dirty, slimy friends do it. Can't you see that? He's getting back at you for the beating."

"That dirty, rotten son of a bitch!" James had returned with two lanterns and had heard what Dory had said. Wiley appeared with just his pants on over his union suit. His shotgun was in his hand.

"Stay in the house with Dory, Wiley. If anyone comes to the door besides me or James, shoot the son of a bitch." Ben took one of the lanterns from James. "Let's see if they left any tracks."

After carefully searching the area from the end of the porch to the edge of the trees, they found one fresh hobnailed boot track.

"It sure as hell wasn't Indians." James peered at the track. "That's the kind of boots a river pig wears."

Ten minutes later they found where two horses had stood recently. The droppings on the ground were fresh.

Ben and James hurried to the barn and saddled their horses.

"They'd not hang around here after they took her." Ben led his horse out the big double doors.

"I'm going to the mill." James blew out the lantern and hung it on the saddlehorn. "The men will help search. One of them might know where Milo would take her." He checked his sidearm and shoved a rifle down in the saddle scabbard.

"I figure she's been gone twenty-five or thirty minutes," Ben said as he mounted. "There were bugs on the horse dung. One of the horses shied and stepped in it. Could be it was not used to carrying double."

By the time Ben had finished speaking, James was a dozen yards ahead and riding hard.

Ben didn't allow himself to think beyond the moment. He couldn't afford to let hate and revenge confuse his thinking. He followed James, trusting his horse to navigate the trail, while his eyes surveyed first to one side and then the other.

James suddenly hauled up on the reins. His horse reared. When he settled down James turned him to backtrack, then jumped from the saddle. He picked up something that lay on the ground, something that Ben had ridden by without spotting.

"She's been this way. I gave her this today." James stashed what he had found inside his shirt without showing it to Ben. He mounted and dug his heels into the sides of his horse, and the big black's powerful haunches propelled it forward.

When they reached the mill, James rode past the bunkhouse to the back of the main building. He dropped the reins to ground-tie his horse and went swiftly to a door. Without hesitation, he kicked it open. The room was black as midnight. He struck a match and held it aloft. Both bunks were empty.

Back in the saddle, James followed Ben to the bunkhouse. Through the one windowpane they saw a group of men playing cards. The rest were watching or lounging on the communal bed that stretched the length of the building. All turned as James threw open the door.

"That son of a bitchin' Milo has taken Odette Waller. When I catch him, I'm going to shoot the bastard. We need all the help—"

"James, wait." Tinker stood.

"Can't wait. We've got to find her and—"

"Wait," Tinker said loud enough to override James's voice. "It couldn't have been Milo. He's lyin' over there drunk as a skunk." Tinker jerked his head toward the end of the bed. "He's been here since mid-afternoon."

"The hell!" Ben went to look down at the man sprawled on his back, his cut and bruised mouth hanging open. He smelled as if he'd been dunked in a privy. "Where's Louis?"

"He left this afternoon to go back up to the cutting camp. He's mad as hell 'cause you're not up there."

"Jesus, my God, what'll we do?" James took a trembling breath. "I was sure it was Milo."

"Are all of Milo's dogs here?" Ben demanded.

Tinker looked around. "I don't see anyone missing, do you, Billy?"

The old man scanned the room. "Nope."

Watching the men closely, Ben saw the flicker of a grin cross the face of one of the men who had backed Milo the morning of the fight. He was on the bed leaning up on one elbow. Ben went to him.

"Get on your feet."

"What fer?"

" 'Cause I want to see you fall flat on your ass when I bust you in the mouth."

"What'd I do?" The man's eyes scanned the room seeking help, then he got off the bed.

"It's what you're going to do, Rink. You're going to lie, when I ask you who took my girl."

"How the hell would I be knowin'? I been here all—"

A rock-hard fist connected with the man's jaw, knocking him off his feet. Ben was on him in an instant, dragging him up and propping him against the wall.

"You're Milo's top dog. You do his dirty work. I'm going to ask you once more and then I'm going to carve you up." Ben drew a thin blade from a scabbard hanging beside his gun.

With blood running down his chin, his eyes pleading for help from the other men, Rink tried to sidestep away from Ben. When he realized he couldn't get past the big man, he looked past him.

"For God's sake! Ain't you fellers goin' to help me?"

"If you know anything, you'd better tell him, Rink. He's a mean son of a bitch. You saw what he did to Milo." Tinker came to stand beside Ben.

"Why'er ya pickin' on me? I ain't the only friend Milo's got."

"You've always been so proud of bein' his top dog, Rink. If you've had a hand in doin' something to Waller's girl and you don't make it right, you'd better not work around me or any of these men ever again. A little shove here or there and—" Tinker drew his finger across his throat. He was playing on the fear all men had who worked near the spinning steel blades.

The what-the-hell smile the men were used to seeing on James's face was gone. It was a cold-eyed, grim-faced stranger who stepped up to Rink and shoved the barrel of his gun in the man's belly.

"You set this up for that son of a bitch! You turned a young, innocent girl over to a pack of river pigs!"

"Naw, James. I been workin' here off 'n' on fer two years. I ain't never done ya no harm."

"We're not talking about me, you shithead. Who took Odette and where is she? Start talking or I'll blow you straight to hell!"

"Don't kill him yet, James," Ben said. "He'll spill his guts if he suffers enough. I lived with the Shoshone for a while and I know a place to drive a splinter that will make this bastard scream his heart out before it kills him."

"My God!" Rink's eyes were wild with fear. "Air you fellers goin' ta let 'em kill me?" There was dead silence from the hostile-eyed men. "I ain't done nothin'. I ain't never seen that dum— I ain't never set eyes on her. I ain't—"

"Ain't what?" James moved the barrel of the gun down and pushed it hard against the soft organ that hung between Rink's legs. "Go on, you piece of horse shit. Milo hired someone to take her, didn't he?"

"Stop! Fer God's sake, stop!" Rink yelled and tried to wedge his hand between the gun barrel and his manly parts.

"Talk, damn you!" James jabbed hard with the gun barrel. "I don't have the time to drive a splinter in your gut," James gritted. "Tell what you know or I'll shoot your pecker off, then one ball at a time. Is Milo payin' you enough for that?"

"Milo told me . . . he said . . . nobody'd know—"

"You stupid bastard. Milo got himself dead drunk so he

couldn't be blamed." James pulled the trigger. The bullet passed between Rink's legs and into the wall behind him. The man screamed.

"No! Please!"

"I only nicked your balls, you gutless asshole!" James gritted. "The next time, I'll blow 'em away."

"Don't shoot! I only done what he told me. For God's sake, don't shoot—"

"What's God got to do with it? Do you think he'd care if I blew away everything you got down there?"

"Milo's boss. I can't buck 'im."

"I'm boss now, and I'm not asking you again." James fired another shot.

Rink screamed and began to babble and cry. "Oh, oh, God! Don't. Please. I'll tell—"

CHAPTER
* 25 *

Odette was wonderfully, supremely happy when James pulled her into the hallway and told her that he loved her and wanted to marry her. He said they would live together, make babies together, spend their lives together. He wanted a home of his own, a family. He wanted her.

She feared for an instant that this really wasn't happening; but when she saw the tender look of love in his eyes, she was too stunned with happiness to think of anything but him.

Standing in his arms, her eyes on his lips, she read every word he said. He repeated over and over that her not being able to hear was unimportant. He would hear for both of them.

His kisses were sweet and gentle. She returned them with all the love her young heart had to give. She clung to him. Her hands moved up into his hair and down the strong line of his back and shoulders and up to clasp around his neck.

He gave her the heart pillow and she read the words *I love you* on it. He held it to her nose so that she could smell it, then kissed it and tucked it into the neck of her dress. After sharing gentle, loving kisses, he looked down at her and in his magnificent eyes there was the glow of love. He was so great a miracle that she trembled with the happiness that she could hardly believe was hers.

It was over quickly.

As soon as they stepped back into the kitchen and she saw her father's grim, disapproving face and Dory's sad one, she knew that something was terribly wrong. Was it because she couldn't hear that her papa didn't trust James's intentions?

After the two men left the kitchen, Odette and Dory sat at the table. Odette's stomach was so knotted that she thought she would be sick. She had not dreamed that Ben would be anything but happy that she had a love like the one he shared with Dory. It was no comfort to know that Dory shared her misery. Her green eyes were bleak and she looked as if she would burst into tears any minute.

When Ben returned, he told her that James had gone to the mill and that he didn't know when he would be back. Odette wanted desperately to know what was wrong, but he had walked out without giving her an explanation.

Until they came here there had been only two people in Odette's life: her mother and then Ben. From the moment her mother had told her that Ben was her father, she had adored him. He was everything she had hoped her father would be. With Dory and Jeanmarie she had learned that she didn't have to live in a closed-in, silent world. She could communicate with people, enjoy life, give love, and teach. She was teaching Jeanmarie her ABC's, teaching James to cipher.

James. How she loved him. From the first it had seemed to Odette that her soul had reached out to him, and his lonely soul to her. They had bonded together without either being aware of it. Now they were being torn apart, and she didn't understand why.

Odette was relieved when supper was over and she could

allow her shoulders to slump, her lips to tremble and the tears to fall from her eyes. She and Dory took their time tidying the kitchen after the evening meal. While Odette washed the dishes, Dory bathed Jeanmarie in the washbasin, then took her up to bed. Odette finished the cleaning and carried the dishwater out to the end of the porch.

There was nothing to warn her.

As a hand closed over her mouth, she was jerked off the porch. The arm that hooked around her middle and lifted her up cut off her breath. By the time she got over her surprise and began to kick and lash out with her arms, the man had her pressed tightly against him and was running toward the woods.

In the silent darkness Odette's fear was so great that she swooned. When she came to, she found herself hanging head-down, her arms dangling. The jarring movement told her she was on a horse, lying face down across a man's knees. She panicked. Her struggles caused the frightened horse to side-step and fight the bit. A heavy hand dealt her a stinging blow across her bottom.

Her skirts were up and all that covered her flesh were her underdrawers; she felt exposed, terrified, defenseless. Pinpoints of fire, like tiny stars, blossomed behind her tightly closed eyelids. Her fear was so suffocating that it pushed her into a swirling black void. She hung, draped over the man's knees, half-conscious, without thought and without pain, while the horse trotted on through the dark night.

Odette awakened from a dream in which she was in a deep black hole and was slowly rising to the top of it. She strained to push herself upward, but her head was too heavy and her arms were like lead bars. She wanted to hold her head with her hands, but they were somewhere behind her and she couldn't find them. Wincing with pain, she finally drifted up from the suffocating pit, opened her eyes and blinked against the light from a lantern that sat on a box beside her.

She was on a dirt floor, her back against a wall, her legs out in front of her. She was looking at her feet when she became fully alert and discovered that she was bare to the waist, her hands were tied behind her back, and two men were staring at her.

Long black hair hung to the shoulders of one of the men. His eyes were as black as coal. He was watching her with his mouth open and his tongue resting on his lower lip. The other man's face was covered with a thin straggly beard, but she could see that most of his teeth were missing.

Their mouths were moving. They were looking at her, talking about her!

"She's waked up. Hit's 'bout time. Hit's no fun humpin' 'er if'n she ain't knowin' what she's gettin'."

"I ain't never had me no dummy. Rink said it was what she was." Both squatted down beside Odette.

"Rink said 'er could talk too. I wanta hear 'er say somethin'."

"Say somethin'." The black-haired man shoved his face close to Odette's and shouted. Odette turned her face away and closed her eyes. The man shouted again.

"She ain't hearin' ya an' yore hurtin' my ears."

"I get to have 'er first 'cause I carried 'er off."

"I ain't carin' if ya have 'er first. Look at them titties." Dirty fingers reached out and pinched her nipple. Odette sobbed.

"She be right pert fer a dummy." The man scratched his crotch. "Them titties is shore purty." Rough hands curled around the soft breasts. "Go on, touch 'em. They be gettin' me all itchy."

"Wal, scratch yore itch so I can get me a turn."

"Rink said ta just leave 'er here when we're done."

"I ain't goin' ta be done right soon." The black-haired man grabbed Odette's shoulder and tried to push her over on her back.

Odette's eyes glazed over in fear. She turned and twisted in an effort to get away from her tormentor. The man bending over her no longer looked human. His mouth was open with lust, and spittle ran from the corner. She lashed out with her feet and tried to butt him with her head. A slap sent her head reeling back against the wall.

James! James, I love you—

As her ankles were grabbed and her legs pulled apart, a scream of terror tore from her throat. It was the first sound she had made. The men were startled; they paused and stared at her as if she were from another world.

"Shee-it! The bangtail can holler. This's goin' ta be a real set-to. Ain't nothin' like dippin' yore pecker in a woman what—"

The black-haired man had spoken his last words. A big red splotch appeared on the side of his face and he fell across Odette's legs. She screamed and sobbed in terror as the bearded man, the top of his head a bloody pulp, was suddenly flung back against the wall. A beloved face floated into her field of vision as darkness engulfed her.

James lifted the black-haired man off Odette and flung him as if he were a rotten carcass. He knelt down beside her, gathered her in his arms and pulled her dress up to cover her breasts.

"Is she all right?" Ben covered her legs with her skirts.

"Untie her hands, then get away from her," James snarled. "I've got more right to her than you have."

"We'll not argue that now." Ben slipped out of his coat. "Put this around her."

The shack they were in was no more than ten feet square. It had been thrown up as a shelter many years ago by some wandering trapper. Tinker stood inside the doorway and four armed men stood outside.

"Did they— Did we get here in time?" Tinker asked.

"Just in time from the looks of it," Ben answered. "Do you know these men?"

"I know 'em. Betcha James does too. They're timber scum. They been kicked outta ever' timber camp in the Bitterroot. No loss."

"I suppose we'll have to report this to the marshal."

"I ain't seen nothin' that ort to be reported ta no marshal or anybody," Tinker snorted. "Ya men see anythin' what ort to be reported?" he asked the men behind him.

"All I seen was two dead polecats. We jist ort ta dig us a hole an' bury 'em so they don't stink up the place."

"Come to think on it, it's what I saw too," Tinker said. "That is if anybody asks."

"I'll help dig the hole," Ben said.

"Ain't no need. Ground's soft. Won't take long. You and James take the little missy on home. Me an' the fellers'll clean up the mess."

Ben stuck out his hand. "I'm obliged, Tinker." He thanked the other men and shook their hands. "When Milo sobers up, tell him to stay clear of me and mine. If he don't, I'll roast his ass over hot coals and send him down river on a pike."

"Rink said Milo only wanted to scare the girl, but I don't believe that fer a minute. Louis is goin' to have to do somethin' with him, or the company's goin' to hell." Tinker backed out the door when James stood with Odette in his arms. "Have ya seen anythin' of Steven? He's been gone a couple of days an' we've got a pile of plank that needs to go out."

"I haven't seen him," Ben said.

James stepped outside the hut. "Is there anyone up there who can tally?"

"Wal," Tinker scratched his chin. "Cook's helper can tally some. He did it once down on Saint Joe."

"Get him on it. Steven will straighten out the mess when he gets back."

The men went inside the hut as James went to his horse. Ben followed.

"Hold her while I get on the horse," James said curtly. "Then give her to me."

"What's put your tail out of joint?" Ben took the girl from James's arms.

"You have," James replied. He reached from the saddle and lifted Odette up to sit across his lap and eased her head back against his shoulder.

"Hell. It wasn't my brother that stole her," Ben said irritably.

"No. To your way a thinkin' it was her *papa*. Damn you!" He turned the horse, and with Odette held protectively in his arms, he rode away.

Ben slapped his hand against his thigh, said a few swear words and went to his horse.

They had not yet reached the trail that would take them to the homestead when Odette came partially out of her swoon and tried to pull away from him. James stopped the horse and held her face so that she could see him. She was still in the throes of terror and began to lash out at him. He held her tightly with one arm while he reached into his shirt for the sachet pillow he had found on the trail. He held it to her nose. She snatched it from his hand and held it against her chest.

"James! James," she screamed and began to sob.

"I'm here, darlin' girl. It's James. Don't cry. You're safe with James."

James turned Odette's face up to him, hoping she would see the movement of his lips. When Odette became aware that it was James who was holding her, she wrapped her arms around him and sobs shook her slender body. He held her and kissed her and loved her.

"Darlin' girl," he whispered in her ear. "I know you can't hear me, but I've got to tell you that I've been through hell tonight. I died over and over. Sweetheart, I don't know how I'm going to live without you. All my life I've dreamed of someone like you—sweet, gentle, loving. I know you were hurt today when I didn't come back, but that goddamn Ben told me something that knocked the wind out of me."

Odette felt his lips move against her ear and knew he was talking to her. She had never before wanted so desperately to hear as she did at this moment. She moved her lips against his neck and hugged him with all her strength.

"I'm going to marry you, darlin'. I don't give a hoot in hell if it's against the law. We can't have the family we wanted. It wouldn't be right. There's ways for us to love each other without making babies. I'm not strong enough to be with you and not want you that way."

Ben rode up beside them. "Is she all right?"

"She's all right. Go on."

"I'll follow you."

"Goddammit! Get the hell away. This is my time with her!"

Ben shook his head and walked his horse on down the trail. James was an angry man. He was angry at the hand fate had dealt him. Ben couldn't fault him for that. The man had been half-wild with worry when he had charged into that hut and killed those two men. He might have killed Rink too; Rink had been bleeding like a stuck hog when they left. The only thing that had saved Milo was that he had passed out. His day would come.

When Ben reached the house, he stopped the horse as soon as he came out of the woods and yelled his name. Dory and Wiley were on the porch when he reached it.

"We found her and she's all right." He dismounted and tied his horse to a post.

"Where is she?" Dory asked anxiously.

"She's coming with James."

"I've been so worried." Dory went back into the kitchen and sank down in a chair. "Who took her? I know she didn't wander off by herself."

"One of Milo's top dogs hired a couple of timber bums to steal her. It was to scare her, he said. When we found her, they were fixing to rape her. James killed both of them while I was getting my gun out of the holster."

"That poor little thing," Dory said. "I know she was scared half out of her mind."

"I'd hate bein' in Milo's shoes when James gets ta him." Wiley had leaned his shotgun against the wall and eased down in a chair. "That Rink's got no sense a-tall. He follers along like a cur dog a hopin' fer a handout."

"He's going to be limping for a while if he walks at all," Ben said. He went on to explain how James had forced the confession out of Rink.

"I hope James . . . ruined him good and proper." Now that she was over her fright, Dory was angry.

"There's a good chance of that. A very good chance."

"What about the dead men? Will James be in trouble with the marshal?"

"Tinker and some of his men are burying them. That should be the end of it."

"Wal, if ya be stayin' here, Ben, I'll be takin' me off ta bed." Wiley stood and reached for his shotgun. "Lucifer! It's plumb queer what all's been goin' on."

"It should be over soon, Wiley. Things are coming to a head." Ben spoke evenly, his eyes on Dory.

Dory waited until Wiley went out the door before turning frosty eyes to Ben.

"I'm surprised that you let James bring Odette home, considering your attitude toward his courting her."

"I had no choice. It was either back off or fight."

Dory looked steadily at him. "You're a cold man, Ben. Cold and . . . possessive."

"You think I want to keep her with me, hold onto her? You think that's why I'm against a match with James? You're wrong, Dory."

"What made you decide that I'm good enough for you when my brother isn't good enough for your daughter?"

Ben studied the stubborn look on her face and decided that now wasn't the time to try to reason with her. Hell, he should have known that it wasn't going to work out between them. If Dory went away with him, there would still be that contact with James. It would take a long time for Odette to get over him, if ever.

She was looking at him, waiting for him to answer her question. Her brown curls tumbled about her face and framed her dark-circled eyes. Tears that she was too proud to allow to surface brightened them. She was hurting. It was a shining pain he saw in her eyes and a reaction to an intimacy that should not have happened. Of this Ben was dismally certain.

What could he say in the short time they had before James arrived with Odette?

His silence pushed Dory into a sense of helplessness that threatened to destroy her composure. To further question his motives was useless, She began to sink lower and lower into the deep pit of loneliness where she had lived for so long. Unable to sit still, she got up and went to the door. The awkward silence was suddenly relieved by the sound of a snorting horse. Dory stepped out onto the porch to greet her brother.

"Come hold onto her, Sis. I don't know if she can stand."

Ben had followed Dory to the porch. He stepped out ahead of her and lifted Odette down. He stood her on her feet and then helped her up onto the porch. She clung to him for a moment.

"Papa. Oh, Papa, I was scared." She hugged him tightly, then reached out to Dory. "I'm glad to be home, Dory."

"Oh, honey," Dory murmured. "You poor little thing." She could see the blur in the darkness that was Ben's face. He looked lonely standing there, like an outsider. *What are you thinking? Can't you see that we love her and she loves us?* She felt tears burn her eyes and after a long look at him, she turned Odette toward the door.

Ben waited until the women were inside the house, then untied his horse from the porch post and led him to the corral beside the barn. James was there.

"Thanks for what you did tonight," Ben said as he lifted the saddle from his horse.

"I didn't do anything for you."

"I know that."

"I love her, you stupid son of a bitch."

"Watch your mouth," Ben growled. "I've had about as much of your lip as I'm going to take."

"I suppose you'll take her and run."

"Not until I explain to Dory. I took on the responsibility of caring for Odette. I can't let my own personal feelings interfere with that."

"I'm going to marry her."

"Like hell you are. It's against the law."

"You can't prove one of my half-brothers fathered her."

"No, I can't. But it's likely. Do you want to see her fall to pieces when she gives birth to a half-wit?"

"Goddammit! Anyone with half an eye could see that she couldn't be part of one of *them*."

"That's what I thought when I looked at Dory. Yet the same blood flows in her veins that flows in theirs."

For a long while they faced each other, with Ben vainly trying to find words that would fill the void and make James understand that he was trying to do what was best for Odette.

"You don't quit, do you?"

"I can't afford to."

After James closed the corral gate and carried his saddle to the barn, he went to the house. Ben leaned against the rails and looked at a sky full of stars. A light shone from the upstairs window. Dory would comfort Odette. She needed a woman after the ordeal she had been through. The look in her wild frightened eyes when they burst into that shack and saw that filthy pig on top of her would stay with Ben for the rest of his life. If James hadn't killed them, he would have.

What to do now? Dory and he, James and Odette, all had been caught up in events that were not of their making.

Ben wasn't a man who acted without thought. He owed Dory an explanation. He also owed one to Odette, but he was undecided about how much to tell her. Should he put it to her straight that he might not be her father? Would she be able to handle it or would she retreat into the silent, timid girl she was when they came here?

Ben moved toward the house, paused at the edge of the porch and waited. When Dory came into the kitchen and sat down at the table, he went into the house. Her eyes were bleak. The skin on her face was white beneath the fading bruises. Ben realized that she had lost considerable weight this past week.

"How is she?" Ben asked.

"She'll be all right. James is sitting with her. They deserve this time together," she added, as if expecting him to contradict her. He didn't. He reached for her hand and pulled her to her feet.

"Come with me. I want to talk to you where we won't be interrupted." He wrapped a shawl around her shoulders.

Dory allowed him to lead her out of the house and into a night lit by a million stars.

CHAPTER
* 26 *

Ben was not sure where he was going to take Dory when they left the house. He only knew that he wanted to be alone with her. He damned his heart for beating so fast that it made him feel like a callow youth.

"Is it too cold for you out here?"

"No. The shawl is warm."

"I'll get a blanket from my bedroll." Keeping her close to him, he opened the barn door.

With a blanket beneath his arm they went back out into the starlit night and walked to the open shed where the wagon was kept. Ben spread the blanket on the end of it. Then, as if she weighed no more than Jeanmarie, he lifted Dory up to sit on the tailgate.

"From here I can keep an eye on the house. I don't think anyone will show up, but I want to know it if they do."

"The family has finally broken apart. I don't know what James will do when he sees Milo."

"Milo will be lucky if James sees him before I do."

The flat statement jolted her. "What will you do?"

"Depends on when and where."

Ben leaned against the end of the wagon, his arms folded

across his chest. His eyes were on a level with Dory's. She swung her legs until they touched him, then she drew them back and they remained still.

He stood and she sat thus in an awkward silence broken only by the usual night sounds: the hoot of an owl, the snorts of the horses and the wind rattling the tin roof of the shed. The sky was studded with a million stars, and a half moon was making its way up over the treetops.

"This is the first time we've been alone."

"We were alone the other night."

"Not like this. There isn't much chance of someone walking in on us out here."

In the silence that swirled around them, Dory closed her eyes. She wanted to hold onto this moment for as long as possible.

"Do you like looking at the stars?"

"Yes. I have one of my own."

"Which one?"

"That one." She lifted her arm and pointed with her finger.

"The little one or the big one next to it?" Ben's voice was low and warm and had a chuckle in it.

"The little one. It looks lonely."

"Like you've been lonely?"

"Yes."

"So have I. I thought my lonely days were over."

"Are you saying you've changed your mind about wanting us to be a family?"

"Never! I'll never change my mind about that. But things have come up now that will make it hard, if not impossible."

Dory took a deep, painful breath. "What things?"

A tremor in her voice caused him to ask, "Are you cold? I'll get another blanket."

"I'm not cold." Her voice now was small and resigned.

"I told you about the summer I was at the boardinghouse.

in Seattle. I didn't tell you all of it. That summer Milo and Louis were there. They didn't pay any attention to me, but they paid plenty of attention to the girl who was to be Odette's mother. She swore to me that I was the only man in her bed that summer, but I can't be absolutely sure."

Dory turned her face away from him and for a long moment there was silence. He heard her catch her breath as she had done before. Finally she spoke.

"What were they doing there?"

"Seeing the sights, they said."

"What was her name?"

"Virginia."

"Would she lie?"

"I've thought about that. She might have decided that I was the best out of those she had to choose from."

"You think she's Milo's daughter or Louis's?"

"I don't know for *sure* whose daughter she is. Look at me, Dory." With fingers beneath her chin he turned her face toward him. "But I took her for my daughter when her mother gave her to me."

"She *could* be my niece, and James *could* be her uncle. Is that what you're saying?"

"I guess it is."

"Then she can't marry James." Tears rolled from Dory's eyes. Silent tears.

"It would be against the law of God and man."

"You wouldn't have to tell anyone." The whispered words barely reached him.

"But I would know, sweetheart. And you would know."

"Are you in love with her? Are you making this up so she won't marry James?"

Her words hit Ben crushingly. He remained absolutely still, then he said quietly, "You know better than that."

"But I don't understand why you kept her with you when you didn't know if she was yours or not."

"What else could I do? What chance would a young, deaf girl have in a place like Seattle? She would have been raped before the week was out. After that she would have been grabbed up by some money-hungry hustler and put in a whorehouse to be used by any jack-tar that had two bits. Even if there was only one chance in a hundred that she was mine, I couldn't let that happen to her."

Dory was crying silently. Ben moved closer and put his arm about her shoulders. She didn't resist. He pulled her to him and held her against his chest, cuddling her, rocking her, stroking her hair, whispering to her.

"Ah, sweetheart!" The words seemed torn from him. "I don't know what to do about us." He placed small kisses on her forehead. He took a deep, quivering breath. "There's something about you that makes my insides melt when I look at you, makes me long to touch you, hold you." Dory heard a tinge of resentment in his voice.

She tilted her face up to look at him. It was too dark to see his eyes, but she knew they were looking into hers. She placed her palm against his cheek. The love, the warmth, the yearning was all there in her touch.

"You may not want to hear this, but I feel I must tell you that I love you." The words rumbled out of her mouth even as tears rolled out of her eyes. It seemed to Dory that everything she had ever dreamed of having was within reach, and yet it was slipping away.

"I never wanted to make you cry." A low moaning sound came from his throat. His lips moved to sip at her tears. "I wanted you to know why I acted as I did. I told James. He isn't thinking straight right now."

Dory pulled back from him. "Do you love me? Or do you

just want to take me to bed? I've got to know," she asked in quiet desperation, discarding all pride.

"I love you and I want to take you to bed," he said harshly. "I like to think that I'm a normal man. I have the urge to mate with *my woman* like any male. You are the woman for me." He held her tightly to him, giving her no chance to resist. "Why do you think I stayed here when every instinct told me to take Odette and go? I was ready to leave the night we came here, and then I saw the loneliness in your eyes. I was almost grateful to the storm. The second time Odette was sick, and after that I was hooked good and proper. I couldn't leave. I wanted to be with you and the little mop-head." The last words were a husky whisper against her cheek.

"I don't want you to feel *hooked* or *obligated* to stay because you think something will happen to me if you leave. James will get the mess straightened out with the judge."

"Dammit! I am hooked. I am obligated to take care of the woman I love." His arms had tightened to the point that she could scarcely breathe. "I could have killed Milo as easily as I would a rabid dog for what he did to you. Then I thought of prison, of being locked up away from you. That's what made me decide to use my fists and not my gun if I didn't have to."

"If you love me, then why did you say it was impossible for us to be together?" She tried to push herself away from him, but he held her tightly.

"Be still!"

"No! You're casting me aside because one of my brothers could be Odette's father."

"Are you willing to go away with me? Far away?"

"Why? To put distance between Odette and James? Or is it that you want to get me away where it isn't known that I had a child out of wedlock?"

"I could shake you for that. Answer me. Will you go away with me?"

"I would go to the ends of the earth with you for the right reason. Tell Odette what you suspect and let her and James decide." She snuggled back in his arms and pressed her face to his neck. "I don't want to lose you."

He embraced her roughly, but there was nothing rough in the way he kissed her. It was a tender kiss. His lips touched hers like some newfound treasure. He fit his fingers around her soft breast and squeezed gently. He didn't know what to say to her. He held her for a long time, hoping to quiet his pounding heart, wanting and loving her in silence. After a while she moved her face so that they were cheek to cheek.

"Ben . . ." She held him as if he were a dream that would fade away if she let go. "Don't let anything come between us."

"Shhh . . . Don't think about it anymore, sweetheart."

"I can't help thinking about it. I've thought of you every night and wished that you were with me."

"I've thought about how it would be if you were all mine, and I had the right to touch your breast, your belly, your secret places. I've wondered if you'd want me or would just let me have my way with you. Right now I want to hold you, feel all of you, kiss you—"

Her arms encircled him. "Is that all you want?" Her voice was thick and unsteady.

"No, dammit!" He groped for her hand and pressed it against his elongated organ. "I'm rock-hard and aching," he said hoarsely. "But I'm a man, not a rutting stag. You needn't fear me."

"It never entered my mind to be afraid you'd force me. Sit up here with me and hold me."

He lifted his head. "You sure, honey? It could lead to something you may regret."

"I won't regret it. I lost my pride minutes ago when I realized that I might lose you."

"I'll get another blanket."

He was back in seconds. Soon they were sitting with their backs to the sidewalls of the wagon. He took off his gunbelt and placed it beside him within easy reach before he put his arms around her.

Dory delighted in the sensation of being cuddled against him, feeling the warmth of his body. The blanket he spread over their legs and pulled up to her shoulders closed them in their own private world. Never had she felt so safe, so filled with tenderness. And never had she been more determined that nothing or no one would take him away from her. She slid her arm up about his neck and kissed the corner of his mouth.

He didn't know what to say. He held her, hoping to quiet his pounding heart, wanting and loving her in silence. After a while she moved her lips to his ear.

"I do love you." Her voice was merely a breath of a sound.

"I never thought I'd hear a woman say that to me."

"Odette loves you."

"It isn't the same. She depends on me."

Their lips met in joint seeking, her mouth as hungry as his. His hands roamed over her, caressing every inch of her back and sides. One hand shaped itself over her breast, the other flattened against her hip and held her to him. Moving her hand between them she worked on the buttons on her dress, then took his hand and slipped it inside. His palm was rough, but warm, and the feel of it against her nipple sent waves of desire through her.

"Dory. Oh, sweet Dory." The words came from his tight throat in a tormenting whisper. "Godamighty! Sweetheart!" A tremor ran through him as if the earth beneath the wagon were shaking.

"I like for you to touch me. I want you—" Her hand worked its way inside his shirt. With spread fingers, her palm stroked his chest. "Have I shocked you?" Her mouth sought his in a soul-searching kiss as an insistent, primitive desire grew in both of them.

"Honey, you smell so good." He sniffed her neck, her hair, her breast. You smell like a sweet woman should smell." His voice trembled.

"When I was with Mick . . . it was out of pity. I want to be with you because I love you." She pressed her hand against the hardened evidence of his desire and felt the jolt that passed through his body.

Then he was kissing her, his mouth taking gentle possession of hers. Every instinct urged him to bury himself in her body, but an even stronger need overrode the physical one—the need to have love and trust. He whispered her name. His long fingers slid into her tangled curls to hold her head so that his mouth could part her lips in desperate search for fulfillment.

She met his searching lips and surrendered to the excitement of his touch, her mouth responding to the insistent persuasion of his. She clung to him, bonelessly melting into his hard body. The kiss deepened. His hunger seemed insatiable, and his caressing hands became almost savage. An acute aching sensation gathered in the region between her thighs. She moved restlessly closer to him, a hunger gnawing at her relentlessly.

The kiss went on and on as if it were impossible to end it. The taste of her, the smell of her filled his senses. Ben wanted to pull her inside him and keep her there forever. His heart was pounding against her soft breast. He hadn't meant for this to happen when he had brought her here. Even as he was kissing her, a small voice told him to stop. She deserved more than to be taken in a shed on a wagon bed.

"Dory . . . sweetheart. As much as I want to join with you . . . I've got to stop."

A small growl of protest came from her.

"No, don't stop. I want this night with you. It may be all I'll ever have." Even as she spoke, her hands clutched him; her breathing and her heartbeat were all mixed up.

"Honey, listen. There will be other nights."

"Are you sure? I'm afraid to believe it."

"Believe it, sweetheart. When we're together for the first time, I want to hold you in my arms without anything at all between us. I want to see your face when we're joined together. I've never done this when it was an act of love. I want it to be our special time that we can remember always. Afterward I want to hold you while you sleep, wake you up and love you again." The words were groaned thickly in her ear.

"Will that happen, Ben? Will that really happen?"

"Yes, sweetheart. I'll make it happen."

"Promise me." Her hand against his cheek kept his face against hers. "Promise you won't let this thing with James and Odette come between us."

"I promise. Now kiss me again."

His kisses came upon her mouth, warm and sweet. Dory heard his harsh breathing in her ear, and his hoarsely whispered words. He told her that he wanted to hold her naked in his arms and feel every inch of her against him. She murmured that she wanted it too, and said that she would thank God every day of her life for bringing him to her. He trembled and groaned a muted, strangled, incoherent sound and moved his lips from her warm wet mouth.

Ben shifted his body slightly to form a more comfortable cradle for her. They sat quietly. Passion ebbed. They were content to be close. As the moon shone on her face, he could see that her eyes were closed, her lips slightly parted. He was certain now that she held his heart, and he could never let her go.

There wasn't another woman in the world like this woman, Ben thought. She was not only lovely, she was proud, calm, and intelligent. He had not met many men that would have been more courageous than she had been. The thought of another man putting his hands on her, hurting her, caused Ben's arms to tighten around her, his muscles to quiver, and a feeling close to panic to knot his stomach.

"I have never been this happy in all my life," she whispered.

"I'm happy too." He kissed her forehead.

They sat in the wagon bed until the moon disappeared behind the pines on the western side of the homestead. A restless lobo howled his frustration at being unable to find his mate. Far away she answered his call. Then there was silence except for the wind that moaned softly over the tin roof of the shed.

Breakfast was an awkward affair. James was sullen and quiet. Knowing his unhappiness, Dory tried to douse her exuberant spirits. Her eyes went often to Ben and his to her. Odette had given in easily when Dory had suggested she stay in bed until Jeanmarie awakened and they could come down together.

After the meal, Ben picked up the water bucket and went out to the pump. He was back almost immediately.

"Someone's coming." He plucked the rifle off the pegs over the door, checked the load and went out onto the porch. James and Dory followed. James shaded his eyes with his palm and looked down the two-wheel track that led toward Spencer.

"It's one of McHenry's boys."

Dory felt a spurt of relief before she thought of Steven. "Do you suppose it's Steven?"

"Could be. He wasn't in very good shape when I saw him."

Ben took the rifle back into the house and came to stand behind Dory. Needing for her to know that he was there, he put his hand on her back.

Hugh McHenry was a couple of years younger than his brother Howie. McHenry had named his girls after flowers, and his boys' names all started with the letter H. It was sometimes confusing to everyone except the McHenrys.

The slender, freckled-faced lad rode his horse straight to the watering tank. It had been a long, fast ride from Spencer, and McHenry had taught his boys to take care of the animals before taking care of themselves. While the horse drank, the three on the porch walked out into the yard. The lad dismounted and snatched off his hat.

"Mornin', James. Mornin', Miss Dory."

"Morning, Hugh. You've been riding that horse hard," James said.

"Yes, sir. My pa said ta get up here fast."

"Is it Steven?" Dory asked.

"No, ma'am. It's Mr. Louis."

"Louis?" Dory and James spoke at the same time.

"Yes'm. Miss Clara, the whor . . . the woman that works at the Idaho Palace shot him early this mornin'."

Dory felt the blood drain from her face. "What was he doing at the Palace? I've never heard of him spending much time at places like that."

"Pa said to tell ya that ya ort to come. He's gut-shot and ain't goin' to last long."

"Hugh." James held out his hand in a helpless gesture. "Do you know why she shot him?"

"She told Pa and the marshal that he'd ra . . . forced her"—the boy's eyes went to Dory and back to James—"and was chokin' her when she shot him with a little Derringer."

"James," Dory took hold of her brother's arm. "It must be Milo and not Louis."

"No, ma'am," Hugh said. "It's Mr. Louis, the bald-headed one."

"Heavens. This has been such a shock."

"How is Steven, Hugh?" James asked.

A grin spread over Hugh's freckled face. "Ma told 'im that if he died on 'er, she'd be so mad she'd not go to his buryin', so he's eatin' now."

"James, if Louis is dying, we've got to go."

"You don't have to, Sis. I'll go."

"Of course I'll go. He's as much my brother as yours." She turned to Ben, a question in her eyes.

"I'll go with you, Dory, if James has no objection."

Dory turned to her brother. "Shouldn't someone go tell Milo?" she asked.

"He was so drunk last night, he won't know which end of him is up this morning," he said with disgust, then turned to Hugh, as if he were still trying to comprehend what had happened. "Louis tried to kill Clara?"

"Pa said he choked her so's she cain't hardly talk, but she told him that Mr. Louis went kind'a crazy, didn't even know who she was when he was doin' it."

Dory's hands flew to her mouth. "It's hard to believe it of Louis. He's mean-mouthed, but I don't remember ever hearing of him hurting anything."

"I don't want to leave Wiley here alone until this thing with Milo is settled." James shot a glance at Ben. "I'll go tell him, then hitch up the wagon. Sis, get Odette and Jean-marie ready. Hugh, I'd be obliged if you'd ride on up to the mill and leave word with Tinker about what happened. He'll tell Milo if he's sober enough to tell heads from tails."

"Hugh, I'm sorry. I was so dazed I forgot to introduce you to Mr. Waller."

"Howdy."

"Hello, Hugh." The two shook hands.

"Did you have time to eat before you left this morning?" Dory asked.

"No, ma'am. But I ain't hungry. Not a-tall."

"I can't believe that. Come on in and eat something before you go to the mill."

"Yes'm."

CHAPTER
* 27 *

Still in shock over the news Hugh had brought, the group was quiet as they left the homestead a short time later.

"Wiley, what more can happen to the Callahans? Milo has gone crazy, Steven was ambushed and now this with Louis. I can't believe he forced himself on that woman and then tried to kill her. It's not like him."

"I'd not a thought it, but don't worry yore mind with it, Dory. Ya'll know all the ins and outs when we get there."

Dory dreaded facing the townspeople. Although not as much as it had a day or two earlier, her face still showed signs of the beating she had taken. But her looks were a small concern compared to the disgrace of the family name if the marshal and Mr. McHenry were right about what Louis had done. Minutes after Hugh had broken the news, Dory had choked down a terrible suspicion, and until now she had not dared to voice it.

"Wiley, could it be that Louis is the one who killed those other women?"

"Don't be a-jumpin' the gun, Dory." Wiley spit over the side of the wagon and slapped the reins against the backs of the team.

"I'd not be surprised at Milo doing something like that."

"Sometimes what's on the inside of a man don't show up on the outside," Wiley said thoughtfully as he flapped the reins again.

Jeanmarie was excited. She called out to James and to *Papa,* who were riding behind the wagon as they had done the day they went to the Malones. Over the last few days the child had stopped calling Ben *Odette's papa.* Neither Ben nor Odette seemed to mind, and Dory gave up trying to think of a way to correct her.

When they reached town, people were gathered in small groups along the boardwalks on each side of the street. They turned to watch the Callahans come into town. Their eyes on her made Dory's heart thud and goose-bumps climb her arms. Several lifted a hand in greeting; others stared with accusing expressions on their faces.

Wiley turned the wagon at McHenry's store, then turned again to stop in the space behind it. Hugh had said that Louis had been taken to the McHenrys' sprawling living quarters. Mag McHenry was the nearest thing to a doctor within twenty-five miles. She lanced boils, set bones, stitched cuts and dug out bullets.

James lifted Dory down from the wagon seat, and the two of them went to the door. McHenry was there to meet them.

"Is he—?" Dory left the question hanging.

"He be alive still," McHenry said bluntly. "James, can I be havin' a word with ye?"

"Stay here, Dory," James said, and followed McHenry into the building.

Confused, Dory sought Ben's eyes. He had Jeanmarie in his arms and Odette stood close to them. Suddenly she felt as weak as a baby. She wanted to go to him and stand within the curve of his arm, lean on his strength.

Ben saw her take a deep, quivering breath. Wordlessly, he looked at her and admired the proud way she held her head even though her breasts rose and fell with each breath, telling him that she was not as calm as she pretended to be.

When she removed her wide-brimmed hat, the bruises on her cheeks and around her lovely green eyes were prominent against the creamy skin of her face. Even in her drab skirt and shirtwaist and in shoes that had seen many years of wear, she was magnificent. This morning when he had kissed her, he had caught the scent of breakfast, of soapsuds and the pure, sweet, musky smell of woman. Just thinking about it caused his flesh to ignite and his nostrils to quicken.

"Ben—?"

"Don't worry about the baby, honey. Odette and I will take care of her, and we'll be nearby if you need us."

"I do need you," Dory said softly. "All of you."

"Dory," James said from the doorway. "McHenry tells me that Louis is out of his head and that you might not want to hear his ramblings."

"Poo! I've been listening to his ramblings all my life. He is Papa's son, and we should be with him during his last hours on earth regardless of how we feel about him or he about us." Dory looked past James to McHenry. "Mr. McHenry, this is Ben Waller and his daughter, Odette."

"Howdy, mon. We be hearin' of ye." The two men shook hands. "Come in. Be making yerself ta home. The young lassie can be lookin' 'bout in the store an' findin' goods fer her papa to buy—huh?" McHenry said with a twinkle in his eyes.

Just inside the door was a small room McHenry had set up for Mag to do her doctoring. He waited until Ben and Odette had gone down the hall toward the store before he opened the door. Mag was bending over the cot where Louis lay. She turned when they entered and Dory saw Mag's shocked expression when she saw her face. Her dark eyes went from Dory to James and back to Dory.

"How be ye, Dory? It's been a while since ye been to town."

"Hello, Mag," Dory said softly. "How is he?"

"I ain't be knowin' what keeps him a breathin'."

At that moment Louis tried to rear up, and Dory could see that a band of cloth across his hairy, naked chest held him down. There was another across his legs. A blood-soaked cloth covered his stomach. He was writhing in agony, his arms straining at the strap that held him down. His gasps for breath were loud in the quiet room. Dory went to the side of the cot. Louis's eyes opened and he stared up at her.

"Ya goddamn bitch! Ya come—"

"Of course. James and I both are here."

"Then get on . . . an' ride, ya goddamn . . . slut!"

Dory backed away. "James, what does he mean?"

James glanced quickly at McHenry. "Sis, he's out of his head. He doesn't know what he's saying."

"Jean!" Louis yelled. "Ya gived it to that red-headed bastard an' to that ol' man, but ya warn't givin' nothin' to me. I knew what ya was doin' when I heard them bedsprings a squeakin'. Ya ain't nothin' but a . . . whore nohow!"

Dory and James stood side by side and stared down at the man on the cot. Dory willed herself not to faint at the sight of the red blood that soaked the cloth on his belly and the bloody froth that came from the corner of his mouth.

Louis lifted his head off the pillow. "I swore I'd kill ya an' I did!" Hate-filled eyes stared up at Dory. "Ya goddamn Malone bitch!" His voice was filled with rage. He tried to spit at her. "I choked the life outta ya. Ya begged, but I choked till yore tongue hung out. Ha . . . ha . . . ha—" His dry cackle was the most evil sound Dory had ever heard. "Ya give that old man what ort a been mine an' I killed ya for it."

James touched Dory's arm. "Do you want to go?"

Slowly she shook her head. Louis was talking about her mother. He had carried that hatred all these years. Was it hatred or love? He was killing her mother each time he had killed one of those poor women.

"Oh, James, I never dreamed he hated us so much."

"Jean!" Louis shouted, his eyes wild. "Why'd ya come back for?" He tried to rear, then fell back and closed his eyes. "Jean, you're so . . . pretty—" he cried hoarsely. A few seconds later his eyes flew open and he looked at Dory with pure hatred on his face. "Ya goddamn bitch!" he snarled, and for a moment there was recognition in his eyes. "I'll choke the life outta ya and that blasted Malone brat." Blood covered his lips and his lids fluttered down. "Jean, why'd ya have ta—?" Bubbles came from his mouth.

Dory turned her face away, and when she looked back, his eyes were closed and he lay still. Minutes dragged by. Mag went to the head of the cot, felt for the pulse in his neck, then raised his eyelid. It remained open.

"He's gone," she said, as she closed the staring eye and laid a cloth over Louis's face.

With his hand against Dory's back, James guided her out of the room. The McHenrys followed and closed the door.

"Don't ye be fearin' that what he said 'bout yer mather will be prattled 'bout. He be goin' on like that since Mel, not wantin' to look after him, but not bein' willin' to kill him fer what he done to Clara, brought him here."

"He killed those other poor women, didn't he?" Dory asked.

" 'Tis what he be sayin' he did."

"Clara knew him or she'd not have let him in that late." James turned to Dory to explain. "She has a room above the saloon."

"Someone would have seen him go up there."

"Not if he used the outside stairs."

"Mel would not be thinkin' 'bout the other women or he'd a throwed him to the hogs."

"The marshal knows?" James asked.

"He heard Louis rantin'. Mel had given Clara the derringer to protect herself knowin' they be a mon killin' whores."

"I knew he hated me and considered me a loose woman. I wonder why he didn't kill me?" Dory thought of the many times she had been alone in the house with Louis and began to feel a chill.

"We not be knowin' how a mon's mind be workin'," Mag said. "To be sure he'd a harmed ye, is my way a thinkin'."

"We're obliged to you and Mrs. McHenry, Mac," James said. "Tally up a bill and I'll see that it's paid. Sis, you stay here and I'll go see about a box."

"Shouldn't we wait for Milo? He's more kin than we are."

"We'll bury him at sundown whether Milo is here or not," James said firmly. "I'll go talk to the preacher. I doubt there's anyone in town that'd help bury him. Ben and I will dig a hole, but not near Ma and Pa."

Head bent and shoulders slumped, James went out the back door and McHenry down the hallway to the store.

"Ye don't have to be goin' in the store, Dory," Mag said when she saw Dory's eyes follow McHenry.

Mag McHenry had been the rock Dory had clung to after her father died. During the days following Mick's death and when she realized she was to have a child, Mag McHenry had been Dory's only friend. She had come to the homestead and delivered Jeanmarie and stayed to help Dory through the difficult days that followed. Dory went to her now and put her arms around her.

"Dear friend, you must be wondering what happened to my face."

"The marshal be tellin' the McHenry it was Milo who hurt ye." Mag clicked her tongue. "And 'bout yer Mr. Waller killin' Sid Hanes."

"Milo was the mean one. I wouldn't have been so surprised it he had been the one who killed those women. It's hard to believe it of Louis. He kept that hate bottled up all those years."

"Ach! It's sad. George Callahan be a fine mon, but he sired two sorry sons to my way a thinkin'. It seems Louis ha' been overly fond a Jean, and he bein' a lad and all."

"The Callahan name will sure enough be held up to scorn now. Papa doesn't deserve that."

"That be so, lass. Would ye be wantin' to see Steven?"

"James said that he doesn't want anyone to know he's here. Not even the marshal. Don't you think that's kind of strange?"

"He be scared, lass." Mag clicked her tongue as was a habit of hers. "The mon be more dead than alive when he came to our door. That marshal be snoopin' round an' found Steven's horse in the barn. A bullet dug a hole in the flank of the poor beast. I think he be knowin' that the McHenry not be tellin' all."

"Will Mr. McHenry get in trouble?"

"The McHenry has broke no law."

As they talked, they had walked a few steps to another door. Mag paused and looked up and down the hallway before she took a key from her pocket and unlocked the door. They went inside and Mag relocked the door.

Steven lay on the bed, his head elevated by two fluffy pillows. The planes of his face were sharp and boney; his mustache, usually so neatly trimmed, was long and scraggly, as was his hair. Dory hurried to the side of the bed.

"Steven, my goodness. When James came home and told

us what happened, I couldn't believe that someone would ambush you.''

''*Us*. Who else did he tell?'' Steven asked anxiously.

''Only me, Ben and Wiley. We haven't said a word to anyone. Louis is gone, Steven. He died right after James and I got here.''

''I could say I'm sorry, Dory, but it would be a lie. McHenry told me what Louis did.''

''Are you as shocked as I am that Louis was a murderer?''

''In a way. But I sensed something sinister in Louis after Jean died. He changed, and it seemed that all he thought of was his hatred for Chip Malone.''

''But Mama loved Papa.''

''I know she did. Louis was consumed with a deep-seated anger and was warped where Jean was concerned.''

''James says we'll bury him at sundown. Steven, so much has happened.'' Dory told him briefly about Odette being taken and that James had killed the two men who had taken her. ''I don't know what will happen when Ben and James see Milo.''

''If ye want ta be stayin', Dory, I best be seein' to me brood.'' Mag spoke from the end of the bed.

''I should go and let Steven rest. James and I will be back. This morning he said we'd spend the night at the hotel.''

''Dory,'' Steven called before she reached the door. ''Waller beat hell out of Milo for what he did to you. I never saw a man take a more vicious beating.''

Dory took a few steps back toward the bed. ''He wants to marry me, Steven, and take me away from here. He doesn't want my shares in the company.''

Steven chuckled, then winced. ''Did you think the only reason a man would want you was for that damn stock?''

Dory answered his grin. "I guess I heard it so often, I believed it."

"Marry your man if you want to, Dory. But don't leave just yet. Wait until I'm on my feet."

"Why, Steven Marz, I'd not think of leaving until you're on your feet," she scoffed. "Mama would look down from heaven and be disappointed in me."

"Ye be drinkin' that broth, mon, else I'll be takin' a stick to yer backside," Mag threatened.

"It's cold, Mag," Steven complained.

" 'Tis yer own fault. 'Twas hot when Iris brought it. He be better, Dory. He be up to bellyachin'."

"Ye better be takin' care, Mag McHenry," Steven said, using her Scottish brogue. "I be likin' ye too much 'n' be fightin' McHenry for ye."

"Ach, me darlin' mon, ye're as full a blarney as a Irishmon." Mag's eyes were twinkling as she ushered Dory out the door. "I had feared he'd die while I was diggin' the bullet out of him. It is good he be feelin' up to doin' some joshin'."

"He's usually so serious. I don't know if I've ever heard him tease before."

At the door leading into the store, Mag paused. "Ye know, lass, the news be sweepin' the town like wild fire when folks be seein' yer poor face."

"I know, Mag. But I've done nothing wrong and I don't feel I should hide. What happened was done to *me*. The person who did it should feel the shame. If someone should ask, which they won't, I'll tell them who beat me."

Mag chuckled. "Ye be more like yer mather every day."

"You couldn't say anything that would please me more."

Dory longed to tell Mag about Ben and the new happiness

that had come to her. But there was no time. As she followed her into the store, the first thing she saw was Ben, arms crossed, one shoulder against the wall. His head was bent and he was watching as Odette worked with a button hook on the soft kid shoes she had put on Jeanmarie.

"Mama! Look! Papa buy me new shoes."

Dory looked up at Ben and joyous tremors fluttered inside her.

"Oh, Ben. *Red* shoes?"

"She likes them." His face was wreathed with smiles and his eyes danced with laughter.

Ben and James climbed up and out of the hole they had dug and sank down on the grass near Wiley. The old man was whittling on a stick with his pocketknife. A chaw of tobacco bulged his cheek.

The quiet was absolute.

"Not a damn soul offered to help dig this hole," James said, wiping his forehead on his sleeve. A slight breeze felt cool on his face.

"Folks are pretty well worked up over this."

"I don't blame them for that, but hell, they don't have to act like the rest of us Callahans have smallpox."

"What'd the preacher say?" Wiley asked.

"Nothing much. Said he'd read a scripture if we wanted. I told him Dory'd want to do it proper."

"The marshal was in the store asking a couple of fellows about a horse in McHenry's barn that had been creased by a bullet." Ben took off his hat, placed it on the ground beside him, and mopped his forehead with a kerchief. "He said McHenry told him it wandered in. He asked who it belonged to and if it was saddled. He seemed to be a hell of a lot more interested in that horse than in Louis."

"Maybe he's got a line on something. He said he wanted to talk to Steven about what happened the night Milo and Sid came to the house. I don't know what the hell for. He talked to Tinker."

"When I told him about it the day he stopped at the house, he seemed to think that as long as Sid shot first and either Marz or Tinker backed me on it, I'd be in the clear."

"There isn't any reason for him to hang around now that Louis confessed to the killings."

"I wonder why he didn't kill Dory. He had plenty of opportunity." The thought tightened Ben's nerves and he ground his teeth each time he thought of it.

"It's somethin' we'll never be knowin'," Wiley answered. "When he'd go off for a day or two, ever'body thought he was out spying on Malone."

"Speak of the devil—here he comes." James got to his feet and put on his hat. "Malone's got the damnedest habit of showing up where he's not wanted."

"Chip's all right. He ain't never done ya no harm." Wiley folded his pocketknife and put it in his pocket.

"Yeah? What about last spring when he put a jam on the upper river so his logs could hit the fast water first?"

"That was business. Ya'd a done the same if'n ya'd thought of it."

"How could we do that when we're up river?" James glared at Wiley and the old man glared back.

Ben stood and leaned on the spade he had been using to dig the grave and listened to Wiley and James argue. Only men who were fond of each other would be so blunt. It had been that way between him and Tom Caffery.

Chip Malone and a thin, bowlegged man with a large handlebar mustache left their horses at the edge of the church grounds where Wiley had left the wagon and walked through the acre of gravestones to where James, Ben and Wiley waited.

"Howdy," Chip said. "Need help?"

"We're all done, but thanks," James replied.

"I'm surprised by what has happened. I would never have suspected Louis."

"Surprised, but not sorry," James said with raised brows.

"Hell, no! I'm not sorry for *him*. I'm sorry for the women he killed. He got what was coming to him. Saved the town the trouble of having to hang him." He looked over at the man with him. "Dave, meet James Callahan, Ben Waller, and the best damn smithy in the Bitterroot, Wiley Potter. Dave Theiss is a friend from over east of Coeur d'Alene."

"Pleased to meet ya." The men shook hands. Dave Theiss raked Wiley with sharp blue eyes. "The best smithy, huh? I've done a speck of that myself."

"Chip said it, I didn't," Wiley snorted, in spite of the pleased look on his face. "But Chip ain't knowed fer stickin' ta the facts."

"Wiley and I go back a long way. My pa tried to hire him away from George Callahan, but the old goat wanted a half-interest in the business before he'd make a move."

"There ya go. See what I'm tellin' ya?" Wiley said to Theiss.

"Sure do. You got to take what old Chip says with a grain a salt."

"This will go hard with Milo." Chip turned a serious face back to James.

"Yeah. It was always him and Louis against the rest of us."

"Most folks hate Milo's guts anyway. What Louis did won't help matters any."

"I don't give a goddamn about Milo." James picked up a

shovel and sank the blade in the pile of dirt beside the hole. "I'm going to bust his head wide open when I see him."

Chip laughed. "You won't find anything in there but hot air."

Ben squinted at the sun. "We'd better get back and wash up if the burying is at sundown."

CHAPTER
* 28 *

Wiley drove the wagon that carried Louis's body to the graveyard. Ben, Dory and Odette followed in McHenry's buggy. The McHenry girls had offered to keep Jeanmarie, and Dory was grateful her young daughter would be spared the ordeal of seeing a body put in the ground. And, it was a rare treat for the child to be with other children.

James, on horseback, rode beside the buggy. As they rounded the corner to enter the main street, Chip Malone and his friend Dave Theiss fell in behind the buggy, and James moved back to ride beside them.

"What'er you doin' here?" James growled.

"Payin' my respects."

"That's a pile of horseshit."

"Yeah, it is." Chip's eyes scanned the two dozen or more men that lounged along the street.

"Well—?"

At that moment a clod of dirt hit the box in the back of the wagon. Then a barrage of clods were thrown. One hit the horse pulling the buggy. The frightened animal danced sideways and tried to rear. Only Ben's strong hands on the reins held him.

Chip spurred his horse ahead to face a group of angry men. Theiss moved up beside the buggy.

"You stupid bastards! If you hurt one of those women or that man driving the wagon you'll get my quirt across your back." Chip's strident voice carried to every man on the street.

"He's a goddamn murderer!" a man yelled.

"Yeah, he *was*," Chip replied. "And he's dead. You're not going to hurt him with clods."

"He's gettin' a decent buryin'. It ain't right after what he done."

"They're burying him. What did you expect them to do—drag him out in the woods and let him rot?"

"He ort ta be drawn 'n' quartered!"

"You want to do it, Tidwell? After he's buried I don't give a hoot in hell if you go out there and dig him up. But he's going to be buried, so pull in your horns and act civil for a change."

James edged his horse between Chip's and the crowd. "I don't need you to fight my battles," he said low-voiced.

"It wasn't for you, hot-head, it was for Dory. Now get on before you get them more riled up than they are."

Seething, James fell in behind the buggy. "You're pretty high-handed, Malone."

"Yeah. I guess I am."

"This is no concern of yours."

"I guess not."

"They why are you here?"

"You'll find out." They were at the edge of town. Chip looked over his shoulder to see if they were being followed. "Do you think Milo will show up?"

"Doubt it. Young McHenry went up to the mill to tell him. Tinker said when he sobered up this morning he lit a shuck. He knows I'm going to beat his brains out."

"What's he done now?"

"None of your business."

Chip grinned a lopsided grin and shrugged.

Wiley stopped the wagon at the edge of the graveyard and climbed down. Dory and Odette stood by while the men pulled the box from the wagon bed. With Ben and James on one side and Chip and Theiss on the other they hoisted the box to their shoulders and carried it to the open pit where the minister waited with Bible in hand.

"Now you know why we came," Chip said in a low tone to James as they lowered the box onto the ropes Wiley had laid out on the ground.

"I'm obliged," James growled grudgingly.

Dory stood with Wiley and Odette while the men, using the ropes, lowered the box into the gaping hole. She felt neither sorrow nor hatred for the man they were burying. If she felt anything at all, it was a sort of vague relief that she no longer had to fear his outbursts nor endure his insults. Dory had half expected Milo to show up at the graveyard and cause trouble. She wondered now if that was the reason Chip Malone and his friend had come. It certainly wasn't out of respect for the dead.

"—Ashes to ashes and dust to dust—"

Dory's mind absorbed some of the minister's words; then she watched as Ben and James filled the grave. Dear Ben. What would they have done without him? She was sure James was grateful for his help even though his heart was breaking over Odette. Now they would never know if it was Louis who had fathered her.

It was over. The minister shook hands with Dory and James and went back to the church. Dory had seen Chip looking at her face and had avoided his eyes. There was no avoiding him now. After tipping his hat to Odette, he stood in front of

Dory and stared. She met his eyes unflinchingly. She saw a muscle jumping in his jaw as his teeth clenched. If it had not been for his treatment of Mick, she could have liked him.

"Milo did this to you." A breath hissed through his teeth.

"How do you know?"

"It's why James wants to bust his head."

"You're wrong. Ben already did that."

He turned on James. "How did you let that happen?"

"Don't you dare blame James," Dory stormed. "James wasn't there. Neither was Ben. It's a family matter and no business of yours."

"Seems like I heard that once already today. Are you going to marry Waller?"

"Yes, but it's none of—"

"—my business. James, Dave and I would like to have a private word with you and Ben after you take the ladies back to the hotel."

"Say your piece. Anything you have to say can be said in front of Dory and Wiley and Odette."

Chip saw James looking at the young deaf girl when he spoke and saw her watching his lips. Adoration was in her eyes when she looked at him; love and concern in his. *He loves her. He's all swagger and brag on the outside, but inside he's soft as a down pillow just like Jean.*

"This will take a little time."

"We're in no hurry," James replied.

The group gathered at the end of the wagon. Ben lifted Dory up to sit on the tailgate. He turned to lift Odette, but James was there and lifted Odette to sit beside Dory.

"Dave is a federal marshal," Chip said. "He was sent up here by Judge Kenton to look into a matter—a couple of matters."

"We've already got one marshal here," James said.

"Kraus is not a marshal. He's a bounty hunter." Marshal Theiss's voice had the sound of the south in it. "Norm Kraus was a marshal for a short time. Now he hunts men for money."

"There's nothing wrong in that," Ben said. "Why did he pretend to be a marshal?"

"People open up more to a marshal than a bounty hunter. Judge Kenton sent for me yesterday morning. One of McHenry's boys had brought him a packet of papers from Steven Marz, the bookkeeper at Callahan mill. Someone put three bullets in Marz but he made it to McHenry's. He asked McHenry to tell no one he was there and to get the papers to the judge."

James and Dory exchanged glances. "So you know that Steven is at McHenry's?"

"Yes. The boy told the judge. I take it he's still alive?"

"Mrs. McHenry thinks he'll recover. How do you fit in with Malone?" James sent a glance at the tall, red-haired man before looking straight at the marshal.

"I've known Malone a long time and thought a stranger in town wouldn't be so noticeable with him."

"James, don't let your dislike for me cloud what Dave is trying to tell you." Chip spoke irritably.

"McHenry sent the judge every scrap of paper he found in Marz's belongings to make sure he was carrying out the man's wishes. In the papers the judge discovered that Steven Marz is Maxwell Lilly, who for years was a wanted man. Five years ago it was discovered that he was not guilty of taking money from his father's business and thereby stealing from the stockholders. His brother had taken the money, and his father made restitution. Later that year his father, mother and brother went down in one of Lilly's ships."

Dory let out a breath she had been holding. "Well, land-sakes. No one ever knew that."

"George did," Wiley said. "Steven told George. George told me a'fore he died, so I could keep a eye out fer one of them fellers. Steve didn't know I knowed."

"The judge knew that a Maxwell Lilly had inherited the shipbuilding business from his father. It's being run now by Forest Lilly, a cousin, who stands to gain a fortune if Maxwell turns up dead. When the boy told the judge there was a marshal here by the name of Kraus, the judge put two and two together and came up with three. Kraus is known for bringing his men back slung across a saddle. The judge thinks Forest Lilly sent Kraus out here to find Maxwell and make sure he doesn't come back to spoil things."

"That dirty son of a bitch shot Steven!" James looked over at Ben. "No wonder he was interested in that horse."

"What horse?" Theiss asked.

"Steven's horse is in McHenry's barn. It has a bullet crease."

"How did Kraus know to look here for Marz?" Ben asked.

"He has probably scouted every company in the territory that could use a man with Marz's skill at keeping books. Somehow or other he discovered that Marz fit the description of Lilly."

"If that's the case, we'd better get on back to town and guard Steven before Kraus finds him at McHenry's." Ben reached for Dory and lifted her down from the wagon.

"There's no way we can prove he shot Steven," James said.

"There's a chance if we could find one of the bullets. Like I said, Kraus brings in dead men, and in order to prove he killed them, he marks his bullets. I heard this from a marshal down around Idaho City. You say the horse was only creased?"

"Along the flank," James said.

"Mag, Mrs. McHenry, dug a bullet out of Steven. She

told me this morning.'' Dory was holding tightly to Ben's hand.

''If it's got a K scratched on it, it came from Kraus's gun, but it's not proof Kraus fired the gun.''

''Hell,'' James said. ''It was three days ago anyhow. She'd not find it now.''

''There's a big payoff in this one for Kraus,'' Marshal Theiss said. ''If he went back and looked along that trail for a body and didn't find one, he's reasonably sure Marz is in Spencer.''

''If he finds him, he'll kill him?'' Dory asked.

The marshal shrugged. ''The longer he stays around here the more likely it is that someone will turn up who knows he's not a marshal. I can't see him waiting for two or three weeks for Marz to be well enough to ride. If he did that, he would have to make the pretense of arresting him, then shoot him with one of his marked bullets when he got him out of town. It would be quicker for him to kill him here and shoot into his body later.''

''Poor Steven!'' Dory exclaimed.

''Judge Kenton should be here before noon tomorrow. McHenry's boy is driving him in the judge's buggy.'' Marshal Theiss untied his horse and prepared to mount.

''The judge is coming here?'' James asked.

''Tomorrow.''

''We'll meet with him, Sis, and ask him—'' James broke off in mid-sentence. ''Ask him about what we talked about.'' He lifted Odette from the wagon and stood close to her, his hand on her back in a proprietary way that was noticed by both Ben and Chip Malone. ''We'd better get on back. I'll stay in with Steven tonight.''

''I've got an idea, but I need to talk to you and McHenry about it,'' the marshal said to James. Then, ''Chip, do you suppose you and Ben could find Kraus and keep him occupied for an hour while McHenry, James and I set something up?"

"That should be easy enough, huh, Chip?" Ben said.

Chip nodded.

"We'll need your help too, Wiley."

"Ya got it." Wiley climbed up onto the wagon seat.

"The ladies are welcome to go out to the house for the night," Chip said before he mounted his horse.

"That's kind of you, Mr. Malone. But Ben made arrangements for us at the hotel," Dory said coolly, then turned her back on him and went to the buggy.

James helped Odette up to sit beside his sister.

"James? Is it something bad?" Odette spoke for the first time.

Yes, honey, it's something bad. James spoke to her silently, his lips moving with the words. She watched his mouth as he explained slowly and patiently about the man who had come to the house pretending to be a marshal, and about Steven. He asked her if she understood what Louis had done and she nodded. He then told her that he loved her and that she was the prettiest girl in Spencer. He smiled when her cheeks became rosy as apples.

Sitting beside Dory, Ben waited for James to finish talking to Odette. He was torn by the love James obviously had for her and her for him. *If only he could forget the suspicion he had in his mind about who had sired her.* Dory's hand wiggled under his arm, letting him know that she shared the pain he was feeling.

When James finished, Odette spoke, "Be careful, James."

He nodded, pressed her hand and went to his horse.

It was dark by the time they finished eating at Bessie's. Jeanmarie fell asleep at the table and leaned her head against her mother's side. The excitement of being in town and eating at the restaurant had taken its toll on the child halfway through her meal. It was a treat for Dory to have Ben sitting beside her. His eyes twinkled at her when he caught people looking first at the bruises on his face and then at hers.

He leaned down to whisper. "They think we've been fighting each other."

"If we had, you'd look worse than you do," she whispered back, smiling into his eyes.

Chip and the marshal ate their meal at a table across the room. Wearing down-at-the-heel boots, ragged pants and a faded shirt, Dave Theiss looked like a drifter or a timber bum. Dory thought that he would never be taken for a marshal. She was still trying to absorb all the news he had imparted today: about Steven, the bounty hunter, and the fact that Steven would be a very rich man if he lived to return to San Francisco.

Dory was relieved that Judge Kenton was coming to Spencer. Perhaps he could head off the trouble, the serious trouble, they were sure to have with Milo now that Louis was gone. She feared James would kill him for what he had done to Odette. Should that happen James could be sent to prison. Her heart ached for her brother and Odette. They would never know such happiness as she would with Ben.

Ben insisted on paying for Wiley's meal as well as for himself and the women, and afterward he hoisted Jeanmarie up in his arms to carry her to the hotel. Ben had booked a room for the women, one for himself, and one for James before he knew that James would be staying with Steven. Wiley would spend the night with a friend of his, an old-timer who had come to the Bitterroot even before Wiley.

Leaving the restaurant, they walked down the boardwalk to the hotel. One of Dory's hands was in the crook of Ben's arm, and the other held tightly to Odette's hand. She was proud to be with this man and his daughter. With him she could face anything, even leaving her home and James if it was what Ben wanted. Her place would be with her husband, but oh, it would be hard to leave the brother she loved.

When they entered the hotel, the first person Dory saw was Norm Kraus sitting in one of the two leather-covered chairs in the lobby. He stood politely when Ben paused to speak.

"Evening, Kraus. Yours is one of the few familiar faces I've seen in this town."

"Howdy, ladies." Kraus spoke to both Odette and Dory. "This your first visit, Waller?"

"I was here once before—a long time ago. Would you like to walk down to the saloon later? I'll be down as soon as I get the women settled."

"Why sure, Waller. People kind of avoid being seen with a marshal." The man's face wore a bland smile.

"Good night." Dory almost choked on the words.

"Good night, ladies."

Dory waited until they were in the room and the door was closed before she spoke. "Oh . . . that man!"

With his finger to his lips, Ben pointed at the wall. He laid Jeanmarie on the cot that had been provided for her. Dory took off her new red shoes.

Ben turned to Odette. "Are you all right? You've been awfully quiet."

"I worry for James."

"If Milo shows up, James won't have to face him alone. I'll be here. Chip Malone and Marshal Theiss will be here."

"James says he will kill him."

"He said that, but he won't just shoot him. If he kills him it will be to protect himself or you."

"I love him, Papa."

He pulled her to him and pressed her head to his shoulder.

I've made a hell of a mess bringing her here. Over her head he saw Dory watching him. Lord help him, he couldn't give up this woman who had come to mean the world to him. Yet this poor girl's heart would break if he told her he doubted that he was her father. Whichever road he took would mean heartbreak for her.

Ben dropped his arms and went to the door. Dory followed. He checked the lock and handed her the key.

"When will you be back?"

"In a couple of hours. My room is across the hall."

"Knock on the door so I'll know you're back."

"I will." He dropped a kiss on her lips and went out.

The Idaho Palace was doing a thriving business. Clara was the star attraction. She told her story over and over. In the early morning hours, Louis Callahan had come up the stairs on the side of the building and begged to be let in. He had offered her double her usual rate if she would spend some time with him. After she had let him in, he had thrown her on the bed, ripped off her nightdress and raped her. Some of the men commented behind their hands about that. *How can you rape a whore?* When he had begun to choke her, she had managed to get the derringer from beneath her pillow and shoot him.

If Clara was the heroine of the night, Mel was the hero. He told how he had taken Clara out into the woods and taught her to use the gun after the second and third women had been found dead. The news that Louis had bragged about killing the women rippled through the town like wildfire. It was the topic of conversation when Ben and Norm Kraus entered the saloon.

Ben spotted Wiley and his friend sitting against the wall and led the way to a table nearby. A stout barmaid brought them each a mug of foaming beer and Ben tossed her a coin. She poked it down the front of her dress and winked at him. Kraus eyed her, but she ignored him.

When Chip entered and came toward them, Ben lifted a hand in greeting.

"Mind if I sit?"

"Help yourself. Do you know Marshal Kraus?"

"Yeah. How are you, Kraus?"

"Good, now that part of the reason I'm here has been settled."

"Part?" Chip asked. "I thought you'd be making tracks back to report to the governor."

"I've got a few loose ends to tie up."

"Law work is never done, huh, Kraus?"

Chip talked of the lumber business and asked Kraus about milling operations in various parts of the territory. Ben had to admit that Chip was good at conversation. He acted as if he hung on every word Kraus uttered. The barmaid brought several more rounds of beer. Kraus told about catching a man who preyed on miners coming out of the gold fields.

"He was pretty slick-handed. He dressed the part of a miner with a trained jackass that would take off when he whistled. It was a sight to see him." He stopped talking and lifted his mug to his lips when Wiley's gravelly voice came from behind them.

"I knowed it was Steven's horse the minute I laid eyes on 'im."

"He was shot?"

"Shot three times he was," Wiley lowered his voice, but it still carried to the other table.

"The horse?"

"No, Steve Marz. McHenry says he'll live, but he'll be abed fer a spell."

"That Clara is sure enjoying herself," Chip said, his eyes going from Kraus to Ben.

"Yeah," Ben answered. "Her customers won't dare get rough with her now."

Kraus was silent and taking small sips of his beer.

"Mrs. McHenry's good at doctorin'." Wiley thumped his beer glass down on the table. "Said he was pert nigh dead when he come ta their door an' hollered."

Chip began to talk about the donkey engine while Wiley's and his friend's voices droned on behind Kraus.

"Did ya see him?"

"Yeah. He's pert, but ain't goin' to be doin' no cartwheels for a spell. 'Twas strange. Louis was a dyin' in one room an' just across from it, Steven was gettin' well."

The barmaid came to the table. "How about another round, gents?"

"Not for me," Kraus said. "I think I'll get on back to the hotel."

"I've had enough too." Ben got to his feet. "I'll walk back with you."

"Well, if you two are leaving me, I'll move up to the bar." Chip stood. "I hope to see you again before you leave town, Kraus. You too, Ben."

"Thanks for the beer, Malone."

Ben and Kraus made their way through the tables to the door and out into the night. Ben noticed how men made way for Kraus, or rather for the badge he wore, and how he strutted by them as if he had a right to their deference.

"It's good to be out away from that noise," Ben said when they stepped out into the cool night air.

Kraus paused to light a cigar. "Saloons are filled with a bunch of know-it-alls hashing and rehashing something they know nothing about."

They walked down the boardwalk toward the hotel. Ben was eager to get back to Dory, but from the easy way he sauntered along he appeared to be in no hurry. They passed Bessie's restaurant. A light was on and Bessie was washing the tables.

"She did a whopping business today," Kraus said.

"This town will probably not see this much excitement for a long while."

"Are you staying over tomorrow?"

" 'Fraid so. We'll be here a while. Miss Callahan has some business to attend to."

"You planning on marrying that woman?"

Ben grinned. "That's part of the business we'll take care of while we're here."

"You don't see many bobbed-haired women in the territory."

"Do you have an objection to women cutting their hair? Men do it all the time." A wave of anger washed over Ben. He spoke curtly.

Kraus shrugged. "Just commenting."

They entered the hotel and walked up the stairs. At his door, Ben said good night and fumbled with his key until he saw Kraus enter a room two doors down. Before he closed the door, he heard Dory's open. He watched as she came out, turned the key in the lock and moved swiftly into his room. He shut the door and she came into his arms.

CHAPTER
* 29 *

For a long moment they held each other. Then he raised her chin with his forefinger and placed his lips against hers. The kiss began gently without pressure. His mouth lightly caressed her parted lips. After a long delicious moment, he lifted his mouth and put his lips to her ear.

"Kiss me back, sweetheart."

Without hesitation her lips searched for his. His lips were soft and gentle, but they entrapped hers with fiery heat that created strange and wonderful sensations inside her. She opened her mouth beneath his; the tip of his tongue entered and swirled gently over her inner lips. His mouth moved along her cheek to her ear.

"Darlin', darlin', Dory—"

Her lovely curving form, clad only in a nightdress, nestled close against him. He moved his hands down her back to her hips and pressed her miraculous softness to him. For a brief haunting moment he wondered if this was a dream. This precious curly-haired woman had brought something into his life that he had never expected to be his. She filled his heart with a love that went beyond gratifying his physical needs. He wanted to put all his thoughts, toil and love into building a future with her.

"You'd better get out of here, honey, while I can let you go." Ben smoothed her hair and drew his mouth along the line of her jaw. The kiss on her lips was a tender, leisurely, lingering caress. His strong fingers stroked the quivering small of her back, kneaded her shoulder blades, and down under her arms to cup her near-naked breasts. He held her very close, pressing his long, hard body against her, and said huskily, "We'll be wed tomorrow."

"You may think me shameful, but I don't want to go." She pressed warm lips to his cheek. "I've waited all my life for you."

"We'll be wed tomorrow," he said again. "Then tomorrow night –"

"—Tonight, love. Tonight."

"I want it to be right."

"Ben—" His name on her lips was swept away by his kisses. "Ben . . . how can it be more right than now?" she said when she was able to speak.

He groaned her name, then covered her lips with his and left them there while he whispered, "Sweetheart . . . it's killing me to wait, but I can—"

The little jerky movements of her hips against his hardened flesh were his undoing. His arms slid from around her and he stepped away quickly to remove his vest, shirt and trousers. Without a shred of embarrassment, Dory went to the bed. Ben sat down and took off his boots and the rest of his clothing. When he turned to her, she was waiting to welcome him. He gathered her to him, holding her length against his.

"You feel different without your clothes on," he whispered. "Softer, sweeter—"

"You feel warmer, harder—" With something like wonder, her hands moved along his lean ribs to his muscled waist and down his side to hair-roughened thighs. Her hands explored the muscles on his back and shoulders and the hard flat plain of his belly before going around to his hips to press his hard flesh against the nest of her femininity.

His hand swept away her nightdress and then her nipples were buried in the soft hair on his chest. Their breaths became one as his parted lips sought and found hers. The naked hunger that caught and held them was both sweet and violent. Blindly, passionately, he kissed her breasts, drawing gently on the nipple he took into his mouth. She wound her fingers in his hair and held his head to her, never wanting him to stop that glorious torment.

Her breath hissed when his seeking fingers combed through the soft curls between her thighs and into the warm, wet cavern of her womanhood. The rough touch of his hand sent delicious tremors cascading through her melting flesh. The pleasure his sliding fingers evoked was so intense she cried out his name. Her hand sought and found and caressed his elongated, rigid flesh.

"Dory, Dory—" He said her name on a sobbing breath. She listened to his hoarse whisper, felt him shudder, and caressed him while he trembled.

Carefully he raised his body, lowered himself into the cradle of her thighs and entered her slowly and reverently. This joining, Dory was certain, was unlike any coupling anyone had ever experienced before. There was no room in her mind for anything but the hard, throbbing flesh inside her. She was part of him. He was part of her. He was the world—the earth and the sky. Her heart vibrated with love for him.

"You feel so good—" she whispered and sought his mouth.

"Sweet Dory. This is as close to heaven as I'll ever get," he whispered almost in agony, pulled back and then desperately sank himself deeper into her.

His mouth nibbled at hers while the velvety tip of his stiffened flesh moved deliciously up and over the hard nub hidden in the soft folds of her secret place. His movements were precise, stroking to bring her to completion, striving to ignore his own desire and concentrating only on bringing joy to her.

Every stroke of his throbbing phallus sent fire running wildly along Dory's nerves from her nipples to her loins, and she was helpless to do anything but feel and lift her hips and move her hands down his back to his taut buttocks and hold them to her.

"I love you, I love you," she breathed against his mouth.

His hips jerked in response to her words. There was no way he could keep them still. He could feel the series of small explosions that went off in her deepest secrecies and heard the whimpering cries that accompanied them. Her body arched, pulling him deeper into her miraculous softness. The love that flowed over him was so intense that it reduced everything else to insignificance. He trembled all over. His legs quivered; his center felt like a volcano about to explode. Pleasure washed over him in great waves. It was beyond his endurance to hold back now. With a final plunge, his life-giving fluid pumped into her.

Almost at the instant of his gigantic outburst, Dory's own flesh felt first a spark and then a flame of consuming fire. The ecstasy reached a peak that resembled pain, then burst into a rapture so profound that she thought her whole body would dissolve. Unaware that the little spasms inside her were pulling him, hugging him, caressing him, she was lifted to undreamed-of sensual heights before she was released, groaning, shaking, her whole body palpitating.

Dory became aware that her open mouth was pressed to his shoulder. There were no words between them, only the sounds of labored breathing and moaning kisses.

When he turned on his back, he brought her with him and pressed her head to his shoulder. She cuddled against him, stroking the damp hair on his chest and running her hand over his hard-muscled belly.

"I never dreamed it would be like that," she said and rubbed her cheek against the smooth flesh of his shoulder.

"You're a lot of woman, sweetheart. This part of our life will be good."

"Just good?" she teased and nipped his flesh with her teeth.

"Wonderful! Marvelous!" He reached for her thigh and pulled it up to rest across his groin. "It was so wonderful and so marvelous that I'll be wanting to do it all the time."

"Even when I look like I swallowed a pumpkin?"

"Especially then," he murmured with his lips against her forehead.

They were quiet for a while; his hand caressed her hip and thigh. She was his now, warm and weak from their mating. He wanted to touch her, hold her breasts in his hand, stroke her belly. He turned her on her back, lifted her legs over his and pressed her bottom to his thighs. *She loved him.* The thought awed him. He was determined that each time they mated she would get as much pleasure out of their coupling as he did. His hand moved up her belly to her breast. It fit in his palm as if it had been molded for it.

It occurred to Ben that he had never spent an entire night with a woman; had never slept with one. He had never wanted to. Now he wanted to spend every night for the rest of his life with this sweet woman in his arms.

His palm made circling movements on her breast. Occasionally his fingers squeezed gently. Her nipple grew and hardened from the friction of his rough palm. She murmured his name and arched to push against his hand. He bent his head and held the nipple tightly between his lips before drawing it into his mouth and sucking lustily. The roughness of his cheeks against her breast and the pull of his mouth and tongue thrilled her in her belly and deep, deep inside her.

He lifted his head to murmur, "Do you like for me to do this?"

"It's . . . heaven!"

His mouth attached itself to her nipple again.

Her breath came in small gasps and her belly quivered as his hand passed over it. The heel of his palm rubbed gently the curls on her mound. A cry of pleasure came from her as his fingers dipped into the dark wet cocoon that hungered for his touch. As they moved in and out, she felt a wild, new astonishment and dazzling joy.

"Ben . . . Ben—" His name was muffled against his soft hair.

When he felt the tremors in the warm sheath that surrounded his fingers, he reached between her thighs and inserted himself again, hard and pulsing with life, into her yielding warmth. Instantly they were joined and breathlessly surrendering to the passion that lifted them, held them, transported and incoherent, until the moment of glorious shared completion.

In the throes of her passion, her teeth had clung to the skin on his neck. Now she soothed the spot with her tongue. Tears came from the corners of her eyes, tears of the greatest joy she had ever known. Ben felt the wetness on his shoulder and touched her cheeks with his fingertips.

"Honey? You're crying!"

"I'm silly. The tears are because I love you so much and because . . . this has been so wonderful."

"Ah . . . darlin'." His mouth closed over hers. The kiss was long and sweet and conveyed a meaning more than any words he could say. "There'll be many, many more nights like this."

She laughed. "Promise me, Ben Waller. I think I can face anything, if I have this to look forward to."

"I promise, darlin' girl. I promise. Now don't you go to sleep on me. We've got to get you back to your room."

"I don't want to leave you."

Now he laughed. "You know what would happen if James came in and caught us like this. He'd try to bust my head and I couldn't let that happen."

"You locked the door. I saw you."

"He'll come looking for me if Kraus took the bait Wiley dropped tonight."

"How do they plan to catch him?"

"They didn't tell me the whole of it. I was to come back here with Kraus, and Chip and James were to meet behind McHenry's. Kraus might not do anything tonight. I let him think we were going to be in town for a while in case we have to stay another night or two."

"If he was smart he'd wait until Steven was well and catch him out on the trail again."

"Theiss said he has a pattern of not staying very long in one place. Someone could come along that would recognize him as a bounty hunter and not a marshal. If he doesn't act tonight, Theiss thinks he'll act in the next couple of days or nights. There's a lot of money in it for him." Ben kissed her again. "I can't seem to get enough of you."

"You might have to marry me."

"Would tomorrow be too soon?"

"Tomorrow would be perfect."

A loud knock on the door roused Ben out of a sound sleep. He quickly got out of bed and slipped on his britches. Through the east window he could see the light of dawn. The knock came again as he was taking the few steps to the door.

"Ben! Ben!" The voice belonged to James.

James stood with his hand raised to knock again as Ben opened the door.

"We got him!" James's face was split with a wide grin. "He fell for it hook, line and sinker," he said, coming into the room.

Ben closed the door and reached for his shirt. "Where is he?"

"In McHenry's barn handcuffed to the wheel of a dray wagon. Lord! Was he surprised." James was excited. He paced up and down. "Malone and I watched the back door all night. Then about an hour ago we saw something moving along the building. For a big man he moves easy . . . and quiet. He was inside that door and I never even saw the damn thing open. Malone and I beat it over there. We heard Marshal Theiss say, 'Hold it, Kraus.' "

"Theiss was waiting in the room?"

"He was in the bed, or rather on a cot. Steven's room is down a ways. The marshal said he never even heard Kraus coming until the floor squeaked. He held a knife down close to his thigh and was about to stick it in Dave. Dave rolled over and poked a gun in his face. Kraus knew his goose was cooked. He pulled back his arm to stab Dave even with the gun on him. Malone shouted. It threw Kraus off for a second and I tackled him. We hit the floor and Malone tromped down on the hand holding the knife. Dave wanted to take him alive and we did."

Ben sat down on the bed and put on his boots. "Theiss had him figured right. He didn't want to hang around here any longer than he had to."

"You should have seen that knife, Ben. Talk about a pig

sticker! It's a good six inches long, about a half an inch wide and honed down on both edges. Dave said if he had stuck it in Steven's ribs, it would have left no blood to speak of, and we would think Steven had died from the gunshot wounds."

"The cold-hearted bastard."

"McHenry spent the night in Steven's room just in case Kraus went there. He was half disappointed to have missed the fun. He'd armed himself with a shotgun, a sword his father had brought from Scotland, a Bowie knife, and several tomahawks."

"What the hell was he going to do with the tomahawks?"

James laughed. "Use them, I guess. That is if the gun had misfired, and he didn't have room for swordplay, and the knife had stuck in the scabbard."

"This town wouldn't be much without the McHenrys."

"That's the God's truth. Bessie is opening the restaurant. Malone, Theiss and McHenry are going there for breakfast. Do you want to come?" James went to the door.

"First I want to tell Dory." Ben followed James into the hallway and knocked gently on Dory's door. She opened it immediately. She was fully dressed.

"I heard James's voice."

"We caught him red-handed, Sis."

"Steven is safe now?"

"As safe as he'll ever be. Is Odette awake?" he asked, looking past his sister and into the room.

"We both got up and dressed as soon as I heard you."

"I want to talk to her, Waller," James said tight-lipped. "I want her to know what happened."

Ben glanced at Dory and saw the pleading look in her eyes and felt her slip her hand into his. *Hell, why was everyone against him on this?*

"Go ahead. But you're not making this any easier for her."

"I want to be with her," James hissed angrily. "Can't you understand that?"

"I understand it, but I don't want her hurt. She cares for you." There was no mistaking the raw pain in Ben's voice.

"And I care for her."

Ben saw Odette standing just inside the door, and as he had done before, he tried to imagine what it would be like not to be able to hear what was going on.

How could he deny her the happiness of being with James when they clearly loved each other?

Holding Dory's hand, he pulled her out into the hallway as James went inside the room and closed the door.

Shortly before noon, in the church outside of town, Ben and Dory spoke their wedding vows. The family and the McHenrys were the only wedding guests. Dory considered Wiley a part of her family. He sat beside James, Odette and Jeanmarie.

When the ceremony making them man and wife was over, Ben kissed her and held her close in his arms, whispering that she was beautiful and that this was the happiest day of his life. Then everyone began talking. After James kissed his sister, Wiley and McHenry insisted on kissing the bride. Ben kissed Odette, then lifted Jeanmarie up in his arms and carried her from the church. The child didn't understand what was happening, but she knew her mother was happy.

The morning had been a frenzy of activity. Dory had purchased a ready-made dress—her first. Mag McHenry and one of her girls had altered the dress, made of fine-quality pink lawn with a white yoke trimmed with featherstitch braid and double ruffles edged with lace. Dory had bathed in the tin bathtub that had been set up in the McHenry girls' sleeping room. Afterward, Odette and Jeanmarie had used the bathwater.

As soon as wedding plans were announced, Mag set her girls to cooking the noon meal. They were excited. A wedding was an event, even though there had been more excitement in Spencer the last few days than they could remember.

At twelve o'clock sharp the wedding party, the McHenry brood, Marshal Theiss and Chip Malone sat down to cake, custard, baked chicken stuffed with dressing, fried parsnips, fresh dandelion greens, and a variety of jellies, jams and pickles. Dory's happiness would have been complete if it had not been for the look of longing on her brother's face when he looked at Odette and on hers when she looked at him. Iris McHenry's eyes went often to James, but he had eyes only for Odette.

After the meal Dory and Ben went in to see Steven.

"You are a beautiful bride, Dory. Your mother and father would be proud."

"Thank you, Steven. I wish you could have been at the wedding."

Steven laughed. "I'm just glad to be here. Marshal Theiss filled me in on all that has happened. The best part of it all is that now people will know that I'm not a thief."

"We're going to miss you when you go back to San Francisco."

"Not as much as you think. You've made a good choice, Dory. Ben will take care of you."

"There's still Milo to deal with. He must be very angry or he would have come to Louis's burial."

"He might not have known about it," Ben said.

"Or was too afraid to show up after the stupid thing he did," Steven said. "Howie told his father that the men at the mill were pretty worked up over his part in what happened to your daughter."

"They're not the only ones. I'd have killed him that night

if he hadn't been dead drunk and if I had known then what I know now about what happened. As it is, he caused two men to lose their lives. They were scum from the bottom of the barrel, but human beings nevertheless."

"Rink isn't too happy with Milo either. According to what Tinker told Howie, he may be walking spraddle-legged for the rest of his life."

"Serves him right." Ben laughed. "James isn't a man to fool with when he's riled."

"Judge Kenton will be here today. He'll have some ideas about what to do about Milo."

"I hope so," Dory said, looking up at her husband. "I'm eager to go home."

Ben put his arm around her and pulled her close to his side. Home to him was wherever this lovely, sweet woman happened to be. He prayed she would always feel the same about him.

CHAPTER

* 30 *

Judge Kenton arrived in a strong-springed buggy especially built for a man of his size—which was considerable. Although he weighed close to three hundred pounds, he stepped easily down from the buggy when Howie stopped in front of his father's store. Heads turned to view the impressive figure in a black serge suit and fashionable square-crown hat. After the judge had been greeted on the walk by McHenry, Howie drove the buggy with his horse tied on behind around to the barn.

"Come in, yer honor. It's pleased I am ta be meetin' ye."

"And it's a pleasure to be meeting you, Mr. McHenry." The two men shook hands. "You've got a fine lad in Howie. Fine lad. Capable too. I like a man who uses his head first and then his back."

"It's glad I am to be knowin' Howie presented himself well. Would ye be carin' for a bite to eat or a cold drink a water? Spring water here is the best, if I do be sayin' so meself."

"A cold drink would be appreciated. The inn where Howie and I stayed last night packed food for our noon meal."

"This way then." McHenry led the way through the store and into the living quarters.

Dave Theiss and Chip Malone had lingered after the wedding dinner to visit with McHenry. James had walked Odette to the hotel and returned. The men stood and shook hands with the judge.

"I see you're making yourself at home, Dave," the judge said as he accepted the glass of water.

"Sure do thank you for sending me up here, Judge. These McHenry girls are fine cooks."

"Haven't seen you for a while, Malone. I heard that your wife passed on. Sorry to hear it."

"Thank you. She was in terrible pain at the last and wanted to go."

"Yes, yes." Judge Kenton passed the empty glass back to McHenry and eased himself down on a chair after looking it over to make sure it would hold his weight.

"How are things with you, James? Are you still doing your damnedest to break your neck?"

James grinned. "I may have slowed down a bit, Judge."

"Glad to hear it."

"You figured Kraus right, Judge," Marshal Theiss said. "He was here looking for Maxwell Lilly. We caught him red-handed trying to kill Steven. I'll take him back to Coeur d'Alene to stand trial."

It took the better part of a half hour for the judge to be informed of the events of the last few days and all that had led up to them. James related what had happened at the homestead and explained Milo's part in Odette's abduction. McHenry told about Louis being shot while trying to murder the whore at the Idaho Palace and Marshal Theiss reported on Norm Kraus's attempt on Steven's life and his capture.

"Louis Callahan murdered those women. That really surprises me. I didn't think he had a thought that wasn't connected with the lumber business. Did you say he confessed?''

''It be more of a brag, Judge. Ah . . . the evil in the mon, killin' the poor lassies.''

James was glad when the conversation went in another direction. He feared McHenry would get carried away and tell that in Louis's ravings he had talked of his mother. He didn't want her mentioned in the same breath as that lunatic. He would never forget the hatred that had blazed in Louis's eyes when he had looked at Dory.

''So Dory wed Ben Waller. With your blessing, James?''

''He's all right,'' James replied with a shrug.

''I want to talk to Steven. Then I have some business with you and Dory and I suppose with her husband.''

''We want to talk to you about Milo. I'm not working with that sonofabitch after this. If he's part of the company, I'm pulling out.''

''We'll talk about it.''

''I'll go to the hotel and get Dory.''

Even with Ben beside her, Dory had an uneasy feeling as she walked down the hallway toward Steven's room and the meeting with Judge Kenton. Part of her anxiety, Dory realized, was that she was not used to being away from Jeanmarie. Mag had insisted that Jeanmarie stay and play with her girls.

McHenry had placed a stout chair for the judge in Steven's room and a bench for the rest of them.

Dory greeted the judge and introduced Ben.

''Congratulations, Waller.''

''Thank you, sir. I realize that I'm a lucky man.''

''Is this your daughter?''

''Odette Waller.'' Ben faced Odette. ''Judge Kenton.''

''I am glad to meet you, sir.''

''And I'm glad to meet you, little lady.''

James's eyes lit up with pride as Odette spoke up and offered her hand to the judge.

After they were seated, the judge took a packet of papers from his pocket.

"I have been trying to think of the best way to go about this. Dory, you and James are in for a shock. What I have to tell you will also affect Milo. Without a will, Louis's shares in the company will be divided among the three of you."

Dory's heart began to race. She reached for Ben's hand.

"First, let me say that George trusted Steven and gave him certain papers to keep. His trust was well placed. George took his obligations seriously and so did Steven. George wanted to be fair to all of you. Should things have worked out so that the two of you and Milo and Louis got along, one of these documents was to be destroyed. You still would have known the contents of his letters when Steven thought the time right to tell you."

Judge Kenton selected an envelope and took out a letter. It was several pages long.

"James, your mother wrote this letter to you after she recovered from a serious illness. George kept it for years, then passed it on to Steven with a letter of his own. With your permission, I'll read it aloud, or you can read it and keep the contents to yourself."

James shook his head and the judge began to read.

Dear Friend Steven,

This letter was written by my beloved Jean years ago. When the time is right, give it to our son, James.

The judge placed the yellowed sheet on the bed and began to read again.

Dear James,

Oh, how I loved you, my first born, the moment you were placed in my arms. I was sure that you were the most beautiful baby in the world and your father agreed with me. He was so terribly proud of you. First I want to say to you that a father is not necessarily the man who plants the seed that gives life. A father is a man who raises you, provides for you, loves you, teaches you.

I was pregnant with Chip Malone's child when I married George. I knew it and George knew it. He said he would love my child as his own and he has. In a weak moment I had surrendered to Chip, whom I had known and liked all my life. Afterward I realized that we could never have a happy life together. He was a wild, reckless sort of man and George was so kind, so gentle and so loving. After only a few weeks of marriage to George, I came to love him with all my heart.

I pray you will not think less of me, your mother, or George, your father, for he has been your father in every way except for the blood in your veins.

May God bless you and keep you always.

Your Mother, Jean Callahan

There was a long silence in the room when the judge finished reading the letter. Dory didn't dare to look at James.

"Would you like to read the letter, James?" the judge asked. "Are there any questions?"

James seemed to come out of his trance.

"Hell no!" he shouted and jumped to his feet. He pulled Odette up off the bench, grabbed her around the waist and whirled her around and around. "We can get married, sweetheart!"

"James! Put me down!"

Judge Kenton looked at James as if he had suddenly gone mad. Grinning broadly, James sat Odette back down on the bench and knelt down in front of her.

We can get married. His lips moved without sound.

"James, what did he say?"

He says we can be married.

"But Papa won't be happy. I don't know why."

It will be all right now. James turned to Ben. "Tell her, damn you! Tell her she can marry me." With his fingers on her cheeks, James turned Odette to face Ben.

Ben nodded his head as he spoke. "I'm happy for you and James."

"Why did you change your mind, Papa? What did he say?"

James turned her face back to him. *I'll tell you later, sweetheart. I'll tell you every word and you can read the letter he read to us.* He sat down beside her on the bench and put his arm around her.

"I must say that is a reaction I never expected," Judge Kenton said drily.

"Judge, I can't tell you how happy I am to know that I'm not related by blood to Milo or Louis."

"Harrumph!" Judge Kenton returned the letter to the envelope and pulled sheets of paper from the other.

"It's a long story, your honor," Ben said. "I'll be glad to tell you about it later."

Dory's mind was whirling. James was Chip Malone's son. She didn't think the fact had had time to sink into her brother's mind yet. All he could think about was that the way was clear for him to marry Odette. It was ironic, Dory thought, that she and her mother, her wonderful mother, had both committed sin with a Malone. Her sin had brought her Jeanmarie. Her mother's sin had given her James, her pride and joy. The judge was speaking and Dory's attention turned back to him.

"This letter will be equally shocking to both of you and you will know why I read Jean's letter to James first. The first part of this letter is to Steven, telling him that if matters between the four of you become intolerable he was to bring the letter and the document to me or to a suitable magistrate should I be deceased."

Dory was trembling. Ben loosened his hand from hers, put his arm around her and pulled her close as the judge began to read.

"I am not sure to whom I should address these remarks. My beloved wife is gone and I will be joining her soon. She brought me more happiness during our short time together than any man deserves. She gave me a son and a daughter. I knew from the start that James was not from my seed. It mattered not a whit to me. He was, is, a son any man would be proud of. My beautiful Dory, so like her mother, is the joy of my life. I hope and pray she will meet a man who will love her as I loved my Jean.

I was a lad of seventeen when I came to the Bitterroot. My family had died of cholera on the way west. I mined for gold, grubbed out tree stumps, worked in the lumber camps doing everything from high-climber to river rat to cook's helper to keep body and soul together. The winter I was nineteen, I came down out of the mountains, sick, cold, and hungry. I was prepared to die in the cold when I came onto a cabin where a woman and two small boys had wintered alone. Their cabin was warm, but they were hungry. They had a gun, but no ammunition. I had ammunition, but had lost my gun when I fell in a snow-filled crevice. She took me in, thawed my frozen limbs, and shared what little they had with me until I was strong enough to hunt.

Together we survived the winter. I want to make it clear that I was never in Hattie Springer's bed from the day we met until the day she died. She told the boys that I was their pa and they believed her. At first I didn't mind, because I didn't plan to stay. Then something happened that made me so indebted to Hattie that I stayed.

It was spring and I went out of the cabin one morning to see to the stock and was cornered in a shed by a grizzly. I yelled to Hattie to get the boys in the house. That spunky woman ran at the grizzly with the axe, and as it reared up to strike at me with its deadly paws, she sank the blade in the back of its head. Then she said, "Now you will stay. You owe me."

She was a strange woman. She never showed affection for her boys and certainly none for me. She never spoke of the boys' father. After she was gone, I found several letters from him. As far as I know, she never heard from him during the ten years I was with her. I provided for her but spent most of my time in the woods.

Gradually I got a stake together and started sending logs down river to Coeur d'Alene. My business grew and I hired Wiley.

After Hattie died, I worked with the boys. Louis showed the most promise. He worked hard and seemed to like the business. Milo was a hell-raiser from the start. He didn't take anything seriously except his pleasure. Yet he was a good dogger and would have been a good sawyer, but he was too reckless.

My relationship with the boys was not good, but it was not bad until I met and married Jean. Louis especially seemed to resent her. My dear Jean did everything in her power to win them over. But the more she tried, the more resentful they became. Both boys hated James. Jean was constantly on guard until James was big enough to take care of himself.

I am hoping Milo and Louis will work amicably with James in the business. When Dory weds, her husband can take an active part on her behalf. I'm sure that under Steven's guidance the business will prosper.

Should Steven determine that friction between the four of them will not ever be reconciled, he is to produce and file with the magistrate of the Territory my second will, which divides the property as follows: All my property, with the exception of the homeplace, which I bequeath to my daughter, Dory, is to be sold and the money divided between James, Milo and Louis.

By doing this, each of my children will have more of a start in life than I had. I consider

Milo and Louis my children because of my debt to their mother.

On closing I wish to say that I have not been a perfect man, but I have done the best I could with the hand I was dealt. I paid my debts, I loved my wife, and provided for my children.

George Callahan July 1876

When the judge finished reading, the room was as silent as a tomb. He held the sheets of paper in his hand and looked first at Dory and then at James. Dory looked as if she would cry while James's face was creased with an angry frown.

"Why in hell didn't he tell us that we weren't kin to those two no-goods? They made our lives miserable! All my life I've had to walk on eggs to keep one or the other of them off my back. Dory did the same. Why didn't he tell us?"

Steven spoke. "I don't know, and it wasn't my place to question. But *they* knew George wasn't their *real* father. I don't know if he told them, or if their mother did. But after George died Louis made a remark that let me know he and Milo felt they had first claim to the land because their father had filed for it and their mother had improved it. They resented Dory and James having a claim to it."

"The old man could have told us—"

"Don't you dare say anything bad about Papa." Dory turned on her brother. "He was good and kind and tried to do the right thing."

"I'm not saying anything bad about him. He was everything you said, but he should have put his foot down harder on those two. You should be glad to know that you're not kin to them. I sure as hell am."

"James, please—" Dory's voice softened. "There's no use in hashing over why Papa did this or that. His intentions were good. Now we've got to figure out how we're going to deal with Milo."

"We don't have to figure out anything. We'll sell and divide the money. Malone will snap it up in a minute—" James's voice trailed as the realization of his connection with Chip Malone dawned on him. He got to his feet and began to pace. "Why in hell did it have to be *him*?" He stopped and stared down at his sister. "We're not selling to *him*. Somehow I'll rake up the money to buy Milo's shares."

"I have a suggestion," Steven said from the bed. "The judge tells me that I now have money to invest. I'll buy Milo out and go partners with you, if you and Ben will run the business."

"Count me out, Steven," Ben said. "I didn't marry Dory to gain a foothold in that business. I have plans of my own to open a carpentry shop and produce a finished product."

"In that case I think something can be worked out so that your manufacturing business can be run in conjunction with the mill. I've always thought that Spencer would be ideally suited for such a business."

Ben grinned. "I thought so myself."

"That can all be worked out later." James pulled Odette toward the door. "You're all invited to a wedding."

"When is this event to happen?" the judge asked.

"In about thirty minutes."

"James," Dory said with exasperation in her voice. "You can't do that to Odette. She'll want time for a new dress. Besides it will be dark soon. It's bad luck to be married at night."

"Then, in the morning at ten sharp. Judge, can I have the letters from my ma and pa? I want Odette to read them so she'll understand what went on here today."

"Of course." The judge sent a quizzical glance at Odette as he handed the envelopes to James. "Chip should know what's in the letter from your mother."

"Why? He probably cared no more for her than any other woman he pleasured himself with. He's an arrogant know-it-all, if you ask me. Nothing has changed as far as I'm concerned."

"You may be wrong about Chip."

"I doubt it." James looked down at Odette. *We'll go back to the hotel, honey. I've got a lot to tell you.*

Odette looked at Ben. He nodded and smiled. The smile she sent back was beautiful.

"Bye, Papa. Bye, Dory. Oh, bye, Mr. Marz. And . . . you too Mr. Judge."

James beamed as if she had said something brilliant. "Come on, chatterbox."

After they had gone, Dory said, "Isn't she wonderful?" There was unmistakable pride in her voice. "She's stone deaf, but she reads lips. She's terribly bright and James is crazy about her."

"Remarkable," the judge said, and meant it. "She's just what James needs to settle him down."

On the way out James and Odette passed through the McHenry living quarters. Chip and the marshal were still there, drinking coffee and chatting with McHenry. James stopped and pulled his mother's letter from his pocket.

"I may as well get this over now, Malone. Read this." He dropped the letter on the table in front of Chip.

While Chip was reading, James stood with his arms folded across his chest. His eyes never left Chip's face. He saw the skin pale, then redden. He saw a tic in his cheek muscle and a trembling in his fingers when Chip folded the paper and put it back in the envelope. James reached for the letter.

"It wasn't my idea to tell you. It was the judge's. This doesn't mean things will be changed between us, Malone. I want you to understand that."

Unable to get a word through his clogged throat, Chip nodded.

"Odette and I are getting married tomorrow. You can come if you want to."

Chip looked at the tall, auburn-haired man staring down at him. James's eyes and brows were like Jean's, his nose like Jean's. Chip's most precious memory returned as vividly as if he were somewhere looking down on the scene. His eyes narrowed suddenly and his lids blinked rapidly.

"I'll be there, James."

CHAPTER
* 31 *

"I didn't think I'd ever get you to myself. Come here, Mrs. Waller."

Dory blew out the lamp and slipped into the bed beside her husband.

"I had to wait until Jeanmarie went to sleep."

"Isn't Odette with her?" Ben pulled her into his arms.

She wrapped her arms around him. "She's out walking with James."

"Walking? At this time of night?"

"It's only been dark for about an hour."

"Well, he'd better not . . . take any liberties—"

"Landsakes! They're getting married tomorrow."

"That's got nothing to do with tonight," he growled.

Dory laughed. "I pity Jeanmarie and her sisters. They're going to have an overprotective father."

"Damn right." He nuzzled her neck with his lips. "You can't be too careful nowadays. Young bucks have only one thing on their minds."

"The same thing you've got on your mind right now."

"Yeah, but I'm an old buck and you're my wife." He nipped at her earlobe.

"Mrs. Benton Waller, the wife of *the* Benton Waller whose windows and doors are in houses all over the West. I like the sound of it."

He took her hand in his and moved it up to his chest. She felt his heart leaping under it.

"I like the sound of something else better. But kiss me first . . . then tell me." His words were husky and love-slurred.

His mouth took hers in a kiss that engaged her soul. She touched the tip of her tongue against his mouth and felt him tremble, felt his body stir against her stomach. He cupped her buttocks and pressed them against him.

"If I tell you, what will you do?" she asked innocently, and worked her palm between his hard-muscled stomach and her soft one. She felt his body jump when she touched him and laughed against his mouth.

"What I've been wanting to do all day—get my hands under your skirt."

"Not while we were talking to Judge Kenton!" she exclaimed in a horrified whisper.

"Yup. Even when we went in to look at old Kraus shackled to that wagon wheel and when Jeanmarie vomited in the chamber pot, I was thinking of this." He moved her rhythmically against the part of him that had sprung to rigid hardness.

"My husband is . . . depraved! There's only one way to cure him." She placed her lips firmly against his and kissed him deeply. "Did that help?"

"Lord, no! It'll take a million of those."

She answered the gentle thrust of his hips with pressure of her own. Her forehead rested against his, their eyelashes tangled. She filled her hands with his wild black hair.

"I love you, my husband, my friend, my wonderful man."

"I love you, too, my beautiful curly-haired wife." His hands slid under her nightdress and cupped her bare buttocks. Holding her tightly to him, he turned with her, bringing her on top of him. "I like this. I like feeling the weight of you on me." He lifted her gown up and over her head. "I like it better when there's nothing between us."

"Is that why your heart is beating so fast?"

"That's not my heart; it's yours."

"I believe you're right." She leaned her chin on his and spoke against his mouth. "You'd better get to loving me, or I'll go get in bed with Jeanmarie."

He started to say something, then groaned deep in his throat. With his arms and legs locked about her, he rolled her over on her back. She gave herself up to his kiss and hunger leaped deep inside them. She felt the rough drag of his cheeks, the caressing touch of his hair against her forehead. The strength of him and the taste of him filled her senses.

The hard, swift kisses were not enough. Only by blending together could they even begin to appease the hunger they had for each other. He raised his hips; her hand urgently moved between them to guide him into her. She arched against him in sensual pleasure.

"I'll love and cherish you forever." His cheek was pressed to hers, his words coming in an agonized whisper.

The whole world was this woman joined to him. His mouth and hers were one. Spasms of pleasure that followed were like a gorgeous dance throughout his body. He was at home in her, moving gently, caressing, loving. She arched her hips in hungry welcome, and he wildly took what she offered.

Dory wasn't really aware of when it ended. When she returned to reality Ben was leaning over her, his weight on his forearms. The sweet, familiar smell of him, the light touch of his lips brought a small cry from her. She tightened her arms around him, holding him inside her warmth, and hungrily turned her mouth to his.

Later, lying side by side, they held each other while their

bodies adjusted to the aftermath of passion. Her head rested on his arm; her arm was curled about his chest.

"It's going to take a while, sweetheart, for me to get used to having you where I can touch you and love you when I'm with you."

"I don't want you to ever get used to loving me."

"It won't be soon. Maybe forty years." He laughed against her cheek.

Dory stretched lazily, then moved her head to his shoulder.

"Ben, would it surprise you to know that hardly anything Judge Kenton said today shocked me? Oh, it shocked me to know that James was only my half-brother. But now that I think about it, he didn't resemble Papa in any way. Papa had light hair and blue eyes. I never saw anything of Papa in Milo and Louis either. They were so different from us. I thought it was because we'd had different mothers."

"He said in the letter that their mother was strange. If he never married her, I wonder why the boys took his name."

"And Steven said they knew that Papa wasn't their father. It's strange that they never said anything to me or James."

"They may have thought they wouldn't have had as much of a foothold here, honey. They wouldn't even be step-sons."

"I wish you could have known Papa. It's like him to take another man's son as his own."

"I would have liked him if he was anything like his daughter." His hand moved to her tumbled hair and fondled the back of her neck.

"The most shocking of all was what Louis had done."

"I'll have to admit I was taken aback. I'd not have been surprised if it had been Milo."

"I was never afraid that Louis would hurt me physically. He hurt me plenty the day you and Odette came. I thought I'd die of shame."

"You stood up to him. Held your head high. I admired

you for that.'' He kissed her forehead. ''No one will ever talk to you like that again,'' he said with rock-hard certainty.

''What do you think Milo will do now?''

''I think he'll take Steven's money and leave the country. Lumberjacks are a rough bunch, but they have a code of honor where good women are concerned. It'll sweep the Bitterroot that he used his fists on you and hired men to kidnap and dishonor Odette. He'll find no welcome in any camp.''

She reached up and nipped his chin. ''Oh, Ben, things have worked out so well. I don't think James cared a bit that he was Chip Malone's son, just that it opened the door for him to marry Odette.''

''It wouldn't have mattered after we learned Milo and Louis were no kin to him.'' He kissed her. ''I was about to give in anyway and let them take the chance. I'm never going to tell Odette that I suspected one of those two might be her father. She's my daughter. When I see how smart and pretty she is, I know she's mine.''

''Then what will you tell her is the reason you didn't want her to marry James?''

''Because I was afraid he might turn out to be like his brothers.''

''But she might say that you married me when you thought I was related to them.''

''Then I will say she knew James better than I did, and I had been too protective, but everything has turned out all right anyway.''

''Just all right?'' Dory pouted.

''Just perfect, Mrs. Waller.''

Dory smiled. ''That's better. Now turn me loose and let me go see about Jeanmarie.''

''I'll do it.'' He got out of bed and put on his britches. ''I want to see if Odette is back. It's too late for a young girl to be out with a hot young buck who has only—''

"—One thing on his mind." Dory laughed. "For goodness sake, Ben. Look in on Jeanmarie and come back. I've got only one thing on *my* mind."

Shortly after the sun made its appearance on the eastern horizon, James was at McHenry's store buying wedding gifts for his bride. He bought a five-volume set of books by Longfellow, a porcelain mantel clock, a gold locket, a pair of fancy blue garters and a lacy nightdress. He assured a horrified Mag McHenry that he would not give the last two items to Odette until after they were married. He left the store with a white shirt and a black pinstripe suit. On his way to the barber shop for a haircut and a bath, he invited everyone he met on the street to the wedding.

The McHenrys and their brood took up one pew at the church. Bessie, who had been up most of the night cooking for the wedding feast, wore a large hat she had bought from Marge at the millinery. Marge was there to see the hat she had decorated for the bride. The Idaho Palace was closed for the morning. Mel arrived with Clara on his arm. Clara had tucked a lace handkerchief in the neck of her low-cut gown to make it acceptable to wear to the church.

Judge Kenton and Marshal Theiss delayed their return to Coeur d'Alene with their prisoner in order to witness the ceremony. Wiley and his longtime friend sat in the front row alongside Dory and Jeanmarie. Steven had insisted he was well enough to attend the wedding, but Mag had threatened to tie him to the bed. She hid his britches to make sure he would stay put.

A half hour before the ceremony, Chip Malone parked his buggy in front of the church and carried in baskets filled with wildflowers and decorated with ribbons.

The petite bride was beautiful in a white lawn dress with mutton sleeves and decorated with ivory lace. A white satin ribbon circled her waist and satin bows shone on her white kid shoes. Her large straw hat was covered with pink and white satin roses.

It was a wedding such as the town had not seen before and most likely would never see again. The bride's stepmother as well as her father had blackened eyes as well as bruises on their faces. Odette walked to the front of the church on her father's arm and met her husband-to-be in front of a bank of blossoms placed there by her future father-in-law. Ben stood beside the preacher and repeated his words silently. The bride watched her father's mouth, and when it came time for her to speak her vows, they were loud and clear.

James kissed his bride long and hard when the ceremony making them man and wife was over, and he walked her to the door, where they stood and accepted the congratulations from the guests as they filed out.

Chip was one of the last. He looked his tall son in the eye and offered his hand.

"Congratulations."

James took his hand. "Thanks."

"I'm going to kiss my new daughter-in-law whether you like it or not," he said in a low tone.

"I don't like it, but there's not much I can do . . . now."

Chip clasped Odette's hand and kissed her cheek. "Pull in your horns, Bucko," he said aside to James.

"If you call me Bucko one more time, I'll flatten you out like a flapjack."

Chip ignored him and touched his finger to Odette's nose. "Keep a tight rein on this wild man."

Odette wasn't sure what he had said, but she knew he was teasing James.

"Thank you for the flowers, Mr. Malone. Dory told me," she added.

"You're very welcome. Where will you live, James?"

"In Steven's cabin, for now."

"I'll ride over to see you."

"Don't hurry."

Chip laughed as he left the church. Life had suddenly become a lot more interesting. He stood with the others and watched his son and his new bride drive away.

By the middle of the afternoon the wagon was loaded and the two couples were ready to leave Spencer. Dory and Odette had changed back into their more serviceable clothing. Pinned to Dory's dress was the cameo Ben had given her for a wedding gift. In the back of the wagon were several mysterious bundles McHenry had put in at the last minute after a whispered word with Ben.

All the McHenrys stood on the boardwalk in front of the store to say good-bye. Jeanmarie clutched a book Ben had bought for her and waved to her friends.

James and Odette had said their good-byes and were standing at the end of the wagon when a handsome buggy decorated with flowers and ribbons and pulled by a high-stepping mare came around the corner. Chip stepped down and handed the reins to Odette.

"Oh, no you don't!" James protested. "I'm not taking—"

"Back off, Bu . . . James," Chip said. "This is for my daughter-in-law."

"We don't need anything from you."

"I'm sure you don't, but I can give her a wedding gift if I want to. Now stop being an ass."

Odette's eyes went from one to the other. She accepted the reins and placed her hand on Chip's arm.

"James and I thank you. Don't we, James?"

"I guess so." He lifted her up into the buggy and then got in beside her. "Let's go. I've had about all of him I can take for a good long while." He slapped the reins against the back of the mare and she took off in a trot.

"It's going to take James a while to . . . ah . . . get used to the idea that you're . . . related," Dory said, turning to Chip.

"I've got plenty of time." Chip reached down and picked Jeanmarie up in his arms. "Bye, little red bird."

"You're a red bird," she said and giggled.

"I'd like to come see her sometime." Chip sat her down on the pile of hay Ben had placed there for Wiley's comfort. He continued to gaze at the child.

For a second Dory saw the same wistful look on his face that she had seen on Mick's.

"We'll be at the homestead . . . for a while, I think." She glanced at Ben and he nodded.

"I'll find you." Chip stood back. "Bye, little red bird."

"Bye, big red bird," Jeanmarie called gaily.

Ben lifted Dory up over the wheel and onto the seat. "You settled, Wiley?" he called, before he climbed up beside her.

"Yup. It's jist like ridin' on a featherbed."

"Bye, girls." Dory waved. "Bye, Mag, and thanks for everything. We'll be back to see Steven before he leaves."

"It won't be fer a week or two. Howie be takin' him to Coeur d'Alene in the buggy."

Jeanmarie's cheerful shout was answered by a chorus from the McHenry brood.

The buggy carrying James and Odette was out of sight by the time the wagon left town. The plodding team pulling the wagon wound its way through the knee-deep grass in the valley before starting the upward grade. The sun was warm. Birds, disturbed by their passing, flew up from the tall grasses. White clouds billowed in a blue sky.

It was a perfect day.

Dory moved over and tucked her hand in her husband's arm.

"Ben, I never imagined when we left home the other day that things would turn out the way they have."

"Fate stepped in and lent a hand, honey."

"Are you as happy as I am?"

"I'm as happy as a drunk hoot owl." He grinned at her. "As soon as we get to that big tree up there on the hill, I'm going to kiss you."

"You don't have to wait till then," she whispered, her eyes shining with love.

He glanced over his shoulder at Jeanmarie and Wiley lounging on the hay. When he looked back at her, his eyes shone like polished silver.

"I'm hoping by then they'll be asleep."

"For shame!" Her hand slid from the crook of his arm down to pinch the inside of his thigh. "You've got only one thing on your mind."

"Yeah." He captured her hand and held it tightly against him.

"This is no way for a prospective grandfather to act," Dory said primly, and tried to withdraw her hand.

"Good Lord! I never thought of that. If I had, I'd never have let her marry that—"

"—Hot young buck with only one thing on his mind."

Their joined laughter reached the old man in the back of the wagon. He smiled and yawned and shifted the head of the sleeping child to his knee.